DANCE IN A BEAUTIFUL COAT

Bryan Webster

Copyright © 2022 Bryan Webster

All rights reserved

The characters and events portrayed in this book are fictitious. Any similarity to real persons, living or dead, is coincidental and not intended by the author.

No part of this book may be reproduced, or stored in a retrieval system, or transmitted in any form or by any means, electronic, mechanical, photocopying, recording, or otherwise, without express written permission of the author.

ISBN: 9798334838604
Independent Publisher

*My thanks to Lisa, Janet, Tommy, Brian, Elaine, and many others for keeping me right on the details.
And to Lynne and Mick for their corrections, advice and patience.*

This book, although complete in itself, continues the story of 'Wrapped Together in the Bundle of Life'.

*Other books by Bryan Webster:
On Such a Tide (2005/2019)
Aida and the Soothsayers (Kindle 2011)
Time, Hens and the Universal Significance of Fiddle Music (2012/2020)
Wrapped Together in the Bundle of Life (2020)
Eyemouth and the Hecklescar Stories (short stories from the 60s) (2018/2021)*

CHAPTER ONE

Nudge spent four days a week, sometimes five, driving for Anthony Douglas & Son, a fish processing company in Hecklescar, a small Scottish fishing port just north of the Border. On a normal shift, Nudge drove a forty-four-tonne articulated truck from the port down through England to Channel ports and on into continental Europe. If you have enjoyed langoustines on the Algarve there is a good chance that they were brought to you by Nudge.

Nudge is a quiet man, contained contentedly within his abilities and circumstances. In his early forties, he confines his enjoyment to quiet and peaceable activities. When not pounding along the highways of England and Europe, he likes nothing better than to stretch his legs along the Berwickshire Coastal Path.

After one such walk on a rare fine day in the second week of January, he turned up at the fish yard, just as darkness came on. He had come to see Jakey, the manager, but Jakey was not there. As he turned away, Angela, the woman who ran the fish processing room, greeted him.

'What are you doing here? You're on a rest day, aren't you?'

'Aye, but I'd wanted to see Jakey.'

'He's away home for a break; there's a load coming in from Oban the night, so he'll be back later on.'

Nudge hesitated.

'What is it?'

Nudge stared intensely at Angela for a few seconds, then muttered,

'It's Jen, I saw her up by Hawks' Ness, on the cliff.'

'Jen? At Hawks' Ness? What was she doin' up there? I thought she wis hassled wi' the bairns.'

'Aye, I ken,' mumbled Nudge and fell silent.

Angela felt she should say something.

'Why did ye want to see Jakey?'

'To ask him . . . . '

Nudge stopped, and Angela guessed he didn't want to reveal his concern about Jen, whatever it was, to her.

'Look,' she said, 'John Henry and Peter are up in the office. Go and see them.'

'The big bosses! D'ye think?'

'Aye; they're no bogey men. Ye ken them both.'

'I ken John Henry.'

'Well, then; an' Peter's a'right.'

'They'll no mind me buttin' in?'

'Nah! Away ye go.'

Still Nudge did not move.

'D'ye want me to come wi' you?'

'Would ye?'

Together they made their way up the stair to the office, and were shown in to see 'the big bosses'.

The two men were sitting at the boss's desk; Peter in the chair; John Henry alongside him; papers covered the desk. Clearly the men were in discussion.

John Henry greeted Angela and Nudge.

'You know Angela', he said to Peter, 'and you met Nudge at your reception. He's one of our drivers; long distance, mainly.'

Peter welcomed them both.

'How can we help?' asked John Henry.

'Nudge wants to see you about Jen,' said Angela. 'He saw her up by Hawks' Ness.'

'Take a seat,' said John Henry.

'I need to get back to the girls,' replied Angela and left. Nudge sat down but made no attempt to speak. Instead, he looked from one man to the other as if trying to encourage his thoughts into words.

'What about Jen?' asked John Henry gently. 'Why are you concerned?'

Again, Nudge looked from one man to the other, then settled his eyes on John.

John then gently teased out his concern for Jen.

He had been walking along the Coastal Trail, a dramatic walk along the edge of the cliffs that link Hecklescar with the village of Birsett two miles to the south. As he approached Hawks' Ness, the highest point, where a huge bluff soars three hundred feet out of the sea, he spotted the figure of a woman standing on the very edge of the cliff. Then he recognised her as Jen, one of his fellow drivers.

'She was right on the edge,' he said.

'I watched her for a few minutes then I walked towards her; I didn't want to frighten her, so I shouted to her quietly to be careful. She turned and stepped back. Then I walked back with her to the town.'

'Did she seem upset?' asked John Henry.

'She'd been crying,'

'Did she say why?'

'Something about her laddie. I didn't like to pry.'

'What would you like us to do?' put in Peter.

'Somebody should talk to her. That's why I thought about Jakey; he knows about her. But Jakey isn't here.'

With that Nudge stood up. Clearly, he felt awkward talking to the 'big bosses'; to Peter certainly.

'Leave it with us,' said John Henry gently.

After Nudge left the men finished the discussion that Nudge had interrupted, then asked Angela to join them to tell them more about Jen, and Nudge's concern for her.

Angela explained that Jen, one of the firm's van drivers,

generally worked three twelve-hour shifts a week. On these shifts she journeyed over most of north Northumberland, her first delivery being away West to the Coquet Hotel at Rothbury, a good hour's drive from Hecklescar; the last, the King's Head at Alnmouth, the same distance away to the South. She left the fishyard at half-six in the morning and can be seen cleaning her van on the pier as late as seven o'clock at night.

'She was at the reception,' Angela said. 'You would notice her; she stands out when she's dressed up.'

'I think I know who you mean,' Peter said.

'She's a widow, I believe,' put in John.

'She is,' replied Angela. 'Lost her husband about, what, ten years ago.'

Angela went on to tell Peter and John about Jen's son. His name is Callum and for months now has been confined to the Borders Mental Health Unit for his own safety.

'She often stands in for anyone that's off,' continued Angela. 'I've known her work all six days.'

'Why on earth does she do that?' said Peter. 'We shouldn't be asking people to work those kinds of hours.'

'She needs the money,' replied Angela bluntly. 'Callum has a partner and three bairns up on the Poplace estate. Jen tries to provide for them.'

'I see,' said Peter.

'But she gets no thanks from Kiera. As often as not she won't let her see the bairns when she goes up.'

'What concerned Nudge then?' asked John Henry. 'Did he think she was going to throw herself off the cliff?'

'That seemed to be it.'

'Would she?' asked Peter.

'I wouldn't have thought so; she doesn't strike me as that sort.'

'And what sort is that?' asked Peter Munro, solemnly.

Angela gave a reply but neither Peter nor John picked it up. John, because he immediately realised how painful the question must be for Peter whose own wife had committed suicide; in October last year, a few brief weeks ago. Peter, because he had been wrestling with the same question for months now - and drew no nearer to an answer.

John Henry sensed Peter's unease and moved on quickly.

'Nudge clearly thought she might be thinking about it.'

'Well, Nudge is like that. He's very serious, and can be dramatic at times - and he has a thing about Jen.'

'A thing?' queried John. 'You mean he fancies her?'

'Oh no,' laughed Angela. 'Nothing as sexy as that; not Nudge. Has a notion, I would say; at the most. But he needs to watch hissel'.'

'Watch himself? Why?' asked Peter.

'She's aye on the hunt for money. Nudge would do her fine; he must be worth a bob or two with all thae holiday houses.'

John Henry for relief joined in the banter.

'He's a bit young for her is he not?'

'What's ten years when the blood's on the boil?' she chaffed, then added, 'and Nudge was born old, wasn't he?'

'I don't know,' smiled John Henry and brought the conversation to an end.

'What was all that about?' asked Peter after Angela had left.

John Henry explained that Nudge had become something of a curiosity in the town. For a start he attended the Brethren Meeting, an almost clandestine assembly that held services, bible studies and prayer meetings, in a room over Mussen Grumble's shop in the High Street. Originally from Peterhead, he had been brought to Hecklescar by his parents, when his father signed up on one of the large seine-netters that fished out of Hecklescar. They had bought a house on Millerfield, the new executive estate maturing on the outskirts of the town, and settled into the life of the community. Or rather, settled into those activities of the community which did not conflict with their principles. From youth, Nudge had long been driving heavy articulated lorries for Anthony Douglas & Son. Utterly dependable in every other way, Jakey knew better than to ask him to drive a load out of Hecklescar before twelve midnight on The Lord's Day. One minute past, and Nudge would turn up to drive his lorry wherever Jakey directed him.

Jakey's wife, Ina, who interests herself in life's ins and outs and ups and downs of the folk in the town, frequently enquires of her coffee morning companions where Nudge finds the money to buy up all those holiday houses. It is true that whenever a suitable house comes on the market; one in the middle of the town; in one of the old terraces, Nudge makes a pitch for it. Now he owns quite a string of them. (If you want to know which houses belong to him you do not need to Google it; just take a walk through the centre of the town. If you spot a house that is harled in pale blue, with the window surrounds picked out in light grey, the chances are that that is one of Nudge's. He has them painted by the apostolic painters, Peter and John, who are brothers, but not Brethren.)

John Henry explained that there is really no mystery about Nudge's apparent wealth. His parents were well off. He earns good money on the lorry and saves his lodging allowances by sleeping in the cab. Then he spends little of what he earns on the attractions of this Present Age. He doesn't drink, smoke, eat gourmet dinners, attend lavish parties, or take long holidays in the flesh pots of Europe. He drives a second-hand Skoda, cooks his own dinner, furnishes his own house, as he furnishes his holiday houses, from the furniture recycling depot run by the Salvation Army in Gainslaw. And he has never married.

'He's a decent man,' added John Henry. 'Keeps himself to himself, but will put his hand out for anyone. However, he's quite strict, and to some folk, I'm afraid, that makes him a hypocrite. As Ina once put it to me, 'nobody can hold it all in all the time; it's bound to come out."

John Henry laughed at the memory of Ina's serious face

as she pronounced her sentence. Peter smiled in return.

'What did she mean by that?'

'She didn't say, and I didn't dare ask. But you heard Angela. She obviously thinks he needs a woman.'

John Henry stopped suddenly, aware that he may have strayed into an area sensitive to Peter.

If he had, Peter showed no sign of agitation, but changed the subject.

'Everyone seems to call him Nudge. That can't be his real name?'

'No, but I haven't heard him called anything else. You'll need to look it up in the books. I think he got saddled with it when he was learning to drive. Something about the gear stick, or the clutch. He doesn't mind the label and answers to it.'

'Do we need to do anything about - what did they call her?'

'Jen – for Jennifer. No, I don't think so. You heard Angela. You could mention it to Jakey the next time you see him.'

'I'll do that,' replied Peter.

CHAPTER TWO

When Nudge and Angela interrupted John Henry and Peter Munro, the two men had more on their minds than Nudge's doubts about Jen. They had to find a way of saving the firm which employed them and forty others. Anthony Douglas and Son lay on life support.

Until last November, the company had been run by the Son of the title. Anthony, his father, had inherited a fish cadger's business from his father: a rented fish yard, a van, a supply of fish brought fresh from the boats, and fifty or so loyal customers up the country. He had transformed it into a large fish processing operation. His large 44-ton articulated lorries, resplendent in livery of Douglas tartan, picked up prawns and other seafood from ports on the west coast of Scotland and on the Moray Firth to supply his fish processing plant on the pier at Hecklescar. The same lorries then transported prawns, now labelled langoustines, to the gourmet tables of England and the Continent.

The Son, Harold Douglas had taken over the company when his father suffered a stroke, twenty years ago. At first, he had given it the attention it deserved but, believing himself designed for a loftier vocation than running a smelly fish yard in a poky little port, he had set up his own financial services business. Using his contacts and the family name, he garnered the savings of well-off professional people into investment portfolios of his own design. Having neither the experience nor the sagacity to run such a business, in a few short years, he had had to raid the coffers of the fish company to pay for his losses in finance. Just before Christmas, fearing discovery, disgrace and possibly prosecution, he had fled the town, but not before John Henry, a retired banker, had induced him to sell the company to him for £1.

It was worth nothing like that sum! Its debts soared above its assets. Its buildings, vehicles and equipment were dilapidated. It would take many millions to restore the company to anything like operating health. No sensible investor would put a penny into it.

John Henry had acted instinctively. He had sought to rescue Anthony Douglas & Son from inevitable and imminent demise, but did not have the resources to give it a future. He had acted because of the sort of man he is; out of care for the folk who worked there; for Jakey, the manager, Angela who ran the fish room, for the drivers, like Nudge and Jen; for Fiona in the office and all the other workers: fish gutters, packers and fork-lift truck operators, that depended on the work for their livelihood.

He had acted instinctively and, almost immediately, regretted it. He felt as old as his eighty-three years; every day trying to stitch together a life of some meaning without his wife and life companion of over fifty years. He wanted peace, to sit quietly at home with his memories, or walk through the town to be greeted and reassured by friends, to watch the telly or to read one of those heavy books he had always promised himself to read. Businesses, finances, and investments no longer interested him; they lay in the past; he had wanted to keep them there.

Then Jakey arrived in distress at the door. Harold, who went by the name of Hercules in the town, anxious to be shot of the company's liabilities, had offered to hand the company over to the employees. (For a small financial consideration, he told Jakey). The proposal had frightened Jakey who knew a great deal about fish, but scarcely anything about finance.

After an agonising week, Jakey had turned up at John Henry's house close to breakdown. John Henry had listened to him then instructed him to turn down the offer. Shortly afterwards, he found himself the putative owner of Anthony Douglas & Son. In no way did he share the relief that spread through the yard and the town. His aim had been to prevent the company falling into bankruptcy and liquidation for he knew that, once that happened, it could not be resurrected. He had acted to prevent that and had succeeded, but then what? He had no plan and no resources to call on. Nor could he believe that any of the company's debtors; banks, investment managers, wealthy and not so wealthy individuals, would be prepared to risk any further investment in such a run-down outfit.

However, as John Henry had worked his way through the long and depressing list of investors and debtors, he had come across a name he knew: Peter Munro. In it he glimpsed a faint light along the dark tunnel of the company's future. Perhaps?

Peter Munro belonged Hecklescar. His father, a builder, had made money by buying up old properties in and around the town, doing them up, then selling them on for a decent profit. When he died, these properties and profits fell to his son, Peter. Shortly afterwards, just over twenty-five years ago, Peter left Hecklescar taking with him his father's legacy. He had invested it to good purpose in developments in London and the East Midlands.

Most people would regard Peter Munro as a success. At fifty-five, with many millions in the bank, he had retired and come back to his home town. But he did not think of himself in such a way. He had arrived back in Hecklescar a few short weeks ago, ill at ease, seeking refuge from regrets that had plagued his life for the past few years.

He had in mind leaving his tangled concerns behind him and hoped to find in his native town, amongst his oldest friends and embedded memories, a peace of mind he had lost.

He did not think of his return as a route to a contented life. It could not be that; it had become the only road left to take.

All others had become ring roads; when he took them, he found himself back where he started. That first deal troubled him, that first deal that set him on the road to riches. Through his contacts in the building trade, he had got wind of possible large-scale developments of the Docklands area of London, and had bought a dilapidated warehouse and site owned by a Norfolk man by the name of Marney Wegg. Harried by the Health and Safety Executive and stretched financially, Marney had sold it to Peter Munro for a rock bottom price. He had not been aware of the site's development potential and Peter did not enlighten him. When Docklands Redevelopment went ahead, Peter sold on the warehouse for eight times the price he had paid Marney. That single transaction had given Peter a flying start. Astute, careful and, we might add, straight-dealing, Peter had prospered in property development and made a lot of money. But that first deceit bothered him. Had he passed on to Marney what he had heard, would Marney have sold him the warehouse? Had he cheated the man?

Whenever Peter bent the ear of his good friend Oliver about his doubts, Oliver reminded him of how Marney had summed up the deal: he had 'unloaded the warehouse onto some mutt with more money than sense.' But such reassurance had not laid Peter's fear to rest. He had, on at least two occasions, rescued the Norfolk man from financial embarrassment and had invested heavily in one of Marney's less doubtful enterprises. Such amelioration salved Peter's conscience, but it had not cured the anguish. He still regretted what he had done.

He had sought and received the patient care of a counsellor, Mrs Rostowski, who had, to add confusion to her task, sought to help him through a compounding regret: Peter had convinced himself that his wife's descent into despair, depression, addiction and eventual suicide was due to his neglect.

We do not need to track the labyrinth through which Peter led Mrs Rostowski. It can be read elsewhere. Sufficient to say that in the end Peter had decided to cut and run. He could not resolve his confusion. He was too good a man to excuse his actions; and too conscientious to ditch his regrets. He had returned to Hecklescar to find a way of living with himself.

Any yearning for a closeted life had been quickly snatched away. He had no sooner entered Hecklescar, than an old friend, John Henry, a retired banker, told him of the parlous state of Anthony Douglas & Son and sought his help to rescue it. Were it to fall, the livelihoods of forty families, families whose faces he knew, would fall with it.

Now he sat in the big chair in the office alongside John Henry and together the men were working on a plan to rescue the company from immediate collapse and establish it as a prosperous, profitable concern. I will not strain the patience of readers by detailing the plans they laid. Suffice it that investors would be invited to sell their holdings to Peter Munro and debtors relieved of their debt should they wish to offload it. If such offers were accepted the company would belong to Peter Munro, who would likely be poorer by over two million pounds. An amount equal to that would be needed to restore the dilapidated premises, plant and equipment.

Welcome home, Peter!

CHAPTER THREE

Had we followed Peter from Anthony Douglas & Son that day, he would not have led us to his home. He had no home in Hecklescar, nor did he have any immediate plans to acquire one. Peter had rented one of Nudge's holiday homes against the day he would buy a house of his own. The finding of such a house had occupied the time and strained the patience of local solicitor, Cockburn Heath and his indomitable secretary, Mrs Somerville, for some months now. That is where Peter is headed.

Peter is not visiting Cockburn to discuss a house in which he intends to live; he goes to talk about Latchlaw, a house and five-acre site that probably already belongs to him, but in which he has no intention of living.

You will recall that as John Henry trawled through the list of Anthony Douglas's creditors, he came across Peter Munro's name. Against it was a hefty sum: one and a half million pounds. Peter had been aware of the loan that his father had made to his friend, Anthony Douglas, many years ago but not of the agreement that cemented it, until John Henry explained it to him on his first day back on his native heath. According to this agreement, if the loan were not repaid, Latchlaw, a five-acre farm on the outskirts of Hecklescar, would be handed over in recompense. The deed assigning the land to Peter's father in default, had never been formally signed, due to the deaths of both men shortly after it had been concluded. The diligent Mrs Somerville, however, had unearthed a letter of agreement signed by both men. Cockburn in a rare burst of clarity had expressed the opinion that it would be evidence enough to convince a court that Latchlaw now belonged to Peter Munro.

A retired farm labourer, Alistair and his wife, Alice, lived in the Latchlaw farmhouse by permission of Hercules. We must credit Hercules with some kindness, but ought also to mention that he had calculated and calculated correctly that, if the old couple lived in the house, their son, Duncan, a builder, would maintain it.

Duncan had taken on Hercules' youngest son, Hector, as an apprentice. When he left school, two years ago, Hector fell out with his parents. He wanted to be a fisherman; they had in mind university and a profession. The deadlock had been broken by Christine, Hector's girlfriend - and Duncan's only child. She proposed that Hector should join her father's firm and learn a trade. His parents reluctantly agreed. Hector had responded so well that Duncan had decided to train him up to undertake the joinery work that, previously, Duncan had had to contract out. Duncan through a vague agreement with Hercules had taken over steading at Latchlaw to fit it out as a workshop but had put the work on hold until the true ownership of Latchlaw could be established.

Over the past few months, Janet, Duncan's wife, had become aware that Alice was slipping into dementia. Having no faith in Alistair's ability to care for his wife, Janet had recognised that Alice could not long be left on her own to look after the house and her husband. Janet and Duncan had therefore asked Hercules to sell them the farmhouse at Latchlaw. They would then move in beside the old couple. Hercules, however, in need of cash quickly had been on the point of selling the land to a housing development contractor when John Henry discovered that, almost certainly, the land did not belong to him but to Peter Munro.

Peter is visiting Cockburn Heath today to instruct him

to secure legal title to the house and land as soon as possible even if, to avoid a long legal wrangle, it meant paying a modest amount to Hercules.

Shortly before Christmas, Christine and Hector having married, had offered to move in with Alice and Alistair to save Janet the ordeal of moving. Janet had turned down the offer and must now dismantle her home of twenty-five years and reassemble it at Latchlaw. It is not a task she relishes. Some women make a career out of moving house, never quite content with what they have bought, always looking for something a little larger, or in a better part of town, or with a sea view; with a conservatory or en-suite bedroom, or something more up-to-date with underfloor heating, and built-in solar panels. Janet is not such a rolling stone; she has laboured on her solid stone villa in Priory Road since they first moved into it at enormous expense, not long after they married. They took over a tired, neglected property. It had been the home of a Mrs Dudgeon, a farmer's wealthy widow, who had passed on all her wealth to her family and spent none of it on the house. Had not Duncan persuaded Janet he could do most of the renovation himself, they would not have taken it on. It would be wrong to claim that, after twenty-five years of loving care and attention, the house had achieved Janet's ambition for it, but we must put that down to Janet's high standards rather than any deficiency in decoration or furnishing. Now she must part with it – and start again at Latchlaw with a house in a much worse state than Priory Road had ever been. But she would do it. What else could she do? Gentle, old Alice, her husband's mother, needed someone beside her. She could not be left to the attentions of her husband, Alistair.

Alistair would not accept Alice's deterioration. He had seen her dump a cake in the middle of making it; he had come in from the garden to find no meal ready for him; he had missed her from the house and had had to ring Duncan to find her; he had seen the blank look in her eyes as she tried to remember his name. Such evidence he ignored or explained away: 'she was getting old'; 'old folk do funny things at times'; that's all; 'she'll get over it'; 'most of the time she's fine'.

Duncan quietly, Janet bluntly, Christine wheedlingly, the doctor clinically, had all tried to get through to him but he simply did what he had done for all of his married life. He retreated to the fields, the shed or, latterly, the garden. As Janet plans to move into Latchlaw, Alistair and Alice have played their settled parts for forty-nine years. If it is not to be convulsed by Janet's arrival, she will need to 'gang warily'. 'Ganging warily', however, is not in Janet's nature; she was born to take over and run with it. Janet had determined that she and Duncan should not take the house over; it must remain Alice's home for Alistair and herself. However, determination is one thing; execution quite another.

CHAPTER FOUR

'To be honest, mother, I found him dull,' said Olivia to Connie when her mother asked her how she had enjoyed their Christmas meal with Peter Munro.

Three weeks had elapsed since they had sat together around the festive board in Avignon, Olivia's grand house in Alexandra Drive. In spite of the turbulent weeks that led up to the Christmas, Olivia had laid on a sumptuous meal – and, at her best, she could rival any hostess. Peter had worked his way through smoked salmon, turkey, trimmings, sorbet and pudding and had drunk his wine, with only slight satisfaction. He had had little to say; certainly, had listened intently to anything said to him, but showed no animation or enjoyment. Long before the coffee and mints were served, Olivia had formed the opinion that he had come only out of obligation and wanted to be away as soon as he could do so without offence. He was mannerly and polite, but disengaged, Olivia had concluded.

Connie made the enquiry because she remembered the meals they had all shared in the days before Harold Douglas, (whom we have been calling Hercules) had entered Olivia's life. That lay in the past; over twenty years ago. Back then their meals together were friendly, convivial, settled. Olivia was twenty-four, Peter almost ten years older. Connie had assumed that, sooner or later, they would settle down together. Then Harold Douglas swept in with a flashy car, pockets full of money and a pizazz that dazzled Olivia and soon left Peter and Connie taking tea together. Three weeks later, Olivia arrived back in Hecklescar, with a ring on her finger, and started life with Harold Douglas.

A good life it had been; good, that is, in that it suited Olivia. She had money, she had a big house in the best area of the town, she had position, and enjoyed the cream of society that the area had to offer.

Shortly after Olivia's return, Peter had quit Hecklescar to make his life and fortune in England. He had married a Norfolk woman by the name of Dylis Wegg, and had fathered two children.

Now he was back and Harold Douglas gone. No wonder it had crossed Connie's mind that his return might re-kindle the affection (she could not convince herself that it was love) that they once shared.

Ina, Jakey's wife, had chosen as her life's work the rearrangement of the lives of the people around her, and saw, in Peter's return, an inevitable reconciliation. This she had forecast to her companions who gathered regularly in McMaggie's for coffee, as soon as she heard that Peter intended returning to the town. She based her prediction on the evidence she had hoovered up as she had undertaken cleaning and other domestic duties for Olivia. Not long before Hercules' departure, however, Olivia had tired of her interference and innuendos and sacked her. This loosened both her tongue and her imagination. She did not precisely state that Olivia had ditched Hercules to make way for Peter but her listeners easily caught the drift of such a proposition.

We must not take such a suggestion seriously. Hercules had left of his own accord. Hercules had *had* to leave. He was chased away certainly, but not by Olivia. He could no longer hide from his own incompetence, the wrath of his creditors and the inevitable disgrace that would result from his exposure.

We will better appreciate Olivia's reaction by

understanding that, although the double bed that had blessed her earlier years with Harold might now lie abandoned in the master bedroom, it does not mean that she cried on her lonely pillow for their return.

Olivia had sought her fulfilment in the fripperies of life and found herself reasonably content. Any early passion she had felt for Harold had, over the twenty-odd years of their time together, cooled to a convenient accommodation. This suited both. Harold ran the business, played golf with well-off associates at Gullane, lauded it over his minions in Hecklescar, handed out favours when it suited him and generally regarded himself as a man of rank and influence. He also felt free to indulge other inclinations and interests, of which he hoped Olivia would not hear. Not for him the settled satisfaction of a family man; he thought himself made for wider vistas and elite enterprise. When Olivia discovered that Harold, in desperate need of money, intended to quit Hecklescar, she surprised him with her offer to buy Avignon from him and continue living in it; the house of his father, his home as a boy and man; a fine Victorian Villa in Alexandra Drive.

Olivia has no need of a house the size of Avignon. Now that Harold has gone, she will be on her own most of the time. Sally, their daughter, lives and works as a nurse in Edinburgh, coming home only for a couple of days between shifts. Their younger son, Hector, we know, has married and moved out. Alexander, the oldest, has long found the attractions of city life more to his taste than the mundane life of a small fishing town, and rents a small flat in Edinburgh. Whether he can remain in it, is a question he must now face, for he is now out of work. His father had employed him to manage the office of HD Investments, which office, due to the failure of the business, has been locked and deserted for several weeks now. Alexander, however, has shown no enthusiasm for returning to the family home.

For Olivia, the house is much more than a place to live. It is, as they say in documentaries about fine-furnished mansions, a statement of 'who I am'. Without Avignon, Olivia would subside into the ordinary. That Olivia could not face.

'Peter dull?' replied Connie. 'I suppose he is, compared to flash Harry. But then he has much to be dull about.'

She then told Olivia what she knew of the torturous road travelled by Peter Munro. She had the advantage of this knowledge over her daughter for she had met and talked to Peter from time to time over the past few years. Peter lay in Olivia's memory as the quiet, contented, pleasant young man that entertained her with his wide interests and soft humour. Connie, however, had, through his visits and his conversation, tracked his conversion to a thoughtful and at times, troubled man. He had not told her a great deal about his uneasy relationship with his wife, Dilys, but Connie had read between the lines of his narrative and had detected sadness and regret. Peter had met Dylis in Dereham in Norfolk, they had courted, married and had had two children, a boy and a girl. For a while they had been happy living not far away from Dilys's home, then, as his interests in London took hold, they moved to the capital.

'He did not tell me much about what happened there but I can guess,' said Connie. 'I think the big city frightened her. Peter was seldom at home; working all hours; and her with two small children. Peter believed that she stuck it out because she had been brought up to believe that a woman's place is by her husband side, even if that meant for only a few hours each day. I suspect that, in the end, she had a nervous breakdown, but Peter would never admit to that. Eventually they moved back to Dereham and Peter spent the week in London and weekends with the family. I believe the family eventually broke up.'

'She sounds a bit of a wimp,' cut in Olivia sourly.

Connie studied her daughter for a while, then said quietly,

'On the contrary, I believe she simply pushed herself beyond her strength. Peter never had anything but praise for her. His only criticism, if it can be called that, is that she kept her fears and her despair from him until it broke her. Not a wimp, I think, but a very brave woman. Peter thought so, anyway.'

Connie had more to say; more in defence of Peter, but Olivia had lost interest. She had an announcement to make.

'I came to tell you that next month I'm off on a three-month cruise.'

Connie looked at her daughter in astonishment. She is entitled to be astonished. Olivia has no money of her own. Hercules had drained the family coffers, and Olivia had had to borrow two hundred thousand pounds from her mother to buy out Hercules' share of Avignon. Olivia has a job: she is employed by Borders Council as a Social Worker; a job she has always hated, but one that now must supply her needs and wants. Over the years, using what influence and guile she could muster, she has lifted herself out of humdrum caring for the less fortunate. She now occupies one of those jobs whose title gives nothing away and, seemingly, involves the job holder in little actual work. She is a Senior Area Executive. She has also contrived to work for only three days a week, for which she is paid pro-rata. All of which means that what goes into her bank account each month will not run to a hundred and eight days with Cunard sailing round the world. Price quoted: £11,800. Where on earth can she lay her hands on that kind of money?

She has done what many professionals do when their jobs lose their zest, or their lives turn sour: she has opted for early retirement. She is only fifty, but with thirty years' service can expect a small pension and a decent lump sum. This she will squander in the of two older lady friends from Edinburgh, one of whom is divorced and the other, widowed. They sail from Southampton on 3rd February, having inherited, at a reduced rate, an outside cabin cancelled at the last minute. What will she do to earn her living when she comes back?

When, during the remaining days of January, she is asked that question, she will tell her mother earnestly that she has ideas but no firm plans. She will tell her friends airily that she will cross that bridge when she comes to it. But she will not admit the truth to any of them: she is running away.

CHAPTER FIVE

Olivia's absence will be no deprivation for Peter. He had found Olivia shallow. He preferred the Janets of this world, or even, the Dylises, before her depression flattened her. They grappled with life; Dilys, with courage; Janet, with grit and determination. Olivia had none of these qualities. She is an attractive woman, even now, but, in Peter's estimation, she skimmed over the surface of life rather than battling through it. But then, she had never had to battle; Hercules, for all his faults, had protected her from that.

Not that Peter gave much thought to Olivia. He had more pressing matters on his mind. He came away from Cockburn Heath reasonably sure that Duncan and Janet could proceed with the refurbishment of Latchlaw without risk. He could now concentrate his efforts on Anthony Douglas & Son.

Peter had no ambition to own Anthony Douglas & Son. He had promised to put money into the business, lots of money; it needed lots of money, but he wanted it to go into the building, premises and equipment, not out of the company to those who had invested in the past. Having worked through the accounts with John Henry, he agreed with the old banker that, beneath its debt, lay a productive and viable business. Down the road in, say, two or three years, properly managed, it could well produce a reasonable return for anyone prepared to leave their money in it.

Day by day therefore, Peter and John Henry worked

their way through the long and various list of creditors that Fiona had prepared. Hercules had borrowed widely and indiscriminately. They agreed that creditors would be encouraged to continue their support, but, if they wanted out, Peter would pay back what they were owed. They spilt the task between them: Peter would contact personal investors; John Henry would tackle the institutions. But before they approached anyone the two men started work on a business plan to present to the people they were to approach.

Both familiar with such work; they had done it many a time. Of Dodgy Donald and the Mallaig Fishermen's Co-op, however, they knew nothing at all. Nevertheless, Grubs raised the subject, not with the two boss men, but with Jakey. Grubs had arrived with a lorry load of prawns from Mallaig; a journey he usually made twice a week. As he sat with Jakey enjoying the usual cup of tea before heading back, he made an announcement

'You're lucky I'm here,' he said, somewhat smugly, Jakey thought.

'The Co-op is thinking of suspending operations. Dodgy Donald is asking who he should speak to about doing a deal, now that they're independent. He says they've been very patient, what with Hercules taking off, but it can't go on like this.'

'Have you considered, my friend,' replied Jakey pleasantly, 'that we no longer want your fish? When Mallaig was part of the firm, we had to take whatever rubbish you brought. Now you're going to have to up your act, or you'll need to dump it on somebody else.'

Grubs ignored this assault on his integrity and pressed his question.

'Who does he talk to?'
'He could talk to Peter, Peter Munro.'
'He's a builder, isn't he?'
'Close! Property development!'
'Property? What does he know about fish?'

'Not a lot, I would say, but he knows about money, so the Co-op'll need to have all their buttons on when they talk to him.'

Grub took from his back pocket a creased, grubby piece of paper. He laid it on Jakey's desk and, pressing down on it with both hands, attempted to straighten it. Then he took out a ball point pen, and addressed Jakey.

'How do you spell, (what is it? Murray?)

'No, Munro! M, U, N, R, O. D'ye want me to spell Peter?'

'No. Munro, Peter,' he repeated mechanically, and wrote the name down on the paper. He then carefully folded the paper and replaced it in his back pocket.

'I'll tell Donald,' he said.

Clearly he regarded himself as a man on a mission.

'Who employs you?' asked Jakey.

'You do,' he replied.

'Then why are you doing work for another firm?'

Grubs studied Jakey for a while, then muttered, 'Donald said they're thinking of taking me on.'

'Oh, are they?' smiled Jakey, enjoying Grubs' discomfort. 'In which case I'll get Fiona to make up your books.'

'You can't do that!' exclaimed Grubs. 'I haven't tendered my resignation. I'm still in discussions.'

'And you think we should go on paying you when you're looking for another job.'

'I'm not looking for another job. I'll be doing the same thing; I'll be driving the same lorry.'

'What? With Anthony Douglas on the side?'

'No, they'd change the name.'

'So, they're going to take the lorry as well.'

'Yes, it'll be no use to you . . ..'

'Stop right there! Nothing's been decided about who is going to ferry the prawns through from Mallaig, or whether there'll be any ferrying at all. And, if I were you, I wouldn't let anyone here know that you're thinking of jumping ship. Otherwise, you might get thrown overboard – with or without the lorry.'

Of course, Jakey couldn't leave it there. Certainly, nothing had been decided. Previously there had been nothing to decide. The operation at Mallaig: buying fish from the boats and despatching them to Hecklescar had been carried out under the name of Anthony Douglas, albeit by a separate company; Anthony Douglas & Son (Highland) Ltd. Hercules managed both and agreed with himself the terms of the deal. But he had sold the Highland company to the Mallaig Fishermen's Co-operative. Dodgy Donald, (whose real name is MacKay) skippered The Clansman and had been tasked by the management committee to seek a worthy buyer for their fish. Dodgy Donald relished the power granted to him. He would sell to the highest bidder: Anthony Douglas of Hecklescar, or Watt's of Fraserburgh who had been sniffing the contract for years.

Although Jakey had fobbed off Grubs, he knew that Dodgy Donald would soon lose patience. He had never met the man, but Grubs had frequently reported that Donald believed that Hercules had been ripping off the Mallaig fishermen for years. Not long after Grubs left, therefore, Jakey made his way up to the office to convey his concern to Peter. He found him in discussion with John Henry.

The two bosses listened carefully to what Jakey had to say, then called in Fiona to explain what kind of contract existed between the Hecklescar and Mallaig operations. Nothing in writing, Fiona reported. Now and again Hercules checked the prices of fish in the open market and paid the fishermen accordingly.

'Changed days, eh?' commented John Henry, 'I remember old Davie Rodger auctioning the fish on the quayside, box by box, day by day. When they had bought a box or two, the cadgers or dealers dropped a label into the box to show they had bought it. Quite a spectacle it was. People used to come from Edinburgh and Newcastle to see and hear it. It added excitement to the place. Now no more; it's all done behind closed doors and the fish lifted from the boats straight into lorries.'

Jakey remembered it well, a wispy memory stirred in Peter, but Fiona had never seen it.

Peter turned suddenly to Jakey.

'You could do that, couldn't you?' he said. 'You could agree a price with the Mallaig men from time to time. Fiona here could type up a form of agreement. You'll have done that sort of thing before, Fiona?'

Fiona agreed that she had typed up contracts with other suppliers and customers; she could keep Jakey right on the details. It would be no trouble. She would give him a list of headings to be agreed.

While Peter and Fiona were engaged in this conversation, John Henry studied Jakey and saw alarm.

Peter turned to him.

'Is that agreed then? Jakey, you can talk to Donald MacKay, see what he has to say.'

'Naw, naw,' exclaimed Jakey, 'That's no' for me, I canna' do that. Naw. That's for the boss tae dae. I ken about fish, I no ken onything about contracts. It would be ower much. I explained that to John here afore Christmas.'

Peter smiled. He had met this sort of reaction before. Good, experienced people; men (and mainly men) expert in the practical and nitty-gritty but scared at first by admin and management.

'No need to decide now,' he said pleasantly; 'I'll speak to Dodgy Donald and calm him down. We can wait a few weeks. Talk to John here about it, and Fiona. They'll tell you there's nothing to it. You tackle far more difficult stuff than that every day. Most of it is formal and standard practice. It'll be no trouble to you.'

Jakey gave no reply, but John Henry detected no weakening in his resolution not to venture into a chair behind a desk and a jungle of paperwork.

For John had seen what Peter had not; a frantic man

sitting on the edge of his seat in his front room, on the verge of tears: scared out of his mind by the thought of taking over the management of the company from Hercules.

CHAPTER SIX

'I don't think he'll take it on,' said John Henry to Peter after Jakey left.

'He could do it, couldn't he?' said Peter.

'Could be, but I'm not sure. I saw it at the bank: the boss packs in and the foreman decides to take it over. I remember a classic case here, a few years ago. Do you remember old Seppy Redfern; ran the garage, at the bottom of Northbraes. When he retired Billy Chisholm took it over; a man about your age, bit older maybe.'

'I remember Seppy and I remember the garage; it had an exotic name; what was it? 'Cavendish Motors'. He had a Rolls on the signboard; I don't think he ever had one in the workshop.'

'No, I doubt it. But that was Seppy; real name Septimus; he wore a suit and tie whenever he came to see me. But he ran a good business; a tight ship. Billy sunk it in two years.'

'Billy was in the top class when I was in the fourth. Where is he now?'

'Went on the oil rigs; met a lassie up in Aberdeen; left his wife here; lives up in the North East, I think.'

'And the mistake he made?'

'Two, really: wouldn't let the mechanics get on with their work, and he thought that the manager should spend big money on big ideas; he had the roof lifted so he could install a hydraulic lift, and bought a lorry load of second-hand cars to sell.'

'What about Jakey then?'

'Fear, I would say.'

John then told Peter of the night not many weeks back when Jakey had arrived at his door, frantic and close to tears: scared out of his mind by the thought of taking over the company. Hercules had tried to sell it through an agent, but had been told in the bluntest of language that no-one with any business sense would buy it, weighed down as it was by debts far exceeding its assets. Desperate to take something out of it, Hercules had, through Jakey, offered it to the employees.

'But this is different,' replied Peter. 'We'll put the company on a sound footing; he need not worry about that.'

John Henry studied Peter for a while then asked,

'Have you ever seen anything that Jakey has written down.'

'No, I can't say I have, but then it's early days.'

'You never will, unless Jakey can't avoid it. If he does put pen to paper you will think a child had written it. Jakey is barely literate. I'm sure he could make no sense of the documents that Hercules gave him to read.'

'Then how does he manage the plant now?'

'By word of mouth, long custom and sheer ingenuity. Don't get me wrong. Jakey is no ignoramus. I would think he is very intelligent. But his mother and father were layabouts and he was scarcely ever at the school. If he had had different parents he could have been a doctor or a solicitor.'

'Or a banker?' put in Peter, pleasantly

'Or a banker! Perhaps easiest of all,' smiled John.

'But why hasn't he gone on?'

'Well, first of all, he doesn't need to. He can get by. He's good at what he does and makes a decent living at it. Then there's pride. He'd have to admit his ignorance in front of all the people who work for him and with him. He'd be mortified.'

'Do none of them know what you know?'

'Hercules didn't, but I suspect Fiona has figured it out –

and learned to live with it. She doesn't give him much to read, makes sure he understands – and types up from dictation any written stuff he wants to pass on.'

Peter considered what John had said for a while then asked him.

'Who will manage the company then?'

We must see in Peter's question, his determination not to get sucked again into a life he had abandoned. He wanted to rescue Anthony Douglas & Son, but did not want to manage it. He had come home to escape all that.

He had discovered that day to day the firm ran sweetly enough, with Jakey, Angela in the yard, and Fiona in the office carrying out their daily duties with time-blessed expertise and efficiency. But he did not need Dodgy Donald's gripes to tell him that more would be needed than that. He knew, from experience, that every industry has its own way of life, a subtle network of expertise, information, capability and contacts, ways to get things done and to clear obstacles, known only to those who live with it every day.

He also knew that nothing stays the same for long. *'Established 1951'* on the letter heading of Anthony Douglas & Son meant nothing sixty years on, except, perhaps, that Anthony had been astute enough to steer the company to prosperity and the Son had run from the field before his luck run out.

Or not so much a field as a jungle. In business, at any turn, a competitor may find a more efficient way of carrying out the same activities, subverting suppliers, undercutting costs and prices and winning over customers. If you do not match them, or overtake them, you will be hunted down and eaten alive. You need to know your markets. Folk are fickle: they may want more of what you produce, or less, or something different. Are your old customers going to stay with you? Where will you find new markets? Will your suppliers continue to supply you, or will they find someone to pay them more for what they have to offer? What new restrictions and regulations does the government have up their sleeve that could cost you an arm and a leg – or close you down?

Jakey and Angela know that they need new buildings, plant and equipment, new freezers, new units, new tractors and trailers. But what to do? Replace what you have? Or invest in new systems, flow lines and machines? Which of the clamouring equipment companies know what they are doing; which palming off what they've made but can't offload? Angela had heard that the potato factory up the country had found a machine to do what the workers did and paid them all off. And she'd seen something about a gutting machine for fish, and wonders what that would mean for her girls?

Peter is planning to spend millions on the yard. He must find answers to all these questions before he does, or his money will drain away to no purpose, and leave the company in a worse shape than when he found it. He understands the property business, all its twists and turns, but of fish processing, practically nothing.

'We will need a manager,' he said to John Henry before they broke up for the day.

'Of course,' replied John Henry. 'But don't look at me. I know nothing about fish – and I'm much too old to learn.'

'So, if Jakey won't do it, or can't do it; we'll need to find someone who can. Someone who understands this business.'

'Like Dodgy Donald?' said John blandly.

Peter smiled then, lifting a paper from the desk, stated,

'Or Clouston Pritchard.'

'Who?'

'Clouston Pritchard. Have you heard of him?'

'Clouston? No! Never heard. . ... Just a minute, there was a Pritchard in amongst the minor investors. Could that be him?'

'Almost certainly.'

'Why do you ask?'

'Because he is a director.'

'A director? I thought there were only three – Harold,

Olivia and a nominee from the bank.'

'You'd be correct, if you were talking of Anthony Douglas & Son. But, apparently, Harold created a shell company twelve years ago, by the name of HD Processing Ltd. It has no assets and no liabilities that I can determine, but it has never been wound up. Clouston Pritchard is a director along with Harold and Alexander, Harold's son. Fiona drew my attention to it.'

'So, who is he, this Clouston?'

'Fiona doesn't know, but she thinks Olivia might.'

'Are you going to ask her?'

'I had better, you never know with these subsidiaries; they have a nasty habit of turning up with an old agreement that gives them a claim on the parent firm. We wouldn't want that.'

CHAPTER SEVEN

'She's been put out of her house,' announced Ina to the ladies who gather in McMaggie's to drink coffee and sort out the lives of their neighbours.

By 'she' she means Jen, but let me immediately scotch your suspicion that Jakey, Ina's husband, has conveyed this information to her. Jakey knows Ina better than to tell her anything any of his workers has told him.

Certainly, Jakey has followed up what Nudge told him, but uncovered little he did not already know. He had not mentioned Nudge's fear for her safety. He had not even arranged a special meeting; had not called her to see him; he had just used the routine occasion of planning her round to ask if 'everything was alright'. She had told him that son Callum was still in the Borders Mental Health Unit, but that she hoped he would be allowed out soon. His bairns, Malcolm, Bethany and Gabriella were fine – and his wife Keira, had allowed her to visit on Sunday and play with them. When he had asked if there was anything he could do for her, she had only repeated her constant request to be given more hours. She seemed tense, Jakey reported, but coping.

What, then, is this about the house – and where has it come from? Not from Nudge. When he and Jen met on the cliffs, although he could clearly see her distress, he had done the same as Jakey; asked her if she were alright, and had, more or less, got the same answer. Jen had said nothing about the house on their walk back to Hecklescar. In fact, she hardly spoke at all; neither did he. What they did say concerned fish and deliveries; nothing at all about Jen's tears or her house. They are, after all, merely work colleagues.

Nudge has said nothing to anyone apart from Peter, John Henry and Jakey. Angela wouldn't blab, nor would Fiona. Besides we know that those conversations contained nothing about the house. Why then does Ina believe that Jen is in danger of losing being put out of her house?

Because of the board in Cockburn Heath's window that advertises properties for sale. Jen's house appeared on the board a day ago; Ina thinks she knows why. She knows enough of Jen, knows that she is a widow; knows about her son; knows about the wife and bairns; knows that Jen works all the shifts that are spare; knows that she is always short of money. Ina has wondered, as all the coffee ladies have, how on earth she could afford that muckle house on Millerfield Park, the executive estate on the edge of town, on the kind of money she makes?

Now it is up for sale - *with immediate entry*!

Immediate entry! What does that mean? That she is leaving Hecklescar, has found somewhere else to live, or, that she is being put out of the house. To Ina it is obvious. She has heard no word of her buying anything else in the town, and she knows from Jakey that the woman is hanging on to her job at the yard. That leaves only one explanation: she is being put out of the house.

Ina, however, has more to say: 'I'm not surprised,' she concluded. 'I've aye thought there's a story there. Dear knows what she's been up to. She's what I call a husband hunter.'

'But didn't she lose her husband?' said Margaret. 'He died of cancer, about what, ten years ago. Not long after they came here.'

'He did,' confirmed Ina, 'but I wasn't thinking of that husband; I was thinking about hunting for a new one. Nudge, for instance, needs to keep his buttons fastened. She's after his money. They were out for a walk the other day, ye ken; up by Hawks' Ness.'

'Or perhaps she's after someone else's husband,' put in Pat. 'Jakey, for instance.'

At this, all the ladies laughed. All, that is, apart from Ina.

A few days later the house came up in another conversation: between Peter and Mrs Somerville, who assists Cockburn Heath when she is not telling him what to do. Peter had called in to see the solicitor but found him not in the office. Mrs Somerville, however, who had spent the past few months searching for a house in Hecklescar, drew the house on Millerton Park to his attention, handed him the details and suggested that he take a look at it. He thanked her and returned to the yard. There he found John Henry in serious conversation with Jakey. Something about a load, destined for Spain that had ground to a halt somewhere in the South of England. Nudge had rung John Henry asking for some sort of clearance but John hadn't had the faintest idea what he was talking about so had sent for Jakey. The two men were now waiting for Nudge to ring back.

'Mrs Somerville is very persistent,' said Peter lightly as he entered, laying down the handout on the house. 'She's determined to find me a house whether I want one or not. That's the latest.'

John Henry picked up the handout, scanned it quickly then, by way of diversion announced.

Estate agents have a way of mangling the language. Listen to this:

Crovie, 17 Millerfield Park is a substantial beautifully presented detached villa with three spacious bedrooms, two of which have en-suite facilities, and a large well-appointed bath/shower room. Downstairs boasts two elegant reception rooms, an office/study, a large and well-equipped kitchen in addition to a convenient utility room and downstairs shower and toilet facilities. The whole set in a large and mature garden with off-

street car parking and garaging in a sought-after established residential area. Modern central heating and double glazing throughout. Some attention necessary, but the whole is in good condition throughout.

With immediate entry.

Peter laughed, but not Jakey.
'Where?' he asked.
'Millerfield Park,'
'What was the name?'
'Crovie, number 17.'
'That sounds like Jen's house. She comes from up there, the Moray Firth. So did her man. What did it say: 'For immediate entry'? I didn't know she was moving. She's selling up? Where's she going?'

Questions with no answers from his two listeners. Nor from Fiona when they interrogated her; or Nudge when he rang back. But in all four men a new question: did the sale of the house have anything to do with Nudge's fears for Jen on the cliffs up at Hawks' Ness? It could be no longer dismissed as a misunderstanding nor put down to Nudge's sense of drama. They must make sure the poor woman was not in serious trouble; even if she were reluctant to talk about it. Who could be entrusted with such a task? Peter scarcely knew the woman; Jakey knew her too well. Nudge had neither the skills nor the courage to tackle it, so the burden fell on John Henry. He must find out why Jen is selling her house – and if there is anything the firm could do to help her.

Before he set out for Millerfield Park, John thought he should check the facts with Mrs Somerville. After all, all he had to go on was Jakey's hunch that, with a name like Crovie, a small village on the Moray Firth, the house must belong to Jen. It was as well John Henry checked for when he contacted Mrs Somerville, she quickly put him right. The house is being sold, she informed him, not by Jen, but by a Robert Cowie, of Aberdeen. John Henry would like to have enquired further; to have asked who this Robert Cowie might be, and what claim he had on the house, but he did not dare. Even if he had had the courage to ask the question, he suspected that Mrs Somerville would not answer it.

CHAPTER EIGHT

John Henry left it until almost eight o'clock to call on Jen. Jakey had told him that often she didn't return from her round until well after six. And he knew that the following morning, while many hours of darkness still remained, she would drive her van to the fishyard where she would take aboard fish to be delivered to hotels, guest houses, restaurants, cafes, and shops down into Northumberland. She would not return again until well after dark.

John decided to walk to Jen's house. It lay not far from his own house in Hallydown Terrace and the night, though dry, was cold and dark. The car would be a nuisance, he thought. The houses in Millerfield Park, unlike his own, had retreated from the roadside and could only be got at by a path or drive; their numbers and names almost without exception being displayed on or beside the front door. If he took the car, he reasoned, he'd have to dismount, go down each drive until he found the right house; better to walk. He had the address: 17 Millerfield Park, the top end of the estate; a quiet cul-de-sac, where, he discovered, each 'substantial detached villa', determinedly tried not to be like any other in the street. Number 17 lay at the far end of the street and he knew instantly that this must be Jen's house; an Anthony Douglas & Son van rested in the drive.

As he walked towards the house, John found himself speculating that Jen's affluent neighbours may well turn up their noses at a fish van parked more or less permanently in their exclusive neighbourhood. Could that have anything to do with the house being for sale? Or, perhaps, more brutally, did they regret that someone so obviously financially inferior had inveigled her way into their midst. He then shook himself out of his scepticism. He knew quite a few residents at Millerfield and could scarcely label any of them snobs.

John rang the bell at Crovie, but received no response; he then knocked on the door. After a few moments Jen opened the door and was clearly surprised to see him on her doorstep.

'What's wrong?' she asked.

'Nothing, nothing at all,' he replied pleasantly, 'I just thought I'd pop round to see if there's anything we can do for you.'

Jen studied him for a moment then, remembering her manners, ushered him into the lounge. As she did so, it struck John that she was dressed for bed, with her dressing gown over her pyjamas. He immediately apologised and said he would come back at a more convenient time.

She turned down his offer, explaining that when she came in from work she invariably had a shower and made herself ready for bed; but would not retire for another hour or so. John apologised again. In return she offered him coffee. He accepted, but felt ill at ease.

In the days before bank managers were captured by computers, John Henry had, on occasion, to visit the premises of a failing business. Such firms, he would report to his wife Lizzie, had a desolate air about them; you could almost smell the sense of defeat and despair; of the boss hanging on for dear life. As he sat in Jen's lounge the same feeling swept over him. What was it? The room was large with a wide picture window opening onto the front garden. The walls were tastefully decorated in a muted magnolia while off-white paint picked out the doors, skirting and coping. The furniture, two large settees, armchairs, sideboard, coffee table and occasional table sat on a cream-coloured patterned carpet. A patterned

Persian rug lay in front of an electric mock log fire. Landscape pictures adorned all the inside walls. Someone with taste had decorated and laid out this room. It should have been bright and welcoming; but something about it chilled him. Vapid was the word that crept into John Henry's mind. The framed photographs that stood on the sideboard and mantelshelf should have brought life and warmth into the room but they did not. You can tell a lot from the photographs with which people populate their houses but John Henry could not see them well from where he sat and did not wish Jen to find him prying at them when she returned. From what he made of them, however, he conjectured that only one could be called a family photograph: a man and a woman, and a child. The others were, he thought, of Jen in her younger days with friends. They gave the room, he thought, a dated, tired look. Then he corrected himself. Perhaps, he might be reflecting his own thoughts onto it. Perhaps, Jen never used this room. Why should she? She lived alone; this room belonged to a family.

Jen returned and poured coffee from a china jug, into matching cups. John refused sugar from the bowl but allowed Jen to add some milk. She then offered him a biscuit from a china plate and apologised for the lack of home baking. While she did this, John Henry tried to make sense of it all; tried to fit it into a frame. She struck John not only as an attractive woman, but as a refined one. The house, furnishings, jug, plates, cups spoke of a cultured lifestyle and a comfortable income, yet Jen drove a fish van for scarcely ten pound an hour, for all the hours she could gain.

Eventually Jen sat down on the settee over against him and looked at John with an intensity that disconcerted him. He had come anticipating a quiet chat, some innocuous conversation about the weather, the time of year, what she made of the country through which she passed on her round, her family and friends. Once he had established contact, he would casually introduce the riddle of the house. Her look ruled that out. He could read her mind: what have you come for? I am afraid of what you are going to tell me. In her look, John Henry learned what Nudge had seen at Hawks' Ness: she stood on the edge.

While John searched for a beginning, Jen spoke.

'Is it about the job?' she blurted out.

'No, no,' said John, 'Not at all.'

Still John scrabbled for a place to start. Chat was out, but what could he say that would not cause offence, or alarm - more alarm. Jen shifted her gaze and sipped her coffee. John out of options, plunged in.

'You may well see this as interference, but let me assure you of our concern. Nudge told us about meeting you on the cliffs; he thought you were distressed. Then Jakey mentioned that your house is up for sale. We wondered if they were connected. But, as I said...'

John stopped. He had half-expected anger, resentment, an explosion of animosity. But Jen had broken down in tears. John rose from his chair, sat down beside her, and gently laid his arm on her shoulder.

'What is it?' he asked quietly.

'I'm sorry,' she sobbed, 'but it's so distressing. I don't know where to turn, or who can help me. The house . . .'

She stopped. John Henry said nothing; he would give her time. She sat for fully ten minutes, every now and again attempting to speak, then breaking down and falling silent.

Each time John murmured, 'take your time,' and continued sitting beside her.

Then suddenly she stood up.

'This won't do,' she announced in a trembling voice. 'Would you like more coffee?'

John thought about refusing then joined her in her defiance by accepting the offer. She smiled. Then, lifting the coffee jug, she walked out of the room to go into the kitchen.

John Henry's heart went out to her.

When she returned, she poured out the coffee before launching into her story. John Henry recognised and admired the woman's resilience. Whatever storm raged in her mind she had determined (once again) not to be overwhelmed by it.

'I am not selling the house,' she said, 'my husband's family are doing that.'

She then explained to the old banker that when she and her husband, Charlie, married, he was much older than she; twenty-three years; and he already had three children, two girls and a boy; all of them, by that time, grown up; the oldest twenty, the others in their teens.

'I made the mistake,' she said sadly, 'of trying to be a second mother to them.'

'That is a mistake?' enquired John sympathetically.

'In this case, yes.' She made to go on, then glanced at John and, he suspected, cut short what she was going to say.

John suddenly became aware of how he must appear to her: an old man, her employer, a rusty banker nosing into her affairs. None of these, he sensed, qualified him to counsel her. Or even to understand her. He saw that she had come again close to tears, so he switched to territory more familiar to him in the hope he could save her pain and calm her down.

'I think I see where this is going,' he said gently. 'Your husband, Charlie, wasn't it? Left the house to his former family. Is that it?'

Jen nodded her head.

'Yes, that's it,' Jen replied, her words rattling out, as if she wanted rid of them. 'But the will did grant me the right to live here until Callum, my son, reached eighteen.'

'I see,' said John Henry, and left it there, although many questions raced through his mind, not least that Callum had long passed that age, was married and had a family of his own. Yet Jen had clung onto the house.

'So, you need somewhere to stay,' said John shifting to practicalities. 'I think we can help with that.'

'Thank you,' said Jen, 'but I've spoken to Nudge. He's going to let me have one of his houses.'

CHAPTER NINE

John Henry left Crovie and stepped into the cold darkness of a January night. At the end of the cul-de-sac he stopped, turned and looked back at Jen's house. It had relapsed into darkness.

That troubled him. It struck him that night had swallowed up the woman. This arose not as conscious thought, but from an impression that had settled on him as he slogged with his own wife Lizzie through her last days. Since then, he could think of no one else's distress without being overshadowed by the same dark cloud.

What had his visit accomplished? Nothing. His visit may well have made things worse. He had not been able to comfort the woman, had not found it in him to give her the support, the listening ear, and understanding heart she needed.

His brief encounter with Jen had persuaded him that Nudge had been right to be concerned about Jen when he saw her standing on the edge of the cliff. John felt he must not leave it. He could not walk away. What if to-morrow he heard that . . .? And he thought he knew what must be done; a question asked – and answered.

He went back and knocked on the door.

Jen answered almost immediately and invited him in. Once seated in the lounge again, he immediately said, stated in such a way that it could not be turned back.

'This is well outside my territory, but, Jennifer, I feel it is necessary that you talk to someone. I'm not the right one, but is there a friend you can confide in?'

Jen stared at him intensely. For a moment he thought she would refuse to answer his question and ask him to leave. Then with a sad smile, she said,

'When you do not come from Hecklescar you have no friends, only acquaintances.'

The weariness in her voice, and pleading in her eyes, confirmed in John that he had guessed correctly. Jen felt alone in her distress; she had no-one, no friend, to whom she could pour out her grief; no-one to help lift the weight crushing her; no-one who would hug her and cry with her.

'But acquaintances can become friends,' said John gently, 'I know; I'm not from Hecklescar, but I have a few good people here I would call friends now. Is there no-one?'

Jen dropped her head and said quietly,

'I understand what you are saying. I have thought about who I could talk to. I met a lady in the Bridge Club, and we became quite friendly. She told me her troubles; I told her mine, but when Charlie died, I'm afraid I went into a tunnel and hid myself away. I could talk to her then. But that was ten years ago. . ..'

She stopped and looked at him wearily. He couldn't quite understand her. One moment she seemed to be crying out for help, the next shrinking back, bringing down the shutters. He felt ill at ease. Should he be troubling the woman further. He'd already pushed his interference too far, hadn't he? Yet he was anxious to continue the conversation, to understand what Jen really wanted – and what she needed.

'What was her name?' he asked.

'Connie', replied Jen, 'Connie, an older lady, I think she was some sort of relative of Hercules. I have seen her once or twice down the street, but we haven't spoken for years. She has probably forgotten all about me.'

John breathed a sigh of relief.

'If it's the Connie, I know, she will not have done that. You could not have a better friend. She's not from here either and as they say here, 'she has not had her troubles to seek'. She's the mother of Olivia, Hercules wife, and you know what they've been through lately. She's utterly reliable, and, because she isn't from the place, will keep what you tell her to herself. You can rely on that. Do you want to ring her or will you leave it to me to contact her?'

This last was too much for Jen.

'Oh, no. no! You can't do that. I cannot inflict my troubles on her after all this time. Please, I should not have suggested it. Leave it, please. Leave it. I'll be alright. I'll work it out. Please.'

When John reached home, he felt miserable - and in two minds. What should he do? What Jen had asked him to do: leave it? Or do what his instinct demanded: contact Connie? Although it was not yet eight o'clock, he set about his usual nightly routine. He measured out his porridge to steep over night, set the breakfast table, put a hot water bottle in his bed. Whether he had done what he had set out to do that day or not, these simple tasks marked the end of his accomplishments. The day's work over, he could now set it aside and relax: read the paper or a light book, watch the telly, play a few tunes on his organ.

But to-night he could not relax, could not shift his mind from Jen sitting bereft in that lifeless room. He had stirred her up; perhaps she had already written off her day and had been anxious only to reach her bed and turn off the light; to numb herself, as she had learned to do, and hope for sleep. Then he had turned up on her doorstep, opened up her anguish but provided no cure or comfort. Everything about his visit counselled him to let it go; he had blundered: leave it. But as often as he laid this injunction on himself, so often did the insistent claim continue knocking on the door of his concern: she needs help. Now!

It would not lie. He had settled himself in his chair

before the fire and had switched on the telly. Now he stood up, picked up the phone and rang Connie. It was almost nine o'clock. How should he explain his call at such a late and inconvenient hour? Hardly the time for a chat - that he had bumped into Jen and discovered that they used to play bridge together? That would not do, but what would?

He needed no answer to such a question. Connie answered his call almost immediately. He had scarcely introduced himself before Connie replied.

'Oh, hello, John. I thought it might be you. I've had Jennifer Reid on the phone. I believe you went to see her earlier this evening.'

CHAPTER TEN

Had Connie not learnt what Jen is now learning, the meeting between them would not have taken place. Although, in the immediate resolve of John Henry's evening visit, Jen had rung Connie, and asked her if she could talk to her; although she had agreed to come to Connie's house the following evening, the meeting did not take place; not then. The following morning as Jen climbed into her van, drove to the yard, loaded her packets and boxes of fish and checked it out with Jakey, her resolve had begun to wane. By the time she had driven along familiar roads, had delivered her first order to a regular restaurant in Rothbury and the second to a friendly chef in Elsdon, the first fingers of dawn and the bracing normality of her daily routine had persuaded her that she could battle on without exposing her weakness to a comparative stranger. Half way through her round she had pulled into a layby, rang Connie and called off the meeting.

Although Connie had accepted Jen's excuses: that she had been delayed and that by the time she cleaned the van, she would be running late, Connie understood that once vans and fish, deliveries and customers, roads and destinations fell behind her as she drove into her drive at Millerfield the bracing protection of the ordinary would fall away; understood that, as she opened her front door, the old demons would crawl from the shadows and no warming cup of tea, no refreshing shower, no blaring television would shut them out. She called

Jen at nine and said she'd call at seven the following evening. Jen, apart from the feeblest of protests, made no attempt to dissuade her.

For years she had bottled up the seething emotions that troubled her waking hours and startled her awake in the middle of the night. She had resolved to find her own way through to the settled life she had believed to be the deserved destiny of everyone. But as year added to year, no relief had lifted the load, false dawns had come and faded. Over the past few days, these cursed dark, bleak days of January, her resolve had disintegrated. Had Nudge not arrived on the cliff when he did . . .? John Henry had thrown her a lifebelt. She had grabbed it. Could she trust a comparative stranger with her anguish? Could she not?

(Before they meet, I ought to correct an impression I may have given by reporting Jen's membership of the Bridge Club. I don't want you to think that Connie and Jennifer come from the same stable. Connie, now in her seventies, grew up in affluence and refinement. Her father was Professor of Medieval History at Edinburgh University; her mother, daughter of a partner in a shipping company. As a girl she lived in Morningside and attended Gillespie's school there before moving on to Edinburgh University, where she graduated with a second-class degree in French. All of which secured her a sophisticated but shallow lawyer husband who brought her to Hecklescar as the Town Clerk's wife. When she meets Jen, she has been a widow for thirteen years.

While Connie's refinement is the product of her upbringing, Jen, as we shall see, has had none of the advantages of Connie's early life. She gained her membership of the East Berwickshire Bridge Club by accident, and her china cups by acquisition.)

After two or three meetings the old casual acquaintance deepened into friendship and mutual sympathy. As it did so, Jen showed less and less reluctance to talk about her past life.

'When we married,' she explained, 'Charlie was a widower and I was divorced. He was a good bit older than me; over twenty years older,' she stopped, looked at Connie for understanding, then with a weary smile added, 'but I'd tried the younger ones.'

Connie smiled in encouragement.

'His wife had died a few years earlier. They had had three children, the oldest girl not much younger than me. It was never going to work; I should have seen that, but when you're thirty and desperate for things to work out for you, you believe all is possible. It was my third marriage. I had married Billy from school when we were eighteen, and separated soon afterwards. Round about the same time, I met Lionel, an army captain, from Fraserburgh. When my divorce came through, I married him.'

She stared at Connie for a moment or two, then added,

'He didn't want a wife, he wanted an ornament, or should I say, a shelf of ornaments, of which a wife was one. You understand me?'

'I'm afraid I do,' murmured Connie, 'I'm not sure that, at one time, I became something of the sort. I remember once going to Kelso races with Fordyce. It struck me vividly that the wives and girlfriends were being paraded as well the horses. He denied it, of course.'

She smiled and thereby coaxed a smile from Jen. Connie eased her forward in her story.

'Then you met Charlie?'

'Yes, dear old Charlie,' said Jen almost lightly, then corrected herself.

'Oh, what a way to describe your husband! But he was a dear man and very good to me. I only wish I could say I was as good to him.'

Jen stopped. Connie thought she would go on to explain what she meant, but she stopped and dropped her head, in embarrassment, Connie thought, and filled the gap.

'What did Charlie do?' she said.

'He had had his own boat,' Jen replied. 'In Peterhead, but sold up when his wife took ill. The Dutch were offering big money for the quota, never mind the boat, so he just took the chance and stayed at home with his wife until she died.'

Connie wanted to ask how long that had been before Jen had met him, but did not need to ask.

'I had known Charlie for many years; he had been a good friend of my father; he crewed for Charlie at one time, I think. I'd taken a job at the fish shop on the pier, and Charlie used to come in. I suppose he felt lonely, and I was, as you say, disillusioned with young men and staying clear of them so, when he asked me out, I accepted. It went on from there, I suppose. After a couple of years, he asked me to marry him. I was thirty, he was fifty-three. I thought, 'Why not? He is a good, decent, thoughtful, kind man.''

As she heard the heaped-up adjectives, Connie wondered whether Jen sought to commend Charlie to her, or to convince herself that she been right to marry him.

'I really loved him,' said Jen at last, 'and we were blessed with our son, Callum. I miss him; he was just there, always; you know what I mean.'

'I think I do, but I am guessing. Not all wives welcome their husband always being there.'

Jen studied Connie for a few moments, then asked tentatively,

'Including you?'

'Including me, I'm afraid.'

Connie, seeking common cause with Jen would have gone on to explain what she meant: that her husband Fordyce irritated her with his shallow sophistication and posturing. She would have shared with her that, when her husband heard that she had cancer, he left her to face it alone – and that relieved her of keeping up the pretence of being a happy couple; that she would prefer to battle through on her own.

Jen, however, absorbed in her own story, had no attention to give to Connie's.

She smiled.

'I have something to be thankful for?'

'You would seem to.'

Her answer brought no comfort to Jen. Her smile vanished, banished, thought Connie, by some disturbing recollection.

Connie sought safer territory; but did not find it.

'You call your house, Crovie. That's up on the Moray Firth, is it not? Is that where you come from?'

'No,' replied Jen bleakly. 'Charlie named the house; his parents were brought up in Crovie; I'm from Peterhead.'

'Of course, I should have remembered that,' said Connie lightly, then added, 'so what brought you to Hecklescar?'

If Connie thought this innocent question would lighten Jen's mood she miscalculated.

'Charlie wanted us to come,' she said flatly. 'To get me away from the family, I expect. It had not worked out. I think they resented me. Perhaps they thought I was after his money,'

Jen smiled weakly,

'Being so young didn't help. Charlie saw it. I wanted to battle it out. (Oh, that's the wrong word! I don't mean I wanted to fight them! No, I didn't want that!)'

'Work through it?' suggested Connie gently.

'Yes,' clipped Jen. 'But Charlie thought we should make a fresh start. He loved us both, he said, the family and me. He knew Hecklescar from his fishing days. He supplied Hercules for a while, and the house came up for sale. So here we came and made a home of it. Callum liked the school here; he didn't take to it in Peterhead.'

Again, Connie tried to lift the conversation; to find some inert topic that would shift their conversation to a happier theme.

'I'm a stranger too, I think you know that - from Edinburgh. But Hecklescar's a good place to live is it not?'

Jen would not be shifted.

'I thought that at first, but after Charlie died, I felt

isolated. Still do.'

As Connie sought her next comforting counsel, the enormity of Jen's despair struck her. She had called to mind the consolation, the reinforcement that she, Connie, drew from the love and attention of her granddaughter Sally, but no family refuge beckoned Jen. Connie knew that her son Callum languished in the Borders Mental Health Unit; and she had been told by John Henry that his wife Keira, and his two children lived on the Poplace Estate; had also been told that sometimes Jen was allowed to visit them, sometimes not. She upset the bairns, complained Keira, talking about their father.

Connie realised then that the long hours of work Jen sought were a distraction from a life that lay desolate elsewhere, and that she had nowhere to hide, save in that house that would now being wrenched from her.

What then could she say? This:

'Look, Jennifer, 'I want you to promise to call in and see me, every day, when you come from your work. I'll have a cuppa ready for you, and a shoulder to cry on. Promise.'

'No,' exclaimed Jen, 'I can't do that.'

'You must,' stated Connie, 'I insist.'

'I don't work every day. My regular shifts are Wednesday, Thursday and Friday. I'm no fit company after twelve hours on the road. But I could come on Mondays and Tuesdays.'

'Yes,' replied Connie, 'Of course – and on Sunday.'

'On Sunday, yes; after I've been to see Callum. That would be good.'

CHAPTER ELEVEN

Hector, at the best of times, never had much to say, but one day in the last week of January, Duncan could scarcely get a word out of him. As the young man opened his lunchbox his complaint revealed itself.

'Me and Christine have fallen out,' he griped, contemplating the contents of his bait tin.

Christine, you will remember, is Duncan's daughter.

He and Duncan were sitting in the builder's truck taking a break from a job on which they were working: putting a new roof on the garage of Mrs Purdie's house up on the Redhills Estate. Mrs Purdie, an old friend of Janet, had offered them soup and a sandwich but Duncan preferred the solace of the cab and a bite of whatever Janet had packed in his tin. On a cold dull day, they had driven the van a little way along the cart track that leads to the fields that blanket the cliffs to the north of the town, then pulled off the track to take in the view of Coldingham Bay and distant St Abb's Head.

'How long have you been married?' asked Duncan pleasantly.

'Six weeks,' replied Hector.

'You've done well,' commented Duncan. 'We fell out on our honeymoon. What did you fall out about?'

'Me knockit. She said I should get it myself. She said that I knew where everything was and she had her work to go to.'

'And had she?'

'Yes.'
'What time did she have to start?'
'Six o'clock.'
'This morning?'
'Aye, this morning.'
'Way before you. Were you up?'
'I was but, when I asked her about ma knockit, she said, 'Ye'll need to get it yersell."
'That no' sounds like a fall oot to me.'
'But she's aye made it up before.'
'That may be, but she's pit doon a marker. You'll get it when you get it, but no expect it.'
'That's no' what Craig says. He says that women like to be dominated by the men in their lives.'
'Did he now? Craig that goes to the crabs with you? Him?'
'Aye'
'Craig knows about women?'
'He says he does. He found it in a magazine he read in the Turkish barber's.'
'Is he married?'
'No.'
'Girl friend?'
'He was biding with this lassie but she pit him oot.'
'She pit him oot! And this is the man that's giving you advice about women.'
'He said she pit him oot because he was too feeble. She liked strong men. That was before he read the bit in the magazine.'
'Oh well, that makes him an expert. Did he say if the article mentioned any Christines - or Janets?'
'Well, no it wouldn't. It was a about women in general.'
'Women in general, eh? As far as I can see, and I haven't read the magazine, there's no such thing as women in general; they're all different.

Duncan detected that Hector, with Craig and the

magazine behind him would not be persuaded by an old married man. Hector pressed on.

'Janet pits your knockit up every day. Christine should do the same for me.'

'Janet no' starts work at the Co-Op at six o'clock in the morning.'

'I'll defy her. I'll no' ask her; I'll make up ma ain tin.'

'I wouldn't advise that. I know our Christine. It'll make things worse. She'll think you've fallen out.'

'But we have.'

'Yes, I know you have, but if you want to make up your own tin for the rest of your working life, you'll make it up to her.'

'Make it up! But it wisnae' me that. . . '

Duncan held up his hand to silence Hector.

'That's no' the point. The point is to make sure that tomorrow morning, when she's not at the Co-Op, she makes up your tin – and makes it up, when she can, for the rest of your natural. This is not the advice ye'd get from Craig, and ye'll no find it in any magazine, but as a general rule, when Janet pits her fit doon, I accept that it's my blame. It might not aye be. I know that, and Janet knows that, but it makes for clarity – and gets ma tin made up every day.'

'So, what do I say?'

'Not 'say', 'do'. What time does she finish her shift th'day?'

'Three o'clock.'

'That's nae use.'

'No?'

'No, I wis goin' to suggest you made something ready for her when she came it, but she'll be in afore ye.'

'Me? Make something?' Hector sounded alarmed.

'Ye can open a tin o' beans, can y'no?'

'Aye'

'Well, then - beans on toast; and mind y'butter the toast afore y'pit the beans on. But that's nae use if she's in afore you.'

'So?'

'Well, you'll know, won't you? If she has your tea on the table when you go in, you'll know the storm has blown over.'

'I wouldn't call it a storm,' muttered Hector. 'She hardly said anything. Just 'get yer ain.' Then she was off.'

'So, what makes you think you've fallen out?'

Hector glanced nervously at Duncan, but made no reply.

'Whit is it? Maybe she wis jist in a hurry.'

'Naw, she wisnae' pleased.'

'How do you know?'

Hector glanced again at Duncan and reddened.

'Well,' he mumbled, 'she no' gie'd me a kiss, like.'

Duncan laughed.

"Oh aye,' he said. 'The gilt's aff the gingerbread.'

'What was that?'

'The gilt's aff the gingerbread.'

'Whit does that mean?'

'It means the romance is over, son. Welcome to the true state of matrimony. Get your lunch, there's a woman needs a roof on her garage.'

Hector opened his lunch box and pulled out a large oatmeal biscuit, a chunk of cheese and a banana.

'It wis all I could find,' he explained.

'Well, then,' replied Duncan, offering him his tin, 'take ane o' these ham sandwiches.'

For a few seconds Hector struggled with his principles. Should he take a sandwich from a man that didn't dominate his wife? What would Christine say when she heard about it? In the end, hunger overcame scruples. He took the sandwich and the tub of yogurt that Duncan said he wouldn't be eating.

He salved his conscience by declaring,

'Mind you, it's up to Christine to make the first move. She wis the one who walked oot.'

'She had her job to go to.'

'All the same,' began Hector.

Then his mobile phone rang

'It's Christine,' he said, glancing at Duncan with a slightly superior smile on his face.

However, there was nothing to smile about. Christine had Alice, Duncan's mother with her. Alice suffers from dementia and lives at Latchlaw, a good kilometre outside the town. Yet Christine had found her wandering up the aisle of the Co-op looking for bread.

'Tell ma fither tae come and take her hame.'

Hector did as he was told.

CHAPTER TWELVE

Duncan took Hector back to Mrs Purdie's garage, then drove to the Co-op. Alice had not done any of her own shopping for months; not since she'd called into Janet's with a pint of milk she had bought. Janet had walked her home, and discovered four pints already in the fridge. Nowadays, Duncan or Christine took her to the Co-op or into Gainslaw on a Friday to do the week's shopping. If she needed anything during the week, she told Janet or Christine and they fetched it for her. That was the arrangement; until to-day.

When Duncan reached the Co-op he found an agitated Christine and a cheery Alice wondering what all the fuss was about. They needed bread so she had come to buy a loaf.

How had she got there? She had put on her coat and hat, walked out the back door and found her way to the shop. It was cold, she reported, but not wet. Christine took the loaf, checked it out, and put it in a bag, then Duncan drove her to Latchlaw. All the way there Alice chatted pleasantly, as if they were out for as run, and Duncan replied in kind. But his mind and his concern were otherwise occupied. What if she had got lost? Had she gone straight to the Co-op? Where else had she been? How long had she been away from Latchly? Where was Alistair, Alice's husband?

He came across Alistair hurrying towards them as he turned into the lane that leads down to the farmhouse: When he saw Duncan's car, Alistair stopped and waited for Duncan to pull up alongside.

'Ah, you've got her,' he grunted. 'I rang Janet, but she wasn't in. I left a message.'

After they had settled Alice in her kitchen with instructions to make a cup of tea, Duncan took his father into the sitting room and asked him about Alice's excursion. Alistair's answer surprised him.

'She did it once or twice afore I locked her in.'

'You lock her in?'

'I just turn the key in the kitchen door, when I'm going into the garden.'

'How long have you been doing that?'

'Two or three weeks now. She'd wandered away up the lane.'

'Why didn't you tell us?'

'I found her so there was no need,' he growled. 'And she found her ain way to the Co-op th'day, didn't she?' he added.

Then Alice entered cheerfully with tea and scones.

'He's still in denial,' stated Janet, when Duncan reported to her that evening. 'She could have been anywhere. At this time of year, too. If she got out and Alistair didn't notice, she'd freeze. You know how he is; gets in that garden or greenhouse and forgets the time. She could be miles away, God knows where. We'll have to do something.'

Janet is mistaken, and is so because she is a spectator. She does not live at Latchlaw with Alice; Alistair does. He spends all his days there; nights too. He may not yet admit to Alice's condition, but he recognises what is happening and fears for his wife – and for himself.

Since he settled down with Alice forty-nine years ago, his path, apart from the odd diversion, has tracked along a familiar road. He has worked on the land, grown and cared for his flowers and vegetables, repaired what needing repairing then sat down with Alice for tea and relaxation. He has had little interest in anything else. He has felt no need for it. His settled life (narrow you may be inclined to call it) has given him all the satisfaction, yes, and enjoyment, he needs. We know this because when he found himself confined to a poky little house on the Poplace Estate with a backyard the size of a pocket handkerchief, his dissatisfaction almost destroyed the man. (None of us is much aware of the hidden foundations on which we depend until they begin to crumble. It is then we realise that what we have taken for granted is not guaranteed by circumstance.)

Had Hercules not come to his rescue and allowed them to take over the house and land at Latchlaw, Alistair and, for that matter, Alice, would have shrivelled and died. As it is, Alistair continues to live comfortably without wealth, position or success. (Provided you ignore the cups that grace their old oak dresser; won year after year at Beanston Show for his dahlias. And discount his boast that there is a woman who regularly travels from Edinburgh to buy his courgettes.)

Alistair has never sought company. He has friends, or rather a few men that he is acquainted with, and with whom he might have a conversation if he ever met them. They are either companions from his working days, on the farm at Fairnieside, or men who, like him, grow flowers and vegetables for the shows in the neighbourhood. There are a couple of women too. The one we have mentioned, who travels from Edinburgh to buy his produce, and Mrs Stewart who organises the Beanston Show. None of these he sees often. He seldom steps outside Latchlaw. He leaves only to take the collie for a walk each day, but seeks out the solitude of quiet country lanes; no-one calls in to see him, stops him in the street, or rings him up for a chat. Unless Alice precisely forbids him, he absents himself when anyone arrives at the house.

But he cannot do without Alice, and, in his heart, he knows it. His solitary existence has always depended not only on her astute husbandry of their meagre income and resources, the meals she puts on the table before him, and the comfortable home she provides but also on her companionship; on the conversations they have, secrets they share, programmes they watch together, and books they enjoy; on their shared remembrance of times past, and of the laughs that occasionally punctuate their life together. For these two, incongruous as it may seem to readers of romantic fiction, are lovers. They like living with each other. Every night when they settle down in their old double bed, each says to the other, 'goodnight, sweetheart'.

From the days of their courtship, through their days together in the farm labourer's cottage at Fairnieside, their short sojourn in Poplace, and their seven years at Latchlaw, the couple have devoted their lives to each other. On the whole, they have enjoyed doing so. Not that it has always been sweetness and light. They lost a baby girl a year or two before they were blessed with a son, Duncan, and it almost broke young Alistair's heart. They found it hard to leave their home at Fairnieside when mechanisation robbed Alistair of his job on the farm and his pride in what he could do. Then there were those miserable, debilitating years at Poplace.

They have not always agreed. Alice has been known to rebuke him for coming home late, and to castigate him for not treating as a treat the new meal she has spent half the day preparing. Nor does she share Alistair's antipathy to company, and, in the days when they owned a car, had to insist on Alistair driving her to the WI for their weekly meeting, on Sunday morning to the kirk, and to Hecklescar when she needed something from the shops, or when she fancied getting out of the house for a while. The fact that Alice does not look upon his renowned Kohl Rabi as a proper vegetable, irritates Alistair as does her habit of washing his work clothes without telling him, and lecturing him on the need to get his hair cut. And, whereas Alice's reactions were explosive and short-lived, Alistair has been known to sulk for hours on end. Then, when he sees his wife close to tears, he says he is sorry and promises not to make her suffer again.

Like many married (and unmarried) couples these

two had stitched together a life of purpose and relative contentment from circumstances not always favourable to them. Alice found in Alistair's steady devotion a relief from to-day's incessant clamour for change, and Alistair had come to depend upon his wife's ingenuity, understanding and resilience. Thus, Alistair has never had to accommodate to anyone. It is not in his nature. I do not mean that he joined battle with any forces arrayed against him; he is no fighter. When he meets opposition, he either falls into line or walks away. He has left it to Alice to fight their corner and chart their path. She had provided his happy home at Fairnieside, had dragged him through those miserable years at Poplace and has blessed his later years by billeting him at Latchlaw. He relies utterly on her.

Although to his son and daughter-in-law he still protested that Alice suffered only from old age and forgetfulness, he saw daily something much more sinister at work. As a general rule, the steady rhythm of their life continued. There were days, however, when he came in from the garden to find no meal waiting for him, potatoes unpeeled, or table unset. Once or twice, he had found all the ingredients for a loaf or a cake half-mixed on the table but Alice sitting in the room reading the People's Friend. Always an early riser, there were mornings now when she lay in her bed well past eight o' clock, and rose only when Alistair pointed out the time. Some evenings she would not settle to watch the telly, but would get up and walk about the house, or rummage through the drawers, looking for what? She couldn't say. Names, too; she would stop in the middle of a story searching for the name of someone they knew well. Often Christine's name eluded her, although she saw her every day.

All this Alistair experienced and had put it down to his wife's age – and worry, perhaps, about the house. Then came the day when she looked at him across the table as if he were a stranger. It lasted only a fleeting moment, but it barged through the fast-locked door of his self-deception and demanded attention.

In denial? Of course! Frightened? Certainly! He could not do without Alice. What else could he do but block it? He could stomach no other conclusion.

When Duncan, Christine and Janet arrived for a family conference they had to drag him in from the garden to take part.

CHAPTER THIRTEEN

Later the same evening, Duncan, Janet, Christine and Hector gathered in the sitting room of Duncan and Janet's house, to discuss what could be done to help Alice.

This was not the first time the family had convened on this subject. For months now Duncan and Janet had been planning to sell up their house in Priory Road and move into Latchlaw alongside the old couple. This had been decided last September when, at the height of a storm, Alice had called them in distress in the middle of the night. The gales had almost ripped the flat roof from their kitchen and had driven rain through all the frames of the east- and north-facing windows. The roof of the main house had been penetrated in several places, including the room in which Alistair and Alice slept.

The plan had been made back then, but not much had been done to implement it. This is not neglect or inattention. As we know, the ownership of Latchlaw lay in doubt, but Peter Munro, having discussed the matter with Cockburn Heath, and Cockburn having consulted legal counsel in Edinburgh, now believed he had good title to the house and land. In any case he had had Cockburn contact Hercules' solicitors in Edinburgh to persuade Hercules to agree to his claim and thus avoid a time-consuming and costly legal wrangle. For this Peter offered to hand over one million pounds. The answer from Hercules is still awaited; he is proving difficult to track down. (We must remember the man set out from Hecklescar weeks ago with the intention of disappearing. He is anxious that his creditors and investors do not find out where he is.)

Hercules had already given Duncan permission to use the old steading at the back of the house as a workshop, so Duncan had had plenty of time to assess the condition of the farmhouse and to determine what it would cost to bring it up to an acceptable standard. It lay in poor shape. Nothing had been done to it for decades, apart from the odd patching and maintenance that Duncan had had to carry out to allow his parents to continue to live in it. To Janet's alarm, Duncan had estimated the cost of repairs at fifty thousand pounds. What he had learned from further investigations at Latchlaw had not encouraged him to reduce his estimate. The renovation of Latchlaw would be a major and costly undertaking.

Understandably, their plan had been put on hold until the question of ownership could be settled. Now that Peter Munro had assured them that he would acquire the property and that he would sell them the house to live in, the steading for Duncan and Hector to work in, and a plot in which Alistair could continue to grow his vegetables, Duncan and Janet felt confident they could go ahead with their plan. But that would take time; Latchlaw must be made fit to house both families. Duncan planned to carry out the work himself with the aid of Hector and any other tradesmen he could bring in to help him. However, such a project must take second place to that of earning the family's daily bread. Then, of course, they would need to sell their own house in Priory Road. Clearly it would be some months, could even be a year, before Duncan and Janet could move in to take care of Alice. Yet Alice needed help now.

No-one at the present meeting disagreed with such a decision; they had decided that she could not be left any longer in the house alone with Alistair. Duncan did try, somewhat feebly, to defend his father, pointing out that he had, on his own initiative, started locking Alice in the house when he went into the garden. Alice's arrival at the Co-op, however, had somewhat undermined his advocacy.

In Janet's opinion, Alistair still hid his head in the sand. He had told them about her leaving the house, but that, surely, was not the only danger. Alice still cooked meals, using oven and hot stove; what if she left something on the hob and it blew up, or she simply left it on and forgot to switch it off when they went to bed. Could she be left safe with electric equipment - the hoover, kettle, iron, or mixer - and with her kitchen knives? Janet and Christine had gained some control over the old couple's diet by providing the ingredients with their weekly shop, but what was Alice doing with them? What were they actually eating, and in what condition was it when they did so? No, someone needed to be in the house with her; someone as well as Alistair.

Christine then resurrected her proposal that she and Hector move into Latchlaw. When first proposed, they had plans to marry but nowhere to live. Would it not kill two birds with one stone, she had suggested, if they moved into Latchly with the old couple? The proposal typified Christine; she loved her granny; often called in to see her, and could see no difficulty in sharing the house with her and Alistair. Besides, Hector spent a considerable amount of his working life in the steading at the back of the farmhouse at Latchlaw; it would be convenient for them to live there as well, would it not? Janet and Duncan had scotched the idea; they saw Alice as their responsibility; they would not have the young folk setting out in life cramped by the care of old people. Besides Janet and Duncan's present house, in Priory Road would have to be sold to provide the wherewithal to buy and renovate Latchlaw. In the end, Christine and Hector had rented a house on the Poplace Estate and moved in on the first of day of the year.

Janet now immediately repeated her objection to the scheme; they would have to find some other solution. Perhaps they could share it; they could maybe hire someone to do a couple of days; she knew of a woman that did that for a paralysed woman; she stayed overnight for a couple of nights to give the woman's daughter a spell. If Christine could maybe do a couple of days when she wasn't working, Janet would do the rest. But even as she presented it the idea appalled her – as it did Duncan.

Then Christine, who had learned from her mother not only what to do, but also how to wheedle it, explained that she wasn't proposing moving to Latchlaw permanently, only that she and Hector would fill in for her father and mother until they could take over. This softened Janet's resistance. Then Christine closed the deal with an appeal to Janet's concern for her daughter and new husband.

'It would save us the rent,' she said bluntly. 'That poky little house at Poplace is costing us an arm and a leg. We're paying £350 a month. When I get my pay from the Co-op I hand over half of it to McConachie.'

'McConachie owns that house, does he?' snapped Janet, 'I didn't know that!'

'Because we didn't tell you. You would never have let us take it. But we couldn't find anything else.'

'He's a bandit! He'll be ripping you off!'

'Yes, he's a bandit, but no he's not ripping us off; he wanted four hundred and twenty-five for it. But Lucy that works beside me in the Co-op knows what he charges so we beat him down. But it still sticks in my craw. If we could move into Latchly we wouldn't have to pay him and we could keep an eye on granny.'

Duncan saw that Janet had been shifted and pitched in.

'It'd only be until we were ready to move along there, right?' he said, addressing Christine but looking at Janet.

'Aye, and in the meantime, we could pit our names down wi' the council.'

'Did you not have to pay McConachie up front?' asked Janet

'Yes, but only for a month. We could get out of it after that.'

Janet turned to Duncan.

'Where would they stay in Latchly? There's nowhere fit, is there? Since the storm only your mother and father's bedroom is habitable. That's what you said.'

'One of the back room's no' bad. We could sort it.'

All eyes turned on Janet. Still, she hesitated. She could not rid herself of the suspicion that Christine was wheedling her way into Latchly – permanently.'

'But Alice and Alistair would have to move out when we started doing the house up. Now you'd have to move too.'

Christine blundered into a hole.

'We could go and stay with Olivia, Hector's mother, until the house was fit again.'

'But when the house is fit again, you're going to move into a council house, aren't you?'

'Well, yes,' she admitted, then saved the day by adding, 'I tell you what; we'll put oor names doon wi' the council now. Then we might have a hoose from them before we need to move out of Latchly.'

Janet yielded. After a week of improvements at Latchlaw, Hector and Christine paid off McConachie and moved into Latchlaw. Temporarily!

They were greatly welcomed by her granny – and, it may be assumed though not admitted, by her grandfather. He had half feared that Janet might move in and take over.

CHAPTER FOURTEEN

Peter Munro came away from Avignon relieved that his visit to Olivia was over. She had welcomed him, settled him in the lounge, produced coffee and nibbles for them both and had gone out of her way, he believed, to be friendly. Nevertheless, he had felt awkward in her company, and now headed for John Henry in a more equable frame of mind, there to report what Olivia had told him.

Peter had volunteered to visit Olivia to discover what, if anything, she knew about Clouston Pritchard, He is, you may recall, the man who had been, still is, apparently, a director of HD Processing, a company that Hercules had set up twelve years ago. Peter had agreed to ask Olivia about the man, but he had not relished his visit to Avignon. Fortunately, he is not like we who, when faced with a task we do not like, put it off until it trips us up and demands to be taken seriously. Had he postponed it for a week, he would have missed Olivia for, as we know, she is off on her cruise in the early days of February.

He had last entered Avignon on Christmas Day, when he had enjoyed a festive meal with Olivia and her mother Connie. Is enjoyed the correct word? Yes and No. Yes, the food had been enjoyable and, to a certain extent, the occasion. Olivia had been the ideal hostess, welcoming him into the house, settling him in comfort in the tastefully decorated lounge with an aperitif and her mother. He knew Connie well and they chatted comfortably until summoned into the dining room for an excellent meal.

Peter recognised - and appreciated that, in spite of the turbulent month or two through which she had laboured, Olivia had done her best to make both him and her mother welcome. But he had found her aloof; going through the motions; laying it on for appearance, as a project, an achievement; to impress rather than please. He welcomed the presence of Connie who kept the conversation lively – and human.

He saw clearly, or thought he saw clearly, that Olivia had lost contact with her own deepest feelings. Vulnerable himself, he recognised that Olivia had accustomed herself to living without love, without guilt, without that acute sense of her effect on another human being. We must be cautious, however; at the moment he is still viewing life through the lens of his own recent painful experiences.

He had been glad to be clear of Avignon on Christmas Day; he felt the same this bleak evening to be welcomed by John Henry; to sit down beside a blazing log fire.

'She has never heard of HD Processing,' he reported, 'but she knew all about Clouston Pritchard. Apparently ten or fifteen years ago Olivia and Harold were quite friendly with Clouston and his wife. She remembers him as the Managing Director of a frozen food factory at Livingston, by the name of Arcticus.'

'I've heard of it. Quite a big operation, I believe. It belonged to a Scandinavian Company. Then last year or, the year before that, it closed, taking down something like two hundred jobs, something of that order. It caused quite stir. Apparently, they'd been receiving some sort of assistance from the government, but overnight they pulled the plug. So, our Clouston must have been involved in that.'

'Could be, but Olivia didn't think Clouston had any stake in the business; he only managed it; a sort of native placeman to keep the government happy. He seems, however, to have managed it well and had done so for a number of years before he met up with Hercules at a food fair. Olivia believes he steered quite a bit of business in the direction of the fishyard.'

'Where is he now? Did Olivia know how we could get in touch with him?'

'She had their home number. They live in North Berwick, or did. I'll give him a ring and see what his interest is in HD Processing.'

'If they're still there. Did Olivia say how old he was?

'No but I got the impression she thought that they were a little younger than themselves.'

'And how old are they?'

Peter knew precisely. Olivia is six years younger than he is and knows that on her birthday she will turn fifty. He also knows on what date that birthday falls; he knows because before she met Harold Douglas he celebrated a few of them with her.

'Hercules is coming up to fifty-one' he replied; 'Olivia, a year younger.'

'Clouston Pritchard must be in his forties then. He'll not have retired. He may have moved on.'

'Could be, but I'll ring the number and see if I can raise him.'

After which decision, John sent out for fish and chips, and the two men set aside executive affairs and settled down to enjoy their supper in the glow of the log fire and the comfort of each other's company.

Peter left it a couple of days to call Clouston Pritchard at his home, and found to his surprise that Clouston had been expecting Peter to contact him. Olivia had rung them to check if they were still in North Berwick and had told him of Peter Munro's interest. Peter started to ask about HD Processing, but Clouston interrupted him and said pleasantly,

'Look, Peter, I'll be down in your neck of the woods next week, I'd like to have a chat. Could we fix up a meeting - on Wednesday say, or Thursday?'

'Of course,' answered Peter, 'Wednesday would be fine.'

'I'm intrigued.' he reported to John Henry.

'About HD Processing?'

'No, about Clouston Pritchard. He's after something.'

'What makes you think that?'

'Whenever a man tells me he'll just happen to be in my locality next week, I think of Marney Wegg.'

'Who on earth is Marney Wegg?'

'He was a man I did business with in London. If you wanted to see him you could never find him but, if he wanted to see you, he'd tell you he would be in your neck of the woods and could he pop in. When he came you discovered he had some sort of proposition to put to you. He once went on holiday for two days down to Tavistock and came back with a JCB and an interest in a row of farm cottages.'

John laughed.

'You think Clouston might be another . . .. what's his name?'

'Marney!'

'He might be just coming to Hecklescar for a visit. People do!'

'True. But when people come to your neck of the woods by choice they know which day they are coming, and what they are coming for. If they don't know which day they are coming it is because they are coming deliberately to see you. They just don't want to admit it.'

'We'll see. Am I invited to the meeting?'

'Of course, if just to prove my point. Believe me, he's after something.'

CHAPTER FIFTEEN

As the year slogged into February, Jen made arrangements to quit her house. How easy that sounds. However, we know Jen well enough to understand that it will be far from easy. The house Nudge will lend her he normally lets out in the summer months, a week or fortnight at a time, to visitors looking to escape the multi-stories of Glasgow, Edinburgh, Newcastle or beyond for a few days by the seaside. They are families largely, so the houses are fully furnished. But Jen has a house full of furniture. What can be taken; what left; what put into store; where to store it? Questions daunting for anyone; for Jen insuperable.

Such questions Jen poured into Connie's ears, none of which Connie could answer. Speak to Nudge, she advised. And Connie had a question of her own; one that had bothered her since Jen first took her into her confidence; a question Connie had dared not ask until now.

When John Henry had first talked with her about Jen, he had asked the same question and could suggest no reasonable answer. Why is Jen so short of money? He knew that Jen worked all the hours she could muster and that she spent much of what she earned on the family of her son. But such indigence jarred with the apparent affluence of her other circumstances. Crovie, the house in which she lived, was one of the grandest and best furnished on Millerfield. Charlie her husband, a successful fisherman and boat owner, had been well off. Indeed, Jen had told Connie that he had received hundreds of thousands of pounds for the quota, let alone the boat, when he sold it to the Dutchmen. From her account he loved her and they were happy together. Why then had he not left her enough to live on?

Connie, sitting in Jen's lounge, decided that she might risk venturing into such sensitive territory. She had thought long and hard about how she might approach it, but could think of no question that might not cause offence. Yet it must be tackled.

'Jen,' she said softly, 'I hate to ask this, but do you need help with the cost of your removal?'

'No,' replied Jen showing no sign of resentment, 'I can manage; there's not a lot. Paul is arranging it.'

Then, noting Connie's confusion, she added, 'Nudge! His proper name is Paul.'

'I think you must be the only person in Hecklescar to know that,' smiled Connie.

This pleasant interchange encouraged Connie to press forward with her wider concern.

'And the rent?'

'I'm talking to him about that; he's being very reasonable.'

She sat and studied Connie for a while, then answered the question she knew lay on Connie's mind.

'I know what you are thinking,' she said quietly. 'I always seem short of money. Well, I admit it. I am. I have nothing at all behind me. When we came here we had Charlie's pension, but that died with him; he couldn't pass it on for I was his second wife.'

She hesitated.

'I think he hoped that the family, his family would look after me. I didn't argue but I knew that would never happen. He invested a lump sum. He hoped it would provide an income but it never has. . . . '

Her voice tailed away. She studied Connie for a moment,

as if willing her to understand something she did not want to articulate.

'Quite a large sum, over two hundred thousand, I think. But I have had little income from it – and now, I believe, it has all gone.'

The penny dropped. Connie understood.

'He gave it to Harold to invest in one of his schemes? That's it, isn't it?'

'Yes, I'm afraid so,' confirmed Jen. 'But I didn't want to tell you because he is your son-in-law, isn't he?'

'That is true,' replied Connie grimly. 'But no friend of mine. I'm awfully sorry at what has happened. You're not the only one in Hecklescar to have suffered. If you don't mind, I'll talk to John Henry about it. He's looking into it but I don't hold out much hope.'

'No, I don't suppose so. But I'd be grateful if you'd speak to him. I have the papers, if he wants to see them.'

'Makes sense,' replied John after Connie had reported Jen's predicament. 'From what she said about her husband I was sure he would not have left her destitute. Hercules has a lot to answer for.'

Then he continued.

'I've been doing some investigation of my own. I can't see that Jen can afford to rent a property. That's probably why she's been hanging onto the Millerfield house as long as she can. At the moment all she pays is the council tax, that's about a thousand pounds a year, say, eighty-five pounds a month. I reckon she'll have to pay in the region of four hundred pounds a month to rent a decent sized house. I've been checking on what she earns for her driving. She works three shifts of twelve hours. That makes thirty-six hours, but, technically, she's not paid an hour each shift – that's her lunch break. I say, technically, because Jakey tends to ignore it and hands her three hundred pounds a week. That means that the monthly rent will swallow up a week and bit's pay – and she can scarcely manage now. Then she's apparently trying to support her son's family. He's not being paid, as far as I can find out. He's a graduate, would you believe - in Media Studies, but he's never done anything with his degree, except trying to set up as a web site designer. Nothing came of it. He worked for a while at Fullerton's, the Printing Company at Gainslaw, but it went bust four or five years ago. He then had a succession of short time jobs; driving, mainly, I think. For a while he stacked shelves in Morrisons. I suspect that would be casual work and his pay would cease when he took ill. The only money going into his house is what his wife gets from social security – and whatever Jen can give them. So, as well as having a low income, she's got a lot to do with it. Now she's thinking of taking on rent. I don't see what she is going to do? Certainly, the extra shifts Jakey gives her won't cover it.'

'She does have other work, she tells me,' replied Connie. 'She works a couple of hours at the Fishermen's Mission; in the café - and she does some cleaning for the folk in the Old Mill when they call on her. And there's other little occasional jobs she mentioned, but I didn't want to pry overmuch. She says she can manage.'

'I don't see it. Do you think I should have a word with Nudge about the rent?' asked John, 'He was very concerned about her the other day.'

'Paul, you mean?'

'Paul? Is that his name?'

'Jen says it is.'

'Ah, I see.'

'No, I don't I think you should talk to him. We have to leave the woman some independence. I think we've embarrassed her enough already. Nudge will be fair, I'm sure.'

Then, with a sly smile, she added, 'I have my suspicions that there's something going on there.'

Which sentence John Henry heard but did not understand.

CHAPTER SIXTEEN

That John Henry does not know that Nudge's real name is Paul tells us quite a lot about Nudge. The fact that Jen knows it, and has been told it by Nudge, points to something else, but we will leave that for now, for Nudge himself is probably not aware of what it indicates.

In every community; any collection of folk, there are those who detach themselves from the crowd; loners, they are called. We have met one in our story: Alistair, Alice's husband. Nudge, however, is not such a man. Although quite happy on his own, (which is just as well for a long-distance lorry driver) he likes to be amongst other people, particularly men. He can be relied on to volunteer if there is work to be done around the town; will make up a party to put up the Christmas lights, weed the flower containers, or take a mini-bus party of pensioners on their annual trip. He is not a loner; he just has never become a paid-up member of any official or unofficial group; he has always been and remains, semi-detached.

Nudge (and, although we now know his Christian name, we will keep on using the handle we have always used) lives alone – or does he? His mother used to live with him, didn't she? But we haven't seen her for years. Where did she go? If we asked Ina she would guess that she's in a care home up in the Borders somewhere; for doesn't Nudge go up there to visit every now and again. In this, however, as in many of her stories, Ina is mistaken. Her radar had picked up 'care home' and she has allocated Nudge's mother to it, but that is not correct. His mother, a devout supporter of the Brethren way of getting close to God, left Hecklescar some years ago, and, with her husband, headed home to Peterhead, there to re-settle among sounder and larger Brethren assemblies of Peterhead. And his father? Does anyone know what happened to him after he retired from the fishing. Five years ago, he suffered a 'grievous blow', a stroke, and now languishes speechless and half-paralysed in a private care home where Brethren sufferers can suffer together. Nudge, when he collects fish from the Moray Firth never fails to visit both his parents.

You may wonder why Nudge didn't return to Peterhead with his parents. If you asked him (and, to my knowledge, no-one ever has), why he stayed, he would cite his job with Anthony Douglas & Son. That he needs the job to earn his living is true and obvious, but pounding the roads of Scotland, England and the Continent in a forty-four-tonne articulated truck is no servitude; he loves driving. His ambition has never run to anything else. From the age of nine he set his heart on being an HGV driver and now, at forty-four, he is content with what he does.

Certainly, his job is centred in Hecklescar, but are there not more articulated lorries in Peterhead? Is there not a demand there for experienced HGV drivers? Perhaps even, because of the shortage, at higher wages? We must therefore look for other reasons, which, if not completely conclusive, reinforced Nudge's decision to stay in Hecklescar when his parent opted to return to the North-East.

Could it be that Nudge, having been brought up in Hecklescar among atheists, worldly Anglicans, lapsed Catholics and half-hearted Kirk folk, found Brethren life somewhat restrictive? Would that not also account for his love of travelling; escaping the claustrophobia of Brethren belief. You would be safe, I would say, if you classed his continuing sojourn in Hecklescar as a working compromise. His driving long distance for Anthony Douglas & Son distances him from indoctrination during the week, yet allows him to continue to be part of the little flock, remain on good terms with his mother, and find, in his own interpretation of the Faith, a satisfying way of life. The only outward sign of his adherence to a stricter creed is his refusal to drive his truck on Sundays. In the town, however, this is viewed as eccentricity, and does not affect his general acceptance as one of their own; albeit one on the fringe.

Although the general driver of the Brethren movement is the command of Paul to the Corinthians to *'Come out from among them and be ye separate'*, it is interpreted in different meetings in different ways. The Brethren have no central governing body and no paid ministers, so policy, if we can call it that, is determined on the hoof by leading elders in each assembly It also appears that, if you don't like what your particular elders are teaching, you can always gather round you a group of like-minded people, and start your own. You don't even need a hall. Many assemblies start – and some continue, to meet in the front room of one of the believers' houses. In places like Peterhead, whither Nudge's mother has fled, there are well over a score of assemblies. This splintering of the faithful results in a confusion of doctrine. What does *'come out from among them'* mean in practice. At the more generous end of the teaching, it produces anomalies such as some brethren not attending football matches, whereas in an assembly next door, football matches are kosher but cinemas are barred – but not watching 'wholesome films' on television. Then again, some assemblies insist on women wearing a hat when attending the meeting, whereas others allow them to attend bare-headed. Some have an organ to help them with the singing, in others they sing unaccompanied from 'Hymns for the Little Flock.' At the stricter end of the spectrum there are brethren who will not have a television set in the house, do not approve of Co-op membership, and will not sit down to a meal with a family member who is not part of their own little group. All of which, would you believe, is justified by reference to texts and passages from the Bible. The edict about the hats, I believe, has to do with angels taking a fancy to bare-headed women.

Nudge attended the little group that met in the poky room above Mussen Grumble's shop in the High Street. He did this without fail every Sunday and received a warm welcome from such people as Bobby Dobson, an elderly man and his wife, who hailed from Newcastle and had, in the jargon, assimilated many of the Hecklescar ways of looking at life. The leading elder, however, was of a different stamp. He went by the name of Barnabas, a man of fifty, and had come from Glasgow five or six years ago. Barnabas, it should be noted, went about his work for the Lord with diligence but had he shown any signs of wavering would have been stiffened by the considerable resolve of his wife Miriam, who tied her hair back in a Brethren bun and always wore a hat to the Sunday Meeting and, shall we say, *encouraged* the other five women to do likewise.

Both Barnabas and Miriam regarded Nudge as a backslider. They regarded his absence from the mid-week Bible Study as 'a lack of hunger for the Word', and his general friendliness with folk in the town as 'flirtation with the things of this world'. Until now, however, he had managed to live a useful and enjoyable life by steering clear of any looming collision between the two worlds in which he lived.

Nudge had two houses he could offer Jen; one, a long low cottage on the main street just along and across the road from the Co-op: two bedrooms, living room, facilities and kitchen/dinette; ample space for a woman on her own. The other, in School Road, was much larger: an old Hecklescar two-storey terrace house with two public rooms. kitchen and utility room on the ground floor, three bedrooms plus bathroom on the first floor and above them all, a spacious attic. Then, out the back, an old net store, converted into a garage and let out permanently to old Jim Douglas to accommodate his ancient Mercedes. The rent for the smaller house would be three hundred pounds a month, the larger house, as John Henry had predicted, four hundred.

(Before we accuse Nudge of being mercenary, we should add that, in summer, as holiday homes, he charges four hundred and five hundred *per week* respectively - and has no difficulty in letting them out for that.)

Nudge had called on Jen at her house; had been invited by Jen to do so and had been welcomed. Yet he felt uncomfortable as he sat beside Jen on the settee. He had brought a brochure of each property and had intended handing them to her after he had run through the details. But she had moved beside him to look at the pictures.

As she put out her hand to examine the brochure Nudge became acutely aware of her. We know from Peter Munro's description that she is an attractive woman. One of the photographs that John Henry had noticed in her front room depicted her dressed for a ball, wearing a sash declaring her to be 'Queen of the Sea'. In spite of her troubles, Jen had not, as Ina would have described many a woman of the same age, 'gone to seed'. (And, we might mumble that she had herself gone some way in that direction.) Jen, however, in spite of her fears and anxieties, had not neglected her appearance. Perhaps in it lay the last fragment of self-respect she could hang onto; all the others had been stripped from her.

Nudge had had very little experience of women. Reared by a strict, yet kindly mother, he had learnt to fear them. He had worked his way through puberty by avoiding girls as much as possible, and by absenting himself from any activity where he would have to mix with them. Of course, he had had his notions, crushes and excursions but they had been at a distance, private, and, I believe the term is, repressed. His one serious attempt at romance had been with a young woman from an Assembly in Newcastle and chosen by his mother as a suitable future life partner. The venture had begun and ended within a few months just as he turned twenty. One day the chosen one told him bluntly and that she hadn't chosen him. At the time, although his mother was upset, his feeling could best he described as relief. Since then, he had lived his celibate life with discipline, activity, a wide range of interests and not a little enjoyment. He is generally accepted at work and in the town as a lonely man, but a genial one that mixes well. Whereas nowadays, men and women seem to regard a partner as a requirement if not a right, Nudge gave every appearance of getting on quite well without one.

Now Jen, sitting close beside him on the settee and reaching out her slim hand towards the brochure rocked his composure. As his pulse quickened, he felt compelled to edge away from her, but knowing this might embarrass her, resisted the temptation. And concentrated as well as he could on his description of the two properties.

The cottage had all the accommodation that Jen needed but, Nudge noted, she rattled on mainly about the larger house. Clearly disturbed, her questions poured out of her in a torrent of incoherence and indecision. After listening for a while and trying to address her questions as they gushed from her, Nudge began to make some sense of her outpourings.

Crovie, her home, was a large house full of furniture and furnishings she had bought, cared for and treasured for eighteen years. She had lived in it with her husband, brought up her son, entertained her grandchildren, welcomed her friends, consoled herself after those long shifts on the road. Now she had to leave it all behind. Walk out the door – into someone else's house; sit in someone else's chair, eat off their table, stare at their ornaments; all cold, lifeless, possessing no memories and no love.

All this barged its way into Nudge's mind – and heart, we should say, as he sat beside her, witnessed her distress and watched her lovely hand tremble over the brochure. Instinctively, he grasped it gently in his own hand and said,

'Jen, take the School Road house – and take your things with you. I'll move my stuff into store for now. Will that make it easier?'

CHAPTER SEVENTEEN

The year had trudged through most of the bleak days of February before a meeting could be arranged with Clouston Pritchard. Life in the fishyard and town had resumed its dull monotony after the brief brightness of Christmas and the folk of Hecklescar had knuckled down to the long slog to Easter.

Not Olivia, of course. She is not slogging it out but lounging it away. A month into her world cruise she has not yet reached Australia. There we will leave her and pick up her story when she when she returns to tell it to her mother Connie, in the lighter days of May.

Hector and Christine are now safely lodged in a room of their own at Latchlaw having flown their cramped pigeon loft on the Poplace Estate. This had not been straightforward in that their landlord McConachie had claimed that they had entered a three-month contract but had only paid one month's rent. In this he had some documentary support, but what is that when Janet Kerr is ranged against you and knows enough about your affairs to make life uncomfortable if you don't settle with her. Two month's rent, including what had already been paid, sealed a deal.

Christine is learning to be wise and not displacing her granny, and most days, when Christine's shifts at the Co-op allow, Alice, Alistair, Christine and Hector sit down together for their evening meal. Most of the time they had served up to them what Alice had promised; only now and again did Christine have to improvise. Hector also discovered to his satisfaction that if Christine were on an early shift, Alice made up his box, only now and again forgetting to spread something between the bread of his sandwiches.

Jen now lived in Nudge's rented house in School Road, comforted in her enforced migration by having much of her own furniture and effects around her. What of her possessions she had not been able to accommodate in the living rooms, Nudge had stored in the garret. Nudge would have liked to use the garage for storage and had tried to persuade old Jim Douglas to move his old Mercedes out and give it up. Nudge had gently pointed out to the old man that he never used it, could not use it; it was neither taxed nor insured. But old Jim did not want to part with his car; a matter of loyalty, he believed; it had uncomplainingly served him for thirty or more years; he would not desert it now. And he did use it, telling Nudge what Nudge knew already: that he would occasionally bring along a little picnic hamper with a bottle of wine and a simple meal and sit in the car and eat it. It got him out of the house, he said. From this Nudge learned that old folk need familiar milestones to guide them through their declining years. In any case he is not the sort of landlord to force out a tenant, even from an old car, if they didn't want to move.

Was Jen happy in her new quarters? Happy? Of course not, but she had made the move that had hung over her like a guillotine for years, and discovered that it had not decapitated her. The fact that she had not had to part with her furniture gave an assurance that, perhaps, her removal from her own house might be a temporary expedient, and that, in the not - too-distant future, she would once again have a place of her own. That her prospects gave no support to such an assurance did not undermine her thinking. She had long since stopped planning a way out of her difficulties and set her mind only on that which had to be tackled today. Meanwhile, Crovie, her erstwhile home on the Millerfield estate continued to grace

Cockburn Heath's window for sale at £325,000.

In the last week of February, a house we recognise appeared alongside it:

Detached Stone 3-Bay Villa in Priory Road, a sought-after part of Hecklescar. This commodious house offers, on the ground floor: living room and dining room to the front, with large kitchen, utility room and facilities to the rear. On the first floor there are three bedrooms, a study/workroom and a large and well-equipped bathroom. A fixed stair discreetly leads to a large, fully insulated and airy attic which could be used for storage, hobbies, or an extra bedroom. The whole finished to a high standard of design, material and maintenance. A garage abuts the side of the house and is entered via a short drive running alongside the front garden/patio. To the rear lies a larger, well-furnished garden and drying green, the whole surrounded by a tasteful and sturdy stone wall.

An ideal family home in this attractive seaside town, close to shops, schools, health centre and other facilities.

For Sale at offers over £225,000

The house and home of Duncan and Janet. They are on their way to Latchlaw. But not yet.

Entry: September

Duncan and Hector, as paid work elsewhere allowed, had almost finished fitting out the steading as a workshop and were confident that, by the end of the month, they could move into it. In the evenings at Priory Road, Duncan laid out plans for the redevelopment of Latchlaw as a family home for himself and Janet, and had set the entry date now for all to read. Against that fateful day, Janet set out to separate her precious possessions into those she would take with her and those she would have to give up.

By the end of the month, Peter Munro felt confident finance would be in place to set Anthony Douglas & Son on a firm foundation. However, he and John Henry had made little progress in finding someone to cover those duties previously carried out by Hercules: marketing, business connections, contracts, legislation, management. The litany of dissatisfaction from Dodgy Donald of the Mallaig Fishermen's Co-op had been augmented by the whining of other suppliers and producers, whose contracts were already expired or, in their opinion, in need of renewal on more favourable terms. The fishyard continued to run as smoothly and effectively as it always had done under the careful supervision of Jakey, Angela and Fiona, but Peter had become convinced of the need for someone to manage - not the yard, the shops, the vans and the lorries, but the business.

It needed a manager - a Chief Executive, Peter began to insist, whenever he and John Henry discussed it. Whenever John Henry suggested that the salary and perks of such a grandly titled person would put a strain on the business, and that the work would not take up more than two or three days a week, or perhaps as few as five days a month, Peter spotted a ploy and lightly knocked it back as the gripe of a miserly old banker. Peter knew that John was suggesting, it not advocating, that, seeing as Peter already sat in the executive chair, he could comfortably continue to do so without gobbling up much of his retirement.

In this John profoundly misunderstood his friend. From the heights of his own eighty-three years, Peter's fifty-five looked a long way from the summit of endeavour, and well short of a decent contribution to the common good. And he did not doubt that Anthony Douglas gave enough families in Hecklescar a reasonable livelihood to be labelled a common good. However, he had little chance of persuading Peter to sit again at the head of an organisation. The thought sickened Peter. He had done for Anthony Douglas & Son what had to be done. He could not avoid it. Similarly, he had stood by Duncan and Janet on Latchlaw. He had done what only *he alone* could do.

Certainly, he had found refreshment and not a little satisfaction in coming to the aid of his friends but, as his stay lengthened, the old weariness returned. As life for others settled into its normal stride, no normality beckoned him. The brief stimulation of saving firm and farmhouse waned. How could he settle when nothing lay settled? He had not lived in Hecklescar for twenty-five years. Little remained of the town's life as he knew it. The town had changed. Most of the folk who had made up his close company had moved on, out or away altogether. Those who remained were no longer the people he knew, and, apart from John Henry, when they met, spoke only of things now gone. The house in which he had been brought up had long been in the hands of strangers; now he lodged in one of Nudge's holiday houses. Unlike Jen, however, the bed in which he slept, the table from which he ate, the chair in which he sat were not his own. He had brought with him a few changes of clothing and some personal possessions, but they hung in empty wardrobes and rattled in unfamiliar drawers. Everything in his life in Hecklescar lay on the surface. Deep down he remained a troubled asylum-seeker from the far country.

He had come back to the old place but had not found himself at home. Although he had returned to work, he found no deep attachment to it. As morning followed morning in this second month, his dissatisfaction swelled. Increasingly he felt that he must do what he had come home to do: to retire from wheeling and dealing, from cajoling and commanding from managing and manipulating. He had other plans for the few years left to him. Plans? Can we, can he call them that? I think not. He had come with a vision, (or perhaps we should call it a notion) of what his life in Hecklescar might become. Heading up a fish processing company did not feature in it.

They must therefore find a Chief Executive – soon. Peter insisted on it. John, recognising Peter's growing conviction, fell silent. Peter did what he had always done when he needed a new manager; he contacted an agency. We do not need to trouble ourselves with the details of the particular agency or, to be strictly accurate, agencies, that Peter contacted.

Certainly, they came up with the CVs of potential candidates; bundles of them bulked up in brochures praising the expertise and track record of the agency, and setting out in excruciating detail where the hopeful had been born, educated, trained and worked. Their family circumstances were laid bare, their interests listed and their membership of associations spelled out down to the last acronym. When stripped of the packaging, however, none of the candidates appealed. Not a single one of them had experience of fish processing in a yard such as that belonging to Anthony Douglas & Son. The only one that had ever smelt fish on their clothes had once handled fish boxes on the pier at Lochinver, during a summer holiday with his parents.

In the meantime, however, Peter and John Henry welcomed Clouston Pritchard to Hecklescar. Peter had calculated correctly; he had come looking for something: a job, perhaps!

CHAPTER EIGHTEEN

Or not so much a job as a question. He had heard from Donald Mackay that Harold had departed and wondered who had taken his place.

'You know Donald Mackay, from Mallaig?' asked John.

'Well, enough to know no one calls him that,' replied Clouston pleasantly. 'Dodgy Donald, I believe, is how he is known in the trade.'

John and Peter smiled along with him. They were settled comfortably over lunch in The Old Barque. Clouston Pritchard had arrived a half-hour ago and after brief introductions in the cramped office at the yard, they had walked along the pier to the restaurant. Clouston had not arrived until two, so the restaurant, never busy at this time of year, lay empty apart from the three of them.

Hilda, part-owner and waitress for the day, handed them a lengthy and highly descriptive menu, but when Clouston attempted to order oysters as a starter, she confessed that what she had to offer on this day and at this time lay largely in the more popular items on sheet. Clouston accepted the inevitable in good grace, chatted brightly to Hilda and opted for scampi as a main course and would join his two fellows in apple crumble for dessert. Peter joined him in the scampi but John Henry opted for a pensioner's small haddock and chunky chips.

From the start Clouston made himself agreeable.

Although in his late forties, he struck both Peter and John as much younger. He looked trim, fit, well-groomed, and switched on. A confident man, John thought, but not overbearing, as prepared to listen with interest as to talk with enthusiasm; a man easy to like and easy to get on with.

'How do you know Dodgy Donald?' asked John.

'I'm on the board of the Scottish Fish Producers Organisation, a non-exec member, and met Donald at the January meeting. He's always there and always has something to say. Since the Co-op took over the Mallaig business from Harold there is no holding him.'

'So we hear,' said Peter, 'but I'm interested in how you happen to be on the board of the FPO; you're not in the fishing business, are you.'

'Well, no and yes. No, strictly speaking I've never been at the sharp end of fish processing; one row back I would say. Until June last year, I headed up the Scottish Operation of Arcticus. We supplied freezing and refrigeration to many fish producers – including Anthony Douglas here and in Mallaig.'

'Arcticus had a plant at Newbridge, just outside of Edinburgh, didn't they?' put in John.

'Yes, that was the main facility, but we had smaller units, or depots, throughout Scotland; places like Peterhead and Turriff up north and a couple over in the West. There was one at Mauchline in Ayrshire, and another at Newton Stewart – and of course, at Mallaig.'

'What was it Arcticus did, then?' asked Peter.

'And do now,' answered Clouston. 'They're still in operation, only they do it without me.'

He let out a little laugh then added,

'Not so well, of course.'

John and Peter both smiled. Clouston went on

'Refrigeration is the business. Three bits to it, really. The core business is designing, manufacturing and installing particularised freezing and refrigeration to food processing companies – including fish producers. At lower volumes we sold freezers and refrigerators; some of our own, but largely branded, to companies that couldn't afford to contract the design work to us. Then, as a spin off, we did a bit of contract freezing – for smaller firms that couldn't afford to set up their own plants, or who didn't need all of the equipment all of the time. Firms like small seasonal growers, or one-man piggeries, specialist poultry breeders, that sort of thing, charcuterie.'

'What on earth is char . . ., what did you say?' laughed John Henry.

'Charcuterie! Speciality meats; venison, streaky bacon, pork, ham. I think there is one called rillette – and salami. Very tasty. But they couldn't afford their own freezing plant so we set up little operations to do it on a contract basis. There is a woman here in one of the units that does it.'

'Here?'

'Yes, she takes her stuff to markets at Newcastle and Edinburgh. She once told me that an attaché in the French Embassy in Edinburgh thinks her goose rillette the best he's ever tasted.'

'I must track her down and taste it, 'said John.

'Take plenty money with you,' said Clouston. 'A little tub of it costs seven pounds fifty. A little has to go a long way'

Both men laughed. But Peter had other things on his mind.

'Let me guess,' he said; 'that HD Processing of which you are a director, had something to do with that.'

Clouston looked at him for a few seconds. Then said,

'Yes. I introduced contract freezing to Arcticus but, I have to admit, it didn't add much to the bottom line. I tried to develop it but Arcticus found it something of a distraction; thought of it as a different business, I suppose. It didn't get the attention or investment it needed. I thought they might be prepared to off-load it at a discount. I knew Harold, and knew he was getting frustrated with the business here. To me the yard here looked a sound business and had potential for further development, but he had tired of it. I thought he might like to make a pitch for the contract freezing. It would have fitted quite well with the fish business.'

'Did he take to it?'

'At first yes, and set up the company. But it didn't go further than that. He got caught up with this investment lark of his.'

'More than a lark, I think,' said Peter tersely. 'It did a lot of damage to a lot of people.'

'Sorry. Yes, it did - including me,' replied Clouston solemnly.

'Oh dear,' muttered John.

'No, no' assured Clouston brightly. 'Save your pity for others; some have lost their life savings I hear. I pitched in only a little because Harold persuaded me, but I wasn't sure. I never thought he was much of a money man.'

'You lost all your money?'

Clouston smiled.

'No, Not all. It wasn't much - and I still hold M&S units that are not completely worthless.'

'So, HD Processing never traded?' said Peter.

'Died in the cradle,' replied Clouston.

'We can give it a decent burial, then.'

'Yes, with my blessing.'

This easy conversation took the meal past the scampi and the apple crumble to coffee, but Peter still had not fathomed precisely what Clouston had come for, yet had become convinced that he had come for something.

Hilda had ushered them from the dining room to the lounge area, partly to seat them more comfortably over their coffee, partly to allow her to get into the restaurant and clear the table. While Peter settled for Americano and John asked simply for filter coffee, Clouston asked for a Macchiato. John had never heard of such a coffee, and for a moment, suspected a city man showing off. But Hilda immediately recognised the request and produced a cup of something that Clouston commended as one of the best Macchiatos he'd ever tasted.

The change of location shifted the conversation.

'I had been wondering how the yard is coping without Harold,' began Clouston, 'but I see it is in very good hands.'

'Thank you,' said Peter.

John Henry expected Peter to open up on his own desire to move out, but Peter turned along another track.

'Yourself,' said Peter, 'you indicated you'd left Arcticus, but it's still there, isn't it?'

'Yes, and doing well I understand, but not under the old firm. Arcticus sold it last year to an Irish company, FosterFresh. You may have heard of them.'

John admitted he had not. Peter didn't reply.

'That doesn't surprise me, they tend to trade under brand names; they're a bit of a mixture, they produce frozen foods for the big stores: Marks & Spencer, Asda, John Lewis, Tesco, under their own label. But they also do a bit of contract refrigeration like Arcticus. They've kept the Arcticus name.'

'Did they not offer to keep you on?' asked John.

'Oh, yes,' said Clouston. 'With a seat on the local board, but I didn't like . . . . . . '

He paused, picked up his cup, took a sip of coffee, then continued.

'I'd been there a long time. It was my own operation; I'd set it up my own way. I got strong vibrations that they wanted to milk the company; drive down costs, shed labour, rationalise products. I suspected that once they had stripped out the refrigeration business they would sell the skeleton to someone else and concentrate on their core business. I didn't want to be part of that.'

'So, you left?'

'That's about it. I stayed to manage the changeover, then,' he paused, '(how do they put it?), they made it worth my while to move on".

'You fell out with them, and they asked you to leave. Is that it?' put in Peter.

John, surprised by his bluntness, glanced at his

friend and saw a determination he had not seen before. And appreciated a little more how Peter had survived and prospered in the harsh world of property development.

Clouston, however, did not flinch.

'Yes, it came to that' he replied pleasantly.

Then continued,

'And that is why I am here.'

Again, Peter side-stepped the hint.

'How long had you been with Arcticus?'

'Almost twenty years.'

'And before that?'

'IceCap – at their Peterhead plant. Frozen fish fingers and all that. Then Arcticus came knocking at the door.'

John tuned in; chat had finished; they were duelling these two; Peter thrusting; Clouston parrying.

'And wanted you to do what?' Peter asked

'Came as Engineering Director; for the last fifteen been Managing Director.'

'Reporting to the board?'

'Near enough; to the Chief Executive.'

'Who is at Newbridge?'

'No, Hull.'

'So, you were top man at Newbridge?'

'Yes.'

'Would you say the company prospered under your care?'

'I would say so,' Clouston replied lightly. 'But then I would, wouldn't I?'

Peter smiled.

'I agree' he said. 'You seem to have increased return on assets every year for the last seven or eight. Some hiccups, but in the present climate, that's pretty good, I would say.'

'Ah, you've been checking up on me,' said Clouston with a short laugh.

'Not you, the company', responded Peter in such a way that John could not tell whether he were rebuking Clouston or praising him.

Peter lifted his cup and deliberately took a long drink of coffee. John recognised it as a chapter heading.

'Now then, Clouston,' asked Peter, smiling but looking intensely at the younger man, 'what is it you want to ask us?'

'Well, I had thought that with Herold gone, there might be a vacancy for a part-time manager, but you two seem to have it well sown up.'

As Clouston stated this, Peter glanced at John Henry. John acknowledged the signal by raising his eyebrows. Clouston picked up the gesture and asked pleasantly,

'Something I said?'

Peter smiled, but ignored the question.

'What kind of part-time did you have in mind?'

'Well,' replied Clouston, in such a manner that John Henry recognised immediately as a mental script he had prepared earlier.

'I was thinking of two days a week, say, or, perhaps, ten spread over the month.'

'That would suit us, wouldn't it, John?' said Peter immediately.

'It would,' replied John.

'In which case we must see what we can do,' said Peter. 'Let me think about it. I'll get back to you in the next week or so.'

As John listened, he marked distinctly the change of the pronoun. The arrangement would suit *'us'*, but *'I'* will be in touch. Peter alone would determine the future management of Anthony Douglas & Son.

You must believe that this came as something of a relief to John Henry.

'I have my CV, if you'd like to see it,' added Clouston, who'd come prepared for an interview and wasn't sure if he had had one.

'Of course. I'll look it over,' said Peter, then added with a smile, 'or as some call it a Personal History – or should that be

B E WEBSTER

'Personal Mystery".

CHAPTER NINETEEN

John Henry came away from the Old Barque not sure what to make of the meeting with Peter and Clouston Pritchard.

He had had to leave the meeting early in order to keep an appointment with his hairdresser, Nicky. While she shampooed and snipped and kept up a pleasant flow of conversation, information and opinion, John muttered monosyllables and tried to make sense of the encounter between Peter and Clouston.

Did Peter intend taking on Clouston or not? He had thought Peter keen to recruit someone to lead the company, yet showed little enthusiasm for Clouston's approach. Did he have doubts about the man? Did that reflect his true feelings or a ploy? Clouston appeared to be a good fit. He had no actual experience of a fish yard but then, who has? He had been there or thereabouts in food processing; enough, John thought, to understand what was needed at Anthony Douglas. He, John, had been quite impressed with Clouston. At first, he had thought he might be showing off; playing the big shot. Perhaps Peter thought that too. Certainly, Clouston came over as confident of his ability to manage; did Peter think he was too confident? Then Peter had commended him for his work at Arcticus – but in such a way that put the younger man on his guard. That's why he mentioned 'return on assets'. Peter demonstrating that he assessed managers not by their ability to talk a good career but to examine what they had achieved through lens of profit and loss. That would also account for his near dismissal of Clouston's offered CV. Nor did he allow Clouston to finesse his dismissal from Arcticus as his decision not theirs. Peter even seemed to accept that the work could be done part-time; he didn't react against it when Clouston raised it. He could have rebuffed Clouston's approach then and there if he really believed that the job needed a full-time manager; but he didn't.

By the time Nicky had sprayed the spray and whipped off the cape he had still not fathomed Peter's intentions. Never mind. He'd talk to him tomorrow.

As he reached for his wallet to pay Nicky, he felt a sharp pain shoot along the top of his abdomen. He winced. Nicky noticed.

"What is it?' she asked.

'Just a twinge,' replied John attempting to smile. He expected the pain to disappear as quickly as it had arrived but it seemed to lodge under his rib cage and grip the harder.

He handed Nicky a note, received his change, gave her back a pound by way of a tip and put away his wallet. As he did so the pain increased.

'Is it still there?' enquired Nicky sounding alarmed.

'Just indigestion, I think. I'll take some bicarb when I get home.'

'I have Rennies, if that would help.'

'Thank you', muttered John through the pain.

'You'd better sit down till it goes away,' said Nicky, handing him the box of tablets and a glass of water. John took two, gave the box back to her, sat down, and sipped the water. As he did so the door opened and Nicky's next customer entered: Janet.

'What's wrong with you?' she demanded.

John made to speak but Nicky pre-empted him.

'He has a pain,' she exclaimed.

'Where?' she asked John.

'Just under the ribs, along the top of the stomach.'

'How bad is it?'

'It's quite severe,' replied John and sucked his lips with the pain.

'I've told him to sit till it goes away,' put in Nicky. 'I've given him Rennies.'

'Are they helping?'

'Not a lot,' breathed John.

'Sit there, then,' ordered Janet, 'till she's finished with me. It'll not take long. Then I'll see you home.'

'There'll be no need; it'll clear,' said John, but made no attempt to move. Nicky shampooed Janet's hair, then sat her in the chair and started to cut her hair.

John leaned back and closed his eyes.

'How is it?' Janet asked John after a few minutes.

'It's easing, I think. I'll just give it a little longer.'

As Nicky set about styling Janet's hair she glanced towards John.

'Y'all right?' she said.

John nodded.

As she finished Janet's hair, John stood up and let out a howl, doubled up, and slumped back into the chair.

'That's bad,' he gasped.

'Right,' exclaimed Janet, 'I'm getting our Christine. Can I use your phone?'

'Aye, but why are you sending for Christine?'

'She's done first aid – and she's just along at the Co-op.'

Then she turned to John.

'Take another two Rennies.'

John did as he was told. Sucking them provided some comfort but relieved the pain not at all. Within a few minutes Christine arrived, carrying with her the defibrillator from the store. John submitted to having his pulse taken: high but not rapid, Christine reported. She felt his brow: warm but not clammy.

'Where's the pain?' she asked.

John pointed to his left side just below his rib cage.

'It's in there.'

'Sore, would you say, or more like pressure or a cramp?'

'More like a cramp – as if something was blocked.'

'On a scale of zero to ten; zero being . . . .'

John didn't let her finish.

'Nine, no, nine and a half . . .,' he gasped.

'What's wrong wi' him?' cried Janet.

Christine ignored her.

'D'ye feel no weel?' she asked John.

'He's in pain,' rasped Janet.

'Shut up, mother. John, apart from the pain, d'ye feel no' weel, cold, feverish, weak.'

To his surprize John discovered he did not. Just the severe pain.

'Did ye feel it tight round the chest, like a clamp.'

'No'.

'Pains down yer arms.'

'No.'

'Whit d'ye think?' Janet again.

'I no' ken, bit I'm sendin' for the paramedics.'

With that she picked up the phone and dialled 999 and asked for an ambulance. When the call-handler started on the routine of asking what was wrong. Christine informed that she knew her first aid, didn't think it was a heart attack, but had a defibrillator just in case.

'He's in terrible pain; he needs an ambulance quickly. If you insist, I'll put him on.'

She turned to John.

'She wants to speak to you.'

'Hello.'

The call handler started to rattle off questions.

'Look,' gasped John, 'I've been through that with Christine. Get me an ambulance, please. This pain is near unbearable.'

She acceded and said an ambulance would arrive within eight minutes.

Christine turned to Nicky.

'In the meantime, d'ye have an aspirin?'

'No, I've got paracetamol somewhere.'

'That'll do,' said Christine.

Nicky raked around in a drawer and produced the packet. Christine took two and closely supervised by her mother, gave them to John.

The paramedics beat their target time by a minute, but it proved the longest seven minutes of John's life. Throughout, Christine stood with her hand on his shoulder speaking softly to him, while Janet, in an attempt to take his mind off the pain, tried to engage him in conversation, talking to him about Duncan's work at Latchly and Hector and Christine moving in with Alice and Alistair. John being the courteous man he is, even in such an extremity, tried to take an interest, but could scarcely speak for pain. He was relieved when two paramedics barged into the shop. Christine recognised Adrian immediately; an experienced paramedic, he lived in the new houses across the water. Adrian introduced his colleague: technician and driver, Beth.

They were followed into the shop almost immediately by Annie, one of the ladies that meet Ina for coffee in MacMaggie's two or three mornings a week. Like a hoover she sucked in the scene before her, before Adrian ushered her out of the shop. Christine then told the paramedics what she had done and they commended her. Then they set to work. They went methodically over the same ground while wiring his left arm up to an Electro Cardiograph (ECG). For a while they studied the trace, then Adrian applied it to the other arm.

'What is it?' said John.

'Not your heart, I think,' replied Adrian. 'Do you have a stomach ulcer?'

'No, not that I know. . ... Owow! Sorry!'

'We'll need to take you to the BGH.'

John stood up. They commanded him to sit down then strapped him into a stretcher, carried him out of the shop and placed him in the ambulance. All the while watched by Annie and a small knot of spectators.

'Do you want your daughter to go with you?' asked Adrian before they closed the doors.

'No, she's not my daughter,' mumbled John, not sure, or bothered, which of the women he meant.

Once inside the ambulance they wired him up to an ECG, then fitted him up with a mask. Beth left to take up the driving, Adrian stayed with John.

'We're giving you gas and air. It's what we give a mother when her baby is on the way,' he said, with a little laugh. 'But don't worry – in your case it's for the pain. Tell me if it helps.'

In spite of his discomfort John smiled, then sank back into his chair and hoped the gas and air would work quickly. It didn't. By the time the ambulance reached Allanton, the pain had John crying out.

'We'll give you a little morphine.' said Adrian calmly; 'that should give you some relief.'

He signalled to Beth to stop the ambulance and instructed John to turn his back towards him. He then lifted John's shirt and injected 5mg into his lumbar area. Adrian then told Beth to drive on.

'Let me know if that works,' said Adrian quietly.

John found his whole demeanour calm and reassuring. Within a few minutes the pain dulled.

'What's causing it, this pain?' he mumbled. 'It's hellish; I've never had a pain like this before.'

'To be honest, I don't know. I wondered if it could be an aneurism – a swelling of the artery in the gut; that's why I took the ECG in both arms; it's usually different in an aneurism, but they were the same. Mind you I notice that, every now and then, your pulse blips; that could be the heart. But I don't think so. I really don't know, John. The quicker the better we get you into the hospital.'

Then he continued,

'How do you know Christine, then?' he asked. 'Back

there I assumed she was your granddaughter and the other woman might be your daughter. I'm sorry about that.'

John recognised the tactic 'get their mind off the pain', and almost welcomed the opportunity to think of something other than what might be the cause of it.

'No, that's all right. The other woman is Christine's mother, Janet, married to Duncan.'

'Oh, so that's Janet!'

'And good to have by you in a crisis.'

'So, you must be John Henry, the old bank manager, that saved the fish yard.'

'Oh, no. I mean, yes, I'm John Henry, but no, I didn't save the fish yard. That's down to Peter Munro.'

'Ah, yes, I've heard of him. He's a millionaire, isn't he? Good for him. There's a lot of Hecklescar folk depend on that yard.'

He studied John for a while then asked,

'I hear the same man's helping Duncan with Latchly. They're going to be moving in beside the old couple, they say. What was all that about the land belonging to Peter all the time?'

John made to answer but sucked his words back as a fresh spasm struck him.

'Still severe?' asked Adrian

'Yes, but. . ..'

Adrian stopped the ambulance again and administered two more micrograms of morphine.

Adrian kept up the conversation without expecting any more than the occasional grunt, nod or monosyllable from his patient. As the pain dulled a little John began, in spite of it, to feel a little dreamy.

They reached the Borders General Hospital in forty-three minutes from Hecklescar. I have never done it in less than fifty – and I had no stops on the way. Without delay, they hoisted John from the ambulance onto a trolley and wheeled him rapidly to Accident and Emergency (A&E).

CHAPTER TWENTY

In the evening of the day that saw John Henry taken from the hairdressers to the Borders General Hospital, Janet and Duncan set out to visit him. They had rung the hospital two or three times to ask after him but, when they admitted to being mere friends not close relatives, had received nothing but bland re-assurances and the information that he was in the Cardiac Unit in Ward Five. This information did not re-assure Janet.

'They're hiding something,' she said as they set out. 'If he's in the Cardiac Unit it must be his heart. I'll have a word with our Christine when we get back. She said it wasn't his heart.'

'She didn't say it *wasn't* his heart,' corrected Duncan. 'She said that she didn't think it *could be*.'

'Well, it comes to the same thing. He was in terrible pain. What did Adrian say when you rang him?'

'He said that he didn't think it was his heart, but he couldn't discuss it with me.'

'So, he is wrong as well.'

'Janet, we don't know if they are wrong. Let's wait until we see him.'

That satisfied Janet for a few miles. Then,

'He was in terrible pain, shouting out. That's not like him. He's generally very composed. It must be something serious. Even if it's not his heart - which it must be if he is on the Cardiac Ward.'

Duncan drove on. As they headed out of Greenlaw, Janet set out on a new tack.

'We must prepare ourselves for the worst, Duncan. You don't have a pain as bad as that without it being really serious. I'm not sure what we are going to find.'

Duncan let out a little laugh and leaned over and patted her hand.

'Oh, ma lass, he'll be all right. He's in the right place. They're very good nowadays. Adrian said he was taken straight away when they got to the hospital. They didn't have to wait at all. Straight in. They saw him immediately. He couldn't be in a better place.'

'They should have taken him to the Royal in Edinburgh. That would have given him a better chance. Dear knows what we are going to find when we get there. He was in a poor way.'

'I thought you said that he said he was all right apart from the pain,' mumbled Duncan.

'That's our Christine. How can you be alright apart from a pain like that? You can't think of anything else. Christine's like you. Never looks things in the face.'

Duncan let go of his frustration, but only to himself.

'Better than staring up your arse looking for trouble,' he mumbled.

'What was that?' clipped Janet.

'Nothing,' he said. 'We're in Earlston. Not far to go now.'

'And what will we find when we get there?' muttered Janet.

John Henry sitting up in bed, pain gone and a big smile on his face; that's what they found. They had wired him up to a drip but he said he felt fine.

'This is a pleasant surprise,' said Duncan. 'We were worried about you. Janet said your pain was something awful.'

'What with the pain and you being in the Cardiac Unit.' added Janet smiling. 'What a relief it is, John. I had Duncan all worried about what we were going to find. What happened?'

John then, with some enthusiasm and not a little humour launched into his story.

Here I must put in a caveat. There are some people who like nothing better than a serious illness to talk about. But I am not one of them. To be honest, clinical particulars make me queasy. I hope, therefore, you'll excuse me, and let me press on with the story without any more of medical minutiae than is strictly necessary to help it along. From those of you tuned in to medical dramas, I ask forgiveness if my diagnoses, prognoses and jargon are not up to scratch.

John reported to Duncan and Janet that as soon as he entered A&E and Adrian and Beth had departed, the pain left him. It had not come back.

The medics had wired him up to an ECG, taken blood samples, filled in forms and had left him lying in a cubicle, occasionally peeking through the curtains. John, blissfully pain-free and feeling well, had conjectured that they thought him a chancer or a fraud. A succession of nurses, technicians, and young doctors visited him, examined him, asked him questions, then stood over him looking puzzled.

Eventually, an older doctor had arrived and ran through the same questions and concluded by asking if he still had the pain in his chest. John replied that he had never had a pain in his chest, that the pain lay further down. The doctor expressed surprise, consulted the notes and asked him bluntly why he had been brought to A&E. John reported to Janet and Duncan that he had given the doctor the details then added, by way of humour, that he must be something of a disappointment.'

The doctor had not risen to the humour and had said that, in the light of the pain he had had in his chest, they would keep him in hospital overnight to carry out further checks.

'When I repeated that I hadn't had a pain in the chest,' John told Janet and Duncan, 'he just stared at me and left. I haven't seen him again. I have a nice friendly lady doctor looking after me. Doctor Keenan - from Ireland, I think.'

As Janet and Duncan made to leave, a young doctor arrived to inform John that, probably, the pain had nothing to do with his heart, and may have been caused by something in the gut: a stone, or obstruction of some sort, or an ulcer. John would need to come back by appointment to have it investigated. He could go home to-morrow.

'He's enjoying it,' said Janet to Duncan as they picked their way through the dark roads of The Borders back to Hecklescar.

'And our Christine was spot on, wasn't she?' Duncan smiling. 'It wasn't a heart attack!'

Janet laughed and clouted him on the shoulder.

Back at the hospital, however, after the lights in the ward had been dimmed, Dr Keenan arrived to say that, as a precaution, he would be taken next day to the Royal Infirmary in Edinburgh to have his heart checked out. Although his ECG showed no sign of a heart attack, blood samples taken in A&E indicated that he may have suffered one. Better be safe than sorry.

Janet has it correctly: now the pain had gone and nothing serious had been discovered, John Henry relished his expedition into the mystical world of the health service. Perhaps I should encourage him to write a short documentary about his adventures but, for the moment, I will confine myself to the most relevant and entertaining of his experiences.

The following morning, after pleading with Elsa, the charge nurse, she detached him from the drip. He then took a shower and shaved. Back in the ward he bought a Times from the two WVS ladies touring the ward, and spent hour making little headway with the crossword. However, although not ill, he would not be left alone and the nurses still arrived with dreadful regularity to take his pulse, check his blood pressure and carry out other procedures the purpose of which he could not fathom and they would not explain. Then one of them borrowed his pen and forgot to give it back. Deprived of his crossword, he transferred his attention to his three fellow patients, all of whom, it seemed to John, were quite seriously ill.

John discovered that the drip to which he was attached could be wheeled about so he took the opportunity to tour the ward to talk to his three companions. He found all of them glad of the opportunity to smother their growling anxiety about their condition in talk about their family, their home-patch, and what they did or had done for a living.

Eddie from Hawick, had been brought in with a racing heart. It had been two hundred beats per minute, now it was a hundred and twenty and they were aiming for ninety. He told John that since he came in two days ago, the nurses had taken off two litres of water. He admitted that he felt like a wimp. His wife never complained although she had had her kidneys removed and went to dialysis three mornings a week – at half-past seven. She liked the early shift as she called it, because it gave her the afternoon to do what she wanted. A tumour has also been detected in her lung but has not grown on a few months.

'She bears it all without a murmur,' he said. 'But look at me; scared out of my mind.' Later in the day, Eddie was moved to Ward Six and John never saw him again.

Just after nine in the morning, paramedics wheeled in Jim. He looked pale, ill, overweight and frightened. A junior doctor came to run through his history with him, and John heard him say that he had had a stent fitted in April but was now again in pain and ill. When the doctor left, John greeted Jim and thought that would be the end of it; that Jim, would not want to talk, but Jim seemed only too glad to avoid suffering in silence. He wanted to talk.

He confessed to being sixty-seven but looked much older. He had worked almost all his life on a farm near Ashkirk and described how his diseased heart had eaten away his busy, active, happy life. Lately, he had had to be given morphine to reduce the pain. Now he was reduced to sitting making crooks. The shanks were hazel, he told John, the handles different kinds of horn including buffalo horn when he could get it from a supplier he knew. He used mahogany too and, if he could get it, burr walnut. He carved the handles in the shape of a thistle, or a ram's head or other images. He also made thumb sticks. I asked if he sold them but he said he mainly gave them away and would make one for me when he was out of his trouble.

In the afternoon, Jim's wife came to visit him. A tall, elegant, pleasant woman, dressed in cream, she had escaped from Zimbabwe with nothing. She had family in the Borders and that is how they met. They had been married (at least I think they are married) ten years. She looked much younger than he, but then he looked old for his years. When her time to go came they whispered their love for each other, and kissed. From the urgent tenderness of Jim's farewell John Henry surmised that he could well be thinking that he may not see his wife again. However, when the lunch menu came and Jim ordered Chicken Casserole, he began to suspect that he had read some of his own sad memories into what he had just witnessed. Clearly Jim was not a man to give up without a fight – and, for a fight, you need Chicken Casserole.

All morning, doctors sought to relieve Jim's pain but still he suffered. They then decided he should be sent to the Royal. Shortly afterwards, a nurse told John Henry that his own transfer to the Royal had been put back a day. John suspected that Jim had been given his slot at the Edinburgh hospital. At seven o'clock the ambulance crew arrived to take Jim to the Royal. A young doctor, advised, so it seemed to John, by the lead paramedic, gave Jim a substantial dose of morphine and left the ward. As he trundled out of the ward, he raised a feeble hand in John's direction John waved back and shouted, 'a' the best'. John regretted that his transfer to Edinburgh had been postponed, but could not regret giving up his place to Jim.

John never received the crook from Jim and wondered why.

CHAPTER TWENTY-ONE

The following afternoon, John Henry was wheeled out of the Borders General Hospital to an ambulance and taken the thirty-five miles to Edinburgh's Royal Infirmary. The Royal, a new build, struck him not so much as a hospital as a small town; about the size of Hecklescar, John estimated. He offered to walk from the ambulance or, at least, through the hospital. He wanted to walk, for the exercise, but found himself being stretchered through a shopping mall, elevated in a lift, manoeuvred along corridors, bustled though doorways until, finally, he found himself in something that looked like a hospital: Ward 103; forty-eight beds plus fourteen in the cardiac unit, into one of which John Henry was decanted.

He remained there for four days. Free from pain, he enjoyed every one of them. If you are medically astute, you might wish to point out that he had had several doses of morphine, and in those doses lay the reason for his relief. But he knew, as I think most of us do, the difference between a pain that has been subdued by drugs and a pain that has given up and left. He felt certain that the pain had gone for good.

During his stay, he spent most of his time sitting by his bedside, reading, doing his crossword, interrupted by a succession of consultants, doctors, nurses, device-operators, blood-takers, pulse-monitors, and note-writers. He would be x-rayed, scanned, and sampled. By the time he emerged from the process four days later he reckoned he had seen three consultants, six doctors, fifteen technicians and close on seventy nurses. Not that he minded. The turbulence had its own excitement and interest. John Henry had always taken an interest in the folk he met, and here he encountered plenty of them. He asked each new arrival what they were for and why they did what they did – and did they enjoy it.

He took a particular liking to Julie, the woman who came to take blood; a once bonnie woman, now fading into her late fifties. She wasn't a nurse she said; she had come twelve years ago as a nursing assistant, and had held her present job for five years.

'Nobody else put in for it,' she said with a tired smile.

What else did she do apart from taking blood samples? Nothing; that was all; she roamed throughout the Royal Infirmary, all six hundred beds of it. Did she enjoy it?

'It's a job and the pay's better than stacking shelves in a supermarket – and there's a pension at the end of it. If I ever get there; the government keeps shifting the finishing line. I have to work 'til I'm sixty-seven.'

'You've a long way to go, then,' said John Henry smiling.

'Thank you, kind sir,' she replied with a little curtsey. Then added with a smile,

'I have a grand title. I am a phlebotomist. But in here they call me 'the vampire'.'

Then there were his four fellow patients.

Kenneth had joined Tesco, when they came to Galashiels but a few years ago had launched out into the bookselling business and, according to him, had been quite successful until the recession undermined his sales. A devoted Christian, he made a point of sitting by his bedside reading a large floppy bible.

Kenneth had had his angioplasty the day before John arrived and hoped to be discharged soon. He told John that he felt unfairly treated because, although sixty-seven, he ate a healthy diet and took regular exercise. Yet his MI had come out of the blue. John asked him what an MI was. Myocardial Infarction, he replied. As far as John could make out, that is just another name for a heart attack. Then he told John that he had inside knowledge of these matters. His wife is a sister at the BGH.

A pleasant, sociable man, he had a keen sense of humour and, in spite of his health claims, had become mildly addicted to coffee. One morning, after asking, in vain, for a cup from every nurse that bustled into the ward, the sister arrived. He immediately addressed her,

'We've had a vote and if we don't get a cup of coffee in the next half-hour we're going to take our diseases elsewhere.'

All the patients cheered, the sister took it in good part and within twenty minutes the coffee arrived.

Something else intrigued John Henry: the catering arrangements. The hospital apparently didn't belong to the National Health Service but to a private contractor who leased it to the local health board. The contractor also provided all the meals. But not occasional coffee and odd cups of tea; they were made on the ward by whoever happened to be free. If no-one was free then the patients didn't get their drinks - unless they had a Kenneth to organise them. Perhaps they should add coffee-making to the duties of the phlebotomist. It would give her a little variety and put back a little of what she'd taken out!

When John reported that all the patients in the ward cheered when Kenneth demanded coffee, he should have exempted Angus. This patient had little interest in anything other than his own health. At forty-three, he lived in Dunfermline, worked for the local authority and occupied his leisure hours playing golf. Now, however, he had been robbed of both his job and pastime by asthma and angina. He had had pain for three or four months, and believed he would not be rid of it until he had a heart valve replaced. His usual consultant, however, had taken three month's leave and he was hoping that another consultant would fit him into his list.

'After all,' he complained to John Henry, 'I am young and have most of my life ahead of me, whereas there are those in their eighties who have had their lives but are clogging up the system.'

He seemed to be unaware that he was talking to one such eighty-year-old. His mind had fixed on Jock, a talkative old man in the bed across from him who insisted and trying, through wheezes and coughs, to engage him in conversation. He later complained to the night nurse that Jock had likely infected him and that that would put off his treatment once again.

Jock, now approaching his eighty-ninth birthday had lost none of his zest for life, and hoped to get his heart sorted out so he could proceed to the Western to have his waterworks mended. John never did find out what was wrong with him. He was very deaf and listening to his stories proved less strenuous than getting him to hear and answer questions. He boasted three daughters and four granddaughters, but only one solitary male relation, a grandson. Several of them came to visit him and they all lectured him. He also suffered from celiac disease and had to have a gluten-free diet. Nevertheless, he ordered haggis, neeps and tatties and was only prevented from eating it when Kenneth warned off the caterers. He belonged Arbroath and had worked as a Post Office engineer all his life. Now he lived in North Berwick cared for by carers.

John found his stories intriguing, not least because they breathed life into what John already knew of recent Scottish social history. Jock had not studied it as a subject at university, read a tome or two about it, written a learned thesis, or discussed it in academic symposia. He had worked, walked, and wept his way through it. People with names: Hamish, Bert and Margaret, bustled out of his memory into his account bearing, in vivid individuality, their tears and laughter, their constancy and eccentricity, their fears and hopes.

His granny and grandfather hailed from Scalpay and his granny taught him to count up to ten in Gaelic. That is the way she counted the herring into the barrel, he told John. He also told John that his grandfather had missed his train at Taynuilt and had seen the red light move out of the station as he arrived. That train, Jock added dramatically, went down with the Tay Bridge disaster, his grandfather thus being saved. His grandfather put this down to God's intervention and became a church elder. When John asked why God hadn't saved the others, Jock said that his grandfather had an answer for that: they were on the train and he wasn't.

Jock had fought in the bloody battle for Monte Casino in the Italian Campaign in the Second World War. Later he had met an Italian ice-cream man in North Berwick that who came from there. When John asked him about the terrible destruction and slaughter that took place there, he recalled everything being flattened and dead bodies lying everywhere. But he switched back immediately to the impressive fact that Giacomo, the man who sold ice-cream in North Berwick, came from a little village at the foot of the hill at Monte Casino.

How much more John would have learned from Jock we do not know for John was summoned back to his bed place. There a quiet older junior doctor introduced himself as Dr. Hamil and outlined the course of his treatment. They were concerned that the pain in his chest had resulted from a blockage or restriction in one of the coronary arteries, so they would, with his permission, carry out an angioplasty and if necessary a PCT. John replied that he had not had, and did not have, a pain in his chest. The doctor received this information with a patient smile on his face, mumbled, 'I see,' consulted his notes, then carried on as if John had not spoken. John got the feeling that the doctor mildly resented being told by the patient what wasn't wrong with him.

We must not presume that Dr Hamil is incorrect in his diagnosis of John Henry as one of those men (and most of them are men) who are determined not to be ill. In his time, he has met all three types of patients: those who believe that what they have is serious and rare, requiring detailed and lengthy treatment; those who have concluded that they have a fatal illness; and those who doubt that there is anything wrong or, if there is, that it will clear up by itself. We would not be mistaken to count John Henry among the doubters.

John then asked Dr Hamil what a PCT was. The doctor rattled off a definition we know must have been Percutaneous Coronary Intervention, but John made no sense of it until Dr Hamil explained that they would insert a camera into his heart to track down any blockage then, when they detected it, expand a balloon to open it out. If necessary a short wire tube, called a stent, would be fitted to keep it open.

'When will all this happen?' asked John, somewhat impatiently, bearing in mind his belief that there was little wrong with him and now there might be weeks languishing on an NHS waiting list wondering when the appointment letter would arrive.

'You are seventh on the list for tomorrow,' stated the doctor.

'That's bad news,' said Kenneth, cheerfully, when John gave him the news. 'I was sixth and wasn't taken until the following day.'

CHAPTER TWENTY-TWO

Shortly after Dr Hamil left, a visitor for John walked into the ward: Peter Munro. Jakey had told Peter that John Henry had suffered a heart attack in Nicki's hairdressing salon and had been taken by ambulance to BGH in a life-threatening condition. (Here we must remember that Jakey's wife is Ina and that that, almost certainly, is where he heard this version of the truth.)

Peter had arrived expecting his friend to be in intensive care wired up with tubes and cables, but found him sitting cheerfully by his bed looking in the pink of health. He expressed his relief, and enjoyed John's entertaining description of what had happened.

'But a pain in the chest is not something you should. . ..'

John roared back at him.

'Don't you start! I've never had a pain in my chest - and I don't think there's anything wrong with it. All the results are negative. That is, they're positive. They all say my heart is working as it should.'

Peter cupped his face in his hands and rocked back in mock defence at John's assault.

'You wouldn't be in here if there was nothing wrong with you,' he said gently.

'I'm in here because the doctors said it was my heart, so they are going to prove it.'

'You don't believe that?'

'Not entirely. To-morrow they're going to slip a camera into my ticker and take a look. I believe, or should I say, hope, that they will find that there's nothing wrong with it.'

Peter then came to the point of his visit.

'I've asked Clouston Pritchard to manage the yard,' he said firmly.

'Have you now?' replied John Henry in such a way that Peter could not tell whether he was irritated or not.

Peter had not come with the intention of irritating his friend in any way. On the contrary, his object had been to take away any pressure John may be feeling about the appointment. He, Peter, had made the decision. John would not need to concern himself about it.

'Yes,' answered Peter, and to lighten his announcement, added, 'I told him the job would be part- time. Ten days a month, I think that's what you suggested, was it not?'

John smiled.

'Did he accept that?'

'Yes,' answered Peter lightly, 'but he wants to be called 'Chief Executive.'

'And you agreed to that?'

'It's not something I would have offered. It's much too grand. But nowadays it's what managers want to call themselves, so I agreed.'

John looked at Peter and held out his hand.

'You've made the right decision,' he said. 'He's not a fish man, but he's been around and seems to know what he's doing. He could be just what the yard needs. Have you told Jakey and the others?'

'Yes, I brought them in to meet him. I watched him particularly with Jakey. They seemed to make contact.'

Peter had determined that he would not inflict any discussion on John Henry; that he would keep back any doubts he had about Clouston. ('John is ill, isn't he?') But John would not let go, and he could not refuse to answer him.

'Did he not want to see what they did?'

'Yes, Jakey and Angela took him away and showed him round. I believe he had a short discussion with Fiona too.'

Peter wanted to stop at that, but John came back again.

'And what did they make of him after that?'

'They said that it would be okay.'

'You make it sound as if they weren't very keen.' queried John.

Peter stared at John for a little while before responding.

'When I called them in yesterday to tell them I was appointing Clouston as manager they seemed a little jittery.'

'Jittery?'

'I'm not sure what had happened on Clouston's tour, but Jakey asked if he would be interfering; that was his word. I got the impression that he was speaking for Angela and Fiona too. I assured them that they would still run the yard day-to-day; Clouston would be negotiating with suppliers – like the Mallaig Co-op, and the customers – and dealing with company level financial and legislative matters - looking at the longer term.'

'Do you think they accepted that?'

Peter avoided the question.

'Fiona did say that she dealt with some of that now. I told her that Clouston would not be involved in the admin, only in the decision-making. That seemed to content her. I'll have a word with Clouston to make sure he doesn't step over the line.'

John let it go at that, but he had caught sight of what Peter had been anxious to hide. That he had misgivings about his new manager.

'When does he start?' John asked.

'End of the month.'

'This month? That's next week?'

'No, March; last week in March.'

'Will he move to Hecklescar?'

'No; they're settled, the family, in North Berwick and he has other irons in the fire in Edinburgh and Aberdeen, I think. He'll commute from there. He said he'd like a car as part of the pay, and I agreed.'

'Not a Mercedes, I hope,' laughed John.

'Not a Mercedes!'

'A real Chief Executive then,' smiled John.

'Fiona asked about you, too,' said Peter smiling. 'She hoped that 'Mr Henry' would not be leaving, and I assured her that you would still have a role in the company.'

'Thank you,' announced John, 'and here's me thinking I could retire at last.'

'We'll talk about that once you are well,' said Peter gently.

'There's nothing wrong with me,' John protested with a short laugh.

'Let's wait and see what they find when they take a look,' replied Peter firmly.

CHAPTER TWENTY-THREE

After lunch the following day, John and his fellow patients, especially Kenneth, thirsted long for the coffee they had ordered. Obviously, Kenneth's bluff had been called; they were not afraid of losing business. No matter how often one or other badgered a nurse or assistant, by three o'clock the promised drinks had not arrived. Kenneth had spent most of the morning scribbling a long letter and had gained permission to go down to the shopping mall on the ground floor to buy a stamp and post it. He then went round the ward taking orders for coffee from the takeaway in the mall.

During Kenneth's absence, the nurse delivered to John a gown and a pair of frilly underpants. These he must put on for his trip to the angioplasty laboratory, she said. The thought repelled him; he would look – and feel ridiculous. John had dressed in his normal clothes; shirt, pants socks and shoes. In the light of his seventh place on the list and Kenneth's postponement till the next day, he did not feel like sitting around in his comical outfit for any longer than necessary. He therefore left the gown and pants on the bed to be donned later in the day.

Kenneth, in triumph, walked into the ward clutching

three large cartons of coffee. As John went forward to claim his cup, a nursing assistant pushed a trolley containing the ordered and long-awaited mugs of the same refreshment into the ward. Not wishing to brave her wrath, John felt obliged to take a cup from her too.

John now had two cups of coffee and settled himself by his bed to drink them.. He had barely settled into his chair, however, when a brawny porter strode into the ward and demanded to know which one of the patients was John Henry; he had come to take him to the angioplasty laboratory. Alison, one of the nurses arrived to accompany him. John still dressed in his normal clothes had to change hurriedly into the frilly pants and gown under the agitated gaze of both porter and nurse. Clearly, he had held them up.

When ready, they ordered him to lie on his bed. The porter unlocked the bed and, accompanied by nurse Alison, whisked him out of the ward. The pair hurried him down meandering corridors, and eventually arrived at the angioplasty laboratory; one of three, Alison told him, each carrying out about eight procedures a day.

What happened next is simply described. John lay on a large table, covered by a large rubber sheet and given a local anaesthetic. Two consultants inserted a camera on a long lead into a vein on the back of his right hand and pushed it until it entered the heart. Then, using a cantilevered TV screen to view the arteries, the consultants declared one of them to be restricted, and fed in a short metal gauze tube, a stent, to hold it open. After a short recuperation, he was wheeled back to the ward.

In the mouth of John Henry as he described it to Duncan and Janet later, the experience had proved to be a mixture of science fiction, mass production and vaudeville. Lying on the bed being whisked down the corridors he felt like the carcase of a washing machine on its way to be assembled, or a Monty Python sketch. When they reached the lab, he had been parked in a cubicle, resembling the changing rooms at the baths when he went swimming. The lab, he said, reminded him of a warehouse, or perhaps an alien temple. He would not have been surprised to be greeted by little green men with pointy ears. Instead, he discovered friendly white-coated and coveralled men and women, who did their best to make him feel relaxed, chatting among themselves about everything but the operation they were about to perform. There seemed dozens of them. They swarmed around what John described as an Incan altar, on which he was laid as if to be sacrificed. They allowed him to climb onto it from the floor. Had he been smaller, they said, they would have provided a step ladder. John found the whole experience mildly ludicrous. Once laid flat on the altar, a consultant he had never seen before sidled up to him and whispered.

'Now, about this pain you have in your chest.'

John, totally relaxed, answered in good humour.

'Look,' he had said pleasantly, 'I do not have a pain in my chest and I have never had a pain in my chest. If anyone else mentions it, I'll climb off and go home.'

'You never said that to the doctor, did you?' exclaimed Janet.

'I did!'

'What did he say?'.

'He just mumbled something I couldn't catch, then told me what they were going to do.'

John then described watching the whole procedure on a television set hovering over his head. He watched in astonishment as the probe wriggled its way into the blood vessels of his heart. He felt not a thing, he said. Then with the same brisk efficiency he was hustled back into the reception area. He would not have been surprised if the doctor had shouted 'next!'

Safely back in the 'changing room' another doctor whom he had never seen before, but who had apparently been at the altar, came to see him to show him a photo of the restricted artery before and after.

'You have three arteries,' he explained. 'The other two are perfectly healthy. You should have no more pain in your chest.'

Janet and Duncan both laughed.

'What did you say?'

'I didn't get the chance. He was off before I could get my tongue round something.'

'When do you get home?' asked Duncan.

'Tomorrow, if you will pick me up.'

Duncan came the following day and had to wait over an hour before John could join him. He had been corralled by an earnest pharmacist who insisted on instructing John on how he should take the tablets he had been taking for years. At the end of the interview, she gave him a spray she described as glyceryl trinitrate.

'Just spray it under your tongue when you get the pain in your chest.'

'What did you say to that?' laughed Duncan.

'Nothing. If I had said anything, I could have been there all day, I told her she'd been very attentive.'

'Is that you in the clear now?' asked Duncan as they made their way back to Hecklescar.

'You must be joking. Once they get hold of you, they don't let go. No, I have an appointment at the BGH in a week then every so often after that – if I decide turn up.'

'You'd better go,' said Janet, seriously.

'Of course I'll go,' replied John, with a sigh. 'I'm not that brave. I got away with it this time. No damage done to the heart they say. I've been lucky.'

As he said this he thought of Eddie and Jim in the BGH picking their way along the edge that, at any moment, could fall away into suffering and, they feared, out of life.

CHAPTER TWENTY-FOUR

John had not been long back home when Peter called to instruct him not to go anywhere near the yard until fully recovered. Although John protested that he felt fit and well and had been given, more of less, a clean bill of health, Peter insisted. He would decide when John could step through the door of the office again. In the meantime, he would prepare for Clouston Pritchard's arrival to take over the management of the company.

After lunch the same day, Jakey came back to yard to find a jittery Nudge waiting to speak to him. Jakey was surprised to see him for he knew that Nudge had returned from the continent in the early hours of that same day. He should be in his bed, preparing to set out on a similar trip that evening. What could be so urgent? Jakey did not have to wait long for the question to be answered. Nudge, ever diffident and never given to many words, launched straight into his story though not, at first, with any clarity.

'They're letting him out provided he has an occupation to go to. They don't want him sitting in the house brooding.'

'Who?' asked Jakey.

'Callum'

'Jen's son?'

'Yes. He's been in the unit up the Borders for a few months now and they'll let him out if he has a job.'

'What's this got to do with me – or you, for that matter?'

'I told Jen I'd come and see you. She's frightened you'd turn her down.'

'Turn her down for what?'

'A job for Callum.'

'A job for Callum; here in the yard?'

'Yes, I thought there might be something.'

Jakey looked at the earnest face in front of him. Of all the problems Jakey faced in his job this one lost him most sleep: turning down job requests for sons and daughters, uncles and aunts, distant cousins and friends of a friend. He belonged Hecklescar, lived in the place, met people here, was related to many of them. He knew the buzz on the street: 'y'can aye get a job in the fish yard; see Jakey.' That's the trouble with living in the place and belonging to the place. If he gave a job to everyone who asked him, the yard would be overflowing with workers - and broke. It hurt him to turn anyone down so adopted a tactic of telling them to write in for an application form. Sometimes that proved to be the last he heard of it; often not. Then, the boy or girl or man or woman would be turned down or hear no more, and he'd be snubbed in the street, or Ina would come back with tittle-tattle of his bias.

'It's a funny thing, when *I* asked him, I never heard again, but *her* that came from Kirkintilloch, she got her daughter into the fish room – and she hardly stayed any time.

And,

'Him that goes to the Legion with Jakey; ye ken him with the beard and the weird wife, from Fife; he got a job straight away.'

Before him now stood Nudge, a man on whom he could depend; a colleague who had often helped him out with back-to-back shifts and long urgent drives to demanding customers; he is asking, for the first time, for a favour – and not for himself, but for Jen, the ever-willing hard-working Jen. Yet, if he made an exception, he would be pilloried in the town.

His anxiety hardened his answer.

'Nudge, I'd like to help, but you know I can't conjure up jobs because someone needs it. Folk are aye on to me about finding jobs. But we have procedures and I have to stick to them. Fiona sorts all that sort of thing out. If I give to one to the lad there'd be a queue before the day's out.'

This exposition had no impact on Nudge. He simply stood with a tense smile on his face.

'The lad needs help,' he said quietly, 'and so does Jen; this is what she's been working on for months; to get her lad out of there and back with his bairns. Is there nothing at all?'

Jakey then remembered Nudge finding Jen on the cliff, of his fears for the woman, and understood quite clearly Nudge's concern. He moderated his tone.

'Nudge,' he said sympathetically, 'as I've explained to you; I just can't pull jobs out of the air.'

'Jen said she'd give up some of her hours if you took him on for a few hours a week at the fish round. That's all she's looking for, just a few hours, to get the lad back into work.'

'Him in a van, serving customers? He couldn't do that – not in his condition, could he?'

'Jen would take him out with her for a few weeks, to show him the ropes and see how he got on.'

'Naw, Nudge, I no' see it. We couldn't take the risk. We'd lose customers.'

Still Nudge did not move. Jakey relented.

'I tell you what I'll do. I'll have a word with Angela, see if she could fit him in in the yard – temporarily. She has a couple on maternity leave and Diane has gone off with her nerves again. D'ye have any idea if the lad has any experience of the fish? What's has he worked at?'

'I'm not sure,' Nudge replied. 'But I'll ask Jen.'

Then he added,

'Thank you, Jakey. Much appreciated.'

Which last phrase worried Jakey. Had he promised too

much? Had he raised hopes he could not fulfil? He thought about knocking back the appreciation, by down-playing the lad's chances, but the simple, silent gratitude on Nudge's face turned him against it, and he simply repeated,

'I'll see Angela.'

She proved no help. She had already taken on a couple of young out-of-work girls to cover for her absentees. She expressed her concern for Nudge and Jen, but said she'd be in trouble explaining why she'd given a woman's job to a man – and a grown man at that. If we were pedantic we could quote the relevant clauses of the Sex Discrimination Act to her, and she would acknowledge her knowledge of them and swear her allegiance to the high principles of the Act. Nevertheless, when push came to shove, there could be demonstrated a monotonous regularity in the proportion of women to men on the fish benches, which contrasted or, should we say, balanced the ratio of men to women on the fishing boats. In government and tribunals, they call it discrimination In Hecklescar, they call it fair.

To Jakey's relief, Angela did not hide behind him. She expressed her regret to Nudge in person - and went further. She reported a long-held complaint that the company needed another fork-lift truck. Whenever she or Jakey had broached the need with Hercules he had always rejected the request and told them to 'manage it.' When they complained to Fiona about it, she simply said that the company could not afford either the truck or the driver. Now that Peter was prepared to put money into the company, she would raise it again; maybe Jakey would do the same. In saying this she clearly has not been listening closely enough to Peter. Conscious of the optimism arising from his promise of investment, he had put a sort of ban on all capital purchases not personally authorised by him. Similarly, he had banned the creation of any additional jobs. Angela, when she spoke to Nudge, knew of these restrictions; Nudge did not.

It could have been expected that Nudge with such

information would have gone back to Jakey and elicited his support for the fork life truck. But Nudge, ever a cautious man, had gained his wealth as well as some satisfaction from surveying the future before venturing on it. He had followed up Jakey's enquiries about Callum's work experience. Jen had tried to burnish her son's career, praising his degree, regretting the demise of Fullerton's Printing Company and talking up his achievement in gaining his driving licence before he toppled into stress and depression. But whatever she said, Nudge could not expect Jakey to impressed by Callum's career. The company had no need of a Media Studies graduate, and Jakey, if he should need shelf-stackers and drivers, would be able recruit them by the dozen.

He learned something else from the interview, glimpsed something of his own confined youth in the life of this young man. He, like Callum, had a mother who had devoted her life to him. Cramped by her duty to God, family and her husband, she had poured all her energies into those activities that were regarded as acceptable by the group of people to whom she looked for companionship. He had been indulged; he now acknowledged that. He had received every encouragement to succeed in life. Although, as they say, not academically gifted, he had been given every encouragement and inducement to take advantage of the education offered him. His mother – and, to a lesser extent his father – had given up their free hours to work on his homework with him, had called on the teachers in the assembly to aid him. By such means he had achieved a decent set of Highers. He now, however, regarded that achievement as theirs not his. He had wanted for nothing, nothing, that is, acceptable to the unwritten rules of the meeting. He had made the usual progress from scooter, to tricycle, to bicycle to motor bike, and in due to time to car, without having to pay for any of them. He had been allowed a computer, but not some of the more violent games; he had been showered with books, but all of a type and nothing that would expose him to the seedier suburbs of human existence. He had been encouraged to mix only with the children of the assembly and had once or twice been discouraged from taking up with those whose families were thought undesirable. In short, he had been reared in a sort of family greenhouse; cultivated and nourished, isolated from the infections and pollutions of the air into which he stepped when he first entered the yard of Anthony Douglas at the age of sixteen.

However, we had better not criticise his mother in his hearing. He would not tolerate that. He might admit that he should have gone out more, mixed with more children from non-brethren households, sampled the activities and delights that beckoned during his teenage years, loosened the apron strings and applied for jobs and opportunities away from Hecklescar, but he would not lay any blame for his confinement on his mother. She loved him, gave him unstinted devotion and spent most of her adult years seeking his best interests as she saw them. He would point out that she had given him a workable set of values by which to stay off the rocks: decency, consideration for others, hard work, discipline, cleanliness, and frugality. You may think him a little strait-laced perhaps, but would not find him censorious. When someone swore or took the Lord's name in vain in his presence, he did not rebuke them, but fell silent and smiled. We have to admit that he has turned out well, and give the woman the thanks she deserves. Further, what if someone should turn their inspection on us? Would we rate any better? He had had a secure childhood and a safe youth. In his prayers daily, he thanked God for his mother; and why should he not? He is a decent man, at peace with himself.

Although, with Jen, there were no religious or restrictive undertones, Nudge nevertheless saw the same over-concern; the same desire to protect, fence round, to save, Callum. He understood as one who had trod the same road, how easy it is for such a one to fall into the ditch when the guide is no longer walking beside them. He recalled those bleak days and lonely nights after his mother and father left to return to Peterhead. Of his abortive attempts to find consolation – and freedom among his fellow workers in the Harbour Bar, and the gentle rebuke of the Elders when they discovered where he had been. He remembered too, old Mr & Mrs Geddes who, when he fled from his fears, welcomed him to their fireside. They had saved him and he had got through without the despair that had swamped Callum. One thing more helped him: his job. That every day he had to turn up at the yard, and there, as well as being tumbled among other workers, girls and youths, and men and women, he could accomplish something useful - and be paid for it.

How much of this matched the life of Callum we do not need to investigate. There are many differences. Some, we might think, crucial and radically different. But is it not true that when we wish to rescue someone, we find it much easier if we climb into the boat with them? Nudge was drawn to Callum whom he could not remember ever having met. But he knew and yes, loved, his mother - and whom she loved, he loved, and would do all he could to help him – and through him, her.

I would not, however, want you to suspect him of underhand motives. The love of which I write is as yet unknown to him. However, let us give him credit; take love out of the equation and calculate, not entirely inaccurately, that Nudge, being the man he is, would have wanted to help the lad anyway.

CHAPTER TWENTY-FIVE

Nudge knew and accepted that Callum had none of the skills that Jakey or Angela could use. Of course, he could be trained, and it must be admitted that virtually all workers at the sharp end of the Anthony Douglas enterprise had been trained 'on the job'. Normally, however, this started when they stepped out of school uniform into the oilskins provided by the company. Not often did the company recruit anyone of maturer years, not least because they could command the adult minimum rate immediately, whereas teenagers of sixteen and seventeen could be paid less as they worked their way into the job. When older people were taken on they were, almost always, experienced in the work they were about to do. Nudge, for all his innocence and advocacy, knew this and knew that, if Callum were to stand any real chance of work at the yard, he would have to have some skill that the company needed.

We mentioned earlier that, when the need arose, Jakey or Angela had occasionally called on Nudge to drive a forklift truck. Nudge could stand in because he held a Certificate of Basic Training. He had acquired this at a unit on the Industrial Estate run by Scottish Borders FLT, and it had been paid for by Anthony Douglas & Son. They had also paid for the regular refresher training required to keep his certificate valid.

What if Callum were a certificated forklift truck driver? Would not that allow he, Nudge, to offer him as the stand-in when the need arose? Once Callum had his foot (or perhaps we should say wheels) in the door, if and when an additional forklift truck was authorised, he would be in prime position to be appointed as its driver.

On his next free day, Nudge set out for the premises of Scottish Borders FLT. It occupied one of the largest units on the Hecklescar Industrial Estate. The facility lay behind a high expanded-wire fence which, due to age and infirmity, now hung exhausted on the supporting poles, giving the impression that it had given up and wanted only to fall asleep in the ragged blanket of tired weeds that wrapped round its feet. But for a freshly painted sign, a casual visitor might well assume that the site had been abandoned. Nudge wrestled the large gate open, walked across the concrete road and entered the door.

He did so with some trepidation for he knew the reputation of the man with whom he had to deal: the manager of the facility, a loquacious Brummie called Dave to his face and Eatit behind his back. There is nothing, Dave claimed to anyone who would listen, that he could not produce or provide, given the incentive and resources. Quite why he was not a billionaire living on a yacht at Biarritz he did not explain and no one had had the courage to ask him nor the time to listen to his answer.

Stepping inside the building, the air of neglect fell behind and Nudge found himself in a surprisingly neat and bright reception area. He had not long to wait after pressing the bell. Dave, smart in casual trousers and monogrammed sweat shirt, bustled out a door to greet him.

'Hello, Nudge, what brings you to my little enterprise. Looking for a new HGV? I can do that, but not before next week.'

He gave a little laugh. His familiarity grated. Nudge

scarcely knew the man. But he smiled in return and started on the question he wanted to ask: would he train Callum as a forklift truck driver and award the Certificate, even though Callum, as yet, did not have a job?'

Dave listened to Nudge for only half the sentence then interrupted.

'I know what you're chasing, and you've come to the right man. Put it in front of me,' he added, 'and I'll eat it.'

'It's true,' thought Nudge, 'he does say it.'

Dave then launched into a long and rambling catalogue of what he could offer.

'Depends where the lad is at. We do counterbalance forklift training, rough terrain tele handling, rough terrain straight mast, multi-directional side loading, simple side loading, narrow aisle forklift, - and Moffet, the very narrow, telescopic handling, et al, et al. If it's for the yard at Douglas it will be just the basic forklift. Trained them all down there.'

Nudge made to speak, but Dave drove on.

'Forklifts aren't toys; you need to know what you're doing. At the old Sea North place, you know, on the pier there, they put a young lad on one of their trucks. First time out he drove it into the harbour. Wrote it off – nearly wrote himself off too. After that they came to the fountainhead of knowledge SBFLT and we trained the rest of the crew up.'

Again, Nudge attempted to respond, but Dave hadn't finished.

'If he intends operating a forklift for a living it is vital that he obtains a Certificate of Competence in Forklift Operation. Competence is what we do; it is what we are. No-one leaves these premises without a Certificate – no matter how long it takes to win the coconut. We will be right behind him and beside him all the way. He is a man? This Callum, isn't he?

Nudge agreed, and would have said more, but Dave scarcely missed a beat.

'Not that that's a problem. We train the girls too.

Nowadays you have to be careful. Sex Discrimination and all that. We know our employment law. But Callum sounds like a lad and you've confirmed it, so that's kosher. When d'ye want him to start?'

Nudge again started to explain that Callum didn't actually have a job. But got no further than an introduction.

'Time's not a problem – can't do nights or week-ends but any other time. Might even squeeze in a Saturday morning if the devil drives and Satan chases. Now you'll be interested in times and seasons. Then we'll come to costs. How long, you're asking? How long does it take? Well, that depends on aptitude and attitude; with attitude in the front seat. If the attitude's right the aptitude rides in on it. Wrong attitude – show him the door. Not worth our effort; waste of the precious God-given. But no refunds. Not for poor attitude.'

'With good attitude and natural ability, do it in two days. I've done it in a day. But average, give or take an hour or two here and there, say a week; that's five days.'

Dave suddenly stopped. Since Nudge arrived, they had been standing in the reception room. Dave now ushered him into what he called the nerve centre: a large, airy barn, neatly and colourfully set out with roads and routes, depots and dropping off points, pallets and pretend loads, mock-up buildings and made-up hazards. Nudge, of course, had been in the room before, had been trained it, had manoeuvred his way round it. Nevertheless, it struck him once again how closely it resembled a traffic playmat.

'They meet here what they'll meet there,' said Dave as they surveyed the scene. Nudge could almost feel the pride and satisfaction bubbling out of his companion. He felt obliged to praise him.

'Impressive,' he murmured.

'Designed to be. Hit them with efficiency as they come in the door.'

Then he picked up the theme he had dropped outside the door.

'What time and attention they need depends on co-ordination of....'

As he pronounced this he strode to one the forklift trucks, laid one hand on its back just below the gas cylinder and pulled back a cover. A large painted eye stared out at them. Dave pronounced,

'Eye'

He moved to the second truck and repeated the move. This time a large hand appeared.

'Hand!'

Dave pulled back the cover on the third truck and revealed what to Nudge looked like a crinkly lettuce.

'Mind!' announced Dave.

He then stepped back beside Nudge and regarded the three signs.

'Co-ordination of eye' (he tapped his eye), 'hand' (he tapped his hand), and touching his head concluded the demonstration with 'mind'.

Nudge would not have been surprised if Dave had rounded off the message with a short prayer and 'Amen!'

'Yes, I see...' started Nudge, but Dave had not finished.

'Now and again,' he continued, 'you discover what I call an 'Industrial Athlete'; someone whose co-ordination is so precise that it puts them in a league of their own. I used to come across them when I headed up training at British Leyland. I remember one. He was, (how shall I put it? I need to be careful nowadays) from our overseas territories. I spotted him when he walked in the door. We trained him on wheel assemblies. After a few weeks he could outstrip any other worker.'

'He'd do well,' put in Nudge.

'Not really,' replied Dave, 'they sacked him after six months.'

'Sacked him?'

'Yes, he was too good. Assemblers were on incentive pay and he earned twice as much as his mates. They didn't like that. Well, if he carried on like that, management might cut the times, so they sabotaged him. I often wonder what happened to him.'

Nudge mumbled his sympathy for the industrial athlete, but Dave had moved on again.

'This lad now, when does he start work, or is he at the yard already – moving up from the gutting eh?'

'He's not at the yard,' put in Nudge quickly before he could be cut off again.

'Not at the yard! Where is he then? Where's he coming from?'

'He's not coming from anywhere. He doesn't have a job. I just thought. . ..'

'Doesn't have a job? You want me to train him on spec?'

'Yes, so he can apply for jobs.'

Dave studied Nudge for a few moments. Then nodded his head.

'Look, we don't normally accept speculative trainees. We could get swamped. But for you, well. Who would pay?'

'I will.'

'You, personally, yourself?'

'Yes, what will it cost?'

'To you, two hundred and fifty pounds.'

'Agreed.'

'Relative, is he?'

'No, the son of a friend.'

'He's not been in trouble, has he, a hoodlum etcetera.'

'No. he's a good lad fallen on hard times.'

'Hard times, eh? Well, hard times is what I do. Put it in front of me, and I'll eat it.'

Jen was delighted when Nudge gave her the news. A few days later, Callum left the Borders Mental Health Unit and started his week-long training.

CHAPTER TWENTY-SIX

'I've been suspended,' blurted out Christine as soon as she entered the door. She had barged into her parent's house just after nine in the evening of the Friday in the second week of March.

'Suspended?' exclaimed Janet. 'From the Co-op? When?'

'Just the now, the night. I've been sent home.'

She plonked herself on a chair at the kitchen table.

'Sent home? Who sent you home?'

'The manager.'

'Jason?'

'No, Brendan?'

'Who's Brendan?'

'The under manager.'

'He sent you home?'

'Yes.'

'Can he do that when he's not the manager?

'He did.'

'Where's Jason? Does he know about it?'

'Mother would you stop all these questions. I've told you I've been suspended! Pending dismissal!'

'Pending dismissal? Just hold on. I'll get your father. He's at Latchly. He should have been home by now.'

Janet rang Latchlaw and commanded her husband to return home at once. Although she gave him no reason for his summary recall, he knew well enough from her tone that it must be urgent. He was on his way, he said. Janet put the kettle on. She always put the kettle on in times of crisis. Then she went to Christine and put her arm round her shoulder.

'Now then,' she said softly, 'tell me what happened.'

Christine had scarcely begun when Duncan arrived. As he entered, she got up and wrapped her arms round him. He embraced her then gently settled her back in her chair. He sat down opposite his daughter and listened to her story as Janet made the tea and brought a cup each to the table.

Christine had started work at one to complete her shift at ten. But just after seven, she said 'she'd been put on 'reductions''.

If you are canny with your money you will have benefitted from the results of this task. You will, for instance, see, at the end of the fruit and veg units, a couple of trays piled high with fruit and vegetables that have been reduced in price. Each packet bears an orange label stating 'Clearance' and underneath the old price, say £2.20, and the new 'reduced' price, say £1.61. Christine had been assigned this task, a job she had done often before, a job she quite liked; better than humping heavy boxes or kneeling down 'facing up' the products on the bottom shelf. Not only did she like 'reductions', she was good at it having been praised for her quick eye and ready hand by Jason. the store manager.

One feature of the job, however, irritated her. Or not so much the job as the 'vultures' as some of the staff called them. There were a regular set of women, and occasionally a man, who would hover round the clearance tray looking for bargains. No harm in that you'd think and the assistants took it, for most part, as acceptable and indeed responsible; it allowed poorer citizens to pick up good food at a price they could afford. But one of the hoverers, Christine and her colleagues suspected, could well afford to pay full price: Mrs

Humbie. She lived with her partner (he was just as bad!) in their comfortable bungalow on the Millerfield estate, drove a two-year-old Audi and spent February and March every year in their own apartment on the Costa Bianca, then, according to Bella, who once booked it, let it out at top rates to holidaymakers in the summer. She had even been heard bragging that her new Axminster had cost eighty pounds a square metre.

Those who study these matters will tell you that very often rich people are rich because they are mean, not only searching out opportunities to earn as much as they can but also committing themselves to spending not a penny more than they need to. Christine's colleagues, however, are paid just above the minimum rate, are employed on short hours contracts, and struggle every week to pay their bills. Oh, and are not allowed to help themselves from the 'reductions' until the end of their shift – after the vultures have scraped up the best pickings. Christine's companions suffered in silence but, as we know, Christine is not the suffer-in-silence type. Nevertheless, she had held her tongue until this night. As we will discover there were other aggravations plaguing Christine that evening, but Mrs Humbie's bullying interference pushed her over the limit.

Seven o'clock, in a warm store, Christine had been on shift for six hours with only a short break at two. Mrs Humbie knew, as all the vultures knew that reductions were made three times a day. On the 'best before' or 'use by' date, prices were dropped at twelve o'clock, three, and, finally and cheapest, at seven.

At seven when Christine arrived at fruit and veg, she found Mrs Humbie already standing there; in her hand were two trays of plums already sporting orange labels from the three o'clock reduction. Christine ignored her and started working her way through the vegetable items in the trays. Mrs Humbie suffered it for a while then thrust the trays under her nose and demanded,

'How much will these be now?'

'You'll need to wait,' replied Christine with all the restraint she could muster.

Mrs Humble wasn't prepared to wait.

'You could do them now.'

'But I'm not doing them now. I'm doing the veg. You'll have to wait.'

'If you don't do them now,' announced Mrs Humbie, 'I'll leave the shop.'

'Feel free,' snapped Christine and went back to her work.

Mrs Humbie disappeared.

'Good riddance,' mumbled Christine to herself, and carried on with her work. Even as she did so, however, she knew that she had stepped over the mark and was not surprised when the next figure to arrive alongside her was Brendan the under-manager.

'What did he do then?' asked Janet.

'He took me to the office and asked me if I had insulted Mrs Humbie. She had come to him and complained about the girl on the fruit and veg. Brendan asked if that was me. I said it was. Then he asked what I had said. I said I had asked her to wait. Then he asked me if I had told her to leave the shop.'

'I told him that I hadn't said that.'

'Neither you did!' snorted Janet.

'Then he asked if I'd said 'feel free' when she said she was leaving the shop.'

'And you admitted it?' asked Duncan.

'Yes.'

Both Duncan and Janet recognised instantly that Christine had gone too far. But before they could frame a reply, Christine broke down in tears.

'I know I shouldn't have said it but she's a bloody pain in the arse.' she sobbed, 'and I'm tired.'

Normally Janet would have rebuked Christine for the language, but her daughter's distress silenced her. She leant across the table and tapped her hands.

Duncan waited a few moments until Christine had

stopped sobbing, then asked gently,

'What happens now?'

Breathing deeply, Christine spat out the answer.

'I'm suspended for a week. Pending dismissal! For gross misconduct!'

'Gross misconduct! What does that mean?' cried Janet.

Christine couldn't bear to answer the question; Duncan did it for her.

'It means, I think, that if nothing changes, in a week's time she loses her job - instantly.'

'He can't get away with that. I'll see to that.' exclaimed Janet. 'They'll not dare do that.'

Duncan ignored her outburst.

'What else did the manager say?' he said calmly.

'Nothing.'

'Did he not say what you'd done wrong?'

'I know what I did wrong. I shouldn't have spoken to Mrs Humbie like that.'

'Neither you should,' put in Janet, 'but you were provoked. She's an awful woman."

Both Christine and Duncan ignored her. Duncan picked up his question.

'But did the manager not put a name to the offence?'

'I can't remember. It's all a blur.'

'He said that Mrs Humbie had complained. Did he say anything else?

'No. – Yes, he said that she had demanded an apology.'

Duncan, absorbed in some thought of his own, fell silent. But not Janet.

'What're you asking all these questions for, Duncan? Can you not see she's upset?'

'Just wait,' said Duncan impatiently. 'I know she's upset.'

He turned to Christine again.

'Now, listen Christine,' he said gently, 'this is important. Did he say she wanted an apology from the Co-op, or from you.?'

Janet again.

'Apologise! She will not!'

Christine silenced her mother.

'Mother, keep quiet.'

She turned to her father.

'I don't know. Brendan said he had apologised but she still wasn't happy.'

'And that's all.'

'That's all.'

'Okay,' said Duncan, 'I know what I have to do.'

He made to speak on but Janet interrupted.

'What is that?'

'I'm gong to see the manager, see Jason; see if something can be done.'

'Good – and you can tell him that Christine is not going to apologise.'

'In which case, she'll be out of a job in disgrace next week. I'm going to see Jason.'

Then he added,

'In the meantime, we need to ask our daughter why she's so tired - and I think we know why.'

He turned to Christine.

'It's Alice isn't it? Has she been walking the floor during the night again?'

Christine sighed. A defeated sigh, Janet thought.

'Yes, last night she just wouldn't settle. She kept getting up and going to the door. In end I got up and slept in the chair in the living room so I could keep an eye on her.'

'I thought so. We thought that something like that must be happening. Your mother noticed you were getting tired. Hector has been hinting at it as well.'

'I told him not to say anything.'

'He didn't, but I guessed as much from what he said. We need to sort that, don't we, Janet.'

'We do,' replied Janet with a tight smile. She reached out to her daughter's hand across the table. Christine, for all her distress, squeezed her mother's hand and smiled in return.

CHAPTER TWENTY-SEVEN

Once Duncan had decided to see the manager, Janet determined he should go immediately. Now! This evening! Duncan demurred. He pointed out that Jason was not on duty; Brendan was in charge. He would go tomorrow when Christine confirmed Jason would be in.

Janet then listed what he must say. He must remind him that Christine is his best worker – he had often said so, that she often, at short notice, would turn in for a shift when someone called off, that she worked nightshift for him, and what about the time she worked all night on her own, which is against the law, to clear a delivery and get it ready for the shelves the next day. She then added character studies of some of the vultures, especially Mrs Humbie, humbug and hypocrite that she was.

Duncan did what he always did when Janet launched into one of her campaigns; he sat and listened. She needed to vent her spleen on someone, and what are husbands for, if not for that? Then he compiled an agenda of his own – and it contained only one item.

That over, he took Christine home with a promise that he would talk to the manager and see what could be done. He would like to have gone further and given her the assurance that it could be sorted out without her losing her job, but he was not at all sure he could accomplish that.

When he came back, he and Janet spent the rest of the evening deciding what they must do to lift from Christine the burden of looking after Alice. Alice was not incapacitated; indeed, she was fit and well in body – and, most of the time, in mind too. She still cleaned the house and washed, ironed, repaired and mended. She managed, with only the occasional blip, to put a wholesome meal on the table for Alistair three times a day. She still patiently wrote out her menus for the week on a Thursday evening and, on Friday, either with Janet or Christine. walked round the Co-op selecting the groceries she wanted to buy. Certainly, in this last expedition she needed guidance, but on the whole, she bought only that which was useful and paid for it from her own purse. In her leisure she could watch the telly with interest, and occasionally pick up an old familiar novel and appear to enjoy it.

How long such a happy (or should we say, not unhappy), way of life could continue no-one knew, but Janet and Duncan had hoped that it would persist until they were able to move into the Latchlaw farmhouse alongside the old folk. As we know, they reckoned that the farmhouse would not be ready for them until September - six months away. Much needed to be done. The house had had little attention for the past fifty years. Duncan had kept it wind and watertight, concentrating, of course, on the rooms that his mother and father inhabited. Other rooms had been left to the scant mercy of the withering years. The bedroom that Christine and Hector now slept in still sulked in the dingy wallpaper and dull carpet placed by long-forgotten tenants. Christine had refreshed the paintwork and put up new curtains, but it lay a long way from the bright and cosy love nest normally furnished by newly-weds. Perhaps she would have done more, but did not want to reinforce her mother's suspicion that the young couple might be settling in to a more permanent lodging.

Janet had always had misgivings about Christine's plan to move into Latchlaw, even if, as her daughter had promised, it would only be until her parents could make their move. Janet, however, knew her daughter well enough to know what she desired; and that she would eventually wheedle a corner at Latchlaw for herself and Hector.

Whatever doubts, however, Janet may have had about her daughter's intentions, she had none about her commitment. Christine would do her very best to give her granny a safe and comfortable life in the familiar surroundings of the old farmhouse she had grown to love. Now Christine had reached, or perhaps, breached, her limit. She could not stay up half the night superintending Alice, then work a full shift the next day. That is why she had insulted Mrs Humbie; that is why she is on the brink of losing her job.

As Janet and Duncan talked over Alice's need and Christine's helplessness to meet it in full, they lifted then discarded all the old remedies. Could they persuade Alistair to face up to his responsibilities? Not a chance! Was now time to consider settling Alice into Care Home? Certainly not! Hector? Of course not! Could they pack up at Priory Road now and move in? No! Janet had heard from Peter Munro about the woman who came in two nights a week to look after Oliver, his paralysed friend at Long Eaton. Could they find someone in Hecklescar to do the same for Alice? No, it would throw the old woman completely to find a stranger in the house. Besides, such an arrangement could not be kept within the family. They had no appetite for exposing Duncan's mother to tittle-tattlers of the town.

That proposition, however, sowed the seeds of a solution: Janet or Duncan would spend the night at Latchlaw whenever Christine had an early shift the following day. They both readily agreed to such a solution and eventually presented it to Christine as something they could 'easily do'. But there is no ease about it; going into the same bed at the end of their day had become for them, as for many couples, one of the unlabelled essentials of their life together. Whatever vagaries and setbacks the day had brought, here was a fixed point; something on which, someone on whom, they could depend. To be alone, even for a night, would be a sacrifice. For Christine, however, they would do it – and for Alice.

Together that evening, at Janet's insistence, they walked the kilometre to Latchlaw to inform Christine of their decision. Janet did not want her daughter to suffer any longer than necessary. When they got there, however, they discovered the place in darkness. All of them: Christine, Hector, Alice and Alistair, had gone to bed.

Janet proposed waking Christine but Duncan counselled caution. He reminded Janet that Alice, for all her confusion, seemed alert to anything that jarred and would refuse to go to bed until, she would say, 'it was sorted'. And 'sorting it' to Alice's satisfaction could well take hours. He imagined that Christine, going home, upset as she was, would have had great difficulty in shielding her grandmother from her distress. But she had done it and got her into bed and the lights out. They ought not to disturb them, he argued, and Janet, for all her desire to bring relief to her daughter, agreed to leave it for the night.

The task, therefore, of persuading Christine to accept their help would fall to Duncan. He would tell her what they had decided when he turned up at the workshop in the steading the following morning. Perhaps that is just as well, for Duncan would offer it as a proposal for Christine's agreement; in Janet's mouth, we may guess, it could well sound more like a prescription to be swallowed.

On the walk home Janet again listed all the evidence Duncan should lay before Jason the manager; and again, Duncan listened and replied that he knew what he would say. But no matter how much Janet interrogated him, no matter how often she shot down his proposals, no matter how persistently she lamented his lack of zeal for their daughter's worth, Duncan kept hidden the one proposal he would make. It was such a long shot that he scarcely had any confidence in it himself. He did not want it blasted by Janet's opinion. For he knew precisely that she would try to shoot it down.

CHAPTER TWENTY-EIGHT

Duncan met a fragile daughter when he crossed the threshold of Latchlaw the following morning. She had slept little. Yes, she had heard them come in last night, but did not get up in case she wakened Alice. She had had some difficulty persuading the old woman to go to her bed.

'She seemed to know that something was wrong,' she said.

Duncan then patiently explained their plan and gently, but firmly, rebuffed her protestations. She would give them a copy of her shift rota when she received them and one of the them would come and stay the night before her long day shifts.

They then talked about his meeting with Jason. Christine, tired and distressed, could see no hope for her.

'It's company policy,' she said. 'Jason can't change it – even if he wanted to.'

We must appreciate that this short phrase: 'it's company policy' had clattered and banged through her head the whole night long; had clattered and banged and kept her from sleep, had clattered and banged and had driven every faint hope from her. When they retreated, other iron-clad phrases took up the cry: 'gross misconduct'; 'suspended'; 'instant dismissal.' They had driven her to her knees, to tears, and robbed her, not only of her sleep; but of her self-worth.

(Is this what you intended, you who sat at your tidy desk in your neat office in Manchester? When you drafted these phrases did you imagine the distress they would cause to 'a committed colleague'? Or did you simply cut and paste from the latest manual on Human Resource Management? Did you, Executive Human Resource Director, as you skimmed through it, give one moment's thought to the terror and tears that would flow from them. Or had your mind drifted from these hackneyed phrases to a relaxing game of golf tomorrow? Did you, Chief Executive, high chief above all, consider what horrible wounds this 'procedure' would inflict? Did you, Chairman, passing the policy through the board on the nod, calculate what profit and loss these phrases might generate? What profit to the company of a loyal worker humiliated and sickened? What loss to her and her family of job, livelihood, and reputation? Did it not strike any of you that such matters need the sensitive touch of a human hand not the fixed indifference of a sledgehammer policy? That you need to see the face of the employee and the attitude of the customer before you can make a judgement? Why not trust your manager Jason? He values Christine, understands her commitment to Alice, and is only too familiar with the ability of Mrs Humbie to irritate his staff.)

'I will do what I can,' said Duncan, trying to sound confident, but did not feel it. Nor did he tell his daughter what he would propose. He had himself little expectation of its success. Even if Jason agreed to it, he feared that Christine would not – and he had already concluded that Janet would certainly be against it. That is why he had not told her what he intended to say.

Duncan, therefore, made his way to the Co-op wrapped in a lonely cloak of foreboding. So absorbed was he that he almost by-passed Harry - and Harry is difficult to by-pass. Harry worked as a school crossing attendant for the council, but spent the bulk of his life, walking pleasantly through the streets of Hecklescar greeting friends and strangers alike, giving a ready ear to their stories and generally encouraging them to take the best out of life. As far as I know the tourist board does not pay him for the welcome he holds out to visitors, but his efforts are far more effective than the sanitised labels with which they placard the town.

'Off to see the undertaker?' he chaffed, as Duncan came up.

'Something like that,' replied Duncan, and fell silent.

'The Co-op manager, I expect,' said Harry. 'About your Christine. That's an absolute disgrace. She's the best lass they've got in there. She's a menace that Mrs Humble. I'd Humble her if she picked on my lassie.'

'Thanks, Harry.' said Duncan, not at all grateful for his sympathy. The news of Christine's disgrace had leaked to the street, and now delighted the mouth of the gossips. The sickening fear that he felt for his daughter plunged downward another fathom.

There are those who savour a contest, the more demanding, the harder they run to meet it. Duncan is not such a one. By nature, he chose peaceable paths and would rather turn away from trouble than face it. He knew, however, that if he did not take on this particular challenge, and find a way of winning it, his daughter would be out of a job and disgraced.

He understood too, that it fell to him to take it on. Janet, of course, had volunteered to tackle the manager, and there were times in the past when he had not stood in her way, or, perhaps we should say, *dare not* stand in her way. For Janet, with a following wind and all guns blazing, had, in the past, put many an adversary to flight. Ask Duncan and he will tell you of the time his van had been shunted into a siding at Fairburn's garage in Gainslaw; 'waiting for a part', they said. Duncan, not wanting to push them, had explained to his wife, that they should be given time; that many a tradesman had had to wait for suppliers to deliver what he had ordered – and that he himself, occasionally had had to do the same. For a few days, he will tell you, Janet swallowed such assurances, rather, he will add (if Janet is not listening) like a man swallowing his dinner when his false teeth are out for repair. After a week his slack ran out and Janet tightened her grip on the case. Next time Duncan got a lift to check on the van, Janet was with him. The garage foreman launched into his excuses, but got no further than his first 'but', when Janet opened up.

'We came away with a replacement van for a week – at no charge.' Duncan will tell you with more than a hint of pride. Then he will swear that when he took back the replacement to pick up his own van, the foreman shuddered and immediately looked behind him to see if Janet had come back.

Duncan understood, however, that such talent is useful only when you have a decent hand to play with. That was not the case here; the cards were stacked against them. He did not need to consult the Co-op Colleagues Handbook to know that being rude to customers constituted a dismissible offence. And he had heard with his own ears his daughter confess that she, too, now accepted that such behaviour was unacceptable. His only hope lay in clemency – and his single doubtful proposal.

His appointment with Jason, the manager, had been set for ten. By half past he was back in Priory Road reporting to Janet and Christine what had happened.

'Is he giving her her job back?' demanded Janet.

'No, he can't do that.'

'There, I told you,' cried Christine. 'I told you he wouldn't be able to do it. That's me finished.'

'Just a minute,' put in Duncan. 'That's what he said. His hands are tied. The woman, Mrs what th' call her,'

'Humbie.'

'Mrs Humbie, put in a formal complaint. Brendan tried to get her to back off by saying that he would have a word with Christine and tell her she was out of line, but Mrs Humbie insisted that she must be 'held to account'. Those were her words., She said she had been humiliated in the sight of her friends. She even wrote down her complaint and signed it.

Jason said that that means that under company policy, the manager has to suspend the employee pending dismissal.'

'So that's her finished, is it?' snapped Janet. 'I told you you should let me go. You're far too soft. I'd have told him what he could do with his job and his shop if that's the way he treats our Christine. They don't deserve her.'

'Mother,' said Christine, 'you don't understand. If you're instantly dismissed, you're barred from unemployment benefit for weeks. And who is going to give a job to someone who was sacked from their last job for gross misconduct?'

'Anybody that knows you, Christine, would give you a job tomorrow.'

'But nobody I know has any jobs.'

'There's lots of jobs – up on the industrial estate. There's the potato factory – and the fish yard.

'The tattie factory is shut for the winter - and there's no jobs at the fish yard. They wouldn't take me on anyway. You need references.'

'Your father could give you a job; you could do what I do now with the invoices and quotes and ordering supplies.'

'Mother, you do it because Dad can't afford to take somebody on. No, that's me finished.'

Her voice broke and she started to sob. Janet put a hand round her shoulder to comfort her.

Duncan now decided that the time had come to throw out the flimsy life-line he had negotiated with Jason.

'Jason said that if you apologised to Mrs Humbie and she withdrew the complaint, the manager would issue you a warning and let you keep your job.'

Janet blew up.

'What! You must be joking! Apologise! What a nerve he has! I'll give him a apologise!'

This silenced Duncan. But not Christine.

'Is that what he said?'

'Yes, he said if you could get her to accept an apology they could hush it up.'

'And I wouldn't lose my job?'

'No, you'd get a warning, but they'd keep you on.'

'She will do no such thing. She'll be humiliated. Think what they'll make of it down the town.'

'Mother,' urged Christine, 'would you keep quiet? I'm trying to think.'

'What is there to think about it? You're not going crawling to that woman.'

'Please, mother.'

She turned to Duncan.

'What do you think, dad?'

'I think it's worth a try but....'

'Is that all it is - a try!' (Janet again.)

Duncan turned to his wife.

'Janet,' he said quietly, 'have you any better ideas?'

'No way should she apologise to that woman. She'd love it! She'd crow all over us!'

Duncan continued on his way of peace. (He had over the twenty-five years' experience to draw on.)

'Love, I know you're upset and it sticks in the craw, but getting steamed up about it doesn't take us anywhere. If Christine does nothing, by this time next week, our daughter will be out of a job. Is that what you want? You'll be happy she hasn't kow-towed to the woman, but she'll be out of work.'

'I didn't say I'd be happy,' snapped Janet.

'But that's what it comes to, doesn't it? In order to please you you're asking Christine to throw away the only chance she has of keeping her job.'

'It's not much of a chance, is it? She'll turn her down flat and laugh behind her back. That's what'll happen.'

'It might, but I say she should try it. I say she should go to Mrs Humbie and see what she can do. If it doesn't, she's no worse off than if she just sat and got steamed up about it. It might work. The woman might be flattered.'

This interchange had given Christine time to think about what she should do. She turned to her mother.

'Mother,' she said firmly, 'I shouldn't have said that to the woman. I was wrong.'

Then she added,

'And I mind the time when that lassie in Morrisons got your change wrong because she was talking on her phone. You sent for the manager, didn't you? Well, you're no better than Mrs Humbie. You've no idea what happened to that lassie. She might have lost her job.'

At this Duncan smiled and looked at Janet. She avoided his glance. It had happened over five years ago but Duncan had never heard of it till now. Clearly Christine had been sworn to secrecy.

Janet made to protest her innocence, but could not lay her tongue on the right words before Christine continued.

'I know you wouldn't have wanted her sacked, would you?'

Janet avoided the question. Duncan didn't.

'No, she wouldn't,' he replied, placing his hand on Janet's on the table..

'Well, if you must,' said Janet flatly, conceding defeat. 'But I don't fancy your chances – and don't take any cheek from her.'

CHAPTER TWENTY-NINE

Sunday, I suppose, is the appropriate day for confessing your sins and pleading for forgiveness, though most people, including myself, don't care for doing either at any time. It is much easier to adjust your morality to suit your mood, than your mood to your morality. As the man once said, 'I may make mistakes, but being wrong isn't one of them'.

Christine, however, had looked her folly in the face and opted for Saturday. She had come to conclusion that if she didn't offload it; it would offload her. There is nothing profoundly philosophical or even ethical about her decision. She needs the job – and the income. We know that she had been encouraged to this decision by Duncan. Her father goes to church every Sunday, and repeats, as fervently as any there, the bit in the Lord's Prayer that asks for forgiveness. Because he attends the Church of Scotland, it is his 'debts' for which he seeks relief, not his trespasses. Considering that Duncan is a practical man who runs his own business this is quite a commitment, for any self-employed joiner, builder, or painter in decorator in Hecklescar will tell you that getting the money out of some folk is a pain - and all tradesmen, without exception, have had to forgo payment they have been unable to extract from their customer. But such forgiveness is passive;

it is not normally an act of Christian charity, or superior morality, but a gritted teeth acceptance of the inevitable.

Duncan and Janet, however, both recognised that Christine's debt could not be cancelled without repentance. Such repentance stuck in their throats. Unwarmed by any desire for reignited friendship, it formed a straightforward commercial transaction. To keep her job, she had to persuade Mrs Humbie to call off the manager.

On Saturday morning, then, Christine set off on her unpalatable task. Ten o'clock was the time the restoration committee (Janet, Duncan, Hector and herself) had decided would be best for the attack. (Yes, I know that it is supposed to be a retreat, not an advance, but neither Janet nor Christine could swallow such a concept so tactics had been agreed for an assault on the woman. The plan is to bowl the woman over in a wave of regret and humility). Janet therefore scuttled down to the flower shop just after nine to procure a large bouquet, with which to equip her daughter. Thus armed, Christine kissed her mother and her husband, and set out in Duncan's car for Mrs Humbie's house at Millerfield.

Duncan drew up outside the house, and squeezed his daughter's hand. Her determination and courage impressed him and sickened him in equal proportions. He would fain have presented the flowers himself, would have simpered and grovelled and pleaded for his daughter; had, on the journey there, offered to do so. Christine would have none of it. So, with a lump in his throat and a prayer in his mouth, he watched his daughter leave the car and, clutching the large bunch of flowers, walk up the path towards her fate. As with most of the well-bred bungalows on the Millerfield estate, Mrs Humbie's residence had a manicured garden that prevented direct access to the front door. The path led to the side of the house then, at the last opportunity, turned sharply to run along the front of the house and up three wide stairs to a small patio in front of the door. Duncan watched his daughter every step of the way. Then suddenly, at the corner of the path she stopped, laid down the bouquet, and bent down behind large clump of dahlias. For a moment Duncan thought she had fallen or chickened out; had decided she could swallow the indignity no longer. He laid his hand on the door handle to open it, then sat back when he saw his daughter straighten up, pick up the bouquet, make some adjustments to it them carry on to the door. Duncan watched and fretted as she rang the bell. After a few moments, the door opened and Mrs Humbie appeared framed in it. Would she turn Christine away? He saw Christine talking then handing her the flowers. Would she receive them? She took them and the next moment he saw Christine stepping over the threshold into the lion's den. He waited and mumbled to himself vague threats of what he would do if Mrs Humbie did not respect his daughter. After a long quarter of an hour, Christine emerged from the house and walked down the path. At least, thought Duncan, she doesn't still have the flowers. She opened the car door, threw herself into the seat and let out a big sigh.

'Okay?' said Duncan gently as he started the car.

'Okay - I think,' replied Christine and fell silent.

Duncan wanted to ask more but he guessed that Christine was biting back her tears, so drove quietly home.

To Duncan's surprise, Janet proved equally indulgent, and simply hugged Christine and presented them all with a mug of tea. Once she had her hands round the mug, Christine told them of her encounter. At first, she said, Mrs Humbie didn't say much. She acted cold and distant, but as she poured out her apology and expressed her sorrow at causing Mrs Humbie so much distress, and had explained that she had been up most of the night before caring for her granny, Mrs Humbie thawed, accepted the flowers, and the apology – and would tell the manager that she would withdraw her complaint.

'D'ye think she meant it?' asked Janet.

'I think so.'

'Think so? Did she not promise?'

'She did.'

'But you doubt it?'

'No, I think she'll talk to Jason. She asked for his name.'

'Good. Well, we'll just have to wait. But it sticks in the craw that you've had to crawl to that awful woman. She'll brag about it down the town. I know she will.'

Duncan interrupted what he suspected could turn into a long tirade by asking a question that had been on his mind since seeing Christine walk up Mrs Humbie's path.

'Christine, when you were going to the front door, you stopped and bent down behind the clump of dahlias. What were you doing?'

Christine smiled.

'She did what?' demanded Janet.

'She bent down behind the flowers.'

'What for?'

Christine sighed.

'I wasn't going to tell anyone. But I picked one or two flowers from the clump and put them in the bouquet.'

The statement stunned her hearers. Janet's face became a study in incredulity.

'Why on earth. . .?' she started.

Duncan answered.

'A little bit of 'yer own back', perhaps?' he said quietly.

'You could say that!' replied Christine smiling.

They all laughed. Then Janet got up and gave her daughter a big hug.

Later in the day, Jason rang to say that he wanted to see Christine. When she met him at three, he told her that Mrs Humbie had withdrawn her complaint, that he had cancelled Christine's notice of dismissal, would issue her with a written warning, and expected to see her for her shift at six on Monday morning.

CHAPTER THIRTY

Six on Monday morning! An early shift; an early shift that, according to their commitment, meant that either Duncan or Janet would spend the night at Latchlaw to listen for Alice and give Christine a decent night's sleep. A commitment they had made but the arrangements they had not and they must now scurry to do so.

Were Latchlaw to be advertised for sale, you would read in Cockburn Heath's window that *'this mature house has five bedrooms, three reception rooms, a spacious kitchen and one bathroom'*. Then, in anticipation of the reaction to only *one* bathroom for five bedrooms, would add without pause: *'great potential for sympathetic development'*.

It is all true. (Which compliment would send most estate agents scampering back to their desks, wondering what they had overlooked!) Five bedrooms! We know that two of them are occupied; one by Alice and Alistair, the other by Hector and Christine. We inspected Hector and Christine's room when they moved in there a couple of months ago and know that is it is a makeshift. Christine has done her best to make it comfortable, but you must remember that she daren't push it too far in case her mother gets the impression that they're thinking of staying there permanently. Of the other bedrooms, two of them were of reasonable proportions, but largely unfurnished. Alice, in her more active days, had, in one of them, accommodated a double bed, a chest of drawers and a square of old carpet she had been offered by a friend who was throwing them out. The other large room has a square of carpet only and, to be strictly accurate, is no longer a bedroom, but a storeroom for anything that anyone had wanted to store over the years, not only of their residence but for generations before. It is quite probable that it has altogether forgotten that it is a bedroom, and will not wake up to the description until an enthusiastic estate agent rouses it, or somebody sticks a bed in it.

Then there is the 'little end', tucked in at the head of the stair, a child's bedroom, that has never accommodated a child in living memory, yet has a child's bed, a child's wardrobe-cum-dressing table-cum chest of drawers and a child's rug covering what had once been bright pink linoleum. In this room, Janet has determined, they will sleep when on Alice watch, not least because, situated as it is at the head of the stair, they could listen in comfort for Alice's wanderings.

The bed in the little end is short and narrow and Duncan had, at first, thought it might be better to buy a portable bed and set it up in the sitting room. Once he had inspected it, however, he changed his mind and accepted Janet's proposal.

You must not think that this is cowardice. It is true that, like many happily married men, he found it more comfortable to go along with what the little woman wanted, but he had been known to back his own judgement and win the day. In this case, however, he was persuaded to change his mind, not by his wife, but by the sitting room.

Like the rest of Latchlaw, the sitting room had last been decorated by tenants fifty-odd years ago. Duncan had refreshed the paint on the doors and windows and repaired the odd corner of the wallpaper, but by and large, the room reflected the dated tastes of the long-gone sixties. Alice had imported into it her own furniture; time-honoured bits and pieces, hard won from the scant surplus of a farm labourer's wage. Precious as it had been to her, it now had little hold on her devotion. Being cheap and utility then, it lacked any elegance now. It continued to occupy the space it did simply because Alice had never had the wherewithal to replace it. Now age and debility had robbed her of the will to try.

In contrast to the bright and busy kitchen, the room brooded in dingy antiquity. The old couple had never made the decision to abandon the room, but had chosen to spend their days in the large farmhouse kitchen. They ate there, sat there, relaxed there and, since Duncan installed a small set, watched the telly there. Only 'when they had company' did they migrate to the 'best room', or rather Alice did. Alistair usually melted away as soon as visitors stepped through the door. Nowadays they rarely had company. To be blunt, once anyone had been entertained in the best room, they preferred, on the next visit, to be welcomed by Alice in the kitchen.

Duncan too, in his heart, had abandoned the sitting room. For him, home had been, and in his soul still is, the farm cottage at Fairnieside where he lived as a boy. But surely, the furniture in the sitting room at Latchlaw held some hold on him? Of course, like many a child, he had, in his mind, the door of a room that every now and again burst open to pour out its stored joy into his present life bringing the convincing reassurance that as he was loved then, he is loved still. Thus Duncan recalled the furniture of his childhood: the lumpy chair by the fire, the gate-legged table under which he retreated to look at the pictures in his book, the drawer where the pencils were kept, the biscuit barrel on the sideboard with the windmill on it, the stain on the table where Aunty Margaret spilt her wine one Hogmanay, the frightening picture on the wall of hounds bringing down a stag, the singed carpet by the fire, the scratch on the cupboard door made by that bitch of a collie his father used to swear at. Many of these objects still populated the sitting room at Latchlaw but, for Duncan, their glory had departed and they now, in these alien surroundings, tasted only of age and decline. He found the room cold and uninviting. Indeed, if he were fully aware of his own feelings, he would admit that he avoided entering the room, afraid that these decaying objects would corrode memories he held precious.

He would sleep in the cramped bed in the little end.

CHAPTER THIRTY-ONE

By Friday of the third week in March, Callum, Jen's son, had completed his training, and had obtained his Certificate of Competence in Forklift Operation. That is easily said, and if I were more concerned about the plot and less about the characters in it, I would leave it at that. But Dave who ran the Forklift Truck Training Centre in Hecklescar would be mightily offended if we simply grabbed the certificate and made for the door. Certainly, he would not allow any of his trainees such latitude. He loved his acronyms, and drilled his pupils in DIET at every opportunity. DIET, you will want to know, stands for 'Discipline In Every Thing'. Whenever he detects slippage from the 'high standards which inform all we do', he requires the trainee to say 'I need to go on DIET' then recite to him what it means.

You can readily appreciate that Dave could not pass up the opportunity for display the handing over of an award would offer. Certificates must be presented in a ceremony – even though, as in Callum's case, he is the only trainee receiving one. Dave has set the time for ten o'clock. Jen cannot attend for she has fish to deliver, so the sole attenders at the presentation are Callum, Dave, Nudge and John Henry. John Henry is there as second reserve to Jakey who couldn't attend and Peter Munro who wouldn't attend. Both had been nominated by Nudge, but officially invited on pre-printed invitation cards signed by Dave. John Henry, who also received an official invite has turned up to please Nudge; he supports what he is doing for the boy. Nudge is attending though tired, having had a bare two hours sleep since returning to Hecklescar from the Continent in the early hours of the morning.

For the ceremony, Dave has laid out the Centre with especial care. He has carpeted the concrete floor in front of a table with a large green baize cloth. The table is tucked between two large potted parlour ferns, covered with a startlingly purple cloth and bears several cups, shields, and figurines the purpose of which is purely decorative; they will play no part in the proceedings. The table also holds the certificate to be presented, and a carafe and tumbler for the use of the presenter should he need it. To the side of the table, off the green baize, stands an immaculate fork lift truck.

When Nudge and John Henry arrive, they are ushered into the Centre by Martha, whom Dave has borrowed for ten pounds an hour from the garage next door. As he will say if you ask him, 'no expense spared; the lads have worked hard; they deserve their moment of glory.' Dave dressed in a bulging business suit and tie walks onto the baize to greet his guests, then hands them back to Martha who shows them to three chairs set just off the front of the baize. She hands them a folded printed programme then sits down beside them. Dave retreats behind the table. But where is Callum?

Dave stands up and announces:

'Welcome to the two hundred and twenty-sixth award ceremony of the Hecklescar Fork Lift Truck Centre. We are here to honour the achievement of Callum Charles Reid in passing with distinction the course of Competence in Forklift Truck Operation.'

He then announced in a loud voice:

'Come on in, Callum Reid.'

The audience immediately heard the sound of an engine being started, then turned and saw the truck slipping out of a bay at the side of the warehouse.

It came to halt expertly alongside its pristine partner. Callum switched off the motor and dismounted. John and Nudge would have clapped anyway, but Dave led the applause and continued with it until Callum proudly stood in front of the table.

We do not need to describe the handing over of the certificate to Callum. Nor pay much attention to the fulsome praise of the diligence and discipline of the Hecklescar Forklift Training Centre in steering this latest scholar to the sunlit summits of capability. No doubt you have been to such ceremonies in your time and can readily appreciate what took place. There is no harm in us taking a little amusement at the extravagances of such occasions, but let me add this (and I have John Henry's support in saying it), the presentation of this certificate did a lot for Callum. After all he had stumbled through in the last few months, this public acknowledgement of his achievement lit a little light at the end of a very dark tunnel and straightened his tottering steps in a way little else would have done. Well done, Dave. Well done, Nudge. Well done, Callum.

As they made to leave, Dave let Callum and John Henry go ahead, then turned to Nudge,

'A word in your shell-like,' he pronounced somewhat in the manner of a headmaster speaking of a child leaving his care. 'You need to keep your eye on that young man. Very brittle, I would say, bright enough – and conscientious, but brittle.'

I doubt if this analysis took Nudge by surprise. Certainly, John Henry did not need to learn it. He had already gleaned as much from his conversations with Jen and made a point of complimenting the young man on his achievement. Callum accepted his praise, but the way he did so troubled the old banker. The three men then walked along the road to the junction of Priory Road. Nudge and John Henry's route lay down the hill towards the town, Callum's up towards his home on the Poplace estate. They shook hands and made to part, but, something about the young man, made John Henry hesitate. Then he said to Nudge,

'You go on, I fancy a walk; I think I'll take a turn round the Red Hills. I'll head up the Poplace on my way.'

He then set off to catch up to Callum.

We are familiar enough with John Henry and his ways to know that little he does is without purpose. The sight of Callum walking away, on his own, clutching the brown envelope containing his certificate – and, perhaps, his future, struck John Henry forcibly and he thought the least he could do was to accompany the young man to his front door.

They talked of little on the way there. The Poplace estate had been built in the seventies to house the potential workers of the potential industrial firms that would be tempted to Hecklescar and other 'deprived' areas, by council campaigns and government grants. The firms never came, but the people did. Refugees from Tyneside and Glasgow largely, put out of work by the demise of shipbuilding and other labour-intensive industries. They concluded (and who can fault their logic) that if you are to be unemployed it is better to be so by the seaside rather than in a decaying multi-storey in a neglected and noisy conurbation. For them it may have been, and remained a pleasant place to live. Indeed, some had bought their houses from the council and lived happily in them with their children, and children's children. The place, however, depressed John Henry. The houses were, in the local jargon, 'jam-packed'. The architects had done their best to vary the buildings and the spaces around them, but they were under orders from the planners to pack as many houses as possible into the three fields lying to the north of the town.

Callum's house lay in the middle of a row of the most 'compact' houses, none of which had been bought by their tenants, simply because they were not worth buying. It formed a sort of clearing station, where people were housed by the council until they could find somewhere better on their own. The way into the house lay through a high wooden fence into a backyard the size of a large handkerchief. Callum opened the gate then paused.

'D'ye want to come in and meet Keira and the bairns,' he said hesitantly. John Henry took the statement as an obligation, something Callum had been taught as well-mannered, rather than as an invitation.

'No, I'll be getting....'

He got no further. The house door burst open and a young woman, an angry young woman, barged through it.'

'Where the hell....?' she started, then stopped when she saw John Henry.

'This is John Henry,' mumbled an embarrassed Callum. 'He was at the presentation..... I got my certificate.'

He held up the brown envelope. Keira ignored him and stared at the old banker.

'Hello', she said without feeling, then turned back to Callum. 'I need to go to the Co-op,' she rasped, 'and that ane is being a little bugger.'

A tearful little face peeped round the house door. Not tearful only, noted John Henry, but anxious, a look he now associated with neglect; not physical neglect, but that more insidious variety: a child not valued, not loved, not free to dream.

'I'll be off,' muttered John Henry and made his escape.

He did walk round the Red Hills, along the edge of the cliffs overlooking the sea, out over Coldingham Bay to St Abb's Head; a lovely walk, even on a dull March day like this one. John Henry appreciated little of it. He had become absorbed in his own troubling thoughts, chief of which were that Callum's problems – and Jen's, lay deeper than his lack of employment.

CHAPTER THIRTY-TWO

We must not assume that Nudge's care for Jen had not been noted in Hecklescar. And noted not only by those who make it their daily business to enquire into the lives of their neighbours.

Of course, Ina had kept the coffee ladies in McMaggie's up to date with the 'blossoming romance'. These are not my words but hers. I will not contradict her, but would not like to go so far as such a description; I'd prefer for the moment, 'growing friendship'. Unlike an author whose words hit the page and stay there, Ina nimbly retracts any miscalculation and denies she ever made it in the first place.

'He's moved her in,' she informed her hearers on the same March day that saw Callum pass his test, 'and is trying to wangle a job for her son at the yard.'

'She's in one of his holiday houses,' corrected Pat who could always be relied on to stick up for the innocent.

'Ah, but which one?' retorted Ina. 'Not one of his little single ends but the best one he has; the big one in School Road, the one with all the bedrooms. Now why should he move her into that one, if it wasn't that he intended moving in with her?'

'If he was moving in with her, he'd only need one bedroom,' quipped Pat.

The ladies laughed.

'Say what you like,' said Ina trying to recover the attention of her unruly congregation, 'He's intending moving in with her. That's why he's let her have the big house. It's for the laddie and his partner as well, isn't it? One big happy family.'

'Not so happy, if you knew what I know, and saw what I see,' put in Gracie C.

The women turned to stare at Gracie. Normally she never spoke except when spoken to, or to ask someone to pass the scones. What did Gracie know that they didn't? Ina, too, fell silent and looked at her normally timorous companion. The sudden attention directed at her rendered Gracie speechless for a moment or two, then she plucked up her courage and explained.

'They live over the back from me, and they no' get on.'

'What do you mean, they no' get on? Who doesn't get on?' demanded Ina, in the tone of a policeman who suspects the suspect isn't telling the whole truth.

'The son, Callum and his missus – well, partner. They're always rowing. Well, not him. He's feared for her. He doesn't say much. She keeps locking him out.'

It did not take long for Ina to stitch this new patch of information into her narrative.

'You see,' she said, 'that's what they're up to. When she throws him out. . .? What's her name?'

'Keira'.

'Then madam'll take him in. That's what the big house is for – and the extra bedrooms.'

'I heard Nudge let her have the bigger house because she needed somewhere to store her furniture,' said Pat.

'Well, he would say that, wouldn't he?' concluded Ina, before moving onto much safer ground.

'The new manager at Douglas's starts a week on Monday,' she announced. This time no one contradicted her. For isn't she Jakey's wife - and isn't Jakey the manager now?

Their silence covered the question they asked among themselves when Ina isn't there: why is Jakey being replaced? Now we know that he is not being replaced. We know that Peter Munro wanted to make him the manager, offered the job to him, but he turned it down. We also know that the new manager's name is Clouston Pritchard, and that he is to be called not 'manager' but 'Chief Executive'. Ina knows this too, but as a seasoned tittle-tattler, chooses. whilst ferreting out the detail of everyone else life, to titillate her hearers by allowing them only a glimpse or two of what is going on in her own. The ladies, therefore, reluctant to give Ina the pleasure of stringing them along, make up their own version of events. She seems bright enough so they conjecture that she and Jakey must have a plan. The best they can come up with is that Jakey is retiring early, and that, once the new man takes over, he and Ina will embark on a world cruise with his big pay-off, and visit her sister in Australia. This shows that they are learning from Ina how to construct, from a straw or two, a narrative which is much more intriguing than the mundane truth.

We must leave them - and Ina, to it, for the news of Nudge's accommodation of Jen has reached other ears. The Brothers at The Meeting have picked up the whiff of waywardness.

Nowadays the general opinion on the street, any street, is that everyone has the right to do whatever they like, provided it's within the law and doesn't do serious damage to anyone else. The Brethren have no truck with such a view. They expect those that are on the broad way to perdition, (that is, the human race as a whole) to behave as they wish, but those who are born again, who walk in the way of The Word, must toe the line. Which line they toe is by no means clear. It seems to vary from Meeting to Meeting, but attentive elders will, as a general rule, keep an eye out for those who are straying.

The Hecklescar Brethren Meeting, therefore, have commissioned elders Bobby Dobson, and Barnabas to enquire into the matter and if necessary, to restore brother Paul, whom we know better as Nudge. Whether they will do it with meekness is a moot point. Bobby Dobson is a canny man but brother Barnabas, who works in the Job Centre, has a reputation among the town's job-seekers for suspicion and insensitivity. Some admit that he has found them a job, but others report that they come away with the impression that he believes they are fiddling the system, and trying to get something for nothing. More than one will tell you that he has reminded them that 'in Thessalonians we find the Bible saying that *'he who does not work, neither shall he eat."*

If you are beginning to think that I am exaggerating the opinions of these people, let me assure you that I have come across much worse. I have met good people among the Brethren; men and women whose commitment to their faith has blessed the lives of those around them. There are others, I'm afraid, whose beliefs, would, if canned, strip paintwork and disinfect toilets. Their insistence that the Bible is the Word of God and MUST be obeyed trumps any kindly teaching of the man they claim to follow.

I have, however, no wish to venture further into such uncomfortable territory. We have gone far enough, I hope, to give you an appreciation of the risks Nudge is taking in his befriending of Jen. His whole life so far, all his forty-four years, has been lived within the narrow, but not disagreeable, confines of such beliefs. Now Jen has tempted him to the border of his experience, and he must explain himself to those who believe they are appointed by God to act as border guards. As tradition demands, the meeting will take place in his own home - in the evening of the last Saturday in March; the day before the Lord's Day.

Of course, he doesn't have to entertain the elders. He could refuse to admit them. But these people represent his community; he does not want to offend them. He could make an excuse, but it is not in his nature to do so; he is an honest man. Besides. he knows what he is facing; he has been a distant witness of other brothers and sisters who have been counselled about their 'walk'. He does not want to be excluded from the meetings of the Lord's People.

More important than any of these, and binding them all together, is the fear that he might be losing God's favour. That God had watched over him he was sure. He had given him a Christian home and loving parents, blessed him with good health and crowned his years with prosperity. All of which he had taken for granted. He had listened many a time to preachers who had amplified the fate of David who lost his son, Samson who lost his eyes, Judas who lost his life - all because they turned from the Lord's way and sought their own. He had also taken comfort in the general consensus of the meeting that it wouldn't happen to him. The faithful may be chastised but, so long as they remained faithful, they would be restored.

I hope those readers who claim no religion will not despise Nudge for such fears and misgivings. For I have found that those who claim not to believe in God, tend to believe that their way through life is conditioned by something much more nebulous: Fate, Karma, the movements of planets, departed relatives, the ascent of man, genetic make-up, luck or, heaven help them, the next general election.

After a few pleasantries, Bobby Dobson assures Nudge of their brotherly love in the Lord, then Barnabas takes over. He too, assures Nudge of his concern, but does not fail to mention that his is no casual concern – good health and all that, but concern for Nudge's eternal soul. He then presents his bona fides in the form of a quotation:

'We are here, brother Paul, in meekness and humility, at the command of the Lord in accord with the instructions set out by Paul in Galatians chapter six, verse one: *'Brethren, if a man be overtaken in a fault, ye which are spiritual, restore such a one in the spirit of meekness, considering thyself, lest thou also be tempted."*

Has Nudge been overtaken in a fault? They don't know but, from what Miriam has told her husband, he is running neck and neck with one. Miriam has an aptitude for sniffing out faults, and has reported that Nudge's fondness for Jen looks like one in the making. Jen is an unbeliever; no, worse than that, from all reports, she once walked the paths of righteousness but has now fallen from grace.

'We are sure you are aware, brother Paul,' Barnabas continues, 'of the command in two Corinthians six fourteen: *Be ye not unequally yoked with unbelievers.*

He stares at Nudge searching for signs that his assault has gone home. Nudge's vacant gaze, however, encourages Barnabas to open up with the second barrel: *'For'*, he quotes, *'what fellowship has righteousness with unrighteousness, or light with darkness?'*

At this, even Bobby Dobson flinches and makes to speak, but Barnabas surges on.

'News has reached us of your fellowship with Jennifer Reid. You are aware that her walk is not in the ways of righteousness, that, although she once loved the eternal things of God, has cast them away, abandoned the means of grace and embraced the passing pleasures and illusions of this world.'

Nudge listened to all this in a sort of haze. He had grown used to such lectures. Every Sunday for the past forty years he had attended to them, but so accustomed had the language become, that it had no leverage; the words no longer conveyed any meaning. The Brethren might despise the Roman Catholics for using Latin in their services, the Anglicans for mediaeval English, and the Freemasons for gobbledegook but their own formulaic language performs precisely the same function. The words are mere symbols. They give the faithful a unique identity, and reassure them that they have a grip on something outsiders have not.

Only when Barnabas stopped speaking did Nudge realise that he must make some statement of his own. Untroubled by any accusation the elders may have made; (certainly, none had registered with him) he freely admitted that he was helping Jen – and her son. He then told them of Jen' distress, and of his encounter with her on the cliff top. He told them that he had moved her into one of his holiday properties and had provided storage for her furniture. He also informed them of his attempts to secure employment for Callum. He presented all this as he saw it - openly, factually and honestly, as an act of Christian charity. The woman needed help, he had the means to help her, so he would – and should, do so.

He felt sure that he had given an adequate explanation, a righteous explanation, for his behaviour. Bobby Dobson acknowledged his kindness and praised him for it. Nudge had bid them goodbye at his door reassured that his actions were upright and acceptable in the sight of the Lord. Afterwards, however, it occurred to him that Barnabas had not responded at all to his account of his dealings with Jen.

CHAPTER THIRTY-THREE

Until I took an interest in Nudge, I imagined that driving a truck, albeit a 44-tonner, would be straightforward. You climb into the cab, drive to where you are directed, discharge your load, then come back. Nothing complicated in that, you might think; nothing to delay a writer concerned with the ups and down of human experience? No action, appeal or angst? How easy it is to conclude that some people, lorry drivers, for instance, steer their way through their days with only a modicum of strain and stress.

There are, however, several concerns that trouble a long-distance driver. The most obvious scarcely concerns at all nowadays: the reliability of the vehicle. Rarely does an engine or transmission break down; rarely does a wheel puncture at speed. Then there is the great imponderable of road conditions; of hold-ups, diversions, cones and, largely in winter, weather. None of these will trouble Nudge this late March evening as he sets out for France with a full load of langoustines.

Other complications, however. do concern him, and another will arise, whose particulars are not shared by his companions of the road. First, he must find a place to eat, and it must be the right distance away. Lorry drivers are restricted to driving nine hours a day, and must break that with a rest of three-quarters of an hour after no more than four and half hours. This is not an act of benevolence by the owner of the truck, or a bit of wishful thinking by the Road Transport Authority. It is mandatory and, nowadays, difficult to circumvent. Back in the eighties, when the tachograph produced a paper record, it could be (shall we say) 'adjusted'. Now such flexibility is well-nigh impossible, due to digital tachometers that not only store the record electronically but also relay information from the cab to whoever wants to keep an eye on the driver. This includes the kindly owners of the vehicle, who as well as being concerned that their drivers do not become overtired at the wheel, are also interested in whether their truck is gainfully employed in ferrying paid-for cargo or sitting idly in a layby somewhere with the driver asleep or pursuing some interest of his own.

Of course, such snooping is not needed for such a conscientious driver as Nudge, but it concerns him that he must time his arrival at an eatery of his choice for the start of his mid-trip break. Unfortunately, Nudge has found that there is not much to choose from. He will tell you that most of what is available is dire and dear. Located on motorways, with little competition, service stations serve up what they like and charge what they choose. Similarly, such places charge over the odds for the four hundred gallons of fuel that are needed every two or three days to keep the artic moving. Nudge has, however, found a couple of places where he can feed himself, and others where he can feed his truck, provided, that is, that hold-ups and diversions allow him to arrive within his permitted hours.

What fluid goes in has to come out, and as we grow older it comes out more frequently. Nudge is not as old as some of his tribe, nevertheless he must find a convenient spot. There are toilets, of course, of a sort, in lorry parks, but Nudge generally does not choose to use them and will, if intake and constitution allow, make sure that he reaches somewhere more hygienic. If not, there are always laybys out in the country, where a lorry driver may relieve himself against a nearside wheel hidden from the passing traffic by the bulk of his wagon. Nudge when caught short, in spite of his religious principles, not only makes use of such an arrangement but conforms to the general superstition that if you pee on the drive wheel it prevents breakdown.

Then he must find somewhere to park up the truck and take the stipulated break. At the end of his long journey through the length of England, if he gets his timing correct, this is not problem. He arrives just as his four-and-a half hours are ending and takes advantage of the concession that allows him to dip into his rest hours in order to drive his lorry onto the ferry and off again at the other end. Thus, the time taken on the ferry is counted as part of rest period; saves him time and Anthony Douglas and Son a delayed delivery.

On other journeys down South, however, he must find somewhere to stay the night. There are lodges and rooms, but Nudge prefers the bunk in the cab behind the driver's seat, and a berth in one of the lorry parks that populate the main transport routes. For £25 or £30 he can park his truck and bed down for the night in a secure location. In this he is not always a popular bedfellow. In the early days he had often been roused by an adjacent driver in the park, who couldn't get to sleep for the noise of the fish lorry's refrigeration system. He has now, however, found one or two overnight stays where a thoughtful site owner has provided a separate space for such antisocial vehicles.

On the night we are with him, he leaves Hecklescar as daylight is fading with a load of langoustines bound for France. Two hours later, he fills the truck with fuel at a depot not far from Darlington. The roads are quieter at night and no coned overnight roadworks delay him so he makes good progress and, for his mid-journey break, reaches one of his regular halts, Tibshelf, a few miles from Mansfield in the

Midlands; not the best of watering places, but not the worst.

Here, on this particular night, Nudge suddenly realised that he had strayed into unfamiliar territory. He had had his cup of coffee and his sandwiches in the cafe and, with twenty of his forty-five minutes still to rest, having no fellow driver to talk to, had retreated to his cab for a short nap before continuing his journey. Following a well-trodden routine, he slid a CD into the player, set the alarm and pulled his woolly hat down over his eyes. The CD he had chosen was an old favourite: *The Best of Country and Western*. As he closed his eyes his mind drifted to his meeting with Barnabas and Bobby, heard again what they had to say, agreed with them again that righteousness must have no fellowship with unrighteousness, nor light with darkness. He had satisfied them, (had he not?) - and himself, that he had no intention of fellowship with Jen. Then Hank Williams set out on *Gipsy Woman*. Nudge tracked it note by note with increasing excitement until, in alarm, he heard: *'Ivory skin against the moonlight – and the taste of life's sweet wine.'*

Fellowship with Jen? No! But love? He saw her delicate hand, her ivory skin, stretched out to the brochure that evening he sat next to her on the settee in her front room; saw it vividly – and felt again her proximity. It stormed back into his imagination. He saw it, felt it and recognised that it came, not from outside, but welled up from within.

Throughout the rest of his long journey, he thought of little else. It delighted him and shocked him, confused and comforted him, lifted him and dumped him. By the time he arrived back in Hecklescar, he had still not resolved the conflict in his soul. Is this love? Or carnal desire? Am I helping Jen – and her son, out of kindness or because she is a lovely lady? Does it have to be one or the other? How do you know the difference? Is such attraction acceptable to the assembly – and to God, or something that must be supressed, defeated and rejected?

He had no experience to advise him. From his youth up, he had been taught to bring his body under subjection;

that the only expression of sexual desire, much less sexual activity must be within the compass of marriage, marriage to a born-again Christian woman; a woman of the assembly, who like himself accepted that the relationship *'must not to be enterprised, nor taken in hand, unadvisedly, lightly or wantonly, but reverently, discreetly, advisedly, soberly, and in the fear of God, duly considering the causes for which matrimony was ordained:* *'the mutual society, help and comfort, that the one ought to have for the other, and that children might be brought up in the knowledge of God and the praise of his Holy name.'*

Such a woman had never turned up so Nudge had accepted enforced celibacy; enforced, but not, until now, irksome. He had reconciled himself to his single status, had avoided any stimulus that would tempt him from it, and had been relatively content with his lot. After all, he frequently told himself, he could have ended up with someone like Ina or, worse, tied to someone like Miriam, Barnabas's other half. It was no sacrifice, he would mutter to himself, in his more wayward moments, to pass up on such mutual company.

Now such composure and self-control had disintegrated. Questions, long supressed, surfaced, and demanded attention; chief of which presented as simplest of all: how did such rigid advice accord with love, love of another person, love of a woman. Love, the ordinary, human, exhilarating love, he now admitted, he felt for Jen?

CHAPTER THIRTY-FOUR

As the clock in the Market Place struck seven on Monday morning in the last week in March, Clouston Pritchard drove into Hecklescar. He parked his car on the double yellow lines on Harbour Road and strode into the fish yard to take up his position as the Chief Executive of Anthony Douglas & Son.

The contrast between Clouston's arrival and that of Peter Munro could not have been more pronounced. When Peter came last December, he had quietly materialised in the office; no-one could remember him walking through the door. Clouston stormed in in a blare of self-confidence and bonhomie. He stepped into the yard and found Jakey supervising the loading of Nudge's lorry, while haranguing some distant supplier on his mobile phone. Clouston interrupted the call to ask Jakey where he might park his car, and Jakey commissioned Nudge to shift it from the double yellow lines to the safety of the public carpark at the Smiddy Brae, a hundred yards away.

Clouston then made his way to the suspended office, which is easily said but, give the man credit, no mean achievement. The office in the yard is a relic of the days when Anthony ran the firm. He stuck it in the only place in the yard left for it: suspended, literally, from the roof beams in the corner of the yard. It required considerable ingenuity and not a little courage to reach it.

A stranger can only find it with a guide. From the pier he enters the open yard that had, through the years, narrowed as the walls of the building on either side had been pushed out to accommodate additional rooms inside them. Reaching the back of the yard. he shoves open large rubber double doors, dodging, as he does so, any fork-lift truck that may be barging through from the other side. He then finds himself in a fish room among women and men who, when not greeting him with raucous comments, are standing at large stainless-steel benches, gutting and preparing fish. Keeping to the nearside wall, he comes across a short passage leading off it. Straight ahead he sees a door, opens it and finds himself in a poky windowless store room furnished with a desk and computer equipment and occupied by two disconsolate men in waterproof gear. Neither of these is the manager, so he apologies and retreats. They point out a stair tacked against the wall at the end of the passage. He climbs the stair and reaches a wooden landing on which is parked a desk and two large metal filing cabinets. This is Jakey's office when he needs one, which is not often. On the landing is a door; through the door is what he has come to find: the head office. It is a surprisingly large space occupying almost the whole width of the building. The room is lit only by artificial lighting. The one window lies in the inside wall and gives a view of the fish room below. Immediately inside the door sits Fiona at her desk with computer in front of her filing cabinets and cupboards. At the other end of the room is the seat of all power; the executive desk and chair of the boss. He has negotiated the labyrinth.

Had he come in Anthony's time he most likely would not have found Anthony in the chair. The boss could be working at a fish bench, on a fork-lift truck, serving fish in the shop, reversing a lorry at the pier-end or shouting to a skipper landing fish. That is, if he happened to be in Hecklescar, for often he was away, touring the fishing ports of West, Fife, the Moray Firth, negotiating and doing deals. Or down South, across the channel, further afield even, finding outlets for his fish.

Hercules the 'Son' of the firm's title, had grown up with the suspended office, and had put up with it, preferring to meet visitors off-site, or apologising that as he had to stay with the ship he had had to greet them on the bridge.

John Henry and Peter, however, had not apologised to Clouston when he first entered the office. They had found it adequate; it did what an office should do; it provided a place to sit and plan and think about the business. With Fiona at the other end of the room with information at her fingertips and her abilities at their service, both John and Peter had found nothing to complain about. Peter, particularly found being on top of the shop both convenient and commendable.

On his way to the office, Clouston, unaccompanied, entered the fish room. There he was greeted (as all visitors were, especially all attractive male visitors) with wolf whistles and ooohs from the girls who, whilst apparently concentrating on their work, nevertheless detected a delicacy. Clouston took it in good humour, smiled, waved casually and headed for the stair.

The girls did not need to be told who he was; he had been expected and talked about for weeks. Now he had arrived they were impressed. Of medium height and slim build, Clouston bore his forty-seven years well. He had not billowed out as many men do as they approach their fifties, and he had kept his hair which, apart from a scattering of snow around the temples, was dark, wavy and well-groomed. His face was open and his smile relaxed. He walked with the lithe stride of a man who kept himself fit and had set off fast on the road to somewhere. He stood (or rather, strode) in contrast to flabby and fidgety Hercules - and the two stiff old men who had been running the show for the past few months. He breezed into the fish room – and into the attention of everyone else in the company, like a breath of fresh air. In place of the doubts of John Henry and the diffidence of Peter Munro, his demeanour exuded confidence and commitment. The new boss had arrived. First impressions are important.

Fiona, too, was impressed to find Clouston comfortably settled into the boss's chair when she arrived at five to eight. Since he had arrived, Clouston had made himself at home in his new headquarters, clearing away the executive paraphernalia that Hercules had left behind and replacing it with some of his own. One of his first requests to his secretary when she turned up was that she pack Harold's personal belongings in a box and have them delivered to his erstwhile home in Alexandra Drive. I will leave it to you to speculate what kind of welcome they will receive when Octavia returns from her cruise and finds them in her hallway.

Peter Munro had agreed to welcome Clouston to the company at nine but, when he arrived at a quarter to, found his new Chief Executive with his feet already well under the boss's desk. Clouston apologised for his unexpected arrival and explained that he had left his home in North Berwick early to avoid the commuters crushing through its streets on their way to their desks in Edinburgh. Peter did not reject such a motivation, but suspected that another might be at play: that Clouston intended from the start, right from the very start, that he would keep the troops on their toes. After all, thought Peter, Edinburgh lies West, and Hecklescar East, of his home; any hold up would be minor and short. I will leave it to you to question whether Peter is being perceptive or Clouston crafty.

The two men spent most of the morning in conference. Peter had expected to use the meeting to explain to Clouston the history and development of Anthony Douglas & Son and explore its recent neglect. He had then intended to introduce the new man to what steps he, Peter, had taken to stabilise the company, and what would be required of the continuing business to give it a stable and prosperous future. This is what Peter had intended, and, typically of the man, he had prepared a list of topics to be covered. However, as Peter explained in jocular terms to John Henry later, Clouston had picked up the meeting and run away with it. The younger man had an agenda of his own, with background papers outlining his proposals – all laid out on the desk, alongside an open Filofax to receive the objectives, performance indicators and controls to carry forward his plans. (For those fortunate enough never to have had to grapple with a Filofax let me explain that it is a loose leaf portable 'diary' that allows a manager to plan, programme and monitor projects and other planned tasks. In the right hands it is a useful management tool. We must add a caveat, however, that it is also carried round by managers to advertise their grasp of whatever it is they should be grasping, whether they have grasped of it or not.)

Early in the meeting he advised Peter Munro that, this first week, he would spend four days of his monthly contract of ten 'on site', 'meeting the people' and 'getting a handle on the place.' He would take Thursday, he said, to 'mull over what he had learnt', then on Friday, he would address the whole workforce and outline to them 'where the company is headed'.

In the evening of that first Monday, Peter, as he had promised, visited John Henry to let him know how Clouston had settled in.

He handed John a sheaf of papers held together by a bright red spine.

'One for you, one for me,' he said smiling.

John Henry took it from him and read the title: 'Anthony Douglas & Son Riding the Tide: An Outline Strategy for Excellence and Growth.'

'Impressive,' commented John as he glimpsed through its twenty-one pages.

'Does he really have such a strategy?' he added.

'He seems to think so,' replied Peter.

'And so soon? Does he understand the business – and what it has just been through?'

'He reckoned he does,' said Peter solemnly, 'and, I think,

believes that what he does not know now, he will by the time he has mulled it over on Thursday. I did attempt to explain the difficulties the company faced, but found myself rebuked for being negative.'

'Did he really rebuke you?' asked John sounding vaguely shocked.

Peter laughed.

'Not in so many words. He pointedly said that one man's difficulty is another man's opportunity.'

'And you took it that you were one and he the other?'

'Precisely!'

John could not fathom his companion's response. Dry humour (and Peter had scarcely any other kind) was fine, but had he not found the younger man's assertiveness abrasive? How could Clouston possibly appreciate the complexities of the business after such a brief encounter? He, John, had spent months probing the dark corners of Anthony Douglas & Son, yet found himself constantly surprised by what stepped out of the shadows. On the surface, Peter seemed unconcerned but with Peter, John could never quite gauge what churned in the depths. But an attempt at understanding his friend must be made. Surely, Peter must trust Clouston, mustn't he?

'How then would you sum up the session?' he asked of Peter, and asked lightly, not wishing to sound either dismissive or acquiescent.

Peter studied the old banker for a moment then replied, 'It can be summed up in one word: 'forbearance'.'

'Forbearance?' queried John, smiling. 'You'll need to explain that, I'm afraid'

'Well, of all his plans, he asked not once for my 'agreement', only for my 'forbearance'.'

'And?' said John flatly.

'When I got to the office, I found him sitting in Hercules chair. He's already taken over. I am surplus to requirements.'

John detected no emotion in this statement.

'You'll go along with that?' he asked. 'After all, you own

the company.'

'Yes, I'll go along with it.'

Still John could not gauge what Peter really thought about his encounter with Clouston. He must try a direct question.

'Does that not concern you?'

'It does. Quite a lot.'

'So, what are you going to do?'

'I'm going to go away and leave him to it. I can understand where he is coming from. I don't know whether it's the case with bank managers, but in my experience, what the new man doesn't need is the old man hanging onto the reins. He must let go. That, for me, is no sacrifice. I never had them in my hands. I never wanted them. You know that.'

'I do,' said John Henry, 'but can you trust Clouston? You hardly know the man.'

Peter stared at John, spread his hands and grimaced, but said nothing.

'You said you're going away?'

'Yes, for a month or so. There are loose ends I need to tie up in the businesses down south.'

'You're taking a lot on trust,' protested John.

'It's called 'forbearance', replied Peter pleasantly. Then added,

'However, I am taking out a small insurance policy. I am appointing you a director of Anthony Douglas & Son Limited. That gives you the authority to keep an eye on the affairs of the company.'

'But,' began John in an attempt to protest.

Peter cut him off.

'If he is the man I think – and hope, he is, Clouston will extract from Jakey, Angela and Fiona their working knowledge of the business. And from anyone else inside or outside the company. That is as it should be. He will then draw his own conclusions and plan his own actions accordingly. What you must do is the counterpoint. You must keep close to the three of them, particularly Jakey. They will let you know what our man is up to. Don't go tapping them to tell you what they think. That will suggest we're suspicious.'

'But we are suspicious, aren't we?' chaffed John.

Peter smiled.

'Are we?' he said, then continued; somewhat anxiously, John thought.

'It's a tricky time for all of us –especially for Jakey and Angela – and Fiona. Somebody they hardly know is stepping into Hercules shoes. They'll be jittery. It won't be easy for Clouston either. He'll want to make changes and he'll need to 'gang warily'. It'll be a bit rocky for a while. We mustn't muddy the waters - so we'll need to let them get on with it. But I'd be grateful if you would keep your ear to the ground and an open door. You will know where to reach me, if need be.'

'I think I've got that.' laughed John, seeking to lighten the conversation, 'rocky, muddy water, open door and ear to the ground. It sounds painful but I'll do my best.'

Peter acknowledged the humour with a grin. Then John continued.

'I certainly keep in touch - but a director!' he stated. 'I can't agree to that.'

'I didn't ask for your agreement,' responded Peter pleasantly but firmly, 'only your forbearance.'

CHAPTER THIRTY-FIVE

The following day, shortly after eight, Clouston, true to his schedule, left his lofty office and, as agreed, met Angela in the fish-room. She guided him from bench to bench, from cluttered iced fish boxes at the start to neatly packaged polythene containers at the end. She introduced him to the 'girls', and found herself impressed by his rapport with the folk who worked with her.

How easy that is said – and how inaccurate it is. Some of the younger women thought him sexy, others thought him slimy. Some of the older women welcomed his attentiveness, others thought him nosey and officious. Most of the men thought him sleekit, but you must remember that there are not many men among 'the girls', and most of them are old, over sixty even, and therefore jealous of this handsome young buck. Hercules they could dismiss and Peter and John pity; this one constituted a rival for the girls' affections. Generally, however, with these caveats and qualifications, he proved a hit with the residents of the fish-room.

As for Angela, she found herself warming to the man. When she had first met him a few weeks ago, he had struck her as young, not because of his years (he is about her own age) but, as she said to Jakey after their meeting, 'wet round the gills'. Certainly, he talked a good management story, and knew about preparing and freezing, but seemed an infant when it came to understanding the challenges and pitfalls of persuading fish workers like her merry band to do what they knew how to do without fault, complaint or going on the sick again. He seemed to believe they would do it simply because it appeared on the schedule – whatever that might be.

Since that early encounter she had talked of these failings with Jakey, and to a lesser extent to Fiona, and found that they shared the same misgivings. They too, thought him ignorant of the tones and subtleties known only to those who lived in Hecklescar, and worked for Anthony Douglas and Son.

However, after her three hours with him that Tuesday morning, she saw a maturity and thoughtfulness she had not seen before. He struck her as appreciating the frightening precision needed to get the right fish into the right box at the right time. What stilled her suspicions were his readiness to appreciate the fortitude, fears and foibles of her peculiar flock of humans. His patience with bumptious old Bobby, his gentleness with Vulnerable Vera and his ribbing of Scatty Cathy demonstrated what she would have called 'interpersonal skills' if she had come across the term before.

'He'll be all right, I think,' she confided in Jakey at lunchtime.

'Did he not poke his nose into what you were doing?' asked Jakey, suspiciously.

'Only once,' smiled Angela. 'He asked about Cheena Dug?'

Jakey laughed.

'How did she come up?'

'We were in the fishroom and some of the girls were chatting away as they worked – about him, I would think. He asked me if I allowed the girls to talk. I said yes, as long as they kept on working, but some can't – and I pointed out Cheena Dug and said she had been banned from speaking because as soon as her mouth started her hands stopped.'

'What did he say to that?' asked Jakey.

'He asked why she was called Cheena Dug.'

'Why is she?'

'D'ye no ken?'

'I ken the woman, but no' how she got her name. I've never heard her called anything else.'

'She collects china'.

'China dogs? Ma granny had a pair; I think Ina's got them somewhere.'

'A'body in Hecklescar used to have a pair sittin' on their mantelpiece. But no; she disnae collect them – they're ower expensive. No, the 'dug' comes from Douglas – that wis her maiden name and she buys sets of china - dinner sets – and tea sets. Every six months there's a china shop in Edinburgh that reduces the price of all their china sets – and she buys one; turn about, a tea set this time, a dinner set next.'

'What on earth does she do with them?'

'She uses them – for the six months. Then gives them away – or puts them into a charity shop. She says for what they cost it's nice to have a change.'

Jakey returned from this excursion to his main apprehension.

'What did you make of the new man, then – overall?'

'I think we'll be able to make something of him.'

This did not satisfy Jakey.

'That's good to hear. But, ye ken, ye're a poor judge o' character; look at that man ye married!'

'No change the subject,' replied Angela pleasantly but firmly. 'D'ye think this Clouston's going to fit in?'

Thus, forcing Jakey into a response.

'I've no' had a proper look at him yet.' he replied. 'He wants to spend the day wi' me the morn. I'll let you know after that.'

Not all Angela's considerable wheedling powers could draw out any more from him.

In the afternoon, Clouston sat in the office and wrote

up, in the appropriate pages of his Filofax, his encounter with Angela, the fish-room, and its workers. He entered the facts and figures Angela had given him in a statistical analytic tool on his laptop. Then, as all good managers should, but few accomplish, he updated his ToDo list and scheduled time slots to deal with them. All this without the assistance of Fiona who, although she had work of her own to do, could not understand why he did not make more use of her secretarial services. All he asked was that she kept the coffee machine topped up and ready for action.

Then, at the end of the working day, as the fish-yard fell silent and the gutters and packers made their way home, he asked Fiona if she would stay on for an hour or two to help him understand 'the supply chain': the firms, boats, individuals and contractors that supplied fish; and the 'capability resources':

packaging, ice, fuel, vehicles, services, equipment and disposables that allow the company to carry on churning out 'product' as he called it. He also asked if tomorrow evening would she stay back to work through the 'outlets': customers: from local shops and chefs that bought their fish from the vans that toured the countryside, to the big boys and middle men in England and the Continent, who had their own networks to supply.

Fiona agreed and would postpone her warmed-up pizza for a couple of hours in order to spend time with the boss who had virtually ignored her all day. We are entitled to ask why Fiona is being kept back? Why a slot had not been earmarked in Clouston's carefully planned schedule for such necessary work?

No doubt, if we asked him, Clouston would claim to be 'buying time', or 'taking up the slack'. As reasonable people we would accept such a lofty explanation. That, however, does not prevent us salting it with a more mundane motive. He has had a stimulating day, he has been fawned over, consulted, and obeyed; he's been the one on everyone's tongue, all have been anxious to see him, to speak to him, to be in his company. His mind is bursting with new knowledge; he feels exhilarated, pumped up, anxious to forge ahead. But what lies ahead of him now, at half-past five? He must retreat to a poky little room in St Ebba's Guest House, take a shower in an en-suite cubicle the size of a filing cabinet and eat a warmed-up meal alone in an empty dining room. How much better to hold onto Fiona's company for a little longer?

If these be your thoughts, as well as mine, do you not warm to the man a little? And begin to consider that he may be something more than a talking management textbook and a careerist searching for an opening? That, in the business suit, might be a human being trying to get out?

Hold onto that hope, for his opening request to Fiona is not encouraging. He asks that she seeks out a supplier for a set of Executive stationery: letter-heading, business cards, compliment slips. Meanwhile he will work on a company logo: fresh, clear-cut, avant-garde.

'We need an image in the market,' he declared, 'that commands attention and is immediately recognisable.'

During the two hours he spent with Fiona that evening, Clouston became impressed by Fiona's knowledge of the business; it proved detailed, precise and as far as he could tell, up to date. She knew where the fish and supplies came from, knew who supplied them, knew the names of the people who made the decisions and knew who could be relied on to do what they had promised and those who had to be chased until they delivered. She also had an informed grasp of company finances and could give him to the pound weekly trading figures for as long back as he wanted to go. They had not been talking long when he formed the opinion that, clearly, for the last few years, as Hercules' interest in the business waned, Fiona had taken it on herself to keep the business afloat. He became thoroughly convinced of it when she produced a short list of requests for spending that she had approved, and an even longer list of those she had turned down.

'Did Mr Douglas know about these?' asked Clouston

sounding vaguely alarmed.

'Some of them,' replied Fiona, tentatively. 'But he wasn't always here, and said I should deal with them.'

'Off your own bat?' went on her new boss.

'I always asked for three quotations and discussed them with Jakey, or Angela. If I needed to talk about funding I spoke to the accountant. I always got Mr Douglas to sign off the spending,' she stated in a rush.

Clearly Clouston's interest alarmed her. Had she done something wrong? Or illegal? She got up quickly, walked to one of the cabinets and, without hesitating, pulled out a file. She came back to the desk and laid it in from of Clouston.

'They're all in here,' she said, 'and all signed'.

Clouston sensed her unease and quickly reassured her that she had done the right thing. To satisfy her, as well as himself, he skimmed through the sheaf of papers she had brought.

'I'm impressed,' he said. 'It's all very well done – and completely in order.'

Fiona relaxed and smiled.

CHAPTER THIRTY-SIX

At seven Clouston called a halt, asked Fiona to make coffee then sat chatting amicably about the town, the people and her cat. Then, just as they were preparing to leave, he smiled and said,

'Two things, Fiona. I want you to call me Clouston.'

'I'm sorry,' said Fiona sounding flustered. 'I always called Mr Douglas, Mr Douglas.'

'I'm sure that was very proper, and I'm sure that would be what Harold would expect, but I want us to be less formal. We'll be spending a time together and I want you to feel relaxed.'

By way of reply, Fiona smiled nervously.

'And,' continued Clouston cheerfully, "I think we should slip into something more comfortable.'

Fiona started, reddened, stared at him and, wondering what he meant, blurted out,

'What?'

Clouston, laughed, held up his hands in mock surrender, and apologised immediately.

'Forgive me, forgive me,' he purred. 'That was clumsy. Oh dear, what a start. Forgive my warped sense of humour.'

'That's alright,' mumbled Fiona uneasily.

'No, what I should have said is: if I have to spend many more days in this office I'll go stir crazy. As offices go this must be one of the most uncomfortable and inconvenient ever designed.. I don't know how you manage to spend all your days cooped up here. Do you not find it airless and claustrophobic?'

'I've got used to it, I suppose,' replied Fiona.

'You've done well to settle for it, I would say, but I'm sure I'm not even going to try. Where did Harold entertain visitors? Not here, I hope. It gives the wrong impression of the company. It's dull, and dingy. What must they think when they're shown up here? That this is thriving progressive business? No, they'll go away and sneer at it with their business friends. The main office must be a window on the company; must show the world what the company is - smart, bright, going places.'

They were sitting at Hercules' old desk, he behind, Fiona in front. But as the allegory struck him, he rose from his chair and strode to the window that looked out over the fish-room.

'This office does the opposite. The only window, this one, looks in and back. It must look out and forward. These symbols are important.'

'Mr Douglas liked the workers in the fish room to know that he could see them from the window.'

'I'll bet he scarcely ever looked.'

Fiona conceded that he seldom looked, and of late had been scarcely in the office anyway. Clouston continued,

'In any case, I'm pretty sure this office is illegal. In case of a fire, how would we get out?. The stair leads into the building - not outside - and there's no fire escape.'

Clouston stopped. As he delivered his verdict he had been glancing round the room. Now he gave his attention to Fiona – and saw her agitation. He then realised that, although he saw the office with the eyes of someone used to all the trappings of executive privilege, she regarded this room as her home for most of her waking hours.

'I think we can find somewhere much better for you,' he said gently.

Fiona made her way home, but not directly. Her house, an ex-council house that Hercules had helped her to buy, lay on the Poplace Estate; on that part of the estate that isn't totally surrounded by other houses, but which at the back, (if you pardon the contradiction) faced onto the open fields that gave sight of Coldingham Bay and distant St Abb's Head; an attractive location, but to reach it she had to walk almost a mile from the office in Harbour Road, up a long slog of a hill. Even so, on this night she chose not to cut up through the town along its darkened streets, Instead, she walked the full length of Harbour Road, then made her way along the Bantry. She had just turned the corner when she ran into Cheena Dug hurrying in the opposite direction with a packet of fish and chips in her hand. Cheena expressed surprise at meeting Fiona in such a place at such a time of night. Fiona, flustered, replied at length that she had come to see if McMaggie's fish and chip shop was still open so she could buy chips to go with her pizza when she got home. Cheena listened inquisitively to her explanation then informed her that she had left it too late; she had got into McMaggie's just before they closed; they'd had to scratch around to get her what she wanted. Fiona expressed regret and hurried on. But, as Cheena confided to Angela and the 'girls' the following day, (but not while she was working!), she thought it strange because, normally, people don't have chips with their pizzas and would have thought that Fiona ought not to be doing so. They all knew what Cheena meant: after all, Fiona is a bit on the tubby side and should be counting the calories.

 Cheena's doubts were justified, for whatever Fiona said, the reason she took the long way round has nothing to do with chips; it has to do with her long confinement with Clouston Pritchard. She needed fresh air and she needed to mull over all that had happened.

 'Do I like him? Yes, I do, but I didn't like the way he looked at me when he said that about 'comfortable.' Yes, I know he apologised, but was that just because I knocked him back. Suppose I'd led him on? What would have happened then? I mean, he's a married man. And she's a lot younger than me – and a looker they say. He wouldn't be interested in me – in that way, would he? But she's not here; he might be lonely. I've read that some bosses get pumped up when they work hard and need to take it out, you know, relieve themselves - and think their secretaries should oblige. No, Fiona, don't think like that! You wouldn't want that, would you? In any case he probably thinks I'm an old frump. What did I say that made him apologise? I can't remember. I'm older than him anyway. In which case why did he. . .? Hercules never attempted anything like that, not ever. Why did he do what? He didn't do anything he shouldn't have done. Maybe I'm reading too much into it. He's good to work with. Much easier than Hercules. He's organised and has lots of good ideas about where he wants to take the company. Professional too. It could be good for my career. I've had to do it all myself without much help. I never got the feeling that Hercules appreciated how efficient I was at everything. I had to slog along all by myself. Jakey too, doesn't realise how much I do – nor does Angela – and the others. But Mr Pritchard, er, Clouston, does. I think he liked the records – and what I knew about the company; and the way I could lay my hands on what he wanted - and the way I'd carried on even when Mr Douglas lost interest,'

'If it hadn't been for me keeping on top of spending dear knows what would have happened. They were always onto me for being stingy. If I hadn't been, the company could have gone bust. I know John Henry and Peter appreciated that - and I think Mr Pritch . . . Clouston, thinks the same. Like that authorization thing he came across. I thought for a moment he would tell me I'd overstepped the mark, but instead he praised me. I knew I had done it within the law. I looked it up. I knew I had done it properly – and so did he. Maybe he'll let me handle all that accountancy bit. I could take courses in it.'

'I mean, Peter Munro is alright. He's very thorough and we must be grateful for what he's done with the finances – and to John Henry. I like John Henry, he's canny and approachable, but no businessman. Peter doesn't say much and you never know what he's thinking. He doesn't seem that interested in the business and doesn't have any long-term plans for it as far as I can tell. I think that's why he brought in Mr Pritchard. He's got ideas.'

'He's right about that office an' a. It is claustrophobic. I wonder where he'll find another one. There's that room over the café next door; that might do.'

These were her thoughts but if you would understand how she felt, you must spice these raw ingredients with a little excitement and not a little tingling anticipation of spending time with this lively, unpredictable younger man.

As she stroked her cat at the house door she muttered pleasantly,

'Yes, Poppy, I think, on the whole, Clouston Pritchard is going to be just what Anthony Douglas needs.'

Clouston, that same evening settled into his lodging well pleased with his day. He had, in his estimation, 'impacted'; he had left them in doubt that he had arrived, and that he intended to 'penetrate' the business until he knew what was going on where by whom.

He had met the drivers of the business: Peter, Jakey, Angela, and Fiona and so far, had been pleasantly surprised. From Peter he could expect backing – he would not want to interfere because he wanted out of management; he, Clouston, would accommodate him in that. Angela he regarded as a Sergeant-Major; she ran a tight ship and understood her team. Compared to the supervisors and line managers at the freezer companies he had worked in – Arcticus and IceCap, she was an amateur, but a good one – and, he thought, willing to learn the professional skills she would need in the envisioned company.

Jakey, he suspected, would be most difficult to mould. In the few moments he had spent with him those first two days, he had not been able to properly fathom the man, and thought he may have detected some resentment. Perhaps this local man had objected to a new man being brought in over him? If so, he could deal with that. He had done so before. But by tomorrow evening he would pretty well have him in focus – and know what he must do to win them to his vision of Anthony Douglas & Son, or, as it now occurred to him, with its logo already half formed in his mind: ADS.

Fiona? A diligent and sell-organised amateur, but her attitude is staid, unimaginative, pedantic; rooted in a past that must be left behind. A bit of a frump, too. Could she persuaded to move forward?

He doubted it.

CHAPTER THIRTY-SEVEN

On Wednesday of his first week at Anthony Douglas & Son, Clouston Pritchard had pencilled in a morning with Jakey, and thought he had told Jakey he had pencilled it in. We also know from what Jakey said to Angela on Tuesday that he knew that Clouston wanted to see him on Wednesday. However, when Clouston arrived at seven and asked for Jakey he discovered that the chief of his 'top team' had not yet turned up for work. When he expressed his irritation to Fiona, it abated only a little when she told him that this happened quite often. Jakey, she explained, had probably been at the yard for a couple of hours in the middle of the night. He'd been expecting a lorryload of prawns from Mallaig and a load of whitefish from Ballantrae.

'Does he not delegate that to one of his men?' he asked.

'He likes to do it himself,' replied Fiona.

'I had arranged to meet him this morning,' said Clouston, seeking to justify his irritation.

'He'll be in about nine, I expect,' said Fiona.

Jakey proved her right, give or take five minutes or so. Jakey, however, didn't report to the office. Following his usual routine, he turned up at the yard and started organising shipments and deliveries for the following day.

Clouston lingered in the office for a while then made his way down into the fishyard. There he found Jakey gutting fish at a bench chatting enthusiastically to a woman standing beside him.

'We arranged to meet this morning,' he said tersely to Jakey.

'So, we have,' replied Jakey, pleasantly. 'I'll be up once I've got these fish done; Carol at Kelso has run short of haddies, so Jen here has come in and is running them up.'

Clouston bridled at the thought of being put behind Jen in the queue for Jakey's attention. He glanced at Jen, but, professional manager that he is, knew he ought not rebuke Jakey with one of his underlings as a witness, so he studied Jen for a moment, then swallowed his irritation and asked Jakey to come up immediately he had finished despatching Jen to Kelso.

Twenty minutes later, Jakey appeared in the office wiping his hands/

'I'm sorry about that, Mr Pritchard,' he said, 'but Hercules always told us to put the customer first. That's who pays us, he said.'

Clouston ignored this advertisement and quickly submerged Jakey in a sea of questions about what he did and why, and, to Jakey's concern, carefully wrote down his answers. His unease increased when Clouston read them back to him and asked him to confirm that that is what he had said. Jakey had not been brought up to such precision. For him, words counted for little; they were oil that lubricated the gears of activity. What mattered was what happened; if words were needed he would use them and listen to them – and any words would do. At first Jakey tried to knock back Clouston's questions about equipment; vans, lorries, refrigerated units, forklift trucks, boxes, clothing, and all the other bits and pieces, claiming cheerfully that he only used them; if Clouston wanted to know what the company owned he should ask Fiona; she knew about 'a' thae things'. Clouston, however, would not let go and chased down every nut, bolt and location and drew not a little satisfaction from finding yawning discrepancies between Fiona's lists and Jakey's accounts. Where had all the missing stuff gone, he asked Jakey, as each shortfall appeared on his page.

I am not inclined to wash more of Jakey's dirty washing in public than is strictly necessary to carry along our story. I will therefore report only one interchange between the two men. It concerned a van.

'How many vans do you have?' asked Clouston, innocently.

Jakey eagerly replied. He knew how many vans he had at his disposal.

'Four,' he said firmly, and sure of his ground, amplified his reply by nominating the drivers and routes. 'Little Dod covers The Borders from Jedburgh to Canonby ye ken, over by Gretna. Elaine heads North to Dunbar to the shop there then on to Haddington before colliding with the competition from Leith; Jen covers North Northumberland – as far down as Alnwick, taking in Alnmouth, Bamburgh and all thae popular places down there – Seahouses and a'. She logs up over two hundred miles on each trip. Then there's Eddie; he takes on Berwickshire and Berwick, and the shuttle to the Kelsae shop. That's when he's no' at the BGH investigating his bad hip again or complaining aboot it tae anybody that'll listen.'

This attempt at humour drew only the faintest of smiles from Clouston.

'Four,' he responded. 'You say we have four vans?'

'Aye. Four.'

'The inventory says we have five.'

'The inventory?' Jakey queried, having heard of 'inventory' but had never quite understood what it was.

'The inventory; the list of assets of the company. There are five vans listed.'

He stopped talking and stared at Jakey.

'Five vans?' mumbled Jakey. 'We've not got five vans; only four.'

'Let me read you the description and registration of each of the five.'

Long before he got to the end of the list, Jakey knew where they were headed. After the third van, he came clean.

'We used to hev that Peugeot, but we got rid of it. It was knackered.'

'Got rid of it? In what way?' pressed Clouston not wishing to save Jakey any embarrassment.

'Angela kent a young laddie, next door, ye ken, just passed his test. He was lookin' to start up as an odd job man; cutting grass, tidying gardens,, fixing fences, that sort of thing. We'd finished with the van. That wis years ago, when we bought Jen's new van, years ago. So, we let the lad hev it. It wis nae use to us.'

'You gave it away?'

'Aye, it wis unreliable; left her stranded two or three times afore we ditched it. The laddie said he knew a man that could dae it up.'

'But it belonged to the company. It didn't belong to you, - or to Angela. You can't just give the company's assets away. They have to be written off. Did you ask Harold if you could give it away?'

'Harold?'

'Mr Douglas.'

'Hercules! No, he wouldn't be interested. Angela might have mentioned it."

'Fiona then?'

Of course, Jakey had not told Fiona. Of course, Angela had not spoken to Hercules. They had just given the lad the van to get it out of the yard.

Clouston did not pursue the van any further, nor any other deficiencies, lapses or omissions that he uncovered. By the end of the meeting, he knew that he had made his point and put Jakey on notice that the Do-it-Yourself days were over. From now on the company – and its assets would be managed.

Jakey relaxed, therefore, when Clouston broke off the

inquisition and asked him to show him round the yard, the shop and the pier and explain what went on in each of them.

On home territory, Jakey retaliated for his humiliation in the office. He trailed Clouston through every room, alley and passage in building and yard, traipsed him down the pier and into the shop where he repeated the performance. He chaffed and chatted him to everyone they met, demonstrating, for the benefit of the new manager, the friendship and informality that bound them all together in a common enterprise. Steered by Jakey, Clouston toured refrigeration units, cupboards, benches, cages, vans, forklift trucks, pallets, polythene boxes and much more. Jakey led him through the labyrinth of systems, methods and safety procedures that processed the fish, prawns, crabs and lobsters, from boat to box, from box to fishroom, and from room to vans and shops. Expert at gutting himself Jakey invited Clouston to try his hand, but he turned down the offer. Likewise, he eschewed the opportunity to wheel a large bin full of fish guts from the gutting rooms to the disposal point. (Jakey, however, thought it better not tell him that crab and lobster fishermen were invited to raid it to gather bait for their creels; they might be assets! Clouston, to his credit, did try his hand at driving the tanker lorry to the slip there to fill it with fresh sea water to replenish the lobster tanks.

Jakey then marched him down the quay to inspect the boats; the big ones that steam forty or fifty miles out, chasing prawns and white fish and the little ones that potter about the rocks with a fleet or two of lobster pots. He introduced the new man to whoever of the fishing fraternity he could find on the pier. Always announcing him, not by his official -- and self-chosen - title of Chief Executive, but as 'the man that's come in for Hercules'.

Throughout he pointed out pointedly the deficiencies and shortages with which they struggled every day and stressed the need for better equipment, better premises and more people.

As they walked back to the yard, Clouston complimented Jakey on 'his operation', saying he had been impressed by his grasp of the practicalities and the obvious respect in which he was held by the workforce.

'They're my friends,' explained Jakey. 'Well, most of the buggers. Mind you I don't know what they say behind my back.'

Clouston graciously laughed at this admission.

'Thanks to you, - and Angela and Fiona, I have learned a lot this week. Of course, here's a lot more I need to know but what I'd like to do is to meet the workforce and let them into my thinking. Would that be possible on Friday?'

'This Friday?'

'Yes.'

'We should be able to do that. The best time would be afternoon. We finish early on a Friday. We could squeeze it in at two, say. Just before they knock off. The shift finishes at three.'

'Half two will do then,' replied Clouston. 'I don't need long. I'll not go into detail. I want to take the top team through my vision first.'

Here he stopped as he read the questions reflected in Jakey's eyes.

'Top team? Who's the top team? John Henry and Peter? But Peter's away isn't he? And we haven't seen John Henry for weeks. Who's he on about?'

Clouston helped him out of his confusion by adding,

'You, Angela, and Fiona.'

'Oh, us!' Jakey thought, not without some satisfaction. 'We're the top team, - and here's me thinking we were just punters like the rest.'

Clouston continued.

'Just to reassure them. There must have been a lot of speculation, and I want them to go home for the weekend in a positive frame of mind.'

'I'll arrange that,' confirmed Jakey. 'Half-past two on Friday.'

When they returned to the yard, they came across

Jen washing her van after her hurried trip to Kelso. Jakey thanked her and introduced her to Clouston. Reluctantly, Jakey thought, she acknowledged Clouston's greeting, did not put out her hand to shake the man's hand, and did not look him in the face. She scuttled off as soon as she could. As she hurried away, Clouston studied her for a while then turned to Jakey and asked him,

'She doesn't come from Peterhead, by any chance, does she?'

'I believe she did,' replied Jakey.

CHAPTER THIRTY-EIGHT

On Wednesday evening, Clouston left Hecklescar for home in North Berwick. There to review his first few days as Chief Executive of Anthony Douglas & Son. As planned and promised, he would not come back until Friday. He had a lot to consider.

To understand his state of mind, we must remember the old saying that a general's plan of campaign lasts only as long as first contact with the enemy. I also suspect you have gathered that Clouston is the sort of manager who believes in plans. Since his meeting back in February with Peter Munro, and his tour of the plant in the company of Angela and Jakey, he had been hard at work on his SWOT analysis. This is a well-loved management tool for those who wish to reduce the complexities of life to an A4 sheet of paper – or four sheets at the most. The word is an acronym for Strengths, Weaknesses, Opportunities and Threats, and Clouston had identified plenty of each to convince himself that Anthony Douglas & Son lay in need of him. He would now spend Thursday sketching out what might be done to correct the weaknesses and head off the threats. Exploiting the strengths and seizing the opportunities he would develop as the weeks went by. All of which is much easier if you don't know a great deal about the plant in question. Ask any experienced manager and he or she will tell you that the more you dig into a firm, the more worms crawl out of it.

In the last three days with Fiona, Angela and Jakey, he had started excavations and must now give the lengthy list of weaknesses his attention. In his study, he is creating for each item on the list a control sheet, setting out not only the problem but composing a suitable banner for the course of actions he intends to pursue. I tell you this not to elicit your sympathy for the man. Had he found nothing wrong, he would have had nothing on which to exercise his abilities. If you glanced over his shoulder as he creates his control sheets, you will see that they are not entitled 'Problems' but 'Projects'.

I will not try your patience with the whole list, but will give an example to illustrate the technique. We know that he is dissatisfied with the attic office he shares Fiona. We will therefore find a sheet entitled, 'Recreate Executive Office' and will see that the major 'Purpose' of such an action is 'to present a modern dynamic image of the company to customers, suppliers and other contacts'. An ancillary benefit is described as 'providing an efficient, convenient and safe working environment' for the users of the office. He has then sketched out various actions that will be required to carry out the plan. 'Seek out a better location'; 'consult architect', 'review furnishings', and so on. Eventually against each of these actions a date for completion will appear. You get the idea. Clouston will flesh out each of his projects in this way until he has a whole portfolio of plans for Anthony Douglas & Son. It is a sound way to bring things about – provided that you have complete control over every aspect of the project, that no-one with any clout disagrees with you, that you can lay your hands on all the money you need and that everyone who in any way is affected by your proposal will go along with it without dispute, delay or bloody-mindedness. In all of these you need your 'top team' behind you. Now then, has he done enough in the past three days to bring them aboard?

For that we need to switch our attention from the neat sheets of paper on Clouston's quiet desk in his comfortable house in North Berwick to the splash, smell, racket and ructions of the fishyard on the pier at Hecklescar.

I would not like you to underestimate what Fiona, Angela and, especially, Jakey are tackling. They have known for months now, that 'somebody else' will sit in Hercules chair, and, for weeks, that that somebody had the name of Clouston Pritchard who, they had found out, is not yet fifty, used to be a friend of Hercules, comes from Peterhead, once worked at IceCap there, has recently been a big boss of Arcticus, a refrigeration company up Edinburgh way, lives in North Berwick, and asked for, and had been given, a company car.

All this they know. But it makes not a whit of difference to what they do every day. And as they are do it questions seep into their minds, especially Jakey's. Did the company need a Chief Executive? Did they need Clouston Pritchard? Before Peter came, Jakey well understood that the company lay in deep trouble - but not due to anything that he, Angela and Fiona did or didn't do. Peter had told them that. He blamed Hercules for raiding the company's coffers to prop up his dodgy dealings in Edinburgh. That had been put right; Peter had seen to that. He had assured them that the business made money. So why could they not just carry on the way they were? He knew his job; should do - he'd been doing it for over twenty years now. He knew how it fitted in with Angela's job; they didn't ever fall out about who does what. Well, hardly ever. He trod on her toes when, last summer, he took Brenda away to stand in for Carol at Kelso; he thought he'd asked Angela if he could borrow her, but she said he hadn't mentioned it. It had come up suddenly and he had to keep the shop open. But that didn't happen often; they worked together well. He got on with Fiona as well. She isn't so much day to day, and can be a bit tight-fisted when it came to materials, but she knows what she was doing and he respected her for it. The fishyard ran like a well-oiled machine, he had told John Henry way back in December. The old banker had agreed and said that if it had not been for their expertise and hard work together the yard would have been shut years ago. And hadn't Peter said, after he'd taken a look at things, that the business made money and, (and this thought had grown to become dominant in Jakey's mind) he thought company well-managed. Well-managed!

Such rumination had produced in Jakey and, almost by equal degree, in Angela, the notion that they didn't really need a Manager or Chief Executive, or anyone to help them in the running of the company. It ran well enough as it is. Fiona, however, had her doubts. She had worked closely with 'the boss' of the company. Daily, she entered the office and witnessed the empty chair; weekly, she cleared away unanswered correspondence; regretted often that her shorthand notebook remained fast closed in its drawer and regularly advised an irate caller that Mr Douglas had left the company, and no, no-one had taken his place.

So long as the proposition 'someone to replace Hercules', remained a distant ambition of Peter Munro's, it had proved no check on the assumption growing in Jakey's mind that the yard did not need a manager. Then. as the weeks drew on, and the company bustled along, both Jakey and Angela began to believe that no manager would ever step through the gates of the yard; that everything could and would carry on as it always had done.

Such conjecture had not been entirely scotched when they heard that a man called Clouston Pritchard would take a look at the yard. After all, Peter had invited him just to 'explore the possibility' of his taking up a position with the company. We know from Peter's report to John Henry in hospital, that their meetings with Clouston had come as a shock to Jakey, Angela and Fiona. It had sent them scurrying to Peter for clarification of his role in the company. He had reassured them that the new man would stay out of the day-to-day running of the firm; that would carry on very much under their own control.

Now the new man had arrived, he could no longer be catalogued and filed way as the refrigerator man from Arcticus, with a house in North Berwick, or him that once lived in Peterhead. He had walked through the gate and settled into the office. He had come alive; he had moved in beside them.

But what had he come to do? What was his job? Jakey doesn't know. That is clear from his words when he introduced Clouston to the fishermen on then pier. He did not call him by his official title; he had said 'this is the man taking over from Hercules'. Hercules had been the big boss. Peter, however, had said that Clouston wouldn't be that. Hercules owned the company –this man didn't and, most of the time, he wouldn't be here. What? Ten days a month. You can't be boss part-time.

Not much of Jakey's confusion passed his lips that Thursday, even though Angela, on more than one occasion, tried to draw his opinions from him. She reminded him that on Tuesday he had said that after he'd spent Wednesday with the new man, he would 'let her know' what he thought. Nevertheless, when she made her way home that Thursday evening she had not heard from Jakey any serious comment about their new Chief Executive. That does not mean that she had no clue as to what Jakey felt about the new man. Few of us can hide our feelings simply by keeping our mouths shut. Jakey is not one of the few; he is a garrulous, sociable man whose even temper rarely erupted into anything approaching either delight or dejection. On this day, however, it became obvious to Angela that her rather grumpy companion had not found his time with Clouston to his comfort.

CHAPTER THIRTY-NINE

Now that Clouston Pritchard had boarded Anthony Douglas & Son, Jakey could no longer ignore him, nor pretend that it would make no difference to him who took over the wheel from Hercules.

'If you have lived with Hercules, you can live with anyone,' he had bragged over the past few weeks as news of Clouston Pritchard's appointment spread through the town; a message broadcast also by Ina to any audience that would listen.

If you would understand what they mean, you need to turn over the calendar that hangs squint on the wall behind Jakey's desk at the top of the stair. You will note that the calendar was produced by the Aberdeen Mercantile Association and that the month that is displayed is long gone and depicts a photograph of an oil support vessel sailing out of Aberdeen Harbour. Nothing there you would think. But turn over the page and there you will find a cartoon. It depicts a line drawing of a ship. On the bridge stands a fully uniformed captain with his hands on the wheel and a smile on his face. 'I'm in charge,' it says. But look closely at the wheel. Around it runs a cable that goes down through the floor to a similar wheel in the engine room and back in a circle to the bridge wheel. Quite separate from this device, sits a complacent old sea dog with his hand on a tiller that steers the boat. Clearly the boat is under his control, not the captain on the bridge. There is a name scribbled beside the old sea dog. It reads 'Jakey'. The fact that Jakey has kept the calendar long after its year has expired and that he keeps the cartoon covered tells you much about Jakey's understanding of his position in Anthony Douglas & Son.

Jakey had come into the fish yard as a refugee from the fishing. He had stuck it out on heaving decks for three years on David Flett's boat, before David retired and had taken himself and his boat back to Orkney. That left only five big boats fishing out of Hecklescar and all had full crews – Filipinos mainly. No berth could be found for Jakey. So, to the yard he came – and had stayed. For thirty-four years now. He had never been promoted, he had just drifted upwards; taking over the duties of those who had left or retired. For the past ten years or so he had been the acknowledged boss. What title is on his contract of employment, I don't know and, I'm sure, neither does he. It is doubtful if he has one. Fiona might know; she keeps tabs on all these legal requirements.

Jakey, however, enjoyed being the boss. Not for the perks, for there were none, unless you call helping yourself to a few fillets or a lobster or two now and again, and occasionally filling up your car on the company's account. He enjoyed keeping the show on the road. He took no interest in the accounts, the ins and outs – he left that to Fiona, What absorbed him was the busy-ness of the place; lorries and trucks, deliveries and shipments, piles of boxes coming in and polypropylene packages going out. And, especially, the people – his people; he thought of them as *his* people. He expected, they will tell you, every effort from them and would give them a bollocking if they let him down. He took an interest in their accomplishments and disappointments; their ulcers, asthma attacks and arthritis, gave them time off for hospital appointments, family occasions and domestic disasters, and could be sure, if they didn't outlive him, that he would attend their funeral dressed in his dark suit and black tie – whatever the weather.

Although he would never admit it, the way Hercules had managed the yard – or didn't, particularly lately, suited Jakey. Free of the burden of the company's viability, he relished the hustle, bustle and pizzaz of the yard. Hercules acted as a sort of umbrella, protecting him from financial downpours, commercial storms and regulatory disturbances. Because he could persuade himself that Hercules took care of these matters, Jakey did not have to leave the comfort of the life he had grown used to. Through Hercules' negligence, Jakey therefore found his working life full of purpose, opportunity, and free – free to do what he thought best.

Add to that, his status in the town, and you have a happy man; well, as happy as any of us are. (Of course, he would not admit to being happy; that is far too sentimental an opinion for a man like Jakey; you could get laughed at down the pier for confessing to something like that. All he will admit to there is 'no' bad'', which comes a notch higher than 'daein' away ', and well above 'ye see it a'). The truth is, however, that he enjoyed being at the centre of the wheeling life of Hecklescar and the hub of many of its conversations.

'I'll be landing at Ballantrae.' 'Jakey'll send a truck.'

'We're running out of langoustines and we've a busy weekend coming up.' 'Speak to Jakey.'

'Do you have any megrim?' 'I'll contact Jakey when I get back.'

'Has yer son not tried for a job down the pier – see Jakey.'

'Jakey would see you all right with a forklift truck if you wanted to shift all thae chairs.'

'Oh that? That's the fish yard.' 'No, Anthony Douglas is long gone. A man called Jakey runs it.'

'What's his second name?' 'Ah no' ken. A' body jist calls him Jakey.'

His equability, however, had been severely tested in

the dying weeks of last year by Hercules' proposition that he should take over the yard, lock, stock and barrel. This, we know, demonstrated, not kindness from his old boss, but a cynical attempt to extract a little more value from the company he had already plundered. In the end, thanks to John Henry's intervention, Hercules' intention had been scotched and Jakey had been able, after a few anxious days, to retreat to familiar territory. Under the benign leadership of John, then Peter Munro, he had been able to resume his role as general factotum. No harm done; lessons learnt; course corrected; sail on.

Life, however, seldom allows us to sail on unscathed. Jakey, for the first time in his life had been buffeted by a storm he could not master on a sea he could not navigate. He had not been so tested before. Challenges had never daunted him, and every one of his working days had a scattering of them. Certainly, he had sweated over some of them, and puzzled over others, but ultimately he had charted his way through them; they yielded to his ability – and his self-confidence. In John Henry's front room, however, back in October he had been swamped by a wave he could not ride. He had glimpsed a wider, wilder ocean - and had turned back.

That lay almost six months ago, and during those months, his life had returned to normal, his confidence had returned and he felt in control again. Much of this, we must understand is down to the immediate assistance of John Henry in stilling his fears, and the timely arrival of a company saviour in the form of Peter Munro.

And to something else: his determination not to venture into the murky swamps and impenetrable forests of Herculean management. Peter, we know, had offered him the opportunity thus to explore the higher hills of management– and had offered to be his guide, but he had turned him down. He enjoyed what he did and could not clearly see what else, day to day, needed to be done.

Now he did see it. In the last few days, as he listened to

Clouston and watched him in action, it dawned on him that there was a job that must be undertaken. It lay in the activities that Hercules, for all his bombast and lately, his neglect, had carried out for the past twenty years. Unrecognised by Jakey until this moment, it had given Jakey – and Angela - the freedom to do what they did best: running the yard; bringing in the fish, and selling it on. The duties of such a job had always been a mystery to Jakey, and Hercules had never sought to enlighten him. That played into Hercules' belief in his own superiority and confirmed Jakey in his opinion that Hercules played with the paperwork, but we do the work and earn the money.

Clouston, however, had not kept Jakey in the dark. His discussions with Dodgy Donald and the skippers down the pier and that business of five vans that were only four, and other shots and snippets combined to push aside Jakey's doubts. He saw now what needed to be done; understood that it must be done to allow him and Angela to carry on doing what they had always done. He understood it, and to his discomfort, realised something else: Clouston could probably do it – but he could not.

Shocks that smack us about the face are not pleasant, but they are much easier to defend than those that shake us from inside. Battles against a hostile world are more easily won than those that sap our energy before we start. Particularly when those we would look to for comfort appear to have deserted us. This debilitating thought sickened Jakey as he listened to Angela during their tea break on Thursday afternoon. All day Angela had waited for Jakey to respond to her suggestion on Tuesday that they 'could make something of' Clouston'. Back then, Jakey had parried the proposal and had promised to let her know his opinion of the new man after he had spent the day with him on Wednesday. But Thursday having come, Jakey's lips had been strangely sealed. Even now he would admit to no more than an acknowledgement that the man seemed to know what he was talking about. After such a confession he brought the conversation to a close by picking up his mug and mumbling something about needing to be up in the middle of the night to receive a shipment from Mallaig.

Angela watched him leave with a shrug of her shoulders, and wondered what had made her usually garrulous companion so taciturn. On her way she worked it out, and as she entered her door gave a little laugh.

'Jakey's jealous,' she said to herself. 'He's been knocked off his perch.'

CHAPTER FORTY

The 'meeting with the top team' on Friday morning did nothing to dissuade Angela of Jakey's jealousy. Clouston could not have been more considerate or conciliatory. When Jakey and Angela arrived at the appointed time – appointed in consultation with both of them, they found that he had rearranged the office so that the man in the big chair behind the boss's desk could no longer laud it over underlings cowering in front of it.

The desk that loomed large for Hercules, had now, in the hands of Clouston (assisted by Fiona). become a conference table. The ostentatious executive chair had been sent in disgrace to the back wall and comfortable upright chairs brought in to accommodate all on equal footing – or should that be 'seating'? On the table before each chair lay a neat ring binder, a conveniently placed pen, and a glass of water. Angela smiled at the sight of a new coffee percolator bubbling comfortably on the cabinet beside Fiona's desk. Whether Jakey noticed I do not know for his face remained expressionless. Then like the knights of the round table, all equal, no one above the others they took their places and Clouston launched into the first ever top team meeting in the history of Anthony Douglas & Son.

Though it is of considerable interest to me, I will not strain the patience of the reader by describing what happened in the next hour. (That is what Clouston promised: one hour;

no more - and he stuck to it). Suffice to say that he asked them to open the binder set before them and explained that in it they would find three sections, through which he would run in turn.

The first described what he had seen in his tour of each of their operations and his conversations with them: the fish room (Angela); the yard, product in and out (Jakey), and administration (Fiona).

'It is important to comprehend the present reality', he said, 'before we can draw lessons from it.'

Angela thought she knew what that meant - and felt relaxed enough to interpret.

'Ye hev to ken whit ye're lookin' at afore ye can dae anything aboot it,' she said.

Clouston complimented her on putting it 'much simpler than I have managed'.

In the second section, he had outlined what he thought he had learned – and emphasised that, in no way, could he possibly understand the complexities of their operations in such a short acquaintance.

'I am like a child in the primary,' he said, 'baffled by all I see.'

He then asked each of them in turn to confirm that his impressions were not widely inaccurate. Angela responded eagerly by pointing out that her girls worked in squads of five, not six; though sometimes six and at other times four or, if it was a rush job, it could be just one; she would put one of her best on that, because they were all different – but good in their own way. But she always knew who was doing what, she added. She noted with some satisfaction that he assiduously noted down what she said. Fiona, emboldened by Clouston's response to Angela, corrected a few details of Clouston's findings and smiled as he scribbled in the margin of his notes.

Jakey said little, except to damn Clouston with faint praise for his account of the yard, and to add that he would find out, when he had been here as long as he had, that things are much more complicated than they look. Clouston accepted this feedback with a smile and thanks. He promised to be prepared to be educated in the ways of the yard as he went along.

'Besides,' he said affirmatively, 'the yard is your sphere of operations – and in safe hands, I know.'

Jakey showed no sign of acknowledgment, preferring instead to consult his binder for the next item. Angela and Fiona who had sat stony faced as Jakey delivered his homily, both smiled as Clouston replied.

'Who's stolen your lollipop,' nipped Angela to Jakey as they left the meeting.

'Give me Hercules any day' grumbled Jakey. 'He was a rogue – but you knew it. We don't know what this man is.'

'Well, I say, give the man a chance; he's trying hard to fit in.'

Jakey had walked away before her sentence finished.

Friday arrived and with it the prospect of the 'Briefing Meeting' with the whole workforce that Clouston had requested and that Jakey had arranged. Every Friday the hour-long lunch break is cancelled and the yard shuts down at two o'clock. Jakey had agreed with Clouston that half-past one would be the best time for him to address the workforce.

This served two purposes. One, that the meeting would take place without too much loss of productive time. In spite of Jakey's efforts and Angela's threats, Cheena Dug and her companions, and Jakey's Malcolm, Sid, Compo and crew tended to switch off by slowing down, tidying up their work stations, shedding their waterproofs and wellies, and chattering about what lay ahead of them in the weekend. Angela called it, 'the long goodbye'.

Secondly, the choice of one-thirty on a Friday ensured that the meeting would not last longer than half-an-hour. Set it during working time, and the workers (and who can blame them) might well chose to put in their time discussing plans and programmes, rather than scraping the innards out of crabs, filleting cold fish, hosing down the yard or lugging heavy boxes in the rain.

The meeting needed to accommodate the thirty-seven workers on the Friday shift, plus Nudge, Jen and the other drivers. Only the open yard could accommodate such a large crowd, and, fortunately, the day, though cold, stayed fine. At half one, Clouston climbed onto an upturned fish-box and without a note in his hands, outlined a summary of what he had already covered in his meeting with Fiona, Angela and Jakey. It impressed most of the people who stood in the cold yard listening to it. But it didn't impress Jakey – for Jakey wasn't there. Urgent work had called him away, explained Clouston and praised him for his dedication to the firm.

'It is what we have come to expect of Jakey,' he announced, then added, 'and something we are going to need as we take Anthony Douglas & Son forward.'

What urgent work, you might ask, drew Jakey away from the meeting?

Clouston did not know. Neither do I. But I know what Angela thought of his absence.

'He's in the huff', she muttered to Fiona.

In acknowledgement, Fiona smiled and nodded.

CHAPTER FORTY-ONE

The ramshackle arrangement that sent Janet or Duncan to cover for Christine couldn't last. It came apart one Saturday evening at the family home in Prior's Road.

The stand-in had been cobbled together in a hurry with the threat of Christine's sacking urging them on. It couldn't long bear the weight of expectation placed on it. From the start it lacked the bracing of routine and without routine not much in life stands the chance of survival. For however much we may complain about life's plod, and enjoy the excitement of an occasional expedition, or the delightful distraction of parties and celebrations, it is the plod that carries us through.

Duncan and Janet's routine had been twenty-five years in the making and had sheltered them in many a storm and guided them safely past potholes and pitfalls. Of course, the routine had not stayed the same; it had been adapted and amended as needs changed, but such adaptations had always quickly slotted into place. Thus, if Duncan were working a distance from Hecklescar, the six o'clock meal shifted to seven, or, on a Wednesday, when, during the winter months, Janet attended the weekly meeting of the Rural, Duncan's dinner would be in the oven when he came home with instructions of what knobs to turn and what to do when the timer rang.

This covering for Christine, however, volunteered quickly and in good faith, could not be accommodated easily. Christine worked shifts, but not the same shifts each week. On Monday she may be called in from ten until two, on Tuesday, twelve to four, off on Wednesday but back in early on Thursday for a six to twelve shift. Then horrible hours on Saturday: two till nine. If I were you I wouldn't try to add up her weekly hours, for there are facts of which, you (and I, if I am honest) are unaware. For instance, on some of these shifts, because of their length, she merits a lunch break – for which she is not paid, and on others, she may or may not get a tea break for which she is. All in all, she is contracted to work sixteen hours a week. But, and here's the rub; she must be prepared to work any hours the manager decides to give her. Before you feel sorry for her - and you should, let me add to your confusion: she is one of the lucky ones; many superstore workers are on even shorter contracts; some as short as six hours. Nevertheless, they too must be *'available at all times'*. Not necessarily to work their six hours, but as many as the manager requests. And you must be careful not to show any resentment at being asked to turn in on a Saturday, or arrive for work at six on a school day; if you turn then down he may pass you over the next time he has hours to bestow; and you need the extra if you can get them; the bairn needs new shoes.

His generosity however, is constricted by the hours that he is allocated by some remote controller who, though she is fully cognizant of sales, turnover, and hours/sales ratios, knows nothing of Christine's needs, or Jason's temperament. If you conclude that such employment is little better than mediaeval serfdom, I would not contradict you.

We do not need to venture any further into such a labyrinth to understand that such irregular arrangements are not easily built into Christine's routine; or Janet's or Duncan's. They had patched up a contrivance but it creaked, and certainly could not stand further strain.

On that bleak night at the end of April, however, Janet,

thought she detected such strain in her normally easy-going husband. You don't live with someone for twenty-five years without picking up what's going on inside them. If you're sensitive, that is - and in domestic matters, Janet's antennae were finely tuned. Something was troubling Duncan; had been for a few days now, she felt. No one, and certainly not Janet, could call Duncan a complex character. Unlike his much more volatile wife, he went about life in a matter-of-fact way, taking the rough with the smooth, enjoying the ups and not allowing the downs to get him down. But something troubled him, and Janet, having failed, after a week of hinting and wheedling, to flush it out determined to tackle him. Friday night supper time seemed as good an opportunity as any. This time and this occasion had become, through routine rather than planning, the time when they looked back over the week now ending, summed up what they had achieved or not, as the case may be, and set out their ambition for the week ahead. All without writing anything in a Filofax.

'Something's bothering you, Duncan,' she said after she'd plonked down his cocoa in front of him.

'No, there's nothing,' he replied attempting a smile he intended to be confident, but which merely confirmed in Janet's mind that she'd hit the target.

'Is it Latchly? Have you hit a snag or something?'

'No, we're getting on fine. I showed you the layout Louie drew up.'

Janet detected diversionary tactics and moved to cut him off.

'That was weeks ago.'

Duncan pressed on.

'Well, we've been working on the granny flat bit, or should we say,' he said with a little laugh, 'the granny and granddad flat. We've got the outside wall built. It'll link the house with the steading. Once we've got that in place we can start clearing the space, installing the services, concreting the floor, and putting up the inside walls.'

Her husband's enthusiasm to tell her what she already knew increased Janet's suspicion that he was keeping back something she didn't.

'I've seen what you've been doing,' she said flatly. 'Now then, Duncan, what's bothering you? Is it the expense?'

'No, it's all within budget – what we said. I explained that to Louie. It's all costed.'

'What is then?'

'What's what?'

'What's bugging you? Is it your mother? Is she worse?'

'No, not really. No, she's coping fine. Dad's doing a lot more. He's being a bit more co-operative with Christine. The other day, in fact, he said he would stay in to keep mam company when Christine went off to her shift.'

'That's good to hear. But if it's not the building, and it's not the cost, or your mother, what is it?'

'There's nothing, really.'

'It's our Christine isn't it – or Hector? What is it?'

Duncan had no skill at deception. Backed into a corner he opened up.

'Yes, it's Christine. But I promised her not to tell you.'

'And I'm telling you must. She's my daughter as well as yours. She hasn't been suspended again, has she?'

'No, oh no, nothing like that. Far from that.'

'What is it then?'

'She's been offered night shift for the summer.'

Nightshift! Janet understood instantly Duncan's concern and why Christine didn't want her to know.

It could have been forecast. With Easter here and summer beckoning, visitors flood into Hecklescar, and money flows into the tills of the local shops, including the Co-op. When that happens, the distant controller wakes up and drops a few extra hours into Jason's goody bag. He then distributes them as he sees fit. With sales rising and lorry loads of supplies arriving late in the day twice a week, he has seen fit to lay on a night shift – to clear some of the full cages that are clogging the store room and preying on his nerves. That is why he suggested to Christine, that, if she were willing, he could offer her night shift on a Sunday night – and, perhaps, a Thursday for the summer months.

They are strapped for cash, this young couple. A few short months ago Hector found himself without a home. At least, that is the way Christine had viewed it. Harassed by debt and debtors, his father Hercules, as we know, had sailed out of Hecklescar for destinations unknown and untraceable, leaving his family to fend for themselves. Olivia, his mother, who had long since shed her maternal duties, felt no twinge of conscience to prevent her from joining her sophisticated friends on a three-month world cruise. Technically, of course, Hector could have gone on living in the grand house in Alexandra Drive on his own, but to Christine he had become an orphan and needed the love and protection of a home. She had determined to provide it - even in the teeth of her mother's opposition. Unadvised by more sceptical heads, the young couple had entered into a deal with a local landlord, Con McConachie, to rent one of his apartments on the Poplace Estate. Hector, apprenticed to Duncan did not earn much and Christine is paid a mere pound over the minimum rate. 'A living wage', they call it, but they couldn't live on it for, with her hours limited by contract, the couple discovered that, every month, half of Christine's wage had to be handed to McConachie.

Their move to Latchlaw had saved McConachie's rent. But, always, in Christine's mind, nagged the doubt that once Duncan had finished the refurbishment of the old farmhouse, she and Hector would have to move out to make way for her parents.

Janet had approved the move. Indeed, she had negotiated their release from McConachie. Nevertheless, she continued to suspect her daughter of engineering a more permanent residence at the farmhouse. She is correct; Christine likes living at Latchlaw and doesn't want to move out. Where would they go? They have talked about having a house of their own, but they can't afford it. And the thought of paying out their hard-earned money in rent sickens them. Then there's the furniture! How do we save for that?

The nightshifts would help. It would not increase her overall hours but it would increase her pay. For night working she would be paid a premium of time-and-a-third.

'Take a few days to think about it,' Jason had said.

She had thought about it and considered, somewhat apprehensively, how her mother would react when or, rather, if, she plucked up the courage to tell her what the manager had offered. Now her father had removed the option of the 'if'.

CHAPTER FORTY-TWO

If you expected Janet not to tackle Christine about the night shift before Christine introduced it, then I have made a poor job of describing her. In Janet, concern always trumped consideration. She summoned Christine to a family conference on her way home from that horrible shift on Saturday.

Saturday, quarter past nine, on a dark, dreich night; three tired people. A poor combination for a conversation of any sort. But this is not of any sort; it is the most disturbing variety: where none of the participants knows what they really want and are not at all sure of what they don't. But one person will not be there to speak for herself, yet she will be the chief beneficiary of any helpful decision, or the worst sufferer from a poor one: Alice

I'm sure some poet, writer, artist, philosopher or, if none of these, some social scientist, will have defined human life as a matter of width. When young, we shift first from narrow womb to encircling arms and, not a lot later, are hemmed in by the rails of our cot, the walls of our house and, should we brave the great outside world, by the back garden fence. As our strength increases and our imagination flares, we stretch our boundaries to reach out for education, work, fresh fields and fresh faces. When we are old enough and reckless enough we may venture into the world beyond our school, village, town or neighbourhood, and find in it much to enjoy and little to frighten us. Soon, what had been new and exciting becomes familiar and commonplace. Then as our years and prosperity advance we venture further, searching for the pot at the end of the job rainbow, visiting relatives in the Antipodes, holidaying at historic sites, or on exotic beaches, jungle safaris or venturing into any other location that will give us bragging rights over our more sedentary neighbours. Some wait until work is over then raid the pension pot to give Marco Polo a run for his money: 'we're just back from Mongolia; stayed two nights in a ger; next year we're booked on the Silk Road Safari'. Then what? Well, I'd like a pound for every seventy-five-plus-year-old who has confided that nowadays they prefer the local pub, a dander round the houses and their own bed at night.

Alice had never taken more of the earth's space than a short ration. She had spent much of her life looking after a house and, even in her decline, she had continued doing so with only the occasional lapse. But always such work had been enriched with activities outside the house. Way back it had been in the fields, rogueing swedes, planting sprouts, gathering tatties, clearing out hedge bottoms, all in fresh air under bright skies with the sound of gulls or geese in her ears. When Alistair gave up labouring at Fairnieside, she helped in his vegetable plot with the year-long routine: digging, planting, hoeing and weeding, or in gathering, cleaning and storing the produce of his labour.

Her life shrank considerably when they left Fairnieside and found themselves incarcerated in the house-cum-hen coop on the Poplace estate. Even then, although Alistair retreated to his chair and bottle, Alice ventured into other women's more spacious houses, taking over the work they found constraining: cleaning, dusting and washing floors. For a while she had the run of Avignon, Octavia and Hercules semi-mansion in the less cramped part of the town.

Alice had never thought of herself as confined by her dependence on a low wage and what others might reckon a limited sphere of interest and activity. Of course, she enjoyed the occasional week they had spent on holiday; never abroad, always self-catering, usually somewhere north of Perth, but not too far north. No trips to festivals, theatre of even a cinema outside the town, had ever extended her enjoyment. She found enough to please her at home, in the garden, in the shops, down the pier, the local pantomime and, particularly, in the company of friends and her son, Duncan and his family. If she had visions beyond that, they were generated only by her weekly attendance at the Parish Kirk. She wanted nothing more and envied no-one. She was, in the words of Thomas Gray, one of those who *'Along the cool-sequester'd vale of life, kept the noiseless tenor of their way'*. Thomas, if he is listening, no doubt derives not a little satisfaction that his words are still quoted two hundred and seventy years after he wrote them, but he still lies at a disadvantage to Alice. He glanced at such a life in passing and, I suspect, half-frightened, jotted down a few words then hurried on. Alice, however, keeps to the noiseless tenor every day. And does so without brooding on it, or thinking that it might lead to acclaim if she composed a few verses about it. She lives it because no other life has ever presented itself.

Alice had never touched the walls that hemmed her in, but now found herself confined to the house when Christine and Hector left for work and Alistair retreated to the garden. Of course, if Duncan were working in the steading, or Alistair came in from the garden the door would be opened, but most of the time when she went to the door, she found it locked.. Typically, she did not complain, but when Duncan or Janet called in, as they did most days, they often found her asleep in her chair. Drained of activity, interest and purpose, her life had now become delineated largely by the kitchen at Latchlaw.

Longer confinement would be on its way, if Christine accepted the manager's offer and started working nightshift.

She would be out of the house for even longer, and when at Latchlaw, would be in bed needing her sleep, not keeping an eye on her granny downstairs. Christine did not need anyone to explain this. She lived with Alice daily and could not set her aside.

When she arrives for the meeting that dark Saturday night Christine carries with her this troubling item for the agenda - and more. Although they need the money, she doesn't relish creeping through a half-lit silent store with only Solemn Susan for company. She likes Susan: she's reliable and hard-working, but lives on the down slope of life and regularly forecasts that they are not going to get through the work on time. They always do. The day after night shift has to be written off too, and she won't enjoy being in bed when Hector is up and about. The dowdy bedroom, too, weighs on her mind, especially when she wakes up in it at two in the afternoon. She has done her best to brighten it up, but she hasn't been able to do with it what she would like, partly because she doesn't have the money, and partly because she knows her mother is watching her to detect any sign that they are settling in for a long stay.

Janet and Duncan had stepped in to give relief when Christine's shifts demanded it, one of them sleeping the night at Latchlaw to keep an eye on Alice when their daughter had an early start. They did it; and, as far as Christine could tell, carried it out with good grace. Both, however, disliked it. They didn't like leaving home last thing at night; they didn't like the cramped bed in the little bedroom at Latchlaw; they didn't like sleeping apart nor trailing home tired in the morning. Add to these, the sickening knowledge that such sacrifices constituted merely a stopgap not a solution, and you can understand their dissatisfaction with the arrangement. It worked, but it creaked in the mind of both Janet and Duncan. That it provided easier rest for Christine, and security for Alice was all that commended it; in all other respects it chafed.

Listed companies pay their chairmen and Chief

Executives megabucks to steer them through the choppy waters of business life. But when these well-furnished men and women close the doors of their offices at night and retire to their suburban mansions, they are advised to lock their anxieties in their desks and not take them home. They may then find relaxation and relief in the warm bosom of family life.

These three non-executives, however, have no such escape. For it is the family that troubles them. Their concerns must be brought to the kitchen table and dealt with there - without corporate resources to call on. Christine needs the nightshift to pay the bills; Duncan and Janet are strapped for cash; Alice needs care. They must find their own way forward.

'I'd like tae dae it, but I can't see how it can be done,' Christine said after explaining what the manager had offered. She picked up her cup, drank a little tea and studied the tablemat on which it had rested. The words rattled out of her as if she were anxious to be rid of them.

'I'll need to tell Jason I can't do it.'

Now, we may ask ourselves, why, if she is going to turn it down, had she not done so already? Would it not have been better, kindlier, not to mention it at all? Of course, but then, if she did that, there would be no chance of extra money. So, we may suspect that although she says that she can't expect her mother and father to come up with a solution, her hope is pinned on little else. Precisely what solution, she doesn't know. But please do not label her devious. She is young and Janet and Duncan are her parents. They have cleared her way ahead now for over twenty years; to whom else should she turn when faced with such a decision.

'It'd go towards the bedroom suite we're saving up for. But I can't expect Hector to look out for granny when I'm not there. And granddad – I can't speak to him about it. But I can't see how I can do it. It's not fair to ask . . . .'

The sentence died in her mouth and she looked up into her mother's face. She felt wretched for she knew what she should not ask; did not want to ask, not out loud. She understands profoundly that they had moved into Latchlaw on the understanding she would be there for Alice. She felt acutely that she had already let down her mother and father; felt badly that when she had an early shift they had to leave the comfort of their own bed the night before and sleep in the cramped bed in that musty room. Yet who else could she ask?

Janet studied her daughter, her face expressionless. She sat opposite to her across the kitchen table, a mug of tea in her hand. Thoughts careered through her mind, shouting and screaming, colliding and competing:

'You went there to stand by your granny. You never mentioned night shift. I knew it was all a ploy to get to Latchly and you'll not be wanting to leave now. But when it comes to responsibility. . .. Stop, Janet stop, that's not fair; she'd done her whack. I hate having to go there. So does your father. Bedroom suite! Saving up for a bedroom suite! You have a bed; we put one in for you; is that not enough for now? Can it not wait? Do we come second after a bedroom suite? What about Hector? Where is he? Can he not stand in? Of course not, it's not his place to look after an old woman. Well then, where's Alistair? Shouldn't he be doing something. Charging off to that bloody garden. His wife is more important that his. . .Janet. Janet, listen to yourself! This is Christine, your daughter, your own child, your only child, your own daughter, your own dear daughter.'

She glanced at Duncan and saw instantly that he knew what was rampaging through her mind; that he could hear every word.

Christine had dropped her head but was still speaking.

'I can't expect you and dad to cover for the nightshift an' a'. Ye do enough as it is. I'll say to Jason. . ..'

'Don't turn it down,' snapped Janet. 'Your father and I will talk it over to see what can be done. When does Jason need to know?'

'Monday,' replied Christine, hurriedly. 'He said, Monday.'

'Come down tomorrow at teatime. We'll see then.'

Christine made no reply but stood up to leave. She glanced at her mother expecting her to stand up too. But Janet remained seated and simply patted her on the waist as she passed her.

Duncan then escorted Christine out of the door, into his van and drove her through the rain to Latchlaw.

CHAPTER FORTY-THREE

Duncan did not return from Latchlaw immediately, but when he entered the house he found Janet still seated at the table.

Ever since they had decided, back in the dying months of last year, to pack up home at Prior Road and prepare to move to Latchlaw, Janet had dreaded this moment. The moment when all other roads ran out. She knew the evacuation day would certainly come; they had come too far to turn back. She had worked assiduously at her preparations for such a move. (Had she not already carted several cases from her treasured hoard in the garret to the charity shop?) Yet, if she listened to her own heart, she would admit that she taken temporary refuge in Duncan's estimate that the house at Latchlaw could not be made ready for them until September, a full five months away yet.

'You took your time,' she said sharply.

Duncan, who had loved his wife long enough to catch her mood and attract her irritation, sat down at the table across from her and sought to pour oil on troubled waters.

'It's mother,' he said gently. 'When we got there, she had all their shoes on the table. We had to help her to put them away.'

He gave a little laugh. But Janet did not join in.

'Shoes? She had shoes on the table?'

'Yes, her own and Alistair's. Dad's boots as well. She said she was sorting them.'

'Sorting them?'

'She'd cleaned and polished them and taken out all the laces and washed them, then she'd removed all the insoles, and cut them up.'

'Cut them up? Why had she done that?'

'They were dirty, she said. She said she'd get new ones the next time she was in Gainslaw at the shops.'

'But she never goes to the shops.'

'It must have been something she did years ago.'

'Washing the laces? I haven't heard of anyone ever washing the laces.'

'I suppose when they were at the farm at Fairnieside, and Alistair had been in mud, she would do it then, would she?'

'I've never heard of it.'

'The trouble was she couldn't work out which laces went in what shoes or boots.'

'Where was Alistair?'

'He'd gone to bed.'

'And left her with the shoes' snorted Janet, her irritation boiling over. 'Could he not see? No, of course he couldn't see. Or wouldn't see. He never sees.'

Duncan attempted to come to his father's defence.

'He'd probably gone before she started with the shoes. He goes to bed early.'

'Of course, he does', snapped Janet. 'Here are we worried sick about your mother and he couldn't care less as long as he can scuttle off to his garden – or go to bed.. It's his wife! Does he not understand? Alice is his wife! His responsibility! She's run after him all these years and now when she needs him – he goes to bed! And leaves her with shoes on the table! And he knows our Christine is going to find her like that. After a long shift. Knows she worries about her granny. Knows she is going to find her confused with his bloody boots on the bloody ...'

Her words ran out. They could no longer bear the anger she felt. She stood up and gripped the back of her chair. Rarely had Duncan heard Janet swear. But these were no casual expletives but screams of frustration.

'Sh, sh, love, sh', was all the response he could give. That and to stand up and pull her to him. At first she froze at his touch, then melted and let herself relax into his embrace.

For a few moments neither spoke. Then Janet broke away, returned to her seat, and asked quietly,

'Was she upset? About the laces?'

'No, I wouldn't say so, Christine says she doesn't get upset, well not often... '

Duncan hesitated.

'Well, what?' Janet pressed.

'Nothing, really, Christine said she found her in tears the other day. But it was a one off, more or less. It's not important.'

'It's important if it makes her cry,' insisted Janet. 'What is it?'

'Christine said she found her greetin' by the fire. When she asked her what was wrong, she said she'd been thinking about little Mary.'

'Little Mary? Who's Little Mary?'

'Well, that's it. Christine couldn't find out who Mary was.'

'Do you know?'

'I think I do. I think it must be the bairn they lost afore they had me.'

'She lost it early, didn't she?'

'Aye, six months. Something like that. But she must have been told it was a girl.'

'And you've never heard of it being a little girl, or Mary, before?'

'Never.'

Janet fell silent, then said slowly and softly,

'She wanted a little girl and would have called her Mary. Did call her Mary. In her heart has called her Mary down the years and never mentioned it to a soul.'

'Till now.'

'Till now. Bless her.'

They sat for a while without speaking.

'We're going to have to move to Latchly now, aren't we, love?' Janet professed.

'Yes,' replied Duncan.

CHAPTER FORTY-FOUR

John Henry would not forgive me if I gave the impression that only people with problems lived in Hecklescar. Whenever he is tempted to such a conclusion, he takes a leisurely walk through the town to see who can persuade him to change his mind. Please do not accuse him of being on the gloomy side of life himself. As a retired – and respected, bank manager he was, and still is, sought out to steer folk through stormy financial waters. And you do not need me to tell you that such waters are often swept by currents of a more personal nature. We have already seen his hand on the tiller of Anthony Douglas & Son, giving advice to Duncan and Janet, and steering Jen and young Callum into calmer waters.

Now that he has entered his eighty-fourth year, he finds it harder to set aside the concerns entrusted to him and easier to believe that the human race is run over an obstacle course. When he is thus tempted, he takes hold of himself and sets out on a slow walk round the town, hoping that he will meet someone that will restore his belief in the essential goodness of life.

In the Market Place he looks out for Timothy (who refuses to answer to Tim). He hopes to find him sitting on the bench outside the flower shop. Timothy counts cars. If he's there, John will join him on the bench and ask to see today's or even this week's statistics. Timothy, a cultured Englishman in his seventies, arrived in the town twenty years ago, and enjoys, so Ina will tell you, a very good pension, 'which makes you wonder why he lives in that poky upstairs flat in Home Street'.

If he is on the run from the police, Mafia or a mercenary mistress it doesn't show. He doesn't hide and can be found out and about most days. He has been known to leave the town for a few days, but not often and not for long. No-one knows why he came to Hecklescar, and he has never enlightened anyone who asked him. He will, however, enlighten anyone, like John Henry, who sits down beside him and takes an interest in his statistics. If, however, he suspects that you are from the council and would like to use his findings to determine council policy he will clam up and claim his information is anecdotal and confidential. What fascinates John Henry is that he sits on the seat and counts the number of cars that go past, by make, year of registration and colour. What use does he make of the information that he collects? None that John Henry can fathom. Indeed, it seems a point of principle with Timothy that he does nothing with the information – apart from conveying it to his computer when he gets home. 'It's an interest,' he says. and after an hour puts away his pad, goes to the baker's shop for a chocolate slice of some sort and a paper cup of their latte coffee, takes it back to his seat and enjoys it.

'There are now thirty-three percent more Mercedes on the street than there were thirteen years ago,' he told John Henry one day.

'What do you make of that?' asked John, thinking that Timothy may wish to draw the conclusion that Hecklescar had become a little more affluent, or that Mercedes are now cheaper.

'Do we need to make something of it?' replied Timothy pleasantly.

One bleak day, in March John Henry had his spirits lifted by a child he estimated at no more than three years. He spied her trailing along the Bantry with her dishevelled parents hurrying to thaw out in the comfort of their caravan up on Fort Point. But the little girl was no hurry. She had become intrigued by the drainage holes in the sea wall. Spaced every ten yards or so along the path, they allow the water dashed over the wall by the waves to flow back onto the beach. They also allowed smaller citizens to glimpse the sea they could not view over the sea wall. The little girl stopped, looked through every one of them, smiled and shouted down the tube,

'Hello, sea!'

Caught up in her little game she felt neither wind nor rain and brightened the day around her.

Then there is Moira Tait who exercises her dog on the beach but never actually moves. Her daughter decided that her mother needed more exercise so bought her a dog, and elicited the promise that every day she would run it on the beach. She fulfils her promise by walking the dog to the beach then letting it loose to run along the wave line while she watches it from the Bantry, calling it back occasionally to her. If it doesn't look too tired she sends it off on another circuit.

'The exercise,' she says, 'does me good – and the dog likes it.'

If a fishing boat is landing, John will stand to watch the careless rhythm of the landing of the catch: lowering of the derrick, the whine of the winch as it takes up the strain, boxes rising like Lazarus from the hold, to be swung and lifted to the quayside, there to be slotted and stacked sweetly onto a pallet by an attentive young fisherman. John rejoices in the scuttling forklift truck turning and weaving, lifting and layering in the hands of the podgy driver who looks so settled on the truck that you could well believe that he had been bought along with it and has wheels instead of legs. Above all, John welcomed the bustle and the brouhaha, the shouting and banter; men singing, dancing and swearing through their work.

John always greeted the three (or four, or sometimes five) old diehards who sit daily at the table outside Napolitano's café. The kindly café owners do all they can to accommodate these ladies: cushioning the chairs, supplying warm blankets for their legs and, in the coldest weather, placing an electric heater under the table. All this because they like to puff their cigarettes while they drink their coffee. The Great Guardians of our health have decreed that it must be so to protect them from diseases caused by smoking. That the women might die of pneumonia caused by sitting outside in the cold does not seem to trouble them. To John Henry that same undercurrent of exuberant life that he saw in the little girl, Moira and the fisherman runs through the defiance of these old women.

Mark you, there's one old woman (well not so old, she can't be much more than sixty), that he will cross the street to avoid if he is in a hurry. So would you unless you have an hour and a half to spare and an interest in unsuccessful medical procedures.

Again, when he calls in a tradesman to fix something in his house he likes to watch them at work. He admires their skill, patience, precision and general cheerfulness. It is not true that he had his bathroom refitted just because he heard that Martin the plumber was short of work. It happened not long after he lost Lizzie, and no doubt lifted him. Was it for company? To have someone else in the house? Someone to sit with him from time to time and share a cup of coffee, and a chat? Yes, of course. But more than that, he enjoyed seeing Martin at work, creating something fresh, clean and new, with his head and hands and the tools he brought to the task. And the lingering sense of joy, yes joy, that the new bathroom gave him. When he turned on the tap he felt a little of it run through him.

Just as he thrilled to the tiny gift of flowers from the little girl, Finch, two or three, four at the most, who has come to live in the house over the wall from him. It held ragwort, ox-eye daisy, buttercup, with a few strands of grass; weeds, some would call them, but presented to him solemnly by the little girl one dreary morning. They shone for days on his window sill and brought a smile to his lips every time he glimpsed them.

Then there are the young lads, life bursting out of them, tearing along on their bikes, standing on the pedals, skidding to a side-stop, hoisting the front wheel off the ground, scaring the living daylights out of the old biddies on their demur stroll along the prom. The bikers are oblivious to all except their racing companions and perhaps, the girls who are pretending not to watch from a bench on the Bantry outside the Co-op.

If all else fails, his trip to the Porthole for coffee on a Friday morning calls on him to join the busy, bustling, rumbustious energy that runs through Hecklescar and its people. It helps him dodge those dismal ditches that occasionally lie either side of his daily walk. He goes there, he will tell you, as a reward for doing the week's shopping, but do not be deceived, he goes to watch the folk who gather there, to chat, to confide, to gossip and to laugh.

Here is a dowdy woman bragging about the achievements of her granddaughter at university, accompanied by two large companions who, in their contrived interest, give every impression of wishing she would shut up, so they can boast about her man's big share this week, or to report on what the foreigners next door get up to late on a Saturday night. He watches one such 'foreigner' too; Leti the waitress serving them with their coffee and scones; a young woman as graceful as they are clumsy, and speculates that she has come to their little town for love of a local man and a better life for her children.

'We don't have a booking' says a young woman to Leti as she emerges from the staircase into the upstairs lounge. 'There are seven of us; do you have a free table?'

'Certainly,' she replies cheerfully. 'Inside or outside on the balcony?'

The young woman turns, open the door and shouts down the stairs. Five children bubble up the stairs and flood into the room; two boys about ten and three girls aged six or seven. Another young woman follows them in. There then follows an animated conference about whether they should sit in the restaurant or perch themselves on the covered balcony overlooking the street. Fortunately, the balcony loses out on the casting vote of one of the mothers. Fortunately, because it allows John Henry to observe this rollicking group. He purchases another cup of coffee and prepares to drink in the exuberance of the children.

I must stop; John Henry has plenty of time to sit with Timothy and garner these impressions and many more. But we must get on with our stories of those we have chosen to follow. I hope, however, that I have said enough to convince you that in the town of Hecklescar, while Janet and Duncan, Christine, Jakey, Nudge, Jen and Callum wrestle with adversity, there rolls on in vigour a deep and wide current of happiness and hopefulness.

CHAPTER FORTY-FIVE

'I hear there's some at the yard that's had their knuckles rapped,' nipped Madge, at a meeting of the coffee ladies towards the end of May.

Strictly speaking, Madge is not a member of the group, attending only because she works at McMaggies and serves the ladies with the coffee and scones; sort of ex-officio, I suppose. That is not to say she doesn't join in the conversation when she's not otherwise engaged or, in passing, even when she is. The ladies welcome her inputs for she is able to keep them informed of the comings and goings of their neighbours as she presides over the tables of the café, and presides with ears fully attuned to what those tables may have to say. Such opportunism irritates Ina, who likes to be thought of as the best informed of the group. On this May morning she has allowed her irritation to find expression in a complaint that her table is not furnished with little packets of brown sugar.

Ask any McMaggies' regular, however, and they will express surprise at Ina's complaint. Firstly, because Madge takes her responsibilities seriously and is meticulous in the provision of sugar, sweeteners and, where necessary, salt, tartar sauce, tomato ketchup, or any other condiment her customers may need. It is a matter of pride that her tables are always adequately provisioned and each diner leaves with a satisfied appetite and a smile on their face.

(The fact that there is no brown sugar on Ina's table

is not due to neglect, but to Horace from Horsham, a regular who regularly helps himself to the sugar sticks in the bowl to save him buying them. He had occupied the table immediately before Ina and her companions commandeered it.)

The ladies are also impressed by Ina's courage in challenging Madge for Madge runs McMaggies the way a sergeant major of the old school ran his squad of rookies. Customers, any customers, must do what they are told: where to sit, how to order, where to pay. If they obey they will enjoy the best of service and most delicious of meals. It they try to assert their consumer rights they will detect a certain cooling of the atmosphere and a need to ask for what they may have thought should have been provided in the first place. I once observed Madge whip away the fish and chips of a bumptious Edinburgh man with his knife and fork poised over them. It belonged to his wife; Madge advised him. He had not ordered coleslaw. Later, I understand, the wife thanked Madge for rescuing her meal; she had not dared protest herself..

On the day of Ina's complaint, Madge had brought the brown sugar and plonked it down on the table while Ina smirked at her companions. Hence Madge's revelation about knuckles being wrapped at the yard. And she knew whose knuckles they were: Jakey's.

Madge knew, most of the ladies knew, but it immediately became apparent that Ina did not.

Nor did she know that while she blustered in ignorance in McMaggies, Jakey sat drinking coffee in John Henry's backyard, whither he had gone to complain about his knuckles.

'This Clouston man of yours is throwing his weight about,' he complained. 'He made me send young Callum home last night. Ye ken, Jen's laddie, that needs work. I took him on but yon man said he wouldn't pay him. So, I had to send the lad home. You know what that means – to him – and to Jen.'

John Henry agreed it could be serious and asked Jakey to

explain.

You will remember that Nudge, anxious to find employment for Callum, Jen's son, had sponsored the lad through forklift training and that, in March, Callum had been awarded a Certificate of Competence that allowed him to operate a forklift truck. Since then, whenever he had opportunity, Nudge had reminded Jakey of Callum's newly acquired skill and tentatively enquired whether 'there was anything for the lad yet'. Most of these requests had gone in one ear and out of the other for questions buzz around Jakey all-day and every day. But, one day, Nudge's nudge struck at just the right time. Ches, skipper of the Bountiful, had called up Jakey late one evening to say that he was coming in with forty boxes; could Jakey load them straight into a van and ship them to a dealer in Blyth? Jakey agreed; he had the lorry. Then he discovered that Podge, the regular driver, was already occupied loading Nudge's trailer for the continent. The other forklift had gone in that day for repair, having again fallen victim to the potholes in Harbour Road. Jakey, never one to be stuck, had then tried to start the old truck he had kept in reserve. It resisted all his efforts and he found himself regretting again the new forklift truck he had demanded as far back as Hercules's days. In the end he switched Podge to the Bountiful and delayed Nudge's departure, and further frayed his already well-worn nerves. Next morning, he instructed Fiona to buy a new fork-lift truck.

'I had to push her,' said Jakey to John. 'She whined on about paper work and authorisation. But she eventually did what she was told. The truck came the end of that week, and not a day too soon. That weekend was mayhem. We needed all the trucks. So, I called in Jen's laddie. That's when the shit hit the fan.'

'What happened?'

'This morning his majesty arrived and I was summoned to the holy of holies; ye ken, the office up the stair. He asked me if I had taken on Callum. I said I had. He said I had no right to take on staff. I told him I had always called in workers when I needed them. 'No more', he said 'I thought I'd made that clear.' 'Naw, naw, I said, you said I would manage the yard. Well, I need workers for that.. 'Workers that are already on the payroll, already within our resources.' he said. 'If you want to increase the resources – like fork lift trucks and people, it has to be authorised."

'I tried to argue, but he wasn't having it. He told me to go down and lay the lad off. I refused. He said if I didn't do it he would do it himself. I couldn't have that so I walked out and told the lad to go home for the now. I said there'd been a mix up.'

'What happens now?' asked John Henry gently.

'Ah no ken. I thought I'd come to you.'

John Henry needed no reminding of Peter's charge 'to keep an open door' for Fiona, Angela and Jakey, but what could he do? The consequences of Callum's lay-off could be catastrophic – for Jen as well as the lad. The anxious face of Nudge that bleak January morning flashed through his mind; the morning when he had found Jen on the edge of the cliff.

Jakey was waiting.

'Did you explain what effect this might have on Callum – and his mother?'

'I tried, but he wis steamed up. He wouldn't let me speak. He said he'd had enough of my intran... something.'

'Intransigence?'

'Aye, something like that. He said he'd backed off before, but no more. I had to learn to play ball, he said.'

John Henry could find nothing to say.

'I need to get back,' mumbled Jakey. 'I'll leave it with you.'

'Oh, aye,' muttered John Henry wearily.

CHAPTER FORTY-SIX

After Jakey left, John Henry sat for the rest of the morning considering what he had heard. But whichever way he turned he could see no way forward. His dilemma rocked on his opinion that both sides were right and both wrong.

From the very beginning, ever since Clouston Pritchard set foot in Hecklescar six weeks ago until now, he had been aware of Jakey's antipathy to the man. Jakey had made no secret of his belief that the yard did not need a 'Chief Executive': 'what can he do that we have not always done?' John Henry recognised that, in such an opinion, no recollection remained of the crushing anxiety that Jakey had experienced when Hercules offered the company to him in the dying days of last year. Nor did it reflect his downright refusal to consider the manager's job when Peter Munro had offered it to him a few short weeks ago. Jakey had pulled down the shutters and hoped that the storm, whatever it was, that had almost sunk Anthony Douglas & Son had abated and life could go on much as it had before.

John recalled Peter's fears, fears built on experience, that the new man is always resented by the old hands. Peter had assured John that he needed to be away 'on business' for a few months, but John strongly suspected that Peter had removed himself from the temptation to inspect, pick over and, if necessary, intervene in Clouston's management of the company. Such fears, no doubt, lay behind Peter's appointment of John as a non-exec director and his request for him to be a listening ear for any of the staff that had something to tell him. He had even told John where he could be reached if a crisis blew up.

Was this such a crisis? John baulked at the thought. Surely, this scarcely counted as a business crisis? Was it not just a personal spat, an outburst, perhaps, from two tired, and frustrated men, both of whom had the best interests of the company at heart?

John Henry had not yet come to a fixed opinion of Clouston Pritchard. Was he the domineering bully Jakey took him to be? John could find no evidence for such an ogre. Fiona and Angela had not brought to him any complaint. Indeed, they seemed to rub along well with their new boss. John had not had much opportunity to get to know the man well but, had Clouston been as resentful as Jakey believed him to be, would he not have bridled at Peter's appointment of John as a director? Yet John had detected no such ill-feeling. Indeed, Clouston had made a point of sending John a short statistical report at the end of each week, and a fuller summary at each month end. Any questions that John raised Clouston answered quickly, expertly and helpfully. (And the old banker, in order to demonstrate his interest and support, made a point of raising questions.) On the evidence of these contacts, and the buzz on the street, John had come to believe that the yard had started moving in the right direction. Clouston's initiatives in marketing and contracts were paying off, his early investments seemed shrewd and his tighter control of finance were, at least, much more comprehensible than John Henry had ever seen before.

No, he would not trouble Peter with this spat; he would tackle it himself - for now, at least. He would go and talk to Clouston. If he were a reasonable man he would readily appreciate the damage inflicted on Callum - and Jen, by the loss of the job he so desperately needed for his mental stability.

Surely the man would understand that.

With that in mind, after lunch, he walked to the yard on the pier and was making his way through the fish room on his way to the office up the stair when Angela shouted to him.

'If you're looking for the boss; he's flitted.'

'Flitted? Who? Clouston?'

He must have sounded alarmed for Angela laughed.

'Fiona, too,' she smirked.

'Of course!' exclaimed John, 'I should have remembered; he did tell me. When was it? Last week?'

'The week before.'

'Up on the Industrial Estate, I believe.'

'Shangri-La.' shouted Angela. 'You can't miss it. There's a big notice: Anthony Douglas & Son; Head Office Site. We're going to put one up here saying: 'Fish and Guts Department'.

John Henry laughed and made his way up through the town to the new headquarters. Angela may poke fun at it, but the new site made sense.

The yard on the pier was cramped, dilapidated and, as Angela's potential sign hinted, smelly. It lay handy for the harbour, but could not be expected to impress potential customers. The new premises occupied an open site, and consisted of a spacious warehouse fronted by a cluster of offices and a small but airy reception area. As John Henry entered he was greeted by the receptionist, an attractive and smartly dressed young woman, who recognised him immediately.

'Hello, Mr Henry,' she said, 'We haven't seen you here before.'

'That's because this is my first visit - and very swish it is, I must say. It's Clara, isn't it?'

'Carol!'

'Carol! Yes, you sometimes used to serve me with my fish in the shop on the pier. Am I right?'

'Yes, Clouston offered me this job, and I'm getting into it. I'm going to college at the back end to learn a bit about it. Are you here to see him?'

'Yes, if he's around.'

'I'm afraid he's not in today but Fiona is. That's her office along there.'

John Henry thanked Carol and he warmed a little to Clouston Pritchard. Did the company really need such a swanky 'head office'? Could it afford it – and a full time 'receptionist'? Whatever, John thought, give the man credit for not hiring a floosy from the city. He had given this young woman an opportunity – and a dignity she would not otherwise have had.

John sensed Fiona's discomfort before she opened her mouth. In the old fishyard office, she had shared the room with the boss, be it Hercules, Peter and Clouston – or even with John himself for a while. Now she had a small space of her own, a sort of vestibule that led into what John imagined would be the Chief Executive's domain. From what he had seen of reception, John had half-feared that Clouston had treated himself to an executive suite, but Fiona's vestibule, whilst smart and obviously pristine, betrayed no hint of opulence. It appeared to John as a place for work, not leisure.

Fiona, John knew, could be prickly at the best of times, but her attitude this morning struck John as bordering on hostile. Did she feel uncomfortable in her new surroundings? The folk of Hecklescar despise show (unless it is their own). Perhaps she felt vaguely guilty about deserting the yard. (We heard what Angela had to say about it.) Or, perhaps, she had guessed why John Henry had come; had been anticipating it since her spat with Jakey; anticipating it and hoping that her boss might be there when John Henry arrived. Yes, thought John, that is much more likely.

Before John had time to speak she told him that Clouston wasn't in his office today. He'd be back tomorrow. John expected her to follow this information with the usual secretary's offer: 'Is there something I can help you with?', but she stopped suddenly and fidgeted with the papers on her desk as if she were going to carry on with her work. Disappointed, John turned for the door but before he reached it, he heard Fiona's voice.

'This is about Jakey and the boy isn't it?'

John turned and smiled, but before he could reply, Fiona rattled on.

'It's not as black and white as they're saying.'

'As I suspected,' he said pleasantly. 'Jakey's been to see me. But I think there's more to it than he told me. I wanted to hear what Clouston had to say.'

Fiona smiled nervously.

'Let me tell you what I know,' she said. 'Would you like a cup of coffee?'

'I would, if it comes out of that impressive-looking machine you have there.'

His continued warmth melted Fiona a little more and John sensed her relaxing as she busied herself with the coffee. She had something to say, he knew now – and wanted to say it.

After a short innocuous chat about the new premises and the shift to them, John broached the subject on both of their minds.

'Now then, you said it's not as black and white as it seems. But the lad's lost his job, hasn't he?'

'Not really,' replied Fiona, 'he never really had the job. Jakey had no right to tell him to start. He'd been told not to do it.'

'Had he?'

'Yes. Definitely and clearly.'

'Definitely? Who by? Clouston?'

'No by me. I told him that he needed to raise a staff requisition. But he ignored me and went ahead and told the lad to start.'

'*You* told him.'

'Yes, I did, but I was following Clouston's instructions. He told me I had to insist on a requisition. After the forklift purchase.'

Fiona then expanded the story Jakey had told John Henry; expanded it and illuminated it. Certainly, as Jakey had told John, Fiona had been difficult about ordering up the forklift truck. But what Jakey had omitted and Fiona now explained was that she had gone to Clouston before signing off the order, and had been disappointed that Clouston didn't back her up.

'Give Clouston credit', she grumbled, 'he told me to give Jakey one last chance.'

'One last chance?' remarked John.

Fiona sighed.

'Yes, one last chance - after a lot of chances.'

'Chances for what?'

'To co-operate. I'm sorry to have to say it. I didn't want to clipe. But Angela would say the same if you asked her. From the very first day that Clouston stepped inside the yard, Jakey has been a pain. Nothing Clouston does is right. He moans all the time that Clouston has changed things. Certainly, he has – but then a lot needed changing. Hercules kept Jakey under control, but once he'd gone Jakey has done whatever Jakey wanted. Or tried. I had to keep telling him that we couldn't just order things up and take people on. Dear knows what sort of deals he did with the suppliers – and the customers. All by word of mouth. Nothing written down – or on the computer. Nobody, except, Jakey, knew what was going on – and sometimes he'd forgotten what he'd agreed. Every week I could guarantee Dodgy Donald, ye ken, from Mallaig, bending my ear about something he said he'd agreed with Jakey – and no-one here knew anything about it.'

As she recited this litany, Fiona became more and more agitated. John Henry interrupted the flow to calm her down.

'Clouston sorted it out; brought it under control, would you say?'

'Yes, well, he did, but Jakey seemed to take a delight in poking holes in the system. He wouldn't fill in the forms. And he kept trying to bend the rules. A lorry load of polystyrene packaging turned up out of the blue. I didn't know anything about it until the driver turned up with the delivery note. Jakey had sent him. To put me on the spot. I refused to sign it off – but Jakey went to Clouston and he told me I had to do it. He apologised, mind you; said we had to give Jakey time to adjust. I told him that Jakey had no intention of adjusting; it's not in his nature. I was bealing. I'd taken a stand on what the boss wanted and he didn't back me up..

'What about the forklift truck?'

'Jakey tried his old trick of speaking to the supplier. But we'd put out a memo informing them that the system had changed and now there must be paperwork. That stymied Jakey. Then he came to me. I gave him the requisition but he refused to fill it in. Then I think he must have rung Clouston – and Clouston told me to raise it – instructed me to raise it, I should say! I could see Jakey crowing all over when he came to sign it.'

'But he did sign it?'

'He did – and Clouston told me there would be no more like it. No more word of mouth. No more, he said! I could see by his face that he was as pissed off as I was with Jakey's antics.'

'Then Jakey took on Callum?'

'He did - and don't believe he did it all out of kindness; he knew exactly what he was doing. Thought he could get away with it, and poke it at us. Well, we called his bluff. Well, the boss did.'

'Does Clouston understand the background, I mean the lad's mental health=and Jen's?'

'Yes, I think so. I'd mentioned it. And Jakey had bent his ear with the sob story.'

At last John Henry felt he should step in.

'It's more than a sob story. You know his history. This could destroy the lad. What's Nudge saying about it?'

'Nudge is away with a load to Spain. He probably doesn't know anything about it.'

'And Jen?'

'She had an early shift. She went away before seven. She'll not be back 'til six or seven o'clock the night.'

'So, Callum would go home on his own.'

'He has a partner,' began Fiona, then her confidence – and antagonism gave way. She seemed to know what John Henry had discovered the night he walked him to his house. That he would not find much support at home.

'He'd have nobody,' she added seriously. 'He'll be on his own somewhere.'

'I must go and find him,' exclaimed John, standing up.

'Jakey might know where he is. I think I saw him with him when he left.'

CHAPTER FORTY-SEVEN

Jakey knew where Callum had gone. And such knowledge demonstrates both his deceit and his concern. John found him standing on the pier in animated discussion with the driver of a large truck. He had come too early or too late. John, agitated and, we can understand, not a little annoyed, could scarcely wait until the truck moved off before tackling Jakey.

'D'ye ken where Callum is? I've been speaking to Fiona. She tells me that both Nudge and Jen are away. So, where's the lad? He should not be left on his own after what happened.'

Jakey fixed John with a stare.

'I know precisely where Callum is,' he stated, 'because, unlike some, I care about the lad.'

John was in no mood for war games. He sighed and asked brusquely,

'Where is he?'

'He's at the Training School up on the Industrial Estate.'

'What's he doing there?' John demanded irritably.

'Refresher Training for Forklift truck drivers.'

'Does he need that? He only qualified a few weeks ago. He can't need refresher training already.'

Jakey leaned closer to John and smirked.

'I know that. You know that. Dave at Scottish Borders

FLT knows that. But that's where the lad is, and that's what he's doing.'

Jakey's smugness ignited John's frustration.

'Jakey,' he snapped, 'would you stop talking in riddles? Why is Callum re-training?'

'Because I asked Eatit – Dave from Birmingham, that is, to, (what's the word?), occupy him for the day. I agreed it with Nudge. The lad couldn't just be laid off and sent packing. That would have knocked him. You know that. That's what they wanted.'

'That's what who wanted?'

Jakey sneered

'The engineer and the oily rag.'

The reply shocked John. This had gone way beyond what he had anticipated. He shook his head and drew in a deep breath. Jakey took this as a sign that he needed to explain. He did so almost gleefully.

'The boss man – and Fiona!'

'No, they did not!' John growled. 'You created the problem, not them.'

Jakey at last caught John's drift. But pressed on.

'Nah, nah, John,' he protested, 'I took the lad on – and I informed Fiona, and told her why, as instructed. Then the roof fell in.'

'But Fiona told you that if you wanted to take him on you had to put in a requisition, and she would present it to Clouston for authorisation.'

'She never did!'

'She's telling me lies, then! She said that Clouston had warned you when he agreed to the forklift truck that he would let it pass this time but there would be no more off the cuff purchases – or hiring.'

'Aye, he might have done. But he does that all the time. He's the big 'No man'. That's all he does: sits in his new office and tells us what we can't do.'

'There's a lot more to it than that,' started John

Jakey snorted.

'If there is, we never needed it before.'

'Oh, but you did. What do you think Hercules did?'

'Ran the company into the ground from what I make out. Wouldn't listen to us sloggers. It's the same with all these high-heid anes.'

'What, with Peter? Where would the company be if he hadn't bailed the yard out?'

'Peter, aye. He got behind us. Not this man. He's in it for himself. What's the first thing he does? Builds a fancy office up on the estate and hires himself a receptionist. Why can't Fiona do that? She did it before. So, it's alright for him to hire floosies for the office but not fork-lift truck drivers for the fish.'

This had run out of hand with Jakey in full cry. John determined to bring him to heel. He'd try reason once more.

'There's a lot more to running a company than sticking fish in boxes,' he said bluntly. He intended to go on to list what he meant but, before he could pick up the words he needed, Jakey cut back in. He had no need to search for his words, they jostled in his mouth daily.

'Oh, aye, we ken that!' replied Jakey, sarcastically. 'Scribbling at a desk, sitting round the table discussing – (what is it?) strategy! Chatting with other executives 'on the blower'; careering round the country on expenses. Then lecturing the troops on productivity. But productive? How many prawns do they put on the table – in France or Spain, eh? Not a one. Without fish in boxes, we'd all be on the street – and they wouldn't ken it for a fortnight!'

Clearly Jakey had closed his mind to any other opinion but his own, and John understood in full what Fiona (and others, to be sure) had been suffering at his hands. What John said next he had determined never to say – not to Jakey anyway.

They were still standing where John had found Jakey - on the quay across from the Old Barque. The old banker held up his hand to block the tirade, then smiling, said quietly,

'Jakey, let's go inside. There's something I need to say, but it's a bit public out here. Have you time to nip into the Old Barque for a quick cuppa?'

'I'll need to get on,' replied Jakey and, for a moment, John thought he'd turn away. Then, apparently intrigued by what John might have to say, he looked at his watch and replied,

'You go in. I'll make a couple of calls then join you.'

When he entered the restaurant, he found John sitting in the farthest corner of the lounge.

He sat down and ordered tea. John had yet another cup of coffee.

'Jakey,' he said gently, 'I wouldn't say what I am going to say unless I thought it absolutely necessary. And I believe that it is necessary to avoid a disaster – for the business – and for you. If you go on bad-mouthing Clouston Pritchard, there can only be one outcome. He's going to sack you.'

'He wouldn't dare,' snorted Jakey.

'Oh, but he would,' stated John. 'I've come across more than one Clouston in my time – and they don't like their managers slagging them off. In the end it'll come to a showdown. And you'll lose.'

Clearly, the thought that he might lose his job had never occurred to Jakey. He stared at John in disbelief.

'Naw, naw,' he protested, 'the yard can't run without me.'

'I know that,' said John. 'But the chances are Clouston Pritchard does not. So, my guess would be that yard, without you, would close down. It's almost evitable.'

Then he added with a smile,

'You know how to work it – to everyone else it's a mystery.'

Jakey didn't share his humour.

'Peter would never allow that. He's got a lot of money tied up in the yard.'

'And he doesn't expect to get any of it back. If he'd been

looking for a profitable or even viable investment he wouldn't have put a penny in it.'

'But...' started Jakey.

John was not be shifted. He had something to say and he must say it.

'Jakey, let me be blunt. When Peter offered you the chance to run the yard – all of it, you turned him down.'

He studied Jakey's face and saw that his words had gone home. But he pressed on.

'Last November, Jakey, I hate reminding you of it, you came greetin' to my door. Remember. Hercules had offered you the yard, lock, stock and barrel. D'ye mind?'

'That wis different,' mumbled Jakey, but without conviction. He picked up his tea and drained the cup.

'No, it wisnae different,' said John falling into the local dialect. 'Now if there is nothing to it, nothing for Clouston to do, why didn't you take it on? I'll tell you why, Jakey. Because there's a hell of a lot more. You knew it then – and if you'd face it - you know it now.'

Jakey glanced at John for a second or two, then put down his cup. As he did so, John noticed, his hand trembled. Had his eyes filled with tears? John couldn't be sure. He had hurt his friend; he knew that. Jakey had shut out of his mind those dark days at the end of last year. John had broken down the door and let the demons loose. He had had to be cruel to be kind. But what now? What could he say? He felt sorry for the man but did not want to give up the ground he had gained. Jakey must quit his campaign against Clouston, and accept him, yes, as his boss and knuckle down to his way of managing the company - with a discipline and regulation Jakey had never known before.

'I can't see him doing that. He's trapped by his past,' thought John as he scrabbled for something to say.

Then Jakey spoke and John detected that he had turned to face forward.

'I didn't want to hire the lad,' he muttered; 'not put him

on the payroll. I know that. Just call him in for this job. It's what we've always done. Ask Angela – or Nudge, or any of them. We have a whole battalion of workers we can call in when there's a bulge. It's the only way we can operate. We couldn't take them all onto the payroll. I know that.'

'They're on a sort of casual workers' register, are they?' suggested John soothingly, 'and Fiona will already have their PAYE details.'

'If she'd asked I could have got her the lad's details. But she wouldn't listen. She was all stoked up. She was determined to black-ball the lad. Both her and him.'

John saw this outburst as Jakey scrambling back into his dugout.

'Why should they want to do that? Fiona is as concerned about Callum as I am – and you are.'

'Fiona's taking his side, isn't she? She's soft on him - and he kens Jen from way back - Callum's mother. From what the girls say, there's history there, John – and a mystery. He kent her at Peterhead.'

John was not deflected.

'I'm not interested in tittle-tattle, Jakey. I give you credit – and Nudge for giving the lad a chance. But it has to be done properly. Sending the lad for training will do for today, but what happens to-morrow?'

'He can stay there for the rest of the week.'

'No,' said John firmly, 'I tell you what is going to happen. You are going to fill in a requisition, and Callum an application form, and I'm going to see if I can persuade Clouston – and Fiona to put the lad on the casual list. I'll also explain Callum's position to Clouston and try to persuade him to let the lad start back straightway. Fiona will back me up, I think.'

'You've nae chance!' mumbled Jakey, but, John recognised, his voice had lost its spiteful edge. Jakey stood up to leave. Running away again?

But running away from what? Certainly, he resented Clouston and didn't want to conform to his new, more disciplined, methods. But was that all? John suddenly recalled something he had mentioned to Peter when Peter talked of putting Jakey in the top job. He had told Peter that Jakey was 'barely literate?' Could that be trapping Jakey in his belligerence? That he did not want to admit that filling in forms frightened him?

'I tell you what, Jakey,' said John quietly, 'why don't you come up to the house to-night and we'll fill out the requisition together? I'll collect one from Fiona later today.'

Jakey bridled, glowered at John and, for a moment or two, John expected an outburst. John could almost hear the turbulence in the man's mind.

'About half past seven,' put in John before Jakey could speak.

'Aye, a' right; half-seven,' muttered Jakey.

CHAPTER FORTY-EIGHT

Yet again John Henry's instinctive concern harassed him. Suppose it were true, that Jakey's poor literacy contributed to his resentment of Clouston. What did he, John, propose to do about it? Surely he couldn't tackle Jakey? What else? He could help him with this form, but that would simply paper over the cracks. The same thing would happen when Jakey next wanted a piece of equipment or an extra pair of hands.

However, he had set out to help the man and he would carry it through. He trekked up to the headquarters to pick up the paperwork from Fiona. His expedition did nothing to improve his uneasiness. Fiona made it clear or, so he felt, that Jakey had burned his boats and that Clouston would not relent and let him take on Callum.

Such doubts pestered John Henry as he opened his door at half-past seven and showed Jakey into his living room - and to the table where John had laid out the form and a pen. John had studied the form and found it, thanks to Fiona, perhaps, neither long nor complex. It comprised a single A5 sheet and asked only for the job title, a short sentence outlining the duties and where it would be carried out. An additional box asked for a short description of the sort of person who might fill the position; another, for a brief justification for the request. He handed Jakey the form and watched him closely as he studied it. It seemed to him that Jakey scanned the form rather than read it, and very soon handed it back.

'What about it, then, Jakey,' asked John quietly. 'Should we fill it in? Do you want a pen?'

John expected that Jakey would turn down the offer and ask John to complete it, but Jakey took the pen and set about filling in the requisition. John watched with interest. Jakey wrote very much as a child would write, slowly, deliberately, printing the answers rather than writing them. Only once did he ask for John Henry's help. He asked how to spell 'qualified': did it have one 'f' or two?

When the form was complete Jakey handed it to John.

'You could take it,' said John, 'but if you'd rather I did it. . ..'

'You're wasting your time,' snapped Jakey. 'He won't agree to it.'

'We'll need to see,' smiled John, 'I'm seeing him tomorrow morning.'

Had the conversation finished then, John Henry would have been no further forward. Alright, he had established that Jakey could at least read and write. But what is one form, one simple form? What other demands would come from Clouston in the next few months; demands that would overstrain his limited abilities - and, no doubt, lead to further confrontation as Clouston insisted on systematic communication and Jakey persisted in using word of mouth? John could see no way of navigating any settlement between the two men without betraying Jakey's limitations.

John stood up, and with further assurances showed Jakey to the door. Jakey seemed reluctant to leave. As if there were something on his mind. At the door, he turned, looked John in the face and said to him,

'You didn't think I could do that, did you?'

John immediately understood what he meant, but did

not betray it.

'Couldn't do what?' he smiled, then continued deliberately misunderstanding what his companion meant.

'I think a lot of you, Jakey, for coming into line. It takes a big man to do that. It shows sense – and courage. And a way forward.'

Jakey smiled.

'Yeah,' he said bluntly, 'but not that. You didn't think I could write, did you?'

John put out his arm and laid his hand on Jakey's shoulder.

'Fair cop, Jakey,' he said with a gentle smile. 'I've been rumbled. I wondered how you'd get on. But come back in, and we'll talk about it. If you want?'

Jakey came back in, and within an hour, they had agreed that John Henry should arrange some basic literacy education for his friend. He knew just the man to undertake it: Timothy; he whom we met on the bench outside the flower shop counting cars, who, as well as being an educated man, is also discreet. And he doesn't belong Hecklescar.

CHAPTER FORTY-NINE

'Now then', said Clouston pleasantly, as Fiona showed John into his office. 'What can I do for you?'

John settled himself into the chair at the front of the manager's desk and quickly reminded him of Callum's bungled recruitment, and sketched in briefly what he, John, had done since.

'I've had a word with Jakey – and I think he now understands the need to follow procedure', he said pleasantly.

At this he had expected Clouston to relax, but the manager, John noted, seemed to stiffen.

'That's good,' he said, (John thought somewhat tersely). 'Thanks for straightening him out.'

'He has filled in a Personnel Requisition and I have handed it to Fiona.'

'That's good', repeated Clouston, 'I'll have a look at it'.

'I think you understand the lad's position,' John continued. 'He's Jen's laddie, and has been through a rough patch. Nudge paid for him to be trained. But he needs the job. I think that was in Jakey's mind when he took him on. I've passed an application form to Nudge and he will see it is properly submitted.'

As John recounted these words, the manager put his

hand to his mouth, leaned away from his desk and sank back into his chair. When John had finished, Clouston sat for a while looking at John without speaking.

Then, in a low voice, he said, 'John, I thought you understood what I am trying to do here. I had hoped that you may have picked it up from the briefing notes I've been sending you. This company is a mess. It's not really a company at all, not an organisation; just a collection of individuals doing more of less what they like. If something gets up their back, they bring in one of their mates to do it. We have virtually no employee records at all; people just turn up looking for their pay. Fiona seems to understand how it works and keeps the payroll in order, but I don't know how. It's more like a club than a company, and of them all, Jakey's the worst.'

'I see,' mumbled John when Clouston stopped speaking,

'I'm not sure you do, John, forgive me. As soon as I knocked back the boy, I anticipated that Jakey would go bleating to you and you would come pleading his case - and here you are. I'm disappointed, John, I thought you would back me up.'

'That's what I thought I was doing,' started John. 'I told Jakey he must come into line.'

He intended going on to explain that he appreciated that the management of Anthony Douglas & Son needed tightening up; that he himself had experienced something of the casual confusion Clouston had run into; that he would back him up in his efforts to induce responsibility and control. But as he scrabbled for the right phrases. the younger man cut in.

'Yes, I'm sure – into line on this, to get the lad into the job, then what? You know Jakey better than I do – and you know how this place works. Having got his way this time, do you really think, he'll knuckle down to procedure? Frankly, John, I don't. He's a wheeler-dealer. He's using you; he specialises in it. That's what he's good at.'

John found this assault astonishing, yet, it lodged a

doubt in John's mind, a doubt about Jakey's repentance. In his own front room over a friendly cup of coffee, Jakey had seemed contrite; to be genuinely seeking rapprochement with Clouston, but here in the other man's office, picking up his boss's frustration, John could believe that Jakey may well be ducking and dodging. John himself had had little experience of corporate life having spent most of his career in the little branch bank at Hecklescar. Clouston, on the other hand, had steered his way through the shark-infested waters of competing interests and egos in much larger concerns. With a jolt, John, listening to Clouston's suspicions, mentally conceded that he may have a better measure of Jakey's motives and manoeuvres. On the other hand, not all companies are the same. Anthony Douglas & Son had survived – and at times prospered – without the formal procedures that its new boss now thought indispensable. Perhaps, the new man simply hadn't had time to accustom himself to how things worked in Hecklescar. He had already admitted that Fiona had a grip on staffing.

Whatever, John found himself with a loose end. He had thought he had the problem all tied up. He had come to Clouston confident that once he explained Jakey's change of mind and Callum's need of a job, the new boss would relent and go along with what he had planned: that the requisition would be agreed, Callum's application accepted, and the young man could start more or less immediately.

Clouston went on.

'If I concede this one – as I have conceded quite a bit over these last few weeks, it will be taken as weakness – and I can't afford that. A company is like the rest of us; it develops habits. Some of them are good, some not so good, and some pernicious. The trouble is that the people who are caught up in them are not sure which is which. It takes an eye and a mind from outside to distinguish the wheat from the chaff. If he doesn't do it straightaway, it doesn't get done - and he gets taken over by the old bad habits. I owe it to Peter – and the company - for the next three months anyway, not to allow that to happen. I am determined to confirm and reinforce productive habits and root out the wasters. I know that Jakey, and probably others who resent me; believe I'm down on everything they do, but let me assure you of this, John, that there is much about the yard here that is good. Some of what Angela and, even Jakey, do is very efficient. But some of the other practices – particularly by Jakey, the seat of the pants stuff; making it up as you go along, confuses everyone else – at high cost. That has to be tackled. And tackle it I *will*. You can see then, John, that I can't simply back down on this one.'

'I hear what you're saying,' said John feebly, 'and agree with it. You're right; if you don't do it, it won't get done. But the lad needs a job. He's in a bad way – Jen too. If it had been something else I wouldn't have interfered . . . '

He got no further. Clouston held up his hand. When he spoke, it was in a much more friendly voice.

'You weren't to know. Sorry for banging on about it. I'll see if it can be done without serious damage.'

His tone changed. 'Look, while you're here, there is something else I'd like bounce off you. If you have time.'

'Of that I have plenty,' said John, relieved that the tension of the early exchange had softened.

Clouston stood up, walked to the door of the office, the door that separated him from Fiona, and looked out. Then closed the door behind him.

'Fiona is away to the yard. She generally goes down there every morning – to bring back the shipment figures.'

The way Clouston announced this struck John as over-clever - crafty, he thought. As if he were letting John into a confidence. It grated but John played along.

'I see,' he said, smiling. 'She goes to collect the figures? They're not sent up electronically?'

'There's an idea,' laughed Clouston. 'But then I wouldn't find out what was happening down there, would I?'

John joined in the humour. It gave him some small

satisfaction that Clouston had acknowledged what he himself had learned in his few short weeks behind the executive desk: that Fiona could be trusted. But what did Clouston want to discuss that he didn't want Fiona to hear?

In short, Fiona herself.

'You know Fiona well, I think,' Clouston confided, 'I'm thinking of moving her?'

'Moving her?'

'Well, yes. I want to bring in a secretary who can double up as a Personnel Person. Or, nowadays, do we call it Human Resources? I have my eye on someone who worked for me in Edinburgh and she's willing to come. But I don't want to hurt Fiona. She's been very', he paused, then completed the sentence, 'diligent.'

John had anticipated the word 'good', but Clouston had deliberately avoided it. To John's mind, 'diligent' damned Fiona with faint praise..

Clouston went on,

'This business with the lad is just the latest in a series of blunders on the personnel front. It's not Fiona's scene. She copes adequately with the accounts and communicates quite effectively with customers and producers, as far as I can tell. She also seems to have a grip of company legalities, but I think it would over-stretch her to add in Human Resources. There's a lot of employment legislation to get your head round, and I really don't have the time to deal with it myself. I need the resource. Besides,' he added with a knowing smile, 'Fiona's one of them, isn't she?'

John did not need to ask who 'them' were. It signified another shaft in the direction of Jakey and his supporters, even Angela, perhaps.

'So, I thought I'd check it out with you.' continued Clouston, 'How do you think Fiona would react to moving out?'

'You don't mean. . ..', began John sounding alarmed.

Clouston smiled.

'No, no, not out of the company. There's a job for her

here. I meant out of the room next door. We'd give her an office of her own in this building. We could even put her name on the door. Call her Accountant, if that's what she wants, or Finance. No, she's a useful employee. I want her to stay. I could even represent it as promotion. What d'ye think?'

John didn't know what to think. Or, rather, what to conclude. He had thought that Clouston found Fiona, of all the old hands, most acceptable. However, his faint praise and his proposal to replace her – for that is what he intends, tells a different tale. And why is he asking me? What concern is it of mine? Questions that for now, had no clear answers. Clouston is waiting for a response.

'You're the boss,' John heard himself saying. 'It's up to you to do the best you can. I mean to act in the company's best interests. If you think . . . It always seemed to me that Fiona had a pretty good grasp of her job – and she's taken on quite a bit more since Harold departed. But I can see what you mean – the personnel, human resources thing. I can see that. It'll all depend how it's presented to Fiona. Her job is very important to her. It's really all she has.'

'And the cat,' put in Clouston attempting humour. John declined the amusement; he found the comment sour.

'You must do what you think best', he repeated mechanically.

'You'll back me up, if it goes pear-shaped?'

Ah, so that is what he wants! He's anticipating that Fiona will come to me – as Jakey did, and he knows I'm in touch with Peter. He's taking out insurance. But how to reply?

'We'll see how it goes,' said John blandly. 'It all depends how she takes it – and how you sell it to her.'

'Of course,' confided Clouston, smiling and standing up. 'I'll think about it for a few days – and brush you up when I've decided what to do. John, thank you. It's been good to share with you.'

He put out his hand and John shook it.

'Not at all,' he said and made for the door.

Before he reached it, Clouston spoke.

'About Jen's lad; it could be do-able. I'll get back to you on that as well. I may even have a chat to Jen myself. It's always good to suss out the background, eh?'

By the time he reached home, John had deciphered his conversation with Clouston. *He's offering a deal. If I back him on Fiona, and any of the others, he'll give Callum a job.*

Maybe, John thought, Jakey's right about Clouston Pritchard.

CHAPTER FIFTY

John did what he often did when he had something on his mind. He took a dander round the town before going home. The sun shone; the day pleasantly warm. The sort of day when he would find Timothy on his seat outside the flower shop. He had in mind to raise with him the possibility of him tutoring Jakey. But the bench was empty.

When he cut on to the Bantry, however, he heard the same gentleman shouting from a bench overlooking the sea. John joined him and sat down.

'Who is counting the cars if you're here watching the sea?' he chaffed.

'I've given it up for the summer,' replied Timothy in the same spirit. 'I'm taking lessons from my cat – and from the look on your face when you came round the corner, you need the same lesson. If I hadn't shouted, you would have walked straight past.'

'You have a cat?' asked John, ignoring the jibe.

'Yes, at least I think it is mine. One day it arrived in my kitchen when I was preparing my midday meal. That would be about two years ago – in the summer. I'd left the door open. I made it welcome; gave it a few gobbets of meat. Now it keeps me company of an evening. Where it goes after that, I'm not sure. I had a cat flap fitted so it can come and go as it pleases. I call it Kierkegaard.'

John laughed.

'That's a strange name for a cat. What was it?'

'Kierkegaard. You've not heard of him?'

'Can't say I have. Who is he?'

'Not is, was. A long time ago. A philosopher, I think you would call him, but he would have probably objected to the description. He was a thinker who didn't believe in thinking. He argued that we should let life happen to us. At least I think that's what he meant. Like the cat.'

'The cat that gives you advice?'

'Yes or, not so much, doesn't. Nothing he does has any purpose.'

'He has to eat and he finds his way into your kitchen so you will feed him.'

'You're correct. Let me re-phrase: he doesn't have any other purpose than keeping body and soul and together. He is never rushing on to something he must achieve today, or next week, or somewhere else in the future. When he settles down for the night the day is complete; there nothing is left for him to do.'

'So, what advice do you take from that?'

'This. Every day to spend at least one hour doing something completely pointless.'

John laughed.

'And that's why you've abandoned counting cars.'

'More or less.'

Timothy looked at him quizzically.

'You should do the same. Lately, when you have passed me, I gained the impression that you were absorbed in what you are intending to do next. Yet, forgive me for reminding you of this John, the day cannot be far off, when for you – as well as me, there is no next.'

John's laugh subsided to a quiet chuckle.

'You're right, on both accounts. I must take myself in hand.'

'I hope you forgive my insolence,' murmured Timothy smiling.

'It is a word in season. An hour a day, you say.'

'If you can manage it, and it would be pleasant if for a half of it, you could spend it on this bench with me.'

'I will, provided, that occasionally – like now, you will allow me to buy you an ice cream.'

'I approve. But see what happens. We have just agreed to do nothing for an hour. Now you plan to eat ice cream.'

'After eating it we will do nothing.'

John left Timothy sitting in the sunshine and walked into McMaggie's. Standing watching the girl squirting Monkey's Blood onto the cones, he suddenly remembered that far from sitting with Timothy doing nothing, he had come expressly to ask him to do something – for Jakey.

He handed the cone to Timothy.

'Thank you, John,' he said, 'I see you've splashed out on the raspberry sauce.'

'Monkey's Blood, they call it here.'

'Do they now? I am impressed by your generosity, John. I bought a cone a couple of weeks ago; one scoop vanilla with a wafer - no Monkey's Blood, and it cost me two pounds twenty. That's more than my first weekly wage.'

John laughed and after a few silent licks, raised the subject of Jakey's education. Timothy proved to be understanding – and amenable.

'After all,' he said, 'we can scarcely classify licking ice cream and avoiding the drips, as doing nothing. We'll postpone it. If I can help the man I will. I have done something of the sort before. He'll come to me, will he?'

'That is essential,' said John, 'and you'll let me know the charge, won't you?'

'Charge?' exclaimed Timothy. 'I won't hear of it. If I want another cone, I'll take out a loan.'

John laughed.

'I'll be glad to do it.' said Timothy, heartily. 'It will give me a purpose – after I've done nothing for a while, that is!'

CHAPTER FIFTY-ONE

On the eighteenth of May, Janet locked the door of the house in Priory Road, and clutching the box containing her precious Moorcroft vase, walked the few yards to Duncan's waiting van. Without looking back. She climbed in, then, without either of them saying a word, her husband drove her to Cockburn Heath's office in the Market Place. There she laid the keys on the desk of Mrs Somerville and left. The house in Priory Road, their home for twenty-five years no longer belonged to them.

You do not need me to tell you why such a heavy task is being carried out by the woman and not the man. You have previously witnessed enough to calculate that determination and resolve make up a fair percentage of Janet's constitution. Her man had volunteered to carry out the solemn duty; had tried to insist on it, but Janet remained adamant. She would see it through to the end.

April, you'll recall, had not yet petered out when Duncan had related to Janet that he and daughter Christine had found his mother Alice in the kitchen at Latchlaw counting shoes and washing laces. Janet and Duncan had decided there and then that their planned move to the old farmhouse could wait no longer. She had hoped to delay it until September but now determined that they must move in with the old couple immediately to lift from Christine the burden of caring for her granny. She would then be able to take up the nightshift – and the increased pay, she had been offered at the Co-op.

'Give me three weeks,' Duncan had said, 'and it'll be fit for us.'

Three weeks! Corporate managers and council officers take more than that to compile an agenda and convene a meeting. Yet it is impressive what a practical man can achieve in twenty-one days.

We know that, for a little while now, Duncan has been working on the old farm outbuilding attached to the back of the house with the intention that, eventually, it could become a sort of granny flat for the old couple. His work, however, had been largely restorative: strengthening walls, rendering, relaying the floor. He had given a little thought to what the 'flat' would contain, scribbling his ideas on odd bits of paper and the little notebook he always carried with him, but nothing, (if you pardon the expression) concrete. Now he must speed up the whole process, start building internal walls, creating access and entrances, and laying any services that would be required. For that he needed help – and knew where to get it.

The day after he had promised Janet entry in three weeks, he contacted his friend Louie, taking with him a floor plan of the old house and his scribbled notes. Louie now retired lived in comparative contentment on the Redhills Estate in a house built by himself. He had made a decent living designing houses for the more discerning (and wealthier) of those who wished to quit the big cities for the relative peace and quiet of Hecklescar. Would he draw up a plan for the renovation of Latchlaw? Of course. How much? A pint and pie in the Old Barque when the job was complete. How quickly can you do it? Day after tomorrow.

As Louie conceived it, the outbuilding would become a self-contained 'flat' entered by a utility room into kitchen, lounge, bathroom and bedroom. Here would live Alice and Alistair. A short passage would lead from this apartment to the house proper, now designed to have a dining room as well as a large kitchen and lounge. Upstairs, Louie had laid out five bedrooms and a spacious bathroom.

The plan horrified Janet. Not at the apartment for the old couple; that struck her as sensible; all the amenity they needed; all on a modest scale. But the main house! Large kitchen, huge lounge, dining room; why do we need a dining room with a big kitchen and a lounge that could hold a wedding party sitting down? Upstairs, that bathroom! Why all that room in a bathroom; you only go in there to splash water on yourself? Five bedrooms! Five! One for us, then who? Not Christine & Hector I hope. He didn't design it with Christine and Hector in mind; them staying. You didn't mention that to him, I hope?

'It's just a plan,' Duncan reassured her. 'I'll adapt as I go, but we don't have time to keep re-drafting it. I'll need to get started.'

Three weeks! He could not do it on his own, even if he spent all his time on it. He certainly couldn't tackle the roof. With Louie's plan in his hand, he called on JBC, a general builder with a particular expertise in roofs – and a good friend. There had been times when he had helped JBC out, now, he hoped, he would return the favour.

'It'll gobble up your time,' warned Duncan. 'It's a big roof – and I think the timbers will be away.'

'I'll strip it back and take a look. I can put off work on the house we're building at Prior's Cross for a week.'

'You'll let me know what it costs.'

'I will. I'll charge you materials and the young lad's wages. Ye ken Athley, next door to me; he's not what ye call academically gifted, so the school has released him to give him experience of the building trade to see if he likes it, or rather, see if he can stick it. So, I've taken him on for a few weeks. He should be able to tackle roofing; there's not much to it, once you get started. We'll see. I'll tally up the damage, and let you know. But time's short. I'll go ahead - order up the materials?'

'Aye, do that.'

A new roof, JBC concluded after his inspection. Many of the existing Welsh slates could be used on the new roof, but more would need to be bought. To save expense they agreed to use synthetic slates on the back building.

While JBC tackled the roof, Duncan and Hector set to work on the building aided by old Beesknees, and other tradesmen called out of retirement, for interest and a little supplement to their pensions.

What about planning permission, you may ask? With you did it not take months of indecision and wrangling? It did. But Duncan jumped through all the hoops when he renovated the steading for a workshop. That would cover the house, surely. He and JBC know the difference between replacement and maintenance; this is maintenance!

But the expense! Where will the money come from to pay for it all? You may recall that Duncan had originally estimated the cost of refurbishment when he entered into discussions with Hercules, way back at the close of last year. It had frightened Janet at the time. What was it? Fifty thousand - and that was before the plan to convert it into two houses.

How could it be funded? From the sale of their house? Well, yes, but. . . Certainly there would be no delay in laying their hands on the cash paid for Priory Road. Once Duncan had informed Cockburn Heath that they were now open to offers with immediate entry, the house, long advertised, had sold quickly,. Two hundred and twenty-five thousand pounds was the asking price, you remember. They got that – and more. Three committed buyers; a returning native, flush with cash from the sale of a Colinton house in Edinburgh, a well-heeled retired couple from Surbiton, and a local family: Darren, wife Kirsten and three bairns, all offering more than the asking price.

Darren and Kirsten got it, although theirs was not the highest bid. Janet ruled out the Southerners immediately she heard that they intended it only as an occasional holiday home

– and when they weren't using it, to let it out to visitors. Then her heart overruled her head – and her bank balance. She wanted to see a family in residence and welcome the skirl of children's voices echoing through her beloved rooms. Duncan counselled caution; the family had a house to sell. If they could not sell it, he and Janet may have to wait months before they could lay hands on the money they so desperately needed. But after a week's anxiety, Cockburn rang to say that Darren and Kirsten's own house had sold without difficulty – to a couple from southern England looking for a little somewhere to spend the summer months. The same couple? We don't know and don't need to find out.

In spite of his promise to Janet, we must not expect Duncan to have accomplished the entire transformation of Latchlaw into two homes in three weeks. He had in mind – and Janet understood, that the roof could be guaranteed not to leak, and the kitchen, lounge and a bedroom would be ready to receive them and their furniture by the middle of May.

On that day in the third week of May, therefore, after they had dropped off the keys at the solicitors, they sat down in the kitchen of their new home and drank a celebratory – and, for Janet, consoling, cup of tea.

CHAPTER FIFTY-TWO

There is, however, another incident during those three long weeks that merits our attention. It concerns Christine and Hector and, of course, Janet.

Duncan had stepped outside one day to see how JBC's work on the roof advanced. He climbed the scaffold but found only Athley at the top of it. JBC had, he reported, gone down to have a look at the old building at the back of the steading.

In its time Latchlaw farm had run to over three hundred acres, and had boasted a full range of outbuildings. The steading that Duncan had taken over as a workshop had originally served as a threshing barn; behind it lay the crumbling remains of an old horse gin. This building had caught JBC's interest. In days beyond memory, the steading had housed a large threshing machine. This had been connected by wooden gears, drive shafts and drive belt to the 'gin gang' where a horse, walking round and round turned the shaft that drove the thresher. That lay long in the past. Over the years the building had been used for anything and everything, and now lay forlornly full of discarded farm equipment and junk. Its roof, now a mere remnant of what had been a warm covering of old red tiles, had not offered its contents any protection for over fifty years.

Duncan had long wondered what he should do with it. Pull it down, level it? A less sensitive man would have done just that. But such a solution offended Duncan. He had examined the building; had marvelled at the skill of the workmen who had constructed it. Any builder can build four straight walls and stick a roof on it. But this circular building had been crafted; stone by stone, selected, cut, placed precisely to encircle the internal space. Then the roof timbers, sloping to the apex, only two or three still in position, and they rotten and fractured, but still bearing the marks of the saw and adze of the old craftsman who had conjured from them beauty and purpose. Then the warm red tiles, some of them still in position or scattered on the floor; others, no doubt, decorating mock wells in suburbia or broken to sherds to drain plant pots. What was it that John Henry had told Duncan? That the tiles were probably manufactured in an old tile works up the river, where the spoil heaps can still be seen. It offended Duncan that this old horse gin, a repository of skill, dedication, - and yes, beauty. should be bulldozed and levelled. Something should be made of it.

But what? Such a question had long intrigued Duncan. When he found JBC, on that bright May morning, standing amongst its ruins he found the roofer had answer:

'This would make a cracking little olde worlde cottage – for a couple; living room, kitchen, bathroom and bedroom. Keep the outside dimensions and character. The old roof could be restored with new radial beams and tiles - and the stone walls could be re-dressed and rebuilt; that'd be a job worth doing.'

'I hear ye,' laughed Duncan. 'It's a nice idea, but that's a lot of work – and we've plenty on our hands at the minute. And the expense. Naw, naw.'

'Well, down the line a bit,' coaxed his friend. 'It's not often ye get the chance to work on something like this. With the roof caved in, it'll deteriorate quickly. It needs to be done soon, otherwise it'll be beyond redemption.

'Naw, naw,' repeated Duncan, this time with less

conviction.

'Ye might get a grant for it – from the council, or Scottish Heritage –or one of them other outfits that aye seem to have money to throw at auld buildings – see what they did with the Mansion House; whit was it, three million?'

Was it coincidence that Hector, looking for Duncan, should turn up just then? Why not turn the old horse gin into a small cottage for him and daughter Christine? They liked living at Latchlaw, and were in danger of being evicted. Janet had always made it clear that once she and Duncan moved in to care for Alice, Christine and Hector must move out.

However, if Duncan could be persuaded to tackle the horse gin, three obstacles lay in the way: time, expense, and Janet. And the greatest of these is Janet.

CHAPTER FIFTY-THREE

After an anxious week, a week in which John Henry told himself more than once that he should stop interfering in concerns that had nothing to do with him, Jakey stopped him on the pier and told him that Callum had started back at the yard.

The same day, Clouston rang him to report that he had seen Jen and explained to her why he had been so difficult. Following assurances, he had received from Jakey, he had authorised the recruitment of Callum – on a casual basis. John thanked him and, in spite of his earlier misgivings about interference, felt reasonably content with what he had accomplished.

All's well that ends well, then. Callum has a job; Jakey has got his way – and an additional forklift truck driver; Clouston is content that he has brought Jakey into line, has satisfied Jen of his concern for Callum, and Fiona has been vindicated. In addition, John takes particular satisfaction in the agreement of Jakey and the willingness of Timothy to patch up the holes in Jakey's education.

All's well that ends well. Well, not quite all. Nudge is not happy. Certainly, he had shared John Henry's anxiety about what would happen when Callum discovered that his 'refresher' training was a charade and that there'd be no job at the end of it. But he's over that and relieved that Callum will be back working at the yard.

During that week he'd stood by Jen and found her appreciating his concern and company. Then she had changed. When he called on Jen express his satisfaction at the outcome, to his surprise, he had met, not the warmth of gratitude, but a coolness he had not encountered before. Of course, Jen led hm into the lounge; of course, she served him tea; of course, she thanked him for his part in securing her son's employment, but she did not smile, and such words as she uttered were few, clipped and edgy. After a few short minutes, he found himself outside her door, walking home, bewildered and upset. What had happened?

Since we came across him in the cab of his truck at Tibshelf, thrilled and disturbed by his feelings for Jen, he had spent many hours turning over in his mind what, if anything, he should do next. He did not doubt that he was attracted to Jen. But then, what man would not be? She is a beautiful woman. But was it, in his case, mere attraction – of the flesh, as they say in the assembly? Or something deeper? And holier? Of love, pure love? Of God?

Such questions had occupied him for weeks now. He had thought about it, weighed up the pros and cons of it, and prayed about it. Had there been someone in the assembly he could rely on for an open, honest opinion he would have talked it over with them. But such a discussion, he knew, would be over before it started. For had he not already been 'corrected' for his affiliation with Jen and heard from brother Barnabas that they had had reports that while once she had been a true believer, she had turned away from the Lord to walk in the paths of unrighteousness. What fellowship has light with darkness?

Such advice, rebuke, almost, jostled constantly with the thrilling and treasured feelings he now embraced for Jen. He had come to a decision. In spite of what Barnabas said, in spite of what the assembly might conclude, he would ask Jen to marry him. Although nowadays feelings much less insistent than Nudge's lead swiftly to intimacy and intercourse, Nudge could not, would not, consider any other outcome for his love than a respectable Christian marriage. He may be prepared to brave the disapproval of the assembly, but he will not face down his own upbringing and principles. There had been no courtship; there had been no declarations of love, there would be no engagement; he would ask the question.

You must not believe that once Nudge had made his decision he would pop the question when he next met Jen. That is not in his nature; he is a diffident man; has made his way through life so far staying clear of any emotional commitments. He would wait until the right moment. How would he recognise the right moment when it arrived? He wouldn't and hadn't and the days and weeks had dragged on. Throughout those days his fear of refusal had grown along with his love. As his hopes rose, his doubts rose with them. He felt inferior to Jen in every way. Dare he believe that a lovely, elegant and sophisticated woman like Jen would find in him an acceptable husband?

Yet he would try. It could be that relief at Callum's new beginning might provide the best of opportunities. Mustering his courage, he had come on that fateful day intent on declaring his love and making his proposal. He then found himself silenced by Jen's detachment. What had changed?

Perhaps, nothing had changed. Nothing between him and her anyway. Perhaps, something quite unrelated to him – or even Callum, had upset her; with the job or the house? Perhaps! He would see how she reacted the next time they met. He let it lie for a couple of days, then on Saturday morning, he bought a bunch of flowers, (he often brought them – not for you, he insisted, when she balked at the gift – for the house!). She was not at home; at least, she didn't answer the door. She rang later to thank him for the flowers but he detected no softening. The conversation, normally light and lively, he found polite, brusque, and unresponsive. When he dropped in later, he suffered the same courteous but distant reception. What had changed?

Of course, he could have asked her, but this is Nudge, and Nudge has walked, generally alone, out of the throng. He has no experience of what educationalists nowadays inflict on our children - interpersonal skills. He had always hidden from awkward conversations, trusting that the flow of life and passage of time would either solve the problem or would teach him how to live with it. But this question: 'what had changed?' would not resolve or retreat; it hammered at the door and demanded to be let in.

With it came a posse of volunteer answers. Was she warning him off? Had she, that is, suddenly become aware of his growing affection and wished to rebut it; to settle their relationship into friendly acquaintance and that's all. Surely it couldn't be, could it, that she had led him on until she saw Callum settled into a job, and now no longer found the need to cultivate their friendship? Or did it have to do with him being Brethren? Having been of the faith herself at one time, she would know the disciplines and strictures placed on believers' families, and having thrown them off did not want to take them up again? Or could it be simply that she did not find him attractive? That he could understand. He thought of her as an exceptionally lovely lady, and of himself as a pedestrian lorry driver. Was that it?

Two days later he heard another answer and it knocked him off his feet. As he entered the yard, Angela was leaving it. She stopped to speak to him.

'Good to see Callum back on the forklift,' she said.
'Aye,' he replied.
'I warned Jakey. It could have gone pear-shaped.'
'It could, but John Henry sorted it out.'
'Ye think?' she replied doubtfully.
'Aye, he went to see the man – Clouston.'
'And ye think that's what swung it?' she smiled.

'Aye, what else?'

'What indeed? But they've got history thae twae, so Jakey says.'

'Who?'

'Jen and Clouston; they kent each other at Peterhead,' said Angela, then added suggestively, 'and more than that from what we hear.'

This information hit Nudge like a kick in the stomach. Jen - and Clouston! Of course! That's it! She had changed after she'd seen Clouston. Surely not! Jen and him!

'Are ye a'right,' he heard Angela asking through the storm raging in his mind.

'Aye,' he mumbled, and turned and left the yard.

'I thought you were going in for something,' said Angela, but by that time he had gone beyond hearing.

CHAPTER FIFTY-FOUR

'What an insult to Nudge,' pronounced Ina over coffee in McMaggie's. 'In his house too. You'd think she'd be ashamed.'

'Don't change the subject,' chaffed Dorothy. 'We're not talking about Clouston Pritchard. We wanted to know what your husband was doing at nine o'clock at night coming out of the back of Home Street?'

'It's confidential,' stated Ina, and all the company laughed.

'We know where he'd been,' pursued Dorothy. 'He'd been to see the Professor; he's been visiting him regularly for weeks.'

'The Professor?' asked Margaret. 'Who's the Professor?'

'Timothy, ye ken, him from down south, that sits on the seat outside the flower shop.'

'I didn't know he was a professor.'

'Neither do I,' snapped Dorothy. 'But that's what they call him. He talks like a professor. And he lives in Home Street.'

'I know that!' protested Margaret. 'I just didn't know he was a professor – and he isn't.

Dorothy returned to Ina.

'Anyway, we didn't know Jakey knew the Professor. To do with his work is it?'

Ina became aware that all the ladies – and Des the retired haberdasher that often joined them, were looking at her, waiting for an answer. She felt compelled to answer, or risk her reputation as a reliable source of information.

'Well, then,' she whispered, 'in confidence I can tell you that Jakey's taking lessons in French and Spanish – for his work. He often has to talk to Continentals, as he calls them, on the phone and in correspondence, so he thought he'd learn a little of their language.'

'Was that the new man's idea?' asked Margaret.

'Sort of, but Jakey's always wanted to do it,' replied Ina and scuttled back to Clouston and Jen.

'He was seen coming along School Road, ye ken, where Jen has one of Nudge's houses, late the other night.'

'Hold on,' exclaimed Pat, 'just because he was seen in School Road, doesn't mean he had been seeing Jen.'

'What else could be doing there at that time of night?, replied Ina. 'Ten o'clock!'

'He could have been coming back from a walk?' put in Margaret who, wanting to believe Ina, sought to clear up any doubt that might spoil the story.

'Why would he walk along School Road, if he was just out for a walk? He's living up on Red Hills; he's taken a house up there. If he wanted a walk, he'd walk round the cliffs, not into the town. No, he knew where he was going – and so do we.'

'No, we don't,' put in Pat, 'John Henry lives along that way, just round the corner. He could have been to see him.'

Ina ignored her.

'Well, I think it's hard on Nudge, after all he's done for her. I knew it would end in tears.'

Nudge had had plenty of time for tears, for the exchange in McMaggie's did not take place until the first week in July, fully five weeks since he had left the yard sickened by what Angela had suggested.

It had been five weeks of agony; an agony of not

understanding whether Angela was serious or winding him up; the agony of not knowing what, if anything, was 'going on' between Clouston and Jen; agony of believing that they were, (in the barbed phrase that tormented him daily), 'having an affair'. Of course, he had heard about men and women, sometimes married men and women 'having an affair,' but he had always taken no notice of it; or, at least attempted not to take an interest. In Assembly language it lay in the far country 'of the world and the flesh'; from the boundaries of which he had always turned away. But now he could not do that; this is not any man and woman; he could not represent them as fallen creatures in the grip of their sinfulness. It is Jen, the lovely woman he now knew he loved – and Clouston, the man who employed him; a fine young handsome man that had much more to give Jen than he could.

He called to see Jen from time to time, and every time received the same friendly but restrained welcome. As they chatted, Nudge raked over her words and actions seeking to gauge her feelings for him – and for Clouston. A bolder man would have introduced him into the conversation – he was, after all, their mutual boss. Nudge, however, had neither courage nor skill for such subtlety. Besides, the very mention of Clouston Pritchard or any reference to the man, sickened him. Nudge, therefore, simply looked for Jen to reveal her thoughts – and feelings. On the whole he drew a blank, but there were a couple of occasions when he thought that she wanted to tell him something, something personal, something she found difficult to express; a hesitation, a glance at him, then nothing. Of course, he could have pursued it, asked her the question in his mind, or at least hinted at it. But he did not – for the reason I have explained; he is Nudge. He did not - and it added to the growing lump of doubt and fear that growled in his belly.

During these five weeks, his unresolved anxieties pestered his days; at night he lay awake tormented by them. Thoughts and fancies that he had long kept locked in the cellar, hammered at the door and, as the doorkeeper tired, pushed through into his active imagination. In spite of his protests and prayers, images of intimacy between Clouston and Jen burst upon his mind, an imagining that shocked him with its detail, intensity and immediacy.

Five weeks. Then on the day after Ina's revelation in the café, Nudge driving his 44-tonner along Harbour Road rammed into the back of Clouston Pritchard's BMW as it emerged from one of the yards.

CHAPTER FIFTY-FIVE

The police arrived before the ambulance and gave their attention to Clouston who sat slumped unconscious in the driver's seat of his car. The truck had struck the back door and wheel arch on the near side. Having checked that the fuel tank had not ruptured, the officers immobilised the car and, believing Clouston to be in no danger, left him where he sat to await the paramedics. They were not long, a few minutes, but by the time they arrived Clouston had regained consciousness. When he tried to leave the car, however, he found that he could not move his legs; could not feel them. The paramedics eased him out and into the ambulance and left with lights blazing and claxon blaring for the Borders Hospital.

Meanwhile the police officers, a man and a woman, started taking statements of those who had witnessed the collision. They interviewed Nudge first. He had not left the cab of the truck, but sat there unharmed, stunned and silent. He had been driving along Harbour Road, he said, when he suddenly noticed the BMW in front of him; it must have pulled out of the yard. He had braked, he told them, but could not pull up in time.

There were plenty of other witnesses. There always are on the pier, so you would think that the officers should have no difficulty in discovering precisely what happened. Be cautious. Ask any seasoned police officer and they will tell you that seldom from a witness will you hear unvarnished facts. Certainly, in this case we are unlikely to learn the truth from Harry, who lives in Church Street just an alley away from the harbour but is more on the street than in his house and therefore witness to much that goes on in Hecklescar. He happened to be chatting to Janey Lindy just along the road from where the accident took place. He will tell you that he saw the truck coming along the pier, then the BMW pull out of the yard into its path. But, the untidy reality is that, so engrossed was he in telling Janey that there were some children who wouldn't pay any attention to him on the school crossing, that he noticed neither of truck nor car until he heard the crash. He then had looked along the road. The rest of his evidence he had, to use the local word, 'jalouosed', a mixture of guesswork and calculation. Similarly, the two Orkney men loading boxes onto the Shapinsay Lad, looked up when they heard the collision, but could not say whether the car had pulled into the path of the lorry, or the lorry had ploughed into the back of the car.

The police recognised that, apart from a narrow pavement, the yard opened directly onto the road with tall buildings on either side; a car emerging would not be seen until the last moment. Similarly, the driver of the car would not be able to see any vehicle coming along Harbour Road until the front of his car jutted well into the road. The officers examined the road and found little evidence that either vehicle had braked hard. After a short while they allowed Nudge to drive the truck to the garage. Damage to it seemed superficial; at the garage it would be checked out, then, assuming all to be safe and in order, Nudge would be allowed to continue on his way; bound for France with a load of langoustines, a perishable cargo. The woman officer contacted Fiona who promised to arrange for the BMW to be towed away. Harry volunteered to bring his brush and sweep the debris off the road. Within an hour and a half Harbour Road had returned to bustling normality.

No doubt in due time the police will hand a report to the procurator fiscal who will decide whether either of the drivers can be held responsible for the accident. However, we will take no interest in such proceedings. For what interests us is not what the legal authorities think of the accident, but what the folk of Hecklescar make of it. We will catch the flavour of it by dropping in on Angela and Jakey as they take a break one morning a few days later.

'Did ye see Fiona when you were up the hill? Did she say anything about Clouston?'

'He's broke his back.'

'Broke his back?!' exclaimed Jakey

'That's what she said, but she said it wasn't bad.'

'Sounds bad enough tae me.'

'Just twae or three o' thae little banes. He'll be a wee while in the hospital, then they'll fit him up with a corset and let him hame.'

'A corset, eh,' chuckled Jakey.

'Ye're enjoying this, ye auld blaggard.'

'Whae? Me? Naw, I'm sorry for the man. I widna like a broken back – or a corset.'

'Ye no fool me,' said Angela. 'Ye're gloatin' now that Clouston's off yer back.'

Jakey responded by ignoring her.

'Did Fiona say when Peter's coming back.'

'Next Thursday. Till then John Henry's looking in.'

'Just like auld times, eh?' announced Jakey, in a clear attempt to wind up Angela.

'I think ye'll find,' she responded, 'that Peter will tak none of yer mischief. Thae days are over.'

Then, almost without a pause, added,

'D'ye think he just saw his chance and took it?' asked Angela.

'What d'ye mean?' Jakey replied.

'Well, he was bealing at her going off with him, wasn't he?'

'I think I understand you, but just confirm to me, will you,' stated Jakey imitating a magistrate, 'who is 'he' that is bealing, and who is "her' that is going off with the him?'

'Nudge is a' thrown wi' Jen going off with Clouston.'

'I thought that's what you were getting at,' said Jakey patiently. 'You're beginning to sound like Ina. You don't know that there's anything been 'going on' between that pair, and if there is something, surely you don't seriously think that Nudge would try to clobber the boss man, do you?'

'Well, no. Yes, not set out to do it, but when the chance came, he took it. He saw the car in front, then the red mist came down and he went for it.'

Jakey laughed

'Bealing, eh? Red mist? Look, I've known Nudge for years, and I've never seen him bealing yet. He's one of the steadiest men I know: boring in fact, never up, never down. Aye the same. And no red mist.'

'Yea, but lately. . . '

'Lately – he's been tired. Now that could explain it, wouldn't it? No so dramatic, I grant you, but more likely? Wasn't as sharp as usual, didn't see the car until too late? Hasn't been sleeping well, he said. I told him to see the doctor, but he wouldn't.'

'There y'are,' trumpeted Angela, 'he couldna' sleep thinking about Clouston muscling him out of the way.'

Jakey shook his head.

'A'right, a'right, but we'll let the polis do investigating, eh? That's their job,' he pronounced pleasantly, getting to his feet. 'And we've got ours. At least I have. Are ye going to sit here all day?'

If, from this conversation, you take it that Jakey is in a better frame of mind, I would not contradict you. Clouston has injured his spine, and although not in danger, will not be back at work for some weeks. In the meantime, the company will return to the hands of Peter Munro who will, in the next few days, come back to the town after tying up his business affairs down south.

    Also back in Hecklescar is Olivia, having completed her world cruise, but please do not assume from the proximity of these two paragraphs that Peter and Olivia are any closer than they were when we last thought about them.

CHAPTER FIFTY-SIX

When Peter arrived at the new headquarters of Anthony Douglas & Son, he complimented Fiona on the smartness – and sense of it all, and thereby relieved Fiona's mind. She had half-suspected that he would disapprove of the comparative opulence of the new office. He then asked her to provide a report on company activity and, as far as she could tell him, what developments and improvements Clouston had in hand. He then sent for Jakey and Angela.

Peter made them welcome, exchanged pleasantries, thanked them for the improvements they had implemented since he left and invited them to continue to support the initiatives undertaken by Clouston. The company needed such improvements; a mission, he called it, to put it onto a sound business footing.

'I told you,' said Angela to Jakey as they left. 'The auld days are history! Ye'll need to behave yersell. We're on a mission.'

Meanwhile, John Henry, relieved of his slight responsibility, set out on a mission of his own, a mission he'd been thinking about for some months. On his first call, he dropped into Hecklescar Home Bakers to book the Solstice Ceilidh Band to play at a ceilidh in and around his birthday. McColl sucked his lips, shook his head, complained of the short notice, then offered him two dates: Friday 30th September, or Saturday 8th of October, the latter having only become available in the last few days due to Jasmine Coulthard calling off her wedding. McColl, Innes if you want his full name, you will have guessed, is the baker at the shop but also plays the fiddle in the band and takes the bookings

This may seem an odd combination of talents, but think again; when people book the band, they cannot very well look past the bakery to supply the pies, quiches, sandwiches, tray bakes, slices and other nibbles that the occasion demands. John did not hesitate to order up fifty servings of these too. Armed with these dates, John rang Jessica, Session Clerk of the Parish Kirk and booked the Parish Church Hall for the 30th.

Then he had second thoughts. A ceilidh, at his age? The wanderings of a silly old man? These doubts were prompted on his walk to Latchlaw, there to see Janet, to ask her to help with the catering. He knew that Janet had a way of dismantling daft ideas. Perhaps, he thought, he should have put it to her first, before he'd booked the band and the hall, to hear what she thought.

He discovered, however, that Janet had other things on her mind. A familiar friend, he did not need to knock at the door and walked straight in; straight in to a spat between Janet and Christine. Janet sat at the table, shelling peas; Christine stood over against her at the other side of the table. John apologised immediately, and hovered at the door.

'Sorry, sorry, should I just go or do you want a referee?' he asked in an attempt to lift the tension.

'No, come in,' said Janet, 'Christine's just on her away out.'

Christine in confirmation, welcomed John then kissed her mother peremptorily and left. Janet then explained the disagreement, or rather, at first didn't. Her words poured out in a flood of explanations and imprecations, which washed over John Henry but made him no wiser.

'If I could get my hands on that JBC, I'd string him up; putting ideas into their heads. Christine knew the deal; now her and Hector have this hairbrained scheme. And it's JBC that's put them up to it – and Duncan, I suspect. He's gone quiet on it! Given them notions of staying – impossible notions. Where's the money to come from? They haven't thought of that, have they?'

'I see,' muttered John, but didn't, not clearly anyway. 'What is the scheme, then?'

'There's an old shed out the back.'

She stopped stood up and continued..

'Come out and I'll show you.'

She led John Henry to the dilapidated horse gin.

'There,' she announced, 'that's it. They want to make that into a house. JBC put them up to it. He says it would make a nice cottage – with character, he said. He's drawn out a plan and everything. And Duncan's in on it. He didn't tell him it's not on. I said pull it down, but Duncan said he would like to keep it; it's beautifully constructed he said. Can you see it? Does it look beautiful to you?'

John had to admit that it didn't, and added sympathetically,

'I wouldn't like to think how much it would take to make that into a cottage'

'I can tell you that an' all,' puffed Janet. 'One hundred and eighty-six thousand pounds.'

'That's very precise,' commented John pleasantly, trying to ease Janet's disquiet.

'And completely unaffordable! But what do they say, ('we've, notice, *we!* Duncan's been encouraging him). We have the money from Priory Road. That, I reminded them, is to pay Peter Munro for this place - and he hasn't told us yet how much that is. There won't be any change, and certainly nothing like one hundred and eighty-two thousand pounds.'

She then suddenly addressed John directly.

'Are you seeing Peter soon?'

'I am, after this. He came back earlier in the week.'

'Well,' said Janet tersely, 'you might ask him when he's

going to tell us about Latchlaw. How much does he want for it? We need to know.'

'I'll do that.' promised John, and left shortly afterwards feeling for Janet and her battle with Christine and, it seems, with Duncan; a battle, he felt, she had decided she had to win, but didn't really want to.

As he put the key in his own door, he realised that he hadn't asked Janet about the catering for his birthday. It could wait. He had an appointment with Peter.

CHAPTER FIFTY-SEVEN

Peter welcomed John, thanked him for standing in after Clouston's accident and talked him through what he had discovered about the company in his conversations with Fiona, Angela and Jakey.

'Clouston's done wonders in the short time he's been here,' he said. 'The place is much more organised or, perhaps, I should say, systematised. From what I can determine, it's likely to move into profit quite soon. That's impressive. I thought it would take years,'

He stopped and looked at John. John attempted to read his mind.

'But . . .?'

'But he's changing the feel of the place; it's becoming a different company.'

Again, he paused; again, John searched for his thoughts.

'More like Arcticus?'

Peter smiled.

'You see it too.'

'It needed to change, did it not?' pressed John.

'Of course, but a good company has a distinctive life, unique, I would say. It is so entrenched that the people who work in it don't think there's anything unusual about it. They assume all companies are the same. They know their own company; they fit into it the way we do in an old loved jacket. It's just normal; comfortable you could say, but they probably wouldn't. They'd moan about the manager, pay and conditions and equipment. But in their heart of hearts, day by day, week by week, they feel at home; it is where they belong. Destroy that gut feeling and you destroy the company.'

John clapped his hands.

'You should work that up into a book,' he exclaimed.

Peter ignored him.

'You see what I mean.'

'I think so. But you believe Clouston is changing it?'

'Could well be.'

He paused.

'If I'm honest, John, I half-expected it. This firm is small, local; Clouston is a big company man. In a big company you almost always to end up with hierarchy; managers in head office telling workers what to do; workers on the factory doing what they're told. That's the mindset. I suspect that Clouston has brought that with him.'

'Are you sure?'

'I believe so. Look at what he has done. He's moved up here – away from the yard and hidden away behind a receptionist and secretary. He's reduced Jakey's hours. Did you know that?'

John admitted he did not.

'Not in those terms. What he's done is . . . How did he put it to Jakey? 'Lifted the burden of constant availability from you."

'What does that mean?' quizzed John.

'In practice it means that Jakey no longer turns out at all hours of the day and night to receive deliveries in and supervise shipments out. He has a stand-in, who'll turn out out-of-hours two days a week. He knew Clouston at IceCap. A local man, would you believe?'

'Not big Alec Mathews? He's had more jobs than a

washerwoman,' exclaimed John.

'The very man.'

'What does Jakey make of that?'

Peter gave a short laugh.

'He told me himself. 'Good thing, he said, I'll see more of Ina."

John joined in the humour.

'I suspect, however, that he doesn't think it will work. Particularly with big Alec. Too fond of his bed, he said.'

'So I've heard, that's why I'm surprised.'

Peter carried on.

'Then Clouston's talking to Angela about shift-working and short hours contracts.'

'Not short contracts!' exclaimed John, 'I've seen what they do at the Co-op. They only give the assistants, (what is it?), twelve or sixteen hours, but they have to be available whenever they're called in, or they won't get extra hours when the manager has them to give.'

'That's the way of it,' replied Peter. 'But common now in supermarkets and many other firms.'

'He's thinking of doing it here?'

'Yes, apparently he doesn't like Angela calling people in when she needs them – and more or less guaranteeing them a full week's work if they want it. Of course, in cold economic terms, he's right; it makes business sense. As he told Angela, you can't have your employees deciding when they will work for you; we have to call the shots, he said. That's where the early profits will flow from.'

'What did Angela think of that?'

Peter ignored John's question and asked one of his own.

'John, is it my imagination, or have both Angela and Jakey shrunk?'

The question threw John for a while. Shrunk? Then it dawned on him what Peter meant.

'Yes, now you come to ask, I suppose so. You'll have seen the change because you've been away. It's crept up on me. But

I see what you mean. They stand out less. Before, they ran Anthony Douglas, now they don't; they just work here.'

'Precisely. That's what happens when you appoint a big boss.'

'But they had a big boss before – Hercules, Harold.'

'Harold Douglas talked big business management but he never got round to installing it; Angela and Jakey were largely left to get on with it - Fiona too.'

'Talking of which, or whom, did you know that Clouston is thinking of moving Fiona – to accounts or something and installing a People Person – who would double up as his Personal Assistant; someone he knows from Edinburgh. It's not demotion for Fiona he reckons, but it would diminish her. I think that's what you mean'

'I didn't know that. but it doesn't surprise me. Fiona didn't mention it.'

'That's because Fiona doesn't know. Clouston told me or, should I say, sounded me out – in confidence.'

'Ah, I see,' murmured Peter, and leaned back in the boss's chair as if retreating from an unpalatable decision. At least, that's what crossed John Henry's mind.

'What now, then?' he asked gently.

'I don't know,' said Peter tersely. 'If I leave Clouston in charge, I get my money back sooner, but . . . .'

He fell silent.

Perhaps, John thought, this might not be the most appropriate moment to raise Janet's concern about payment for Latchlaw, but he had promised to do so. He found Peter surprisingly well prepared for the question.

'I think Harold Douglas offered it to them for one hundred and sixty-five thousand. Is that it?'

'Yes.'

'Let us say one hundred and fifty. That would be fair, wouldn't it?'

'That's the way it looks to me,' agreed John, but

immediately calculated that if they had that to pay for Latchlaw, and taking into consideration what they had spent on the farmhouse, they would not have much change out of the two hundred and thirty thousand they got for Priory Road.

Peter noticed John's hesitation.

'Something on your mind, John?' he asked gently.

'Well, yes.'

He then told him, somewhat jocularly, about the spat between Janet and Christine about converting the horse gin into a home for the young couple – and the impossible cost. He then donned his old banker's suit and went on.

'There should be a way of making it possible, ye'd think?' he said and looked at Peter.

'Could be,' replied Peter impassively. John expected him to go on, but he stopped and John suspected that he had relegated all matters to the pending tray, save Clouston's management of the company.

John stood up and expected Peter to stay seated behind the desk, but he quit the chair and accompanied John out of the office and into the reception area. There he turned to John and announced,

'I need to speak to Clouston, but not while he is incapacitated. I'll leave it a week or two. In the meantime, I'll come in a little each day.'

'That'll give you time to take stock,' said John in an attempt to read his friend's intentions.

Peter gave a short laugh.

'That as well,' he said enigmatically.

CHAPTER FIFTY-EIGHT

Janet was surprised to see John again so soon, but made him welcome. She even took him into their new sitting room, and sat him in one of her old chairs from Priory Road.

Once settled Janet apologised for his previous reception.

'She's a stubborn brit, our Christine. But it can't be done. They'll have to find a place in the town.'

She sounded firm yet despondent.

John told her he had seen Peter and that the price for Latchlaw would be one hundred and fifty thousand. Janet received the information without comment, but gave John the impression that that figure matched her own reckoning. For a moment John felt tempted to let her know he had mentioned the possible development of the horse gin to Peter, in the hope something may be done, but quickly abandoned it. He had received no encouragement from Peter to do otherwise

He then admitted that he had come to ask her to undertake the serving of the food and drink at his birthday bash.

'It's an awful big splash for a birthday, is it not?' she said.

John smiled.

'It's a special birthday.'

'A special birthday? You'll be what? Eighty-three?'

'Four,' corrected John.

'Eighty-four then. What's special about that?'

'No, no,' said John laughing somewhat nervously, 'I'm holding my ninetieth birthday party.'

He paused then added, 'I promised Lizzie, we'd have a ceilidh when I turned ninety.'

'But you're not ninety!'

'I know that. But remember that scare I had back in March; with the heart. Well, you never know. I might not make it to ninety, so I've brought it forward.'

Janet stared at him for a moment or two, then assured he meant what he had said, shook her head and laughed.

'You old fool! What's the date?'

'The thirtieth of September.'

Janet took down the calendar that hung by the stove and examined it.

'Thirtieth, that's a Friday, right?'

'Yes, Innes McColl can do that date, and I've booked the Parish Hall.'

'What are you looking for? Nibbles or a hand-round supper?'

'I've ordered it up from McColl's.'

Janet looked at him in amused pity.

'McColl's. What have you ordered?' she asked.

John, feeling guilty, explained in too many words that he thought he ought to order the eatables from McColl's seeing as Innes had agreed to squeeze his birthday in. Then he confessed that he didn't know what he'd ordered.

'I'll see Jessie, and sort it out. You'll want to put on a decent spread.' declared Janet.

John, realising he'd lost control of the party, assigned the catering to Janet. She would see Jessie, McColl's wife, and provide whatever she thought necessary.

Janet then scribbled 'John H's 90th do', on the calendar and pinned it back in its place.

John glanced at her nervously.

'Y'don't think they'll say I've lost my marbles, do you?' he mumbled.

Janet studied him for a moment.

'Yes,' she stated, 'they will, but it's probably your turn. If folk are laughing at you they're not laughing at anyone else.'

When John reached home, he pulled out his computer and managed after many false starts to produce a batch of small invitation cards, fifty of them. Over the next few days, he will hand them to his close friends and give them a few each to invite anyone they would like bring along.

He took some with him on his walk down the pier that evening and ran into Nudge. He had come back from his long continental drive a bare five hours ago, had not been able to sleep, and had walked to Hawks' Ness and back by the time he met John Henry. John immediately sensed the agitation of the man. He told him he'd heard of his collision and expressed the hope that he was uninjured and unharmed.

What he then heard from this normally placid man astonished him. His words burst out in a torrent.

What did he make of his collision with Clouston's BMW? He had had few accidents in his career and, (a matter of pride to him) he had never yet been charged for causing one of them. Nor had he received any warning from the policewoman that he would be held responsible for this one. He knew the standard response to a shunt: if you run into the back of another vehicle, it is your fault; you should always drive far enough behind the car in front to stop if it stops. If you're too close to do that, you're to blame. But he had not run into the back of the car, but into the side. He'd been honest; he'd told the truth. As he drove along Harbour Road, the car had suddenly appeared in front of him. He had slammed on the brakes but had not been able to stop in time. The car must have pulled out of the yard in front of him. Yet, he could not remember seeing it do so.

Had he been paying attention? He had loaded up the trailer, driven to the pier-end to turn and was driving back. He felt tired, he remembered that – and that he had a long drive in front of him; but would try to get a couple of hours rest before he set off. He'd seen Jen's van, at least, he thought it might be Jen's van, freshly washed, outside the Netstore fishyard; it might have been Jen's. He'd looked but hadn't see her. He thought she might have finished her shift and gone into the yard – or making for home. Thinking of Jen, he admitted, he thought of where Clouston might be. And there he was, in the car, that BMW immediately in front of him! Could he have stopped? Did he want to stop? He had applied the brakes, he remembered that, but when? Straightaway? Could he have pulled up in time?

He stopped, looked at John; a wild look, John thought, deranged almost, then blurted out the sickening self-discovery that had tortured him since the collision.

'I didn't feel bad about it – the truck smashing into his car - his car. I'm sorry now – in tears and mourning, but then I rejoiced. That he might be killed – or injured! It just came over me, like a wave, a huge wave. Where did it come from? Not from God: 'vengeance is mine,' saith the Lord, 'I will repay.' Not from God; from Satan – Satan himself. But in me, in me! It had taken root – and flourished in me. Evil triumphing over good. Wicked, wicked! I could have killed the man. Now he can't walk. I could have stopped – but I didn't. I didn't want to stop. I wanted the truck to hit the car. I wanted to get back at him.'

The violence of this confession rendered John speechless and the two men stood dumbstruck staring at each other for a few moments. Then John said,

'You'd better come up to the house.'

CHAPTER FIFTY-NINE

Neither John Henry's tea nor his patient attention staunched Nudge's outpouring of guilt. On and on it flowed; the same litany sung over and over again. Vivid flashbacks of the fateful moments before and during the crash, intermingled with bible phrases, confessions of guilt and cries of repentance.

At first John tried to knock back his claims of responsibility for the accident saying that he had heard that they (whoever *they* were, John doesn't know!) thought the car had pulled out in front of the lorry, and that Clouston had been in the process of fastening his seat belt. As John rehearsed this Nudge shook his head and muttered 'No, no.'

John therefore gave up and made no further attempt to contradict or mollify. He recognised that Nudge had become deaf to any explanation other than his own. His story made sense to him; *only* his story made sense. He clung to his guilt; he would allow no-one to take it from him. No longer an attachment he had knitted it into his values and beliefs, into the fears of retribution inculcated in his narrow religious upbringing, unmodified by any experience or acceptance of the ways of modern men and women. John, conceding that Nudge would accept neither contradiction nor counsel, let him run on until the poor man ran out of words, weighed down by remorse, silenced by weariness.

Once Nudge had stopped talking, John gently eased

him away from the accident and teased from him a much-guarded acknowledgement that he liked Jen; that he found her an attractive woman – in every way, not just looks, not just looks. Finally, Nudge admitted, in doubt and disbelief, that he thought he might care for her; that he might love her.

John then probed his fears about Clouston's relationship with Jen. Was he sure that they knew each other in Peterhead – knew each other well, as well as some folk claimed? Angela had said it; others had hinted at it. Is that all? No. What else? Jen had changed; after she saw Clouston; she wasn't the same. Until then she had been friendly, encouraging. I thought, well, I had made up my mind to . . .. His words – and his courage failed him. He continued,

'Then she went to see Clouston about Callum's job – and I found her different; cool, as if she were trying to put me off. He'd. . ..'

John Henry studied the distraught men in front of him; looked into his eyes and saw, felt, his despair. To Nudge a dread sequence fixed the pattern: Jen warming to him, had then met an old lover and attached herself to him again. She had turned away from him in distaste. He could be no match for a handsome, successful man like Clouston Pritchard . . .. Then there he was in front of him, in his car. . ..

A depressing sequence for John Henry too. He could find no flaw in the assumed logic. It led inevitably to a horrible conclusion: Nudge had woken from half-a-lifetime's sleep to discover the exhilaration and adventure of love, had ventured, and had blundered into a nightmare. As doubts and fears tumbled out of Nudge, John added one of his own: perhaps Jen did not particularly like Clouston; perhaps she had been induced to restart their adventure in order to get the job for her son. He had met the woman, had talked to her; knew that her son must come first; before Nudge, before Clouston. She would do anything for her son, wouldn't she?

But what could John say, what could he do? Nudge's case looked lost, yet he must not leave him without hope. Not until there were no doubt left. Not knowing what to say, he blustered, saying that he had heard that Clouston knew Jen from Peterhead, but not that she had been any other than an acquaintance, a woman among the other women that worked at IceCap.

As Nudge stood up to leave, John braved another question, one that had been in his mind since Nudge first buttonholed him on the pier.

'You've seen Jen since the accident?' he asked quietly.

'Yes,'

'What did she say about it?'

'She said she was sorry.'

'Just that?'

'She said she hoped I wasn't hurt.'

John stopped. Should he risk the question that troubled him? He must.

'Did she ask about Clouston?'

'No, she didn't. She didn't mention him at all.'

'But she asked about you?'

'Yes,' said Nudge, but gave no sign that he accepted the thrust of John's questions: that Jen was more concerned about him than Clouston. Nudge, however, had already concluded that Jen had said nothing about Clouston because she already knew all about him. He had stitched that into the pattern too.

To say Nudge went away in a better frame of mind would be a gross exaggeration. He did, however, find a little relief in being no longer on his own; that he had let out what he had battened down; had spoken to someone, someone he could trust, someone who seemed to understand, about his distress – and about his love for Jen.

CHAPTER SIXTY

John Henry's enquiries; careful, tactful enquiries; half-suggestions, really, about Jen's relationship with Clouston all turned up the same dismal story. Dismal that is, for Nudge. There seemed little doubt in anybody's mind that Clouston and Jen had taken up what they had left off at Peterhead over eighteen years ago. No matter how often John comforted himself with remembrance of past Hecklescar fictions, he could see no way of getting at the truth. Only two people knew where that lay and they were not likely to disclose it: Clouston and Jen. John therefore switched his effort to counselling Nudge in his disappointment.

Meanwhile, elsewhere in the town, another elderly counsellor found herself sharing disappointment. I speak of Connie, Olivia's mother. As we know Sally, Olivia's daughter, when she is not continuing her nursing studies in Edinburgh comes home to Hecklescar and stays with her grandmother. She could, of course, have resorted to her own room in Avignon, her parents' grand house in Alexandra Drive, but with her mother away on her cruise, she preferred not to rattle around in the empty semi-mansion on her own.

Now Olivia has returned, however, Sally has gone back to stay with her. One day, soon after her mother's return, she reported to Connie that she thought her mother jaded.

'Jaded?' laughed Connie. 'What on earth do you mean?'

'Sort of bored, she just mopes around and does nothing.

I've even had to cook my own meal at times.'

Olivia had been to see her mother, but Connie had detected nothing out of the ordinary in her daughter's disposition. That should not surprise us; Olivia had for many years kept her mother at a distance. Nevertheless, Connie promised her granddaughter that she would check it out the next time Olivia consented to see her.

'Why don't you go and see her?' asked Sally.

A good question, and one to which Connie had no ready answer. We must remember that their relationship has, for many years, languished on the frostier frontiers of friendship. Due to Connie's compassion (and loan, perhaps!) the frost had eased but not to the extent of cordiality, of popping into each other's houses in passing or visiting with intent.

Had someone other than her granddaughter asked the question, someone older perhaps, Connie would have huffed an answer. But, not wishing to undermine Sally's innocent belief that conversation would help, she promised that she would call on Olivia at Avignon.

Her daughter received her graciously, ushered her into the conservatory, and left to make tea. When it came, Connie found her herself handed a mug, a china mug certainly, but a mug, not a cup and saucer - and saw, laid in front of her, bought biscuits on a plain plate, not home-baked scones or buns on a china platter.

'Changed days,' she murmured to herself, as Olivia sat down.

Changed days, certainly, but has Olivia changed too? Sally seemed to think so. However, in the desultory conversation that accompanied tea, Connie detected only the now customary detachment.

When Connie, having run out of local topics, asked her again if she had enjoyed the cruise, she received Olivia's stock answer.

'Super,' she replied, 'a real break.'

There are two broad kinds of enjoyment: titillation

of the senses and nourishment of the spirit. Olivia's cruise consisted largely of the titillation sort. Would it be unkind of us to say that most of her life up to the present had consisted of the same kind of enjoyment? Let me add immediately that, if that is the case, I scarcely blame her. All her life she has skited comfortably along the surface, never having to struggle in the choppier seas, navigated by others; like Alice, perhaps.

Has Alice enjoyed her life? Of course, substantially. But Alice's enjoyment, perforce, rose from within her life; it was not tacked on to the outside. Since her teens, she had had neither the money nor the husband to indulge much in frivolity. Apart from an occasional delight such as a couple of days on a bus tour, or a pensioners' fish tea at McMaggies with a few friends, she had sought – and found – enjoyment in what she could not avoid; in the workaday activities of her daily life. There she had found a satisfying joy in sitting comfortably in a clean and tidy room, in billowing washing on a clothes line, in shelled pea pods on the kitchen table, in pans bubbling on the stove, or on a plate set down before her hungry partner in life.

All these Alice enjoyed and many more like them. Not Olivia; she classified them as domestic drudgery, and paid others to relieve her of them. In so doing she turned away from commonplace joy and sought enjoyment in titillation. That is why she went on the cruise.

She found it. Relieved of the necessity of work, she could indulge in such enjoyment all day and every day. Croissants for breakfast, coffee from a white-coated steward on the sun deck, dips in the pool, trips to the sights and sounds of new ports and historic cities, shopping in bazaars, bridge in the pavilion, dressing for music concerts, lunch at the captain's table, wine before dinner in the terrace dining room, sparkling conversation with lively sophisticates, and attractive men paying compliments. One man in particular - a Harold would you believe?

A Harold who thought she might be the wealthy widow on which he had set his heart - and his future. Harold, however, ran out of affection at roughly the same time as Olivia's lump sum somewhere between Singapore and Mauritius.

Now she is home; has been for some weeks. She has no job, no partner, no status, and no income to speak of. Life has dropped into a routine, a routine unenriched by any significant excitement. She has had to do her own despised housework. Worse, she has no prospect of improvement; no plan; the plan that is, with which, in January, she put off her mother when she asked what she had in mind for her retirement; the plan that lay unformed, ignored, in the back of her mind during the cruise and the intervening weeks. She had told enquirers that she would cross that bridge when she came to it. Well, the cruise is over, the days are shortening towards autumn, winter lies ahead and, at last, she sees the bridge immediately in front of her.

Her mother is speaking and has the old question in her mouth. The old question of curiosity mixed with awakening concern.

'What will you be doing now?' she asks.

'I suppose I must find myself a job,' she replied. She meant it to sound off-hand, but her anxiety latched onto her words and her mother caught it.

'Anything in mind?' she said gently.

'I'm in touch with the council.'

'The old job?' queried Connie, then wished she hadn't. She meant nothing by it, but sensed that Olivia might take it for gloating. She was not mistaken.

'No, not the *old* job! They don't have any of those, and I wouldn't want it if they had. I don't want to spend the rest of my life sorting out other people's problems. Something administrative.'

Connie thought it best to leave it at that, and rose to leave. Then, at the door, Olivia asked her, in passing, she said, whether Peter Munro had returned to Hecklescar.

CHAPTER SIXTY-ONE

We must not take Olivia's mention of Peter Munro as casual conversation. That is what she wants her mother to believe but her interest goes much deeper than curiosity. In fact, I can report that within a week she will invite Peter for coffee at Avignon. Will anything come of it? How could it? You heard Olivia after their Christmas meal complaining to her mother that he was dull. He found her shallow.

That's quite a gulf and we ought not to expect it to narrow any time soon. It arose from who they are and what they have become; unless they become something different, their opinion of each other will remain the same. Life, however, moves on and if we open our minds it can teach us a sharp lesson or two about what tends to our future happiness. As we have seen, Olivia's life has hit the buffers, and she must find some other way of living it. That is why she is thinking of Peter Munro. At Christmas, when she dismissed him as dull, she viewed him from the secure and lofty perch from which she looked down on those around her. She had hung onto the house and, for the short weeks she spent in it before her cruise, it had reassured her that she had lost little. It had not then dawned on her that with Harold gone he had taken away not only the bulk of the family's income but also her status. Now she is back, it is slowly dawning on her that the first-class carriage she occupies in the train of life has been shunted into a siding.

The little group of sophisticated ladies she counts as friends have, consciously or unconsciously demoted her and no longer regard her with the same distinction. Worse, she has detected a whiff of that philanthropic pity they reserve for those of their number, like Mrs Norris, who have fallen on hard times. Mrs Norris had paid the price of being married to the owner of a knitwear company that could no longer compete with Asian imports and went bust, leaving them virtually penniless. Now she sustains herself from a desk in an estate agent in Gainslaw. Olivia, back in Hecklescar and no longer under the intoxication of exotic climes, is acutely aware that she has fallen to a similar fate and suspects that she, in the minds of her friends, may be heading to join Mrs Norris on the charity rail.

She may pretend to her mother that she intends finding another job. Indeed, how can she do otherwise? But for her mother's loan of (what was it?), two hundred thousand pounds she would be completely disgraced by having to move out of Avignon. She has told her mother she will seek another job, but she has done little to secure one. For years, her old job, that of social worker, had bored her. She had contrived to rise above its particulars and clients (I think that is the word used nowadays for the folk who need help). The job had become largely administrative and sedentary. Now, she has certainly no inclination to concern herself with the depressing lives of those who have fallen on hard times.

She has come to the place where Alice has always been and she doesn't like it. Can she craft from it the happiness, and yes, contentment, Alice has found? How can she? She has no experience of it, no expertise, and no intention of trying to acquire it. She must find another way forward. Perhaps, Peter Munro is not so dull after all.

Peter, however, has come home by the low road, and has lately learned the skills by which Alice has negotiated her way through life. He has had all the advantages that Olivia craves:

position, wealth, influence, status, the cordiality of like people, but he no longer prices them above what he has recently run into back in Hecklescar. He came home looking for solitude and solace; somewhere quiet to lick his wounds and hide his hurt. He finds himself, however, pitchforked into running a clapped-out business, and not able to follow the advice he had always given others so placed; 'if it's dying, let it die; give it a decent burial; then walk away.' He hasn't walked away because he has learnt to respect and value the people who depend on it for their livelihood: Jakey, Angela, Fiona, Cheena Dug and the girls (and men) in the yard; Nudge and the men (and women) in the vans and on the pier; the fishermen in their boats (there are no women) and the bit-time potterers at the poohs. The business would do nothing for him; would cost him; but it would do much for them and their families. In taking such a decision he has found purpose and the early shoots of contentment.

He has also thrown off most of the trappings in which Olivia seeks to shelter from the cold reality of her life. Nevertheless, when the call from her came, he answered it, and turned up at Avignon on a fine Saturday morning in August.

She took him onto the garden terrace and there served him her best coffee in her best bone china cups. An hour-and-a-half later Peter thanked her at the door of Avignon and came away.

'You've been to Olivia's for coffee?' exclaimed John Henny, as they walked along Linkim Beach on their way back to Hecklescar from The Shore. Peter had had the notion that they should walk the Coastal Path. In fact, he had suggested, first, that they walk both ways, taking the cliff top track from Hecklescar, down to Linkim Beach, then scrambling through the tumbling gorse-dressed hillocks and hollows to Coldingham beach, then on past the beach huts and houses to the rock-enclosed harbour of The Shore. Then returning the same way; a distance there and back of over six or seven miles.

Not for John.

'Too far for old legs', he had said but agreed a compromise. They had driven to The Shore and would walk back home, picking up the car later. John had speculated why Peter had suggested the walk, but had come up with no better explanation than that he wanted to talk business in less restricted surroundings than the office of Anthony Douglas & Son on the industrial estate in Hecklescar. Certainly, they had talked about the business but nothing of any significance. John had also asked Peter about his recent weeks down south, and received the news that Peter had used the opportunity to reach a better understanding with his son and daughter. He realised that he had pushed their loyalty to the limit by sharing his regrets and anxieties with Mrs Rostowski, the patient counsellor whom he had, he confessed, led round the houses for months without knowing where he was taking her. He had made a point of meeting her too, and her van-driving husband, Greg. He had even tentatively offered the man a job with the Douglas firm if they wished to leave their home in the Midlands, but Greg turned it down.

'I'll stick to the roads I know,' he responded. 'Then I'll not get lost.'

As interesting as this was, as he walked along and listened, John Henry could not escape the impression that something else lay on Peter's mind. Then, as they walked along lonely Linkim Beach, Peter suddenly announced that he had been to Avignon, to Olivia, for coffee.

'Yes,' replied Peter, amiably, 'and very pleasant I found it. Top class coffee and fresh scones on the terrace in the warm sunshine. Can't fault that, can we?'

John smiled.

'She had made a big effort, then?'

'Yes, I got a Cook's Tour of the house; impressive it is; well furnished; and (what is the word) tasteful. She knows what she's doing with a house.'

'She showed you round?'

'Yes, I even climbed the stairs to the garret, as we use to call it. She called it the roof studio.'

'You were privileged; they say she keeps folk at the door, except those and such as those. Out to impress, would you say?'

'That's the way it seemed.'

'So, what was she after?'

Peter grinned.

'You auld cynic. What makes you think she was after something?'

'Begging your pardon, I must take myself in hand.'

Nevertheless, Peter responded to his curiosity.

'Perhaps she is trying to make the peace.'

'The peace?'

'She talked a lot about 'landing me in it.' That Harold had left me holding the baby, that sort of sentiment. She expressed her gratitude for saving the firm.'

John shrugged his shoulders but made no reply.

'Come on, John, what d'ye say?' pressed Peter.

'Didn't know she cared,' said John. 'There again, I'm not in her confidence. But. . .'

Again, he paused.

'But what?'

'She'll be squeezed financially, I imagine. Her pension won't add up to much; not enough years for that. Perhaps she's after a job.'

'A job?'

'Well, a position. I'm not sure she'd want a job, actually doing something. But something nebulous with a bit status, like 'customer liaison', or 'company representative' – or 'director', even.'

Peter laughed.

'You're getting worse!'

'Well, you did ask! I'm afraid I don't have a lot of time for Olivia Douglas. She doesn't strike me as the most altruistic of people. Rather snooty and off-hand, or, as they say here, regards herself as a cut above the common. Alice, ye know, Duncan Kerr's mother worked for her for years and made nothing of her; found her demanding and distant. Alice preferred Hercules! Olivia could have saved Jakey a lot of grief last back end – when she knew that Hercules intended to sell the yard, but let him suffer in silence.'

'John, John,' rebuked Peter, 'have pity on the woman. She's lost her husband and her income – and, I suspect, her self-respect. She knows what is being said on the street - that they're crowing over her.'.

'She told you that?'

'Didn't need to; it shouts down everything she says'

'She still has the house.'

'With money borrowed from her mother. She has virtually nothing of her own.'

'She told you all this?'

'Not in so many words, but I can add up - and I'll tell you this – in confidence.'

'Ah, thought John, 'this is what he wants to tell me'.

'She's not Olivia Douglas. They were never married.'

'What? She told you that?'

'Didn't need to. I've suspected it for a while. I found her listed as a director of the Highland Company – under her maiden name. But, yes, she confirmed it.'

John walked on for a little while, saying nothing, partly because they were climbing the steep gully out of Linkim, but mostly because he had become absorbed by another thought. When they breasted the slope and had climbed the style onto the cliff path, he ventured to express it.

'Dare I suggest that she has a proposal in her mind? After all, there was a time, I believe, when...'

'Stop right there,' commanded Peter quietly but firmly. 'There has been, is, no proposal. What happened a long time ago, finished a long time ago. John, if there is any thought in your mind, or anyone else's, of the possibility of me and Olivia getting together, scotch it. There is no chance; we were different people then – and I have known and loved – and lost, a much better woman.'

CHAPTER SIXTY-TWO

'Well, what did you expect?' said Connie to her daughter when she reported on her coffee get-together with Peter Munro. 'You told me you found him dull at Christmas, then you invite him again.'

Olivia had surprised her mother by calling on her in the evening after the encounter, and had seated herself in the bright little lean-to that clung to the western wall of her mother's house. A miserable space compared with her own grand sun room, but a favourite of Connie's on a warm summer's evening. From the first appearance of her daughter, however, Connie realised that this would be no comfortable chat of the sort that she enjoyed with Sally. Olivia had come to complain and had flopped into one of the old wickerwork chairs she had repeatedly instructed her mother to dump. She avoided her mother's thrust.

'I'd gone to considerable trouble,' she griped. 'I'd even baked the cherry scones myself.'

Connie smiled as a gibe tickled her humour, then swallowed it and said,

'You think he wasn't impressed? '

'Oh, he thanked me. Said he liked cherry scones.'

'Complimented the scones, but not you, is that it?'

'Oh, he complimented me – but the way you would expect in a restaurant. Officiously, I would say.'

'Officiously?'

'Offhand'

'Offhand?'

Almost patronising.'

'Patronising? Olivia, are you trying to say he didn't pay you the attention you were looking for.?'

'Well, no. Yes. He virtually ignored me. Showed hardly any interest in the cruise – or Avignon.'

'You showed him round the house! Privileged indeed. I don't think you've ever given me that tour.'

'You've never asked, but come round sometime and I'll let you see it.'

'Did Peter like the house? What did he say about it?'

'He said he was impressed, but didn't sound it. He called the roof studio the garret!'

'You must forgive him for that. He was brought hup in Hecklescar so he doesn't know any better. That's what they call it here.'

'Mother, would you stop needling me. I put a lot of effort into pleasing him and got no response at all.'

'What response were you looking for?'

Olivia ignored the question

'He stayed (what?) an hour and a half,' said Connie. 'Surely you didn't spend all that time talking about cherry scones and garrets.'

Olivia was in no mood for humour.

'No, of course not. I asked him about what he'd been doing down south – and he told me – at length!'

'And what had he been up to down south?'

'Buying and selling property as far as I can make out. Apparently, he got into Canary Wharf at the beginning and made a lot of money. Then he said he felt guilty about it. He mentioned a man called Marley, or something. He said he thought he hadn't been entirely honest with him. I got chapter and verse. He'd done nothing wrong, as far as I could see. I told him so but he just shook his head. Why should he feel guilty about making money? Harold never did.'

'But then Harold didn't make it,' quipped Connie then, as Olivia scowled at her, wished she hadn't.

'He then went on about his wife and his two children. Well, they're not children now; grown adults as far as I can tell, and doing well for themselves. He apologised for that too. He said that he hadn't been fair to them either. He had become too absorbed with Dilys their mother and his wife. He felt guilty about her as well.'

'Now then,' chaffed Connie, attempting again to lighten the conversation, 'and what had he been up to to feel guilty about her?'

'Working too hard, and being away too much; moving her to London when she came from a small place in East Anglia somewhere, and him being in London, etcetera, etcetera. To be honest she sounded a bit of a wimp.'

'She took her own life, did you know?'

'No, I didn't. How did you know?'

'He told me.'

'Still...,' Olivia started then could not think of what else to say and switched back to her complaint.

'He rattled on about coming back to Hecklescar and how different it had become. I agreed, but when I tried to remind him of what it was like when we were young, he clammed up; said nothing at all. Just sat there sipping his coffee with a little smile on his face.'

'As I said before, Olivia, what did you expect? You ditched him for another man. Do you expect him to relish a memory like that?'

'I thought he could have made the effort to be sociable.'

'From what you tell me that is precisely how he behaved. But sociable! Come on, my daughter, it's not sociable you are after, is it?'

Olivia studied her mother for a while before replying. Then she stood up as if to leave, – or make a statement.

'I don't deny it. I don't deny that I thought he may like the opportunity to enjoy a little civilised company, after spending his days in the yard. I know Harold did.'

'But Peter isn't Harold.'

'Wasn't and isn't.'

'But twice the man.'

'Mother . . .,' Olivia began sharply, but Connie thought somewhat desperately. As if her little scheme had come unstuck.

'Olivia, I'm beginning to regret helping you keep the house. You seem to . . .'

Overcome by her compassion, she stopped, stood up, and placed herself in front of her daughter. Then she took her by the shoulders and turned her to face the door. Olivia, surprised and confused, submitted to the manoeuvre.

'You need to turn round, Olivia.' said Connie gently. 'The road you were on has run out. You must find another – as I had to do – and Peter Munro.'

Wanting to convey concern not criticism, Connie had come round to face her daughter. For a moment she glimpsed in her daughter's eyes the haughty resentment that had conditioned their relationship for most of her adult life. Then, as Connie reported afterwards, her daughter opened her heart and the Olivia of old, young Olivia, young, lively, loving Olivia stepped out. And, for the first time in thirty years, opened her arms to embrace her mother.

CHAPTER SIXTY-THREE

In shortening days, the year crept into September. The shops notice a fall-off in trade, and the sands empty of bairns dragged back into their classrooms in beachless Glasgow, Edinburgh, Newcastle, and other concrete landscapes. Their places are taken (on benches, not beach) by older folk who, at reduced 'out of season' rates, have booked the caravans and holiday houses vacated by families. Others park their cars and mobile homes wherever they can find a space. Marine Explore and other divers' boats, however, venture out each day and the RIB still adds excitement to otherwise pedestrian days out. But, much to the stated satisfaction of many locals, the town settles back into its off-season somnambulance. To their relief, Angela and Jakey find managing much easier now that Lanzarote, Benidorm, the attractions of Blackpool and Torquay and sundry far-flung relatives have released back to them their gutters, drivers, humpers and general dogsbodies.

The month is no more than three days old when John, at just the back of six o'clock, is disturbed by the distant sound of the doorbell. Distant, because John is sitting in his yard trying to believe that it is warm enough to sit amongst his burgeoning begonias. They are late this year and he has waited all summer for them to reach their colourful splendour. He therefore feels obliged to spend as much time with them as he can afford. His day had been busy but, here in the evening, he has leisure to sit and accept the quiet counsel of his flowers. It is cold and, to be honest, he is relieved to greet Peter at his door and welcome him into the front room.

'I've been to see Cranston,' said Peter once they were settled. 'He's home now. He had a spell in a spinal injuries' unit down south, but they've given him a clean bill of health – more or less. He's a bit limited at the moment, and he says he'll need a corset for a time, but should then be fully mobile.'

'He'll be back with us soon, then?'

Peter looked at John and gave a little laugh.

'Well, yes and no.'

'Yes and no?'

'Yes, he'll come in the week after next. But no, if you're expecting him to take up the reins again. At the moment, as you know, he sells us ten days in the month. We've agreed to cut it to two, or three at the most.'

'Ah,' John ventured, 'you've tackled him. To be honest I didn't think you'd push him just yet. In fact, I wasn't sure whether you had made up your mind about his management of the company. You seemed to be in two minds.'

Peter smiled.

'Still am. But that is beside the point now. He wants to move on.'

'Move on? Well, that didn't take long.'

'He's had a better offer. Arcticus, his old company, are opening up a freezer plant in The Shetlands and want him to set it up, then run it. Too good an opportunity to miss, is how he put it to me. I've agreed. What else can I do? But I've persuaded him to give us a couple of days to complete some of the improvements he's implementing here; a sort of consultancy. I think that's important, even if just to stop Jakey relapsing into his old habits.'

'Who, then, will manage Anthony Douglas & Son?'

'If you won't,' Peter chaffed, 'I'll have to do it, with input from Clouston.'

'You're willing to do that?' exclaimed John. 'I thought you wanted shot of business life.'

'I did, but this isn't a business or, should I say, not only a business; it's a way of life - a way for folk here to earn a living and to ... '

He stopped, embarrassed by his own sentiment.

'You know what I mean,' he said bluntly then continued,

'There'll not be all that much to do now that Clouston's cleaned up some of the mess. Fiona can take more on – and, I believe, Jakey, now that he's more confident with the paperwork. You'll be game to lend a hand when you can, I expect.'

'What else can I do,' stated John, 'if I live long enough. It might just work out well. Best of both worlds, eh?"

'Could be,' agreed Peter. 'We'll see.'

Peter stood up to leave, but John could not let him go without asking a question that kept pestering him.

'Did Clouston say anything about the accident/ Nudge is up to high doh about it. He blames himself. He's beginning to think he deliberately drove into Clouston. Did he say anything?'

'He did. 'Wasn't concentrating', he said. In fact, he'd just taken the call from Arcticus; they'd rung him on his mobile just as he was pulling out of the yard. When he looked up he saw the truck. He told me he would have a word with Nudge when he gets back to the yard.'

'That could help,' said John.

Peter went on.

'He said something else; something that had been bothering him for a while. How he'd got wind of the gossip I don't know, but he went out of his way to tell me there is nothing between him and Jen; never has been. Perhaps, Fiona told him about it.'

'Or Angela, she likes to stir it. He said there's nothing in it?'

'He did, he's emphatic, defensive, I would say. He's obviously been accused of something of the sort before. He said he had heard gossip about her being tangled up with one of the boss men at IceCap up in Peterhead, but he doesn't know where it came from – and it certainly it wasn't him.'

John Henry had lost no time in seeking Nudge out to tell him the good news. He went about it circumspectly. He made no special arrangement to see Nudge; just happened to bump into him on the pier; happened, by hanging around for an hour or two, after he'd checked with Jakey when Nudge would be returning to pick up a load. Even then he passed it off as a footnote to a general report on Clouston and confirming what Nudge told him; that Clouston is moving on.

John detected no great lift to Nudge's spirits. When he told him that Jen had not been involved with Clouston Pritchard, he simply stared back and made no reply. What was he thinking? Did he believe it? John did not ask that question; Nudge did not answer it.

When he did speak, he took up once more his bleak confession - that he had caused the accident; deliberately slamming into the BMW. John had had enough.

'Take off the hair shirt, Nudge,' he commanded. 'It's over. We know what happened. Yes, you might have stopped, but it wasn't your fault. Get over it.'

'But Jen's attitude. . . . . .' Nudge started.

John cut him off.

'Jen! Look, Nudge, how long is this going to go on? If you want Jen, go for it. Stop asking me to guess why she changed – if she did – and ask her. She's the only one who can tell you. If it's true, that is. Then propose. That's the only way you're going to resolve it. It's the only way you'll know how she feels.'

This he had said bluntly, harshly, you might say. Then he added softly,

You're a good man, Nudge. She'd be lucky to have you.'

Nudge heeded neither the lecture nor the compliment.

'It's all right him denying it, but suppose it's true?' he complained. 'What would I do then?'

'You either walk away, or you barge in. Condemn her or forgive her. We're all miserable sinners. But, Nudge, for God's sake, stop whining. Decide what you want and go for it.'

At this assault, Nudge paled, attempted to speak, shook his head, then walked away.

CHAPTER SIXTY-FOUR

'That's what she was after from the start,' pronounced Ina. 'It's a disgrace the way she's taken a lend of Nudge.'

'He's too good-natured,' put in Dorothy, lifting her cup in McMaggie's. A cup – of tea, Pat will tell you, that along with the Malteser slice, costs three pounds sixty, that she seldom pays for herself, never quite having ready the right money to refund whoever goes forward to meet the bill.

'What's she done now?' asked Pat.

Ina glowed.

'She's taken her son and his bairns into the house that Nudge gave her.'

'He didn't give it to her,' corrected Pat. 'She rented it from him.'

'Whatever,' replied Ina. 'She always had in mind to bring the boy and his bairns beside her. That's why she wanted the big house in School Road.'

'What about his missus? Is she coming to?'

'Grace'll tell you,' said Ina, generously giving Grace the floor. Grace seldom added to the conversation but lived beside Callum on the Poplace Estate and had therefore become an authority on his movements.

'She's put him out,' she announced. 'When he came home on Friday night, she'd packed his things in a case and put them outside the back door – and one each for the three bairns. She said it was his turn to look after them; she'd had enough.'

Grace would have continued giving more detail. The ladies seldom gave her any attention and she basked in the brief limelight. But she had served Ina's purpose as an eye-witness with corroborating evidence, so found herself cut off.

Didn't I tell you so,' puffed Ina, 'right from the start? That's what she had in mind all along.'

'He's her son,' put in Pat. 'What else could she do but give him a home – and the bairns? He has three doesn't he?'

'Two girls and a boy,' came back Grace, 'and they're all holy terrors – the wee one especially. Malcolm, they call him.'

'And she won't have the help of the big boss, will she, Ina?' went on Pat, staring at Ina. 'I hear that that was just tittle-tattle that some folk spread around.'

Ina decided at that moment that she needed a drink of her coffee, and lifted her cup, before replying.

'So, I hear,' she muttered, 'but, you can say what you like, I think she's strung Nudge along.'

'Or, perhaps,' put in Margaret, 'he's smitten with her.'

The women all turned to look at Margaret who sat with a satisfied smile on her face. Then they laughed. Solemn, religious Nudge, that keeps himself to himself? That drives trucks and rents holiday houses? Nudge, hardly forty, but aged over a hundred. Nudge! Smitten?'

The gathering in McMaggie's is not the only assembly to take an interest in Nudge's love life. The brothers (and their women folk) are concerned. They have heard of the move of the son and his children into Nudge's holiday house with alarm and assumed the move to be a prelude to Nudge moving in too. They know that Barnabas and Bobby have already had a word with Nudge about his 'walk' and that they came away with no firm promise that he would cease having fellowship with those that had chosen to walk in darkness rather than the light. They have therefore commissioned Barnabas and his wife Miriam to visit Jen. Mark you, not all the brothers are in favour of the visitation. Bobby, for instance, who had lived long enough in Hecklescar to love some of the people of the place, did voice his concern about the visitation and would have voted against it if had been put to a vote. Which it won't be. Barnabas's God frowns on democracy; it is not for us to instruct our Maker, but to obey Him.

If you questioned their insolence, they would pity your ignorance of 'God's Word' and quote several texts from the New Testament authorising them to *'correct a brother in his fault'*. And what goes for brothers goes for sisters too. They will also persuade themselves that, whereas the Ina's of this world are interfering busy-bodies, they have the purest motive, namely, to save brother Nudge from eternal damnation. Of Jen they are not much concerned; they consigned her to the same fate years ago, having heard from other members of the little flock at Peterhead that she refused correction. She would, however, understand that she had become a stumbling block to Nudge and might be prepared to save him by giving him up. That is why they are visiting her.

Let me strain your patience no longer and cheer you by telling you that they will get short shrift. She will let Barnabas and Miriam in, listen to what they have to say then show them the door after ten minutes.

None of which, however, she will bring to the ears of Nudge.

CHAPTER SIXTY-FIVE

Hawks' Ness, where Nudge set off on his journey towards love of Jen, is a wild place. Cliffs soar out of the sea to the height of a hundred metres. On a calm day it is impressive; on a stormy one, awesome.

Here, on a day in early September, nether calm nor stormy, we find Nudge standing where he first saw Jen. Do not be alarmed. Although confused and despairing, he is not about to throw himself over the cliff. He is not contemplating suicide; his principles forbid it. We know that when he is not pounding the roads in his articulated truck, he may be found on one of the many pleasant walks around Hecklescar. Hawks' Ness is one of his favourites. His thoughts, however, on this day are not on the sea, cliffs or rolling landscape. He is here to think, and his thoughts frighten him. He is all at sea, buffeted by contrary gales with no route to safety.

He is tormented by what they are saying in the yard and in the town. He has seen the sickly smile on their faces as they enquire how his holiday lets are going, and is it true that the one in School Road has been taken over on a longer tenancy. What else could he do but let Jen take in her son after his partner put him out? The bairns had to have somewhere to live. And, no, no, no, it wasn't the first step to him moving in too.

Or is it? Is that what he wants? To be beside Jen? But she has changed towards him and he doesn't know why. Or does he? Why would a lovely woman like Jen, who has lived happily with Charlie, a fine upstanding man, a successful skipper; open and confident, as he remembered him, accept him as a partner or, (and this thought scared him most) a husband? Had she strung him along, to make sure she had a place to live – and her son, if he needed it? That she planned that from the start?

What about the assembly; his refuge from the storms of life for forty years? That he should cause offence to them. He shuddered as the face of brother Barnabas, stern, smiling, and unforgiving, stared menacingly out at him. What would his mother think if she knew that he had come under correction - for consorting with an apostate? And mother will know, for is not the promise that those who love the Lord, live on to counsel and comfort their loved ones in their spiritual walk. She would know about the accident too; about him ramming the boss's car and the anger that caused it – and the sin of it.

He had sought refuge in John Henry but now John had turned against him. Propose? He must be out of his mind. What do I do? Suppose she's been seeing the boss man? (He could not bring himself to use the man's name). Sleeping with him? That she is that kind of woman? What then? Surely righteousness must not be yoked to unrighteousness?

Yet the still small voice in his heart would not be silenced. He heard it through the storm. He loved Jen. As its intensity increased, so did his conviction that he wanted to be Jen, wanted her company in his home, wanted (could he believe it of himself?) to take her in his arms and make love to her.

'What can I do? There is nothing I can do!'

Buffeted by such thoughts, he turned away from the cliff to walk back down into the town. Looking down the path he immediately saw Jen making her way towards the cliffs. Picking her way along the narrow track and absorbed in her own thoughts she did not see him until she came within a short distance. She stared at him, shouted a weak 'Hello.' Then turned away.

As she did so, Nudge's mind cleared. He knew what he must do. He must do as John Henry instructed. He must bring it to a conclusion. He must propose to her. Here! Now!

He shouted to her to stop and hurried up to her. Sensing his purpose, surely, she stood, head bowed in the path and waited for him to come up.

'Callum has settled in?' he started.

'Yes, thanks.'

'And the bairns?'

'Yes.'

This would not do. He had no skill in chat – and no stomach for it. His question hammered in his heart, struggling for release.

'Jen,' he stammered, 'I need to speak to you.'

'No,' replied Jen firmly, 'Don't.'

'But you don't know what I want to say. I want you to marry me.'

It was out.

Jen looked him straight in the face and said, bluntly.

'No, Nudge, it can't be.'

'But why?'

'Just leave it, Nudge. It's best if you just leave it.'

'My name is Paul.'

'Sorry,' she said flatly, and turned away.

Instinctively Nudge grabbed her by the arm and pulled her round.

'Please listen to me, Jen.'

'No,' she said, 'I've heard enough. You don't know what you ask. I don't want to hurt you. You're too good a man for that. Leave it, please.'

'You mean you don't like me?' stammered Nudge.

Jen looked at him, stared at him, as if willing him to understand what lay on her mind without her having to put it into words. Words, he feared, that would injure him and hurt her. In the end she simply withdrew her arm from his grasp and repeated,

'Leave it, please?'

Then she turned away and, watched by Nudge, walked away down the path. After a few minutes he followed along the same path, but made no attempt to catch her up.

CHAPTER SIXTY-SIX

'I come to recruit you to a conspiracy,' said John Henry seriously, all the while holding out a bottle of wine. He had come to Connie's door in the evening of the day after Nudge had run into Jen at Hawks' Ness.

Connie, expressionless, took the bottle from John and studied the label. Then smiled and replied,

'It's a long time since I signed up for intrigue, but as there's a decent bottle of wine on the table, I'll listen to your proposal. Step inside, young man.'

Once settled with full glasses on the table in front of them, John asked Connie if she were still in touch with Jen. Connie confirmed that, yes, they still met from time to time, just a couple of weeks ago, in fact.

'How did she seem?' John asked.

'Okay. A little tense, perhaps, but then she always is.'

'Did she mention Nudge at all?'

'No,'

'And did you?'

Connie laughed.

'No, why should we?'

John then told Connie what Nudge had told him about Jen.

'He's fallen for her, I think,' he mumbled uncomfortably. Connie laughed.

'I'm in unknown territory,' he continued, then wished

he hadn't.

'You mean you've never been in love?' Connie chaffed.

'Ah now, that's a different story,' smiled John and gave up.

Connie came to his aid.

'Now there's a surprise. So, it's not just a rented house between them. Who would have believed that about Nudge?'

John then went on to relate Nudge's tortuous love story, ending with his rejection at Hawks' Ness.

'I shouldn't be telling you this,' he added, 'Nudge would be horrified if he knew. He's a very private person. I'm sure he told me in confidence. But there's something not right.'

He stopped, pursed his slips and took a sip of his wine.

'Something not right?'

John then related the gossip about Jen's supposed affair with Clouston. Connie confirmed that she had heard of it – from Sally.

'Did Jen mention anything about that?'

'No, but then she wouldn't. I've learnt that, in Hecklescar, if you're being talked about, you're the last person to find out. Where is all this leading?'

'I'm just scratching an itch. There's something I don't understand. I could understand her turning him down. It doesn't look like a match. I mean she's a lovely, classy, (is that the word?), woman, and he's what? Pedestrian?'

'Not when he's driving his truck,' put in Connie with a little laugh.

John acknowledged her wit with a short smile.

'I could understand it if, from the beginning, she handed him off, but she seemed to encourage him. Then suddenly she changed. At least, that's what he thinks. It happened, he says, after she'd talked to Clouston.'

'And Nudge thought there was something between them?'

'Yes.'

'But there isn't – or wasn't?'

'No, apparently. So, what is it?'

'Perhaps she thought he was getting too serious, and backed off?'

'Could be, but I think there's more to it than that.'

'Like what?'

'I don't know. Something to do with Peterhead. When Peter talked to Clouston he mentioned that she had been linked with one of the boss men at the company she worked for, IceCap, I think they called it. Could that have something to do with it?'

'Why do you think that?'

'Because of the way she turned Nudge down. It wasn't a point-blank refusal. Well, it didn't sound like it to me. He said she kept saying, 'Leave it'. That sounds more as if she were trying to put him off, rather than turn him down, if you get what I mean.'

'No, I don't,' smiled Connie. 'But, if you tell me what's in your mind, I'll see what I can do.'

'Thank you,' said John, sounding relieved. 'I think they could be in a stand-off. I believe she does care for him. Maybe, she values him as a steady, decent, practical man. You couldn't tackle her about it, could you? See if you can find out what she really feels about Nudge – if anything. Or, at least, why she changed since talking to Clouston Pritchard?'

'That's not going to be easy,' replied Connie, smiling. 'However, I'm implicated. I've drunk the wine.'

CHAPTER SIXTY-SEVEN

Janet, at about twelve on the twenty-second of September, thought she heard Duncan's van driving into the back yard. He'd be coming in for his lunch. If he is working in or near Hecklescar he comes home for a bite to eat. They ate their big meal of the day when he came in at night, about six. Hector would join them then if Christine happened to be working the late shift at the Co-op.

Janet heard the van from the old couple's room at the back of Latchlaw. She had gone in there to persuade Alice that she doesn't need to dress for church because it's Thursday, not Sunday.

When Janet came into the kitchen, however, Duncan had not appeared. She had anticipated finding him washing his hands at the sink, expecting to be told off off for using the kitchen, not the downstairs loo that she had had installed specifically to keep him out of the kitchen sink.

She put the soup on the stove and made up the sandwiches. A quarter of an hour went by; still he had not shown up. Perhaps he had gone to the steading. She stepped outside, crossed the yard and pushed open the steading door. No-one was there, nor had they been from the look of it. Yet the van stood in the yard. Then she saw another van parked in the lane outside - and knew immediately where Duncan – and Hector would be.

She walked quietly round to the back of the steading and caught them red-handed: Duncan, Hector – and JBC; in JBC's hands, a large drawing. Janet knew immediately what they were up to: working out what might be done with the old horse gin to turn it into a cottage for Christine and Hector. Caught up in their dream, the three men did not notice Janet. She stood, unobserved, while they discussed details. JBC is speaking, affection in his voice.

'We'd finish off the roof with replaced tiles on this side with Scotch slate on the back two panels. But we need to decide whether we'll level the site or shape it to fit the slope.'

'How much all told?' asked Duncan tentatively.

'Level, thirteen hundred and fifty a square meter; shaped, fifteen fifty'

'How much would that be altogether,' asked Duncan anxiously.

'All told,' replied JBC effusively, 'level, a hundred and eighty-six thousand, say; shaped, one hundred and sixty-eight.'

'Ow,' muttered Duncan.

'And how many bedrooms for that,' put in Hector.

'Just the one, but you could maybe build on at the back, without spoiling the form.'

Janet stepped forward. The three men froze.

For a moment or two they stood stock still. JBC, arms outstretched holding the plan, Duncan and Hector stretching their necks to study it, they resembled a brass sculpture: '*Romulus and Remus lay out Rome.*'

Then a movement behind Janet caught their eye, and they saw Peter Munro peering round the side of the steading.

'Am I interrupting something?' he asked pleasantly.

'You could say that,' snapped Janet. 'Come inside.'

'Thank you, Janet, but before I do that can I have a little look at your layout? I was in the trade, you know; brings back memories; not all of them painful.'

JBC welcomed the intrusion and enthusiastically outlined the plan to Peter. Soon the two men were thick in conversation, most of which Janet did not understand. Nor, to be honest, did Duncan.

Janet ushered Duncan and |Hector into the kitchen where menacingly she said little as she served them with their soup and sandwiches.

'I'm sorry about that,' mumbled Duncan when he calculated that Janet may have calmed down.

'He invited himself, didn't he, Hector?'

Hector nodded and concentrated on his soup.

'He's obsessed with the old building,' continued Duncan. 'He just turned up with the plan.'

'Good for him,' snapped Janet. 'He's going to do it for nothing, is he?'

'He thinks we might be eligible for a grant from Historic Scotland if we keep the original configuration.'

'And there might be is a way to cover the rest,' said Peter's voice from the door. 'I see what he means. It's a quality building – and almost unique. It would be a shame to demolish it.'

Janel invited him in and offered him soup.

'There's enough for all of us,' she said. 'These two are on short rations to teach them a lesson.'

Peter laughed and sat down beside them.

Janet turned to Duncan.

'Tell Peter what his lordship would charge us for doing up the old building.'

'He reckons about a hundred and eighty thousand.'

'If he says that, he's skimping. I don't see how he could do it for that,' declared Peter.

'We can't afford it,' stated Janet, frustration choking her voice.

'As I was saying,' said Peter, 'there may be a way . . . '

Janet cut him off with a stare, then said with some

vehemence,

'We're not looking for charity, if that is what you have in mind. We will either pay what it's worth or do without. We still haven't settled with you for Latchly.'

'Ah, yes,' said Peter, 'That's why I came.'

'We agreed a hundred and fifty, I think,' put in Duncan.

'We did,' said Peter pleasantly. 'But I've been thinking. You know that Clouston is leaving us.'

Duncan and Janet agreed that they had heard as much, but wondered why Peter had changed the subject.

'Well,' continued Peter, 'we have no use for his car so we are giving it up.'

'Ah,' said Duncan.

'We didn't buy it,' continued Peter; 'we leased it.'

'Ah,' repeated Duncan.

Janet sat expressionless and wondered what the car had to do with them.

'The deal is that we pay the lease for a few years and then, if we want to keep the car, we pay what's left of the purchase price.'

The light began to dawn, first on Duncan, then Hector, and finally on Janet.

'So,' she said.

'Suppose I let you have Latchlaw on, say, a ten-year lease, at the end of which I sell it to you for the price of the house minus what you've paid over the years.'

'It would be our house?' asked Janet firmly.

'Yes, we'll put it into a formal agreement. You'll have absolute right to the property.'

Then he added,

'You'd be responsible for maintenance, council tax and all other incidentals.'

Duncan and Hector both looked at Janet. She stared back at them for a moment, then asked,

'The house will be ours?'

'Yes.'

'From the start; from now?'

'Yes'

'We don't have to wait ten years?'

'No.'

'And if we built the bit on for Christine and Hector?'

'That too.'

Hector leaned back in his chair and smiled.

'No ifs and buts?'

'None. We'll have Cockburn draw up a binding agreement. I'll put my name to it.'

Janet studied the three men in front of her. Peter smilingly serious: she could trust him. Hector, barely containing his delight, desperate to charge down to the Co-op to tell Christine the good news. Duncan: her own dear, patient Duncan, who would support her, no matter what she decided.

'I'll think about it,' she said, tentatively. 'Sounds possible.'

Perhaps she would have said more, perhaps one of the three might take her up and press her to make her decision. But they did not get the opportunity. The door to the kitchen opened and Alice stepped in, dressed for church.

CHAPTER SIXTY-EIGHT

Had Connie not been a patient listener, and had she not, in their past meetings, talked freely about her own poor choice of man, it is doubtful whether Jen would have confided in her. Yet that may not have been enough to encourage Jen to be open with Connie had she not wearied of carrying around the burden of her disgrace for so long; a burden that weighed on her conscience – and life, every day.

And had not Nudge been the sort of man he was: decent, generous, forgiving, it is unlikely that . . .. But we must set that aside for the moment.

Sitting in Connie's little conservatory as the sun set on a golden September day, the two women chatted amicably about those little events and incidents that make up our days; trivial we call them, but, in truth, they are what life is made of:

What kind of tea do you prefer?'

'I've been buying seeded batch bread; it's more expensive but it tastes great'

'Yes, when I'm not busy with my quilts, I read quite a bit; mystery mainly.'

'I like Iain Rankin.'

'Of course, you won't have much time to read, not with your job.'

'How far do you go?'

'What, as far as that? And how many calls?'

'Sixty-five!'

'Yes, but my car is seldom out of the garage.'

'You put up your own cupboards? More than I could do.'

'Of course, you won't have as much time now that your son has moved in.' 'How are the bairns?' 'You make my life sound humdrum.'

'I hear that the boss man at the yard is leaving.'

'He is,' answered Jen, then went on. 'I knew him at Peterhead, you know.'

It was not so much the sentence, the words, that alerted Connie, but the intensity of her pronunciation. Connie could almost hear her determination banging at the door; crying to come out.

'Yes, I heard that too,' she said softly.

'And did you hear that there was,' Jen hesitated, '– something between us; between him and me?'

'I heard that too, but . . . .'

Jen cut her off.

'It is not true. It is simply not true.'

She stared intensely at Connie, and Connie recognised that no mere sympathetic agreement would meet Jen's expectation. She needed much more re-assurance than that. She paused before she responded.

'You are a lovely woman,' she murmured gently, 'and I know from experience that a lovely woman attracts not only the attention of men, but the spite of other women.'

Jen smiled, but her smile lacked humour. Connie re-examined what she had said and with a short laugh, corrected it.

"Oh, no,' she exclaimed, 'I don't mean me; I never had any such claim. I mean my daughter, Olivia. She was, what is the phrase, 'swept off her feet' by . . .., well. . . you know who - and abandoned one of the best men I have known.'

'Peter Munro? I think I heard them speak about him and

her.'

Connie leaned forward towards Jen and said quietly,

'Yes. The lesson is, don't turn down the love of a good man if he offers it.'

Jen understood Connie immediately. She smiled seriously, and shook her head.

'You mean Paul?'

At first Connie didn't recognise Nudge by his true name.

'Yes. We should call him Paul, shouldn't we? He's not the handsomest of men, and many think he's staid, but he's a good man, surely?'

'He is. He's been exceptionally kind to me and Callum - and now the children.'

Had it just been a chat; not a commission from John Henry, Connie would have left it at that. Even then, she struggled to frame her next sentence.

'There are some who say that kindness is not all he feels for you.'

Embarrassed by her own words, she quickly added,

'But you know what this place is like; look twice at a man and they have you married, or even...'

She stopped; conscious of the mess she was making of her enquiry.

Jen relieved her embarrassment by giving a short laugh, and saying,

'I believe he does.'

She then stared intensely at Connie and added,

'No, I *know* he does. If I allowed myself, I believe I could,' she paused, then, defiantly Connie thought, 'care for him, but. .. '

She stopped in mid-sentence. Connie took it up.

'But?'

'But! I would not, could not bring him down. I would, you know, if I took him at his word.'

'You mean he has already . . .. proposed?' Connie's heightened voice betrayed her surprise.

'Yes.'

'And you turned him down?'

'Of course. I must. I had a visit from the Assembly you know; a deputation: Barnabas and Miriam. Do you know them? He works in the Job Centre.'

Connie nodded but she did not recognise the man.

'Even apart from that there are the tittle-tattlers. His life would be a misery.'

'Perhaps, he could stand it,' Connie said energetically. 'I don't know him well, but from what I hear he's quite self-contained. I'm sure he knows his own mind. After all,' (and here her enthusiasm led her into a quagmire) 'he didn't back off when he heard the gossip about you and ....'

'You know that?' asked Jen bluntly.

'That's what I heard,' mumbled Connie. 'I know Nudge, er, Paul, spoke to John Henry about it. He was quite upset when he thought ... '

'You see what I mean,' cried Jen. 'You see what would happen if I showed any interest in him. This is really a wicked place.'

'It is. And I have suffered from it all the years I have been here. But there are good people here, discreet and sympathetic. I suspect it is no worse than other close communities - like Peterhead, I would think.'

Aware that, if the conversation continued, it could lead to wrangling, Connie stood up and offered to make another pot of tea and was relieved when Jen accepted.

When they were settled again, Connie made to apologise, but clearly Jen had made up her mind to tell her story.

'You know I came here almost twenty years ago' she said, 'but you must have wondered why?'

Like the tittle-tattlers of whom she complained, Connie had, from time to time, wondered why Jen and husband, Charlie, had come to Hecklescar. They belonged Peterhead, where Charlie had been a successful skipper and a respected member of the community. But his fishing days were over. Of course, he knew of Hecklescar and knew some of the fishing folk here, but had no other connection. So why, for his retirement, did he choose to leave Peterhead, leave the area and settle so far from his ain toon and kin folk?

'I did, a little. I used to think it was strange that you moved here when you both belonged up north – particularly with Callum still an infant. But I could understand you wanting to move away from his other children. One, I believe you said, was not much younger than you. But it really has nothing to do with me – or anyone else. You were free to go where you liked.'

Jen smiled sadly.

'Yes, that as well. It's good of you to credit me with such noble sentiments. But the real reason is much more squalid.'

'Squalid? It can't be!'

'I'm afraid it is. You see . . . .'

She stopped and started again.

'Charlie was a good man. Much better than I deserved. I've told you how we met, in the fish shop. But I used to do an occasional shift at IceCap, the frozen food factory.'

Again, she paused.

'There,' she continued, 'I met Gordon. He was one of the top managers – and a charmer, they called him. He singled me out whenever he came on the line. He made me feel special, and I may as well admit it, tho' I hate myself for saying it, compared to Charlie he was lively, vivacious, good company and when we.. made . . . well, when we were together well, you know what I mean. I suppose you would say that I married Charlie on the rebound, then found him boring. He was over twenty years older than me. I found Gordon exciting. He took me to fancy events and posh places; money was no object; we dined at the best restaurants and he regularly brought me quite exotic presents. What a contrast to skivvying in a fish shop - and the strictures of the holy folk.'

Suddenly she stopped.

'He was married, you know – with two kids.'

'Ah, when you discovered that, that put paid to it, did it?'

Jen shook her head.

'No, it did not. After a couple of weeks, when he persisted, I took it up where we left off.'

She stared at Connie.

'What do you think of such a woman?'

Connie made to answer, but Jen continued.

'I should have ditched him when I married Charlie, but I didn't.'

'Charlie found out!?'

'Yes – and no!'

Her voice trembled as she spoke.

'Yes, Charlie heard of it, but didn't believe it. Would never, all the years we spent together, accept that I would do such a thing.'

'That's why you persuaded him to move away.'

'I wish! No, it was Charlie's idea – to get us away from the tittle-tattlers. That's what he argued and that is what I eventually accepted. But I must admit – bitterly - that I did not have the guts to finish the affair. Gordon gave up when I moved. He didn't care enough to travel two hundred miles to see me.'

This regret struck Connie as perverse. Did she really want to continue seeing Gordon after Charlie had been so understanding?

'You resent that?' she asked.

'No, of course not! By then I had the bairn and glad to be out of it. All the glamour had gone – and the excitement. I just felt guilty – and dirty.'

This last regret by-passed Connie. Her mind had shifted to Callum – and who was his father.

'You had Callum?' she said nervously.

Jen understood her question immediately.

'Yes,' she replied tetchily, 'and he is Charlie's, if that's what you're thinking.'

'Oh no,' not at all,' exclaimed Connie urgently, thereby confirming Jen's suspicions. Jen carried on.

'What I resent is that I never had the satisfaction of telling Gordon what I thought of him – and how inferior he was to Charlie. He finished the affair before I had the opportunity to do it. That has rankled for years.'

'And now?'

'Now the tongues here will start to wag.....'

'No, I assure you,' cut in Connie. 'I will never breathe a....'

'No, no, dear, no. I never thought for a moment that you would. Please forgive me. I didn't mean to suggest. Oh dear. No, what I mean is that now that I know Clouston Pritchard knows about it, it can't be long before it gets out. I know this place well enough to know that that's what will happen. I know they already think that I have taken advantage of Nudge.'

'Paul, I think we agreed to call him. Yes, I believe the gossips do. But you have done a great deal for him.'

'Who? Me?'

'Yes. Through you, love has come into his life. I doubt if there is a greater service you can do anyone. He has come alive. You must see that.'

'If it is true,' said Jen flatly, 'then I am guilty of yet another deceit.'

'Deceit? I take it you mean that you led him on and now must disappointment him?'

'I am not aware of leading him on. He offered friendship and I accepted it. Any more than that, I'm afraid he has read into it.'

Connie became frustrated. This fencing was leading nowhere.

'You mean you don't care for him?' she asked bluntly.

Jen glanced at Connie and paused before answering, and in that pause, Connie learned the truth. Jen did care for Nudge, for Paul.'

'I could not lead him into so much trouble,' she said determinedly.

'By which you mean?' asked Connie, tightly.

'I mean that what is already said about him will get a good deal worse. I've already had a visit from the Assembly, making it clear that he would be forced to leave,' she snorted.

'Or worse, be disciplined - and pitied for linking himself to a fallen woman,' she rattled on in a torrent of words, as if the tap of her pent-up frustration had been opened.

'That is his life. He was brought up among the Brethren, his mother was a saintly woman – but strict. She'd be horrified if she knew. He will be told, if he does not already believe it, that his mother *will* know. That is just the start. Down the pier he will be laughed at. I can hear them even now. His whole life will be turned upside down. How will he cope with a son - and a family? No, it's impossible. I can't do that to him. I can't respond. I can't inflict my disgrace on him. He could not bear it.'

Connie made no attempt to counter her bleak argument, and, thereafter, carefully steered the conversation into calmer waters.

She had, however, learned what she wanted to learn – and what John Henry wanted to know: Jen did care for Nudge – and saw in him a path to happiness, blocked impenetrably by his closest friends, the malevolence of his neighbours and her own foolish wilfulness.

'I give up,' said John Henry, when Connie reported the results of her conversation with Jen. 'You think Jen cares for Nudge; I know Nudge cares for her, but he won't ask her again and, if he did, she'd turn him down – for his sake. There's no way past this.'

'I wouldn't be too sure,' smiled Connie. 'What's the phrase, 'Love will find a way.'

John Henry shook his head and smiled.

CHAPTER SIXTY-NINE

As John Henry stepped out of his house on a calm September evening, he came within the sound of the ceilidh. And his heart danced.

For weeks now he had anticipated this moment. Such was the detail of his anticipation that he saw the room furnished to the last detail: had imagined the hall lighted and dressed for the occasion; floor polished and crowded with rollicking dancers; the band belting it out on the low stage at the front; tables set out round the walls, full of chattering, laughing friends. He had braved Janet to ask for cloths for the tables, but had not had the courage to suggest little vases with a sprig of heather on each of them.

He had dressed himself in his kilt, shirt, Crail jacket. socks and brogues; an outfit he had not worn for many a year, yet one he treasured. In it he had, lang syne, escorted his Lizzie to the country dances they both enjoyed. Not that they were experts, or ever tried to be. Not like the sophisticates: the headmaster and his wife; Gregor and Morag from up the country, or those two whose names they never knew who appeared for the dances then disappeared like wraiths once the session was over. Such connoisseurs regarded dancing a discipline to be mastered; John and Lizzie, a diversion to be enjoyed. Such was their happy disregard for the book, that some of the aficionados contrived never to be in the same set as the banker and his wife.

Dances took place in the old Town Hall that entertained many a generation of Hecklescar folk until the roof fell in during the last dance over thirty years ago. He and Lizzie toured the villages round about: Brisset, Priors Cross, The Shore, Reston; they all had dances in their poky little halls; even the County Town held regular dances throughout the winter months. Allanton, too: a speciality; the dance that saw in the New Year. One year they took to it Maria Heath, Cockburn's eccentric mother, who turned up in a dress made from a parachute she had bought at a jumble sale. She had not had time to finish it so had pinked the edges of the skirt instead of hemming them. As the dance went on the dress slowly frayed from the bottom up.

These were Scottish Country Dances but, had he arranged one of those for his birthday, few of the people whom he had invited would be likely to turn up. He wanted folk he met in the street and in the shops, folk from the yard who could scarcely put a name to any of the dances but who knew how to fling themselves around to the sound of fiddle, accordion and piano.

All this he savoured as he headed for the hall, drawn by the distant music yet nagged by doubt that this ceilidh could not possibly live up to the expectations he had of it. It had been his intention to be there early to welcome his guests, but Janet wouldn't hear of it, and had banned him from setting foot inside the hall until his friends were assembled and the band in full vigour.

As he approached the hall, he thought he saw Christine scuttle away from the door. When he entered, the band struck up 'Happy Birthday to you.' The assembly, all standing, broke into song. Janet came up and, to cheers from the assembly, gave him a kiss. She then took his hand and stood beside him; Duncan joined them. John smiled, waved then glanced round the room. As each kent face came into focus, he nodded and muttered, 'Thank You'. Tears filled his eyes. Then he noticed a, large banner spread along the front of the platform. 'Happy

Ninetieth, John Henry,' it read. He pointed to it and clapped his hands; everyone joined in.

Duncan then escorted him to his place of honour: a table at the front of the hall. There he discovered that he would share the evening with Duncan, Peter Munro, and Timothy. Christine came and handed each of them a glass of whisky and a plate of shortbread. As she laid it on the table, John smiled; in the centre of the table, he saw a small glass with a sprig of heather in it. The three men stood up and drank the health of their friend. Then the dancing began.

When not listening, in happy fellowship, to his companions and laughing at their stories, John looked round the hall; at the people, sitting chatting at the tables; at couples and sets enjoying the dances: Dashing White Sergeant, Eightsome Reel, Canadian Barn Dance, St Bernard's Waltz, Scottish Waltz and more. He knew everyone there; knew that, as well as making their way through the dances, now smug in their competence, now abashed at their clumsiness, they were making much the same progress through their lives. He saw Jakey, inveigled into the Dashing White Sergeant by Fiona and Angela; a progressive dance, where a line of three (in this case the gent in the middle) meets a line of three coming in the opposite direction. The two lines pass through each other to the next trio. Jakey, however, had not got the hang of it, and frequently found himself either in a group of four, having moved too quickly or, more often, on his own, having forgot to move at all.

Had Christine had her way, John himself would have been on the floor with her and Sally, but he claimed the infirmity of age to decline such violent activity and negotiated a quiet waltz later in the proceedings. Christine and Sally, however, had found another victim and he saw them energetically putting JBC, the builder, through his paces. All looking very pleased with themselves. As well they may be, as John was to find out from Janet later.

He spotted Harry, attempting to fend off the attentions

of Gladys who has been chasing him (and his big house) for years. He took in Syd, relieved for a few hours from his crushing anxiety, and Margaret boring Pat, Gracie and Molly about her trip to Australia to see her son who has his own private beach on the Golden Coast. There stood Ina, having been recruited into the catering staff, with teapot in hand, hovering near to pick up any morsel she had not consumed already. He saw Cockburn Heath attempting to teach his new wife the intricacies of the St Bernard's waltz. She's French, Ina had said, from Sardinia; he'd met her while cruising in his yacht in the Mediterranean. A commotion in the corner attracted John's attention: a pair of exuberant youths, friends of Christine's, flinging their screaming partners off their feet much to the enjoyment of all. Two bairns ran by, squealing their delight, pursued then grabbed by their young father whom John immediately recognised as Callum, Jen's son. Smiling he watched them being dragged back to a distant table occupied by Jen and a couple of the 'girls' from the yard.

All this wrapped round John in a bleak contentment. These people, people he knew, some very well, some he loved; these people, he comprehended, were each picking their peculiar way through the hazards and hurrahs of the dance of life, with all its suffering and satisfactions, through heartbreak and happiness, with raw courage and a dour determination to draw from it as much enjoyment and satisfaction as they could.

Then Janet appeared in from of him, plate in hand glancing across the floor and commenting,

'Look at them, love's young dream!'

Christine and Hector, shuffling around the floor oblivious to anyone or anything other than the enveloping delight of each other's arms.

'Don't knock it,' laughed John. 'It's precious and rare.'

'Do you think I don't know that?' replied Janet immediately. She glanced to where Duncan was waltzing his mother Alice gently round the room to her obvious delight.

'I've given in,' Janet said smiling. 'Peter will have told you we've agreed to take the lease. The young ones can have their cottage out the back.'

'No, Peter hasn't told me yet. I'll tackle him if he comes out of that alive.'

He gave a short laugh and pointed to where Peter was being hauled round the floor by Mrs Somerville with all the finesse of an agricultural tractor.

'Call me soft,' continued Janet, 'but to be honest, with Alice the way she is, and Alistair reported absent most of the time, I can do with help.'

She paused then added with a smile, 'and the company.'

Peter returned and flopped down into his chair.

'I'm getting too old for this,' he panted, then added, pointing to a fine figure of a man dressed for the occasions in Argyll waistcoat, white shirt, tartan trews and dancing pumps.

'Now he knows what he is doing – whoever he is.'

As he spoke Angela came by on her way to line up for an Eightsome Reel.

'Who's the man in the gear?' John shouted to her as she passed.

'It's Grubs,' she shouted back.

Grubs! Grubs from Mallaig! That can't be him, surely?

I believe it is!

Peter and John then watched in admiration as the man they had never seen other than unwashed and unshaven, in scruffy jeans and sweaty shirt, tripped nimbly through the reel with consummate skill.

'Didn't know he could do that,' remarked John to Peter.

'Don't know why he wants to,' replied Peter, taking a large swig of his spritzer. 'I've done my bit. Once is enough.'

The words, however, were no sooner out of his mouth than Connie arrived to propose that he ask Olivia for the Scottish Waltz. Much to John's surprise, Peter accepted the challenge.

As he watched them, Olivia opulent, Peter pedestrian,

moving through the floor, John wondered what could be passing between them. Certainly, they were talking to each other, but what about?

When Peter returned to his seat, John ventured a question, the shortest he could think of.

'Well?' he said.

Peter gave a short smile and considered his answer before replying,

'I believe she's on her way home.'

'Is she?' said John and glanced towards where Olivia had been sitting - and where she sat still.

'It's early yet,' he muttered, sounding slightly miffed.

'It is,' agreed Peter cryptically, 'but she has a long way to come.'

John stared at him and caught his smile – then his drift.

'Ah,' he nodded, 'You mean. . ..'

'Yes, she has been a long time in a far country but I believe she is on her way back to us.'

Then he added,

'And I, for one, will welcome her.'

CHAPTER SEVENTY

For reasons not entirely unconnected with Peter and Olivia, John looked across the floor in search of Jen and spotted her in a set with Little Dod, one of her fellow drivers. But where was Nudge? He picked out Bobby Dobson and his wife both of whom had braved Barnabas and Miriam to attend the birthday party of a man they knew largely only as their former kindly bank manager. John hoped that he might see Nudge with them, but he was not in their company, nor anywhere else in the hall as far as he could see. Where is he?

Has anyone seen Nudge? No.

He had been invited; John had handed him the invitation himself; and Nudge had said he would come. Certainly, his acceptance had been hedged with clauses and codicils:

; 'We don't attend dances. But this isn't a dance, is it? It's more of a birthday party.'

; 'You say there'll be drink; I will have to go along with that – and the band, I suppose if you want me there.'

; 'There can be little harm in it. I'll come for your sake, John.'

; 'I might talk to Bobby about it. I'll explain I'd be attending not for the dancing or the music but for your sake, John; to honour your birthday. That would not tend to evil, I think.'

John had smiled at Nudge's seriousness but made it

clear that he looked forward to welcoming him to the hall. But he had not come. Not yet.

John looked round the hall again but still could not spot him. He caught Connie's eye and she came across to see him.

'Do you think he's got cold feet?' she said. 'I thought when you said he'd come that it would be a brave move for him. I don't think he has ever been to a ceilidh before.'

'No, he hasn't, but he did promise. I'll just step outside to see if I can raise him.'

He stood up to carry out his intention but, as he did so, the band played three loud chords, and Innes McColl announced that the Profess..., er, Timothy, would like to say a few words, after which eats would be served.

He handed the microphone to Timothy who announced, somewhat nervously, that he had been asked to pay tribute to John Henry; a task he felt honoured to undertake.

A sheet of paper in his hand, Timothy first apologised for being a stranger; that he had no right to say anything; that there were many in the hall, in fact, virtually everyone in the hall, who knew John much better than he did. But he would do his best. He then recounted what he had learnt of John's career and praised John for his professionalism, helpfulness, and thoughtfulness.

'Without him, I understand the fish yard would be no more and many families in the town would have lost their livelihoods. Well, done John Henry, for this and for your many other acts of service to your neighbours.'

Everyone clapped; all who were able stood up; many cheered.

But Timothy had not finished and stood nervously on the stage, glancing at his paper, until the applause subsided.

'Since asked to perform this little service I have sought to find some little tribute that would encapsulate the debt we owe this man. Then I came across this written by your own poet, George Mackay Brown.'

DANCE IN A BEAUTIFUL COAT

'You must dance in a beautiful coat.'

The hall fell silent.

Timothy paused, looked up from his paper, and took in the bewilderment of his hearers. They had expected a piece of local doggerel, a laugh, a skit on John Henry's age, perhaps.

But what is this? Dance? John Henry? He's a bank manager. He can't dance, can he? Beautiful coat? We've never seen him in anything more than a suit.

'It's about the coat of circumstance; what happens to us in life,' Timothy gabbled anxiously, but detected no easing of his hearers' bafflement.

'And how we live it,' he added.

Still no glimmer of understanding.

Timothy tried again. He glanced at his notes, turned over a page, and muttered,

'The last two lines read:
Between crib and coffin,
You must dance in a beautiful coat.'

Timothy looked up from his notes and surveyed an unchanged sea of bemused faces gawping at him. Then he held out his hand towards to John and proclaimed firmly,

'John Henry, you have helped us all to dance. Thank you!'

For a moment the hall fell completely silent as each of his listeners took in the significance of what Timothy had read to them.

'You must dance in a beautiful coat.'

Has John Henry helped me to dance? Through life? In spite of everything? Of course, he has!

Starting as a murmur, a wave of approval swept through the hall culminating in full-throated cheers, loud enthusiastic clapping and foot-stamping.

Then Innes broke the mood and announced,

'Bring in the cake! John Henry! Happy Ninetieth Birthday!'

Janet, accompanied by Christine, walked into the hall carrying a large two-tier decorated cake and paraded it round the room until everyone had had a chance to admire it.

Then from the stage, Innes again, smiling broadly,

'Baked and decorated this very morning in Hecklescar Home Bakers – for cakes at their very best.'

This announcement elicited cheers and jeers in equal number.

The cake was cut and distributed and eats served: vol-au-vents, sausage rolls, little pork pies, tiny sandwiches, slices of quiche and pies, crisps, little fruit tarts, paradise slice, buttered tea loaf, cherry cake; a feast fit for a king – or a pretend ninety-year-old on a suspended healthy diet.

John, however, had Nudge on his mind.

He excused himself and walked out of the door, through the vestibule and into the cool, dark night beyond. He set off for Nudge's home but as he turned the corner of the church saw the very man, huddled against the wall.

'What are you doing here?' he said. 'Come in.'

Nudge looked at him, almost wildly, John thought, then asked,

'Is Clouston Pritchard there?'

'No,' John assured him, then added, 'but Bobby is - and his missus.'

John expected this to be enough to move him away from the wall. But he stayed put and launched once more into his fears and misgivings.

John cut him off.

'Nudge,' he said, 'I want you at my birthday party. It is little to ask, I think. You don't have to drink, you don't have to dance, you don't even have to enjoy it.'

Nudge stared intensely at John for almost a minute then edged away from the wall.

'But you must eat a piece of my cake,' added John gently. 'Come on in, please.'

Nudge smiled nervously, left the wall and accompanied

John inside. John intended taking him to Bobby's table but that, he saw, was alive with chattering locals, so he seated him sedately at his own table alongside Peter and himself. Nudge sat rooted to his seat for well over an hour then, as the light, colour and song of the ceilidh warmed him, he began to thaw. He took off his jacket then accepted John's offer of a cup of coffee – and helped himself to a sausage roll.

As the ceilidh edged towards its close, John saw Connie approach the stage and speak to Innes. Shortly afterwards Innes announced a dance - a simple St Bernard's Waltz.

'Ladies Choice,' he added, to Ooos around the hall.

The words were scarcely out of his mouth when Jen appeared at John's table and put out her hand towards Nudge and asked,

'Paul, would you like to dance?'

Nudge looked stunned and turned to John Henry. For a moment John thought he would rush out of the room. John smiled and nodded his head.

'Go on, Nudge. It's what the lady wants.'

Slowly, Nudge rose to his feet. John could almost feel the weight he carried as he stood up.

'I can't dance,' he mumbled.

'I can teach you,' said Jen. 'It's simple.'

Again, he glanced at John.

'Go on,' urged John, 'you have a good teacher.'

At last Nudge reached out his hand and grasped Jen's.

She led him into the throng of dancers.

John glanced over the room to Connie and beckoned her to him.

'Are you not going to ask me?' he said pleasantly.

'Of course,' she said, then added. 'So far, so good.'

'Finger's crossed,' replied John. 'Does she know?'

'No, does he?'

'No.'

'Oh dear.'

'My sentiment exactly. Dare we?'

'We must.'

John and Connie circled, keeping Jen and Nudge in sight, and admiring the patience with which Jen steered Nudge through the few simple steps that made up the dance. They caught, too, Nudge's quiet smile.

'I believe he is enjoying it.' whispered Connie.

'Do you think she loves him?' asked John, somewhat embarrassed at the question.

'I'm not sure she knows what love is anymore,' answered Connie quietly

'Do any of us?' muttered John.

They shuffled around for a few more turns, then John tried again to express comfortably what turned in his mind.

'Do you think she would want his company for the rest of her life?'

'Oh, yes,' replied Connie immediately, 'she has already decided that, but is afraid of it.'

John then steered their way to the stage. When he reached it, he broke away and asked Innes if he could say a few words.

Innes stopped the proceedings and handed John the microphone.

Some of the couples began to drift towards their seats.

'No, please, stay on the floor,' declared John. 'There will be no long speech. I just want to thank you for all for coming, for Innes giving us such entertainment, Timothy for his kind words, and my good friend Janet – and all her helpers, for laying on such a sumptuous spread. I have enjoyed myself immensely. I think I might just have another ninetieth next year.'

This brought cheers of approval for all over the hall.

But John had not finished. He gave a little nervous cough and spoke into the microphone.

'And now, my friends, I want to let you into a secret.'

A hush crept through the room. John waited until all was silent. Then declared,

'I wish to announce that our good friend Nudge, or should we call him Paul – and our good friend, Jen, are engaged to be married. Congratulations both.'

He turned and looked towards where Nudge and Jen were standing. The eyes of everyone in the room followed his.

For a moment Jen and Nudge stood stock still. John's heart leapt inside his chest. He glanced at Connie standing wide-eyed beside him. Then, Jen smiled, drew Nudge to her and kissed him. Nudge lifted his arms and threw them round her.

Everyone cheered, and the band struck up 'Congratulations.'

'Didn't I say so?' declared Ina, but no one was listening.

There we must leave them, for we must pick up our own dance where we left it when we sat down to read this book.

And where better than in that warm, bright room, in the company of friends, wrapped round in the cheering tunes of a ceilidh band?

THE END

Printed in Great Britain
by Amazon